LOVE, HONOUR & KILL

Caron Alvarez knows she can trust her husband with her life. He's a wonderful husband and an adoring father — everyone loves the famous TV personality Harry Kravitz. And Caron believes in her fairy-tale life, until Harry suddenly reveals a side that she never suspected — a violent and brutal side. Forced to go on the run from the man she had called her husband for years, Caron cannot convince anyone of his true psychotic nature. Her loving and famous husband now wants to kill her. Where can she run to? Who can she trust? Who will ever believe her . . . ?

Molly Katz is a former stand-up comedian. Her stories and articles have appeared in *Cosmopolitan, The New York Times* and *Psychology Today*. She lives near New York City.

MOLLY KATZ

◆

LOVE, HONOUR & KILL

Complete and Unabridged

ULVERSCROFT
Leicester

First published in Great Britain in 1999 by
HarperCollins Publishers
London

First Large Print Edition
published 2000
by arrangement with
HarperCollins Publishers Limited
London

The moral right of the author has been asserted

This novel is entirely a work of fiction.
The names, characters and incidents portrayed in it
are the work of the author's imagination.
Any resemblance to actual persons, living or dead,
events or localities is entirely coincidental.

British Library CIP Data

Katz, Molly
    Love, honour & kill.—Large print ed.—
    Ulverscroft large print series: mystery
    1. Psychoses—Fiction 2. Wife abuse—Fiction
    3. Suspense fiction 4. Large type books
    I. Title
    813.5′4 [F]

    ISBN 0–7089–4290–3

Published by
F. A. Thorpe (Publishing)
Anstey, Leicestershire

Set by Words & Graphics Ltd.
Anstey, Leicestershire
Printed and bound in Great Britain by
T. J. International Ltd., Padstow, Cornwall

This book is printed on acid-free paper

To the millions of victims and survivors of domestic violence — and the remarkable people who work to help them.

Acknowledgments

Heartfelt thanks for their help to: Andrew Carlin Esq., Robert Ciardullo M.D., Brenda Concepcion, Connecticut Coalition Against Domestic Violence, Eleanor Craig Green, Paul Green, Frank Justin, Daniel J. Kilkelly Jr., Gail Marculescu, Peter McLean, Daveid Nastri, Sky Monhoff, Toba Olson, Bill Parkhurst, Steven Simon and Ami Stokhamer.

And especially: Henry Morrison, Danny Baror, Scott Maus, Det. Mike Marculescu

Prologue

Saturday, January 7, 1991
New York City

There was blood on her shoe, Caron saw, but she was too exhausted to lower her feet from the sofa arm and clean it off.

George Bush and Saddam Hussein were propelling their two nations into war, but the ice-coated New York side-walks were creating buckets of blood all by themselves. Soon enough her beeper would sound and she'd have to hurry from the physicians' lounge to the ER and scrutinize another broken face. Meanwhile, she'd use this precious pause in the action to finish her Coke and elevate her burning feet.

The cold can had just touched her lips when the beep came. She sighed and dragged herself upright, and the unit screeched again. The tiny screen read GYATE, the ER code for urgent: Get Your Ass To Emergency.

★ ★ ★

Just a nasal fracture, a sweet ten-year-old boy, but Caron quickly found out why the rush code: the child's father was Harry Kravitz, and Harry himself had brought him in.

3

'They told me a general surgeon could handle this, but I wanted a plastic surgeon. Just to be on the safe side,' the man said as Caron gently palpated the boy's damaged nasal bone. 'Look, Dr Alvarez, is it okay with you if I ask about your background? And how long you've been here at New York Hospital?' His tone was deferential. This national celebrity was apologizing for asking questions she'd grown used to hearing from the general public all the time. Her Hispanic appearance seemed to prompt that; they wanted to make sure her medical degree hadn't been earned in a tent under a palm tree.

As she answered, Caron was very aware of the hushed attention around them. Other staff pretended to work while listening and sneaking glances. Harry Kravitz's spectacular looks came across on TV and in films, but right next to you he was meltingly gorgeous.

'Smith College, class of '80. Harvard Medical. Residencies at Mass General and Johns Hopkins. I'm in my second year as a full-time surgeon here.'

'I'm impressed. Where are you from originally?'

'Cuba.'

The boy winced under Caron's probing, and Harry gripped his hand and kissed it. 'You're doing great, Josh. Isn't he?'

4

'He's very brave. Adults squirm more than he is. Where did you fall, Josh?'

'East End Avenue. Outside our building.'

'Lucky your dad was with you.'

With his free hand Harry raked back his trademark golden brown hair. 'I snagged a cab and came right over here. Didn't wait to have my car brought. Well? What do you think?'

Caron glanced at the man's anxious face, the dark-lashed brown eyes, the smooth skin. She knew Harry was in his forties — the newspapers and TV kept repeating every fact about the former star of the great sitcom *Scott* who was now the likely successor to Johnny Carson — but he appeared younger. The solidly muscled chest and shoulders under his cotton sweater could have belonged to a teenager.

'I think this needs a simple closed reduction, and Josh will be fine.'

The man smiled his relief. 'You do?'

She smiled back. 'Yes.'

He kissed his son's fingers again. 'Hear that?' Then, to Caron, 'But you'll do it yourself?'

'If you want me to.'

'I do. We do. Hm?' He waggled Josh's hand.

'Yes,' Josh said.

Part One

Sunday to Friday
August 15 – 20, 1993

1

There wasn't a part of Caron that didn't hurt. The arm she gripped Josh's shoulders with ached along its length, and the fingers were raw from her attempts to defend herself. Her vagina and rectum felt macerated. Blood oozed from her lower lip, where she'd bitten it. And where Harry had.

Behind a grille just inside the double doors of the Nineteenth Precinct, an elfin blonde officer was tapping at a keyboard. She looked up at Caron, glanced at Josh's anguished wet face, then back at Caron, squinting at the blood.

She began, 'What can I — '

'I've been beaten up and sexually attacked,' Caron said. She swallowed, and nearly gagged on the leftover taste of Harry's invasion. 'By my husband.'

'The boy too?'

'No. But I couldn't leave him there.' The tears Caron kept fighting to hold back burned to be released; the officer's detachment nearly did it. But Caron desperately needed to put the facts down credibly. She had almost no power up against Harry's position as a national treasure in the entertainment world. If she seemed hysterical, she'd have no chance at all.

'We need to get away from here, from my husband,' she said in a husky but determinedly steady voice. 'He'll kill me if he finds me. 'I *will* kill you.' That's exactly what he said.'

★ ★ ★

In a daze Caron answered questions, supplied words for them to feed into their machines. The police-station indifference changed as soon as she said Harry's name. Word whipped through the precinct. They couldn't get over it. *Harry Kravitz?* They had seen it all, but they hadn't seen this.

Caron felt the pressure of many pairs of eyes staring as she fought for words to describe what Harry had done. The detectives interviewing her, a male and a female, couldn't hide their shock.

'You're saying Mr Kravitz has a Jekyll — Hyde personality?' the man said.

'Yes.'

'And he has never assaulted you before, sexually or otherwise?'

'No. Never.' Caron wiped her mouth, bringing fresh blood.

10

The woman detective gave her a tissue. 'Want to go to the bathroom?' she asked sympathetically, and Caron nodded and went out.

As soon as she was gone, the officer leaned toward her partner. 'I used to watch Kravitz's show every week — *Scott*. He played this sweet bumpkin lawyer. Really funny. Seemed like the nicest guy. And so handsome.'

'It's not on any more, is it?'

'Only in reruns. It was on for seven or eight years.'

'Didn't I just read that he's supposed to start some late-night program?'

The woman nodded. 'I've seen a couple of his movies. I saw him on Jay Leno just the other night. He was a riot.' She paused. 'This is the man who beat the shit out of his wife and wants her dead. Just another asshole.' She shook her head. She shrugged.

God help us, the gesture said.

★ ★ ★

The desk officer traded hellos with a ponytailed plainclothes detective in a summer dress and hi-tops arriving for work. 'Guess who's here?' the blonde said.

'Donald fucking Trump.'

'Better. Mrs Harry Kravitz.'

11

The detective looked up sharply. 'What'd she do?'

'She's the complainant. Assault and rape. DV.'

'DV? *He* did it?'

'So she claims. I'll believe it when he cops out.'

'Yeah. Meanwhile, if she's dumping him, I'll take him.'

'Not if I see him first.'

★ ★ ★

The detectives wanted more from her, but Caron was growing too panicky to remain there. It was a police station, but it was still a public place, and if they went and arrested Harry, they'd bring him here. People had been killed in police stations and courtrooms. People in the process of being protected. Harry could kill her here.

The formal charge and the exam and treatment would have to wait. She simply couldn't stay.

An officer took Caron and Josh to a hotel on Lexington Avenue. The car was unmarked, an anonymous battered old Buick, and the officer was bulky enough to repel a rhino, but Caron slid down low in the hot backseat and made Josh do the same. The hotel was a way station; representatives from a shelter for domestic violence victims would collect them there and take them to the shelter. Its location was kept secret.

There she would be given the medical treatment she had refused to be taken to a hospital for. Hospitals were too open and public and unsafe. If she had to ache and burn a while longer, that was better than exposing herself and Josh. Once she had secured some immediate crumb of safety for them, then she could begin to assemble her resources, think who she dared call, who would believe her. Julie Gerstein again, for sure. Barbara Wrenn, or someone else from Smith . . .

★ ★ ★

Caron found herself rubbing her hands on the chenille hotel bedspread. It hurt, but the cotton bumps on her scraped palms were like cold water in her face.

She got up and went to the dresser mirror. She leaned in and studied her reflection as if it were someone else's. Disassociation.

She couldn't recall specifically where Harry's blows had landed. The pummeling echoed through her still, but she needed to concentrate on each body part, and put that

13

together with this visual examination of the person in the mirror, to assess the damage.

She was fighting to think clinically. It helped to repel the vibrating, nauseating memories of all the ways she had been invaded. The terror of now, and next. *I WILL kill you.*

The dark eyes were numbed-looking but clear, the surrounding area unbruised. Mascara she had put on a thousand years ago this morning trailed down her cheeks. A bite mark with crusted black blood made half a grimace. Her hair, Harry had always called it the color of warm honey, was clumped with tears and mucus; it felt stiff when she touched the curls that hung just below her shoulders. One short sleeve of her T-shirt was stretched where Harry had yanked it, trying to pull the shirt off. He had finally just shoved it up to her neck. She remembered the choking fabric over her nose and mouth. When she'd reached to grab it away, to breathe again, she'd had to let go of the black leggings she was desperately trying to keep on, and Harry had pulled those down . . .

The raw pain down there flamed as she remembered him hammering and clawing at her.

Then, like a channel changing, Caron's mind-picture switched back to how it had

14

been before this hideous day — all the fine sweet treats of her life with her husband and child. She saw her gorgeous Harry standing proudly beside her, caressing her back, as they watched Josh grab a high pop-fly and rush to tag out the batter. She recalled being held protectively close in Harry's arm as he made his way through a flock of adoring female fans, dispensing hellos and thank-yous, but his love shining only on her. She saw herself and Josh tip over on the couch laughing as the three of them watched one of Harry's movies on TV and Harry cracked jokes about himself and the other actors, boom-boom-boom . . .

Josh came out of the bathroom. Caron saw him in the mirror. His expression was dull now, shell-shocked. Not like when he'd walked in on the attack, dumbstruck as he gaped at the tangle of arms and legs, the grunts and curses and stifled yells.

'I shouldn't have told you,' Josh said now for the fifth or sixth time.

★　★　★

East End Avenue was softly twilit. The windows of the elegant buildings reflected the copper of yet another splendid sunset. Harry watched for a few minutes, then walked to

15

the other end of the apartment. He opened the slider and stepped out on to the terrace and let the liquid pink glory that was the East River bring on the tears he'd been unable to shed until now.

He cried for a long time.

Finally it became too much for him — the kiss of the summer night breeze that he and Caron had enjoyed so often . . . the king-size bed behind him, still in violent disarray, blood smears all over.

He rubbed his face dry with his handkerchief. He would go insane if he didn't get out for a while. He had never hated himself so.

A monster. He was a monster.

He looked down at the monster's hands on the terrace rail. There were scratches on two fingers, and a fingernail gouge in the palm. Usually he managed to be left with no marks.

But usually the people could hardly fight back.

Caron . . . Caron was brave and strong, and had fought for her life. He could have been bloody himself. But he was practiced at inflicting damage with hands that remained unmarred.

That thought brought more tears.

It wasn't a human punching-bag this time. It was your wife. Your cuddly, sweet-smelling, wonderful wife.

16

Harry saw his tears falling on his hands. He whimpered with misery. Now he could feel the pain he'd given Caron, inside and out, all the effects of his anatomical weapons.

He would go down and walk by the river, walk off the sick horror of what he had done. Try to think what to do now. How to find Caron and Josh, to begin to make it better.

He could make her see, he knew it. Not him alone; everyone close to them would help. She had already called Paul and Tomas from somewhere, and both the agent and the lawyer had phoned Harry right away to express their concern and support for him. Tomas was asking questions, making notes.

They didn't accept Caron's version of events — and that, though unfair, was as it had to be. What he had done was horrible, indefensible; but it wasn't as if such an aberration had ever happened before with Caron.

He had sworn three years ago that he would never harm another loved one — and he hadn't. He had forced himself to deflect the rage that flamed through him when something or someone blocked his wishes away from his friends and family — a skill first acquired in his twenties. He had learned to substitute. And in the crawling green thickets of New York there was plenty of opportunity for that. Plenty of flesh and blood that wasn't Harry's, wasn't anyone's really.

An evil addiction. But a vital need filled.

Now he would have to squeeze out his reserves of restraint to bend the need back in that direction, away from Caron. He had never hurt her before. They would put this mess behind them and he would never hurt her again. He would honor the promise, as he had honored his promise to Josh.

There was really no one he wouldn't be able to count on for the support that would help them rebuild their marriage. Caron had no family outside Cuba, no friends here in New York who weren't his friends first and foremost.

He'd bring her back home. Show her his desolation, his resolve to start fresh. Caron would be terribly upset, but he would beg her to accept his apology and his promise.

He had the front door open and was setting one of the locks when his phone rang — the business line, not the private one Caron would use. He let the machine answer, but grabbed the receiver when he heard the caller say he was a police officer.

'Mr Kravitz?'

'Yes.'

18

'I'm calling about your wife. Do you know where she is?'

Harry gripped the phone. 'No.'

'She's at the Hotel Norwich. Eightieth and Lex. I just drove her there from the precinct. Apparently you two had a tiff.'

'Well, it's — '

'I'm not asking. You don't need to tell your private business. But look, I'm a fan — when *Scott* was on, I never missed a week . . . they should bring it back, it's better than the dreck they got on the box now. Anyway, I don't want to see this argument of yours become a big schmear, you know? Your wife all upset, the kid crying. How about you hustle over and fix things? I'd hate to see the news guys get interested.'

2

'I'm not hungry,' Josh said.

'I know. I'm not either. But we should eat anyway.' For show, Caron took a bite of the tuna sandwich the big policeman had brought up. To keep from gagging, she quickly swallowed some coffee.

Josh began to cry, tears dripping on the sandwich he held. 'What Dad did . . . It's so hard to believe . . .'

Caron put down her food. She saw the scene again suddenly, felt the trapped horror. She wanted to sob out her anguish and her panic, but she had to hold on. And she had to make sure Josh was fully aware. 'You didn't see most of what happened. He hurt me very, very badly.'

Josh's tears rolled, and Caron wished they were at the shelter, where at least there would be some answers, some advice. Some way to start to be awake in the nightmare.

There was a knock on the door. They both jumped. Thank God — the shelter people.

She opened the door without removing the chain.

Harry reached in and undid it easily.

20

He was himself again, he felt it. The terrible, punishing anger was gone. He believed he could make Caron understand that. Josh was less of a worry. The love and worship in the boy's eyes were undimmable. His son trusted and understood as only a blood tie could.

'You're so important to me. I love you so, so dearly,' Harry told Caron, carefully not touching her. 'I hate what I did. It was all I could do not to heave myself off the terrace. I knew there were scalpels in your bag in the closet, and I thought very hard about using one on myself — '

'How did you find us?' Caron asked.

Harry shook his head. His eyes were red and wet. 'Let me finish. Then you can talk. I'll listen. I'll listen to every word you want to say to me. Please, Caron, have faith. I know what a betrayal that was and I promise that I will never again — '

A knock. Caron ran to the door. It was the policeman. 'Please,' she said, 'stay with us. Don't leave. This man is my husband. He's the one — '

'I know, ma'am. I don't want to interrupt. Just came to see if you'd like anything more to eat.'

Harry gave the man his famous smile, the one that enticed movie stars to tell him things on national television they wouldn't tell their agents over a kir.

Caron made up her mind. There was only one way to proceed. She grabbed Josh's arm. 'We have to leave now.'

The boy hesitated, looking from the door to his father.

'Now,' Caron insisted, pulling him with her, and he went.

Harry followed. 'Caron, I love you. You and Josh. I know how you feel. But please don't leave me.'

Caron turned to the policeman. With a shaking finger she pointed to her face.

'See all this?' she asked. 'Harry did it. He beat me up. He did plenty more, but you can't see with my clothes on. He raped me. Vaginally and anally.' She hated to spell that out in front of Josh, but she had no choice. There was no other way to convince — and she wasn't convincing the policeman. He was gazing at Harry, ignoring her and Josh. His expression said he couldn't believe he was lucky enough to be standing next to Harry Kravitz.

Caron said, 'Harry is not the person you see on TV. He's not Scott, and he's not a charming friendly guy. He is a dangerous,

22

violent, crazy man. He said he is going to kill me.'

Her voice was rising. She was panting for breath, feeling again the choking terror that had come when Harry had held her shirt over her face. She sounded as crazy as she said Harry was. But it didn't matter. The officer was barely listening. He knew Harry would never do such a thing.

'I lost my temper,' Harry said gently. 'I never have before, have I? Tell the officer.'

'Has he hurt you before, ma'am?'

'No. But he —'

'Don't you think you ought to calm down before you make some decisions you might regret?' the policeman asked.

Holding tight to Josh's hand, Caron pushed past the policeman and ran from the room.

* * *

Hurrying along the crowded sidewalk with Caron holding tight to his hand, Josh felt her sweat and his making the grip slimy.

He felt as if a physical part of himself was still back at that hotel with his dad.

He would have given up anything that was asked of him for this not to be happening.

His nose rarely hurt any more, but it did now. The pain was like a headache, but

23

concentrated, as if all the feeling that was usually distributed over his whole head was balled up into his nose. With his free hand he covered it gently as they ran along.

Soon the pain brought tears, dripping over his hand and down his face.

He knew he couldn't, but he wanted to go home. Not just to go; to have it still *be* home. He wished this street, with himself and Caron rushing down it, could evaporate, and they, like Toto and Dorothy, could be plunked back on East End Avenue with his dad holding a phone in one hand and stroking Josh's hair with the other.

At that, the tears ran harder, until he had to stop holding his aching nose and wipe his face.

* * *

'Family Violence Hotline.'

'I'm calling from a payphone.' Caron's heart was racing. Her voice shook. 'I have my stepson with me, and we — we're in danger. My husband beat me and raped me. He'll kill me if he can. We need a safe place to go.'

'What's your first name, honey?'

'Caron.'

'Where is your husband now, Caron?'

'I don't know.'

24

'Is he anywhere near you?'

'Not yet.'

'Are you and the boy injured?'

'I am. He wasn't hurt.'

'Were you unconcious at all? Are you having any nausea or — '

'I'm a doctor.'

A beat. 'Oh. All right, then, Caron. Where — '

'I went to the police. They took us to a hotel, where we were supposed to be picked up by some people from a shelter. But my husband found us somehow . . .'

Caron paused to catch her breath. The memory of Harry's hand reaching around the safety chain, the hand that had squeezed out her blood, was making her gasp as if she'd jumped into ice-cold water. Harry's hand that had once — a million years ago yesterday — comforted her, loved her, guided her. Touched her hair or her ankle, held *her* hand when she was anxious . . .

She shuddered and swallowed back nausea.

Her eyes swept the street and sidewalks continuously. She had taken a taxi across town before making the call, and was sure Harry hadn't been able to follow, but she felt painted in neon anyway, as if she and Josh were pop-up targets in an arcade game. Any of the passing taxis could hold Harry. Harry with a gun.

Would he go that far? Would Harry gun her down on a public street?

And what would she have answered if, yesterday, someone had asked whether Harry would ever rape and beat her?

'Where are you now?' the woman on the phone asked.

'Fifty-fifth and Sixth.'

'On the street?'

'Yes. I'm terrified he'll find me again.'

'I understand. We'll do our best to make sure he doesn't. What — '

'I have to tell you who my husband is. He's Harry Kravitz.'

' 'Scott'?'

'Yes.'

There was a shocked pause, and then the woman went back to business. 'What do you look like, Caron?'

'I'm five-five, thin, light brown hair. Black pants, gray T-shirt. I'm — messed up . . .'

'Do you see a coffee shop or deli anywhere around you? Some place bright and crowded?'

Caron twisted to look, wincing as the cord hit her bruised neck. 'There's a deli next to a restaurant, a few doors in on Fifty-fifth.'

'Go in there. In twenty minutes start

watching for a short woman in a red shirt driving a blue Ford Taurus with Jersey plates. Suzette will come inside and get you.'

★ ★ ★

There were messages when Harry got home, but none from any media. Yet. He returned a call to Tomas, who said he was on another line and would call right back.

Harry slumped in his desk chair. All the way home his mind had replayed the same scene, the one of Josh disappearing as he watched, pulled away by Caron. With every fiber Harry had wanted to run after them, to grasp and cradle his Josh and keep him close.

Harry's arms remembered the feel of his baby son, the squirming little body like a restless kitten. In Harry's nose the hierarchy of smells resided still, babyhood to now: lotion, plastic pants, sand pail at Atlantic City . . . fielder's mitt . . . laptop.

Sliding down further in the chair, Harry was swamped by the terrible forlorn emotion he had seen on people's faces following an accident or tornado, when the camera would catch them freshly mourning a child.

When their precious little one had been sucked right out of life, leaving a crater of pain.

He couldn't lose his son.

Harry sat up and reached across the desk for the picture cube that held Josh in many poses. He turned it to the best close-up and held his eyes on Josh's until he could almost feel the connection.

You're under Caron's influence now, son. You can't hear me. But I am promising you, from my heart to yours, that I will do what I have to, to keep you with me. I will be the father you love and need.

In the picture Josh's hair stood up in the wind, and now Harry touched it. *I'm getting what I need, son. I will see a psychiatrist. I know I did a terrible thing to Caron, worse even than what I did to you three years ago. You have my promise that I won't do any more bad things. You can come back and be with me, and I will never touch you except in love.*

The phone rang. 'Did she come home?' Tomas wanted to know.

'No.' Harry sighed. He put the picture cube back.

'Where were you when I called?'

'Looking for Caron. She's — not herself.'

'I'll say.' Tomas paused. 'Is there something I should know, Harry?'

He didn't answer immediately, and Tomas continued, 'Any public revelations should come first from you. I'm sure I needn't tell you that.'

'Of course.'

'Well? What's the deal? Will Caron be publicly claiming that you attacked her? If she does, what are the facts that we will present?'

Caron had left him with no choice at all. He had to answer — and then he had to act on the answer. His future, his and his son's, were in jeopardy. The threat of Caron was devastating.

He hung up and took a long look at the wall next to his desk. The cast pictures from *Scott* ... the posters from his movies ... Harry and John Goodman in one, tussling on top of a school bus. In another, Harry held Meg Ryan in a fireman's carry while two other lovely women looked on enviously. There were framed shots of Harry on television with David Letterman, with Barbara Walters, with everyone there was.

Harry looked back at the cube with all the pictures of Joshie.

He picked up the phone and called Ronald Brale.

* * *

The shelter was a double brownstone on Seventh Street, near Avenue A, which they had reached by a circuitous series of unnecessary turns and long detours. It was grimy and unremarkable. Women watched TV and ate from bags of chips. An apple hopefully sliced was browning untouched on a coffee table. Several children in pajamas sat or played.

Suzette was a delicate four-feet-ten, but she had announced immediately that she was a black belt and carried a Magnum. She showed Caron and Josh up three flights of stairs to a minute room with a bunk bed in the rear of the house. A window gave on to a fire escape that held a hibachi and big potted plants.

'Rest a minute,' Suzette said. 'Then one of us will be up to do a little intake. Bathroom is across the hall.'

Josh went to use it. Alone, Caron sank down on to the bottom bunk. She needed to clean up, but first she would do as Suzette had said.

In her purse she had found some old Darvocet that she had been carrying around at one time to break in quarters for Josh, when he had fractured his big toe. The pills gave her slight relief, but she was still aching, and filthy. There was blood crusted everywhere. She wanted a shower and clean underwear, but Suzette had instructed her, as the police had, to refrain from washing until medical evidence could be taken.

There was plenty of that.

Her vagina and rectum probably looked as if a wild animal had chewed at her.

She closed her eyes, but didn't doze. A wild animal was it, exactly.

She had heard and read the words in the news, the formal, clinical phrases, applied to rape victims: sodomy, forcible penetration, deviant sex acts. She had seen the women in the ER. But nothing conveyed the reality, the inhuman pushing and tearing, the quaking, sickening monstrousness of being battered and invaded by fists and fingers, teeth and penis.

Nausea came, swamping her. Caron struggled upright, holding the bed frame. She sat, panting and sweating, and the sickness ebbed slightly.

She walked shakily to the window, opened it, and leaned out into the sultry darkness, breathing deeply to calm her stomach. The fire escape rail shimmied slightly. Probably a subway line nearby. Caron listened for the rumble of a train.

She realized suddenly that there was no noise — and that only her part of the fire escape was moving.

One of the potted-plant shapes jumped to

life. A man in black clothing, a gleam of metal. He sprang at Caron.

She screamed and jumped backward into the room. He lifted a black-sneakered foot over the sill. Caron looked around frantically for something to throw, spotted a globe on the desk, and heaved it.

★ ★ ★

Suzette kicked glass aside and leaned out. People buzzed in the hallway. Josh watched the window intently.

'He's gone. No sign,' Suzette said. 'But you're sure it wasn't your husband?'

'Yes. He sent someone.'

Suzette took Caron's hands. 'There's a lot of crime around here. Break-ins, burglaries. No one knows you're here. This location is secret. The chances are a thousand to one that the man was targeting you.'

'He had a knife.'

'That's no surprise. But he's gone to threaten someone else with it. You scared him away.' Suzette started out of the room. 'But you can't sleep in here now, with the window broken. Someone will have to double up.'

'We're not staying,' Caron said.

★ ★ ★

In the cramped bathroom Caron splashed her hot face, wincing as the water hit her wounds.

Suzette and the others were pressuring her not to leave. They were convinced the intruder hadn't been after Caron personally.

But Caron knew.

In the mercilessly shining mirror she saw the difference in her own eyes, in the frozen mouth. Whatever part of her had still been denying, had clung to the filament of hope that this would all go away, knew the truth now. There wouldn't be any explanation, any first aid, that would propel her back to her warm bath of a marriage, her life and her work, her familiar days and nights and months and years.

Her psyche scrabbled for handholds and found only air.

A month ago she and Harry and Josh had been lying on a blanket in Central Park, under a low tree branch near the sailboat lake, Harry incognito in aviator sunglasses and a floppy fisherman's hat. He was feeding her lemon Frozade with a plastic spoon. She had felt the icy tang on her tongue and the flickering sunshine on her face and a limitless contentment she had never experienced before Harry.

Now he wanted to obliterate her. As of the

33

past few minutes she knew he was trying to do exactly that.

The prospect of dying at Harry's hands wasn't just a fear any more. It was real, as real as the blood she still tasted. It had just nearly happened. The man with the knife had been sent by her husband. Her surgeon's reflexes, or a lucky accident, had saved her from where she otherwise would be this second, exsanguinating on the rug of the bedroom across the hall, her heart useless . . . her stepson with his only remaining lifeline gone.

In the mirror her eyes welled and her mouth crumpled, and then her legs lost their power to hold her standing and she sank to the cool floor. She was stranded, she and Josh. They couldn't stay here and they had no place to go. Julie had begged Caron to come to Boston, but Harry could find her there, and Julie would be in danger too. Caron ached for safety but could see nothing but an open dark tunnel ahead.

When she had lost her mother, that tunnel had been there. From the first time that her father smiled falsely and assured Caron and her sister Elisa that their mother would be fine, the tunnel had stretched out ahead of her, unbearably empty, no one else in it, never ending.

In Santa Conda you were rich or very poor, and the Alvarez family was rich.

The city was on the south coast of Isla de Tampas, the third largest island in the Republic of Cuba. Caron's father Horace was Chief of Cardiology at Maria Conda Hospital; her mother Greta had been the head nurse on the unit when they met.

Caron was in her second to last year of high school when Greta, who had never given up her work and was envied for her spirit and energy, began to lose weight. Her skin grew mustardy. A kidney problem; renal specialists were consulted. When none could improve her, Horace crossed the obligatory political palms and flew her to San Diego, California, to see a celebrated doctor there. Rather than good news, what they heard was the worst yet — the man was unfamiliar with the majestic Alvarez status and had no reason to soft-pedal.

Greta had practically no function in her left kidney, and would soon lose it in her right.

Back home in Santa Conda, dialysis was begun. A transplant donor was sought. The girls were incompatible. Finally a cousin of Greta's was approved, but by the time all was ready, Greta had developed sepsis, and surgery was impossible.

Caron remembered the cloudy Monday in March when Greta had lain in her hospital bed and clutched both daughters with thin arms. She was still strong; the bones had pressed Caron's back sharply. Caron welcomed the pain, the momentary reassurance of her mother's aliveness.

They had sat there with her all night.

Horace had wanted the girls to leave, that had been clear. Whatever little moments were left of Greta's presence he wanted for himself alone. But he could no more have confessed that to the girls than he had ever been able to communicate any emotion. He adored Greta and was bereft already. But what love he was capable of was spent there.

Greta died the following noon.

Caron remembered the flower-filled hospital chapel with thousands of candles, and her desolate father, blue-pale, staggering through the mass. He and Caron and Elisa, without the binding warmth of Greta, were three separate broken people who couldn't comfort themselves or one another.

Within a month Horace had had enough of the big family home in Santa Conda. He accepted the offer of a Dr Felhammer at Johns Hopkins School of Medicine in Baltimore, Maryland, who had been after him for years, and left to begin his new position in the States.

Elisa was kind and saw to Caron's needs, but the house boomed with emptiness, and Elisa's disagreements with her husband Reco were disturbing.

Caron would sit in the bathtub, running in more and more hot water to ease her permanent chill, and would hear her parents' voices. They were distant but so real she would sit up in shock. Her mind would leap for the sweet peace of the dream, the chance that it was all a joke, a mistake. Her mother and father were still here. The house was home again, good again.

But the voices would fade and the water would cool and what would be there was what had been all along: the tunnel. The cold black hollow of Caron's days, stretching to forever, with no hugs, not even bony ones, no anything.

★　★　★

Now, in the little shelter bathroom, Caron got to her feet, hugging herself. For her first sixteen years of life, there had always been the haven of Greta — who, knowing her husband's limitations as a father and perhaps guilty at being the only one he had room in his heart for, had given double to the girls. In bad times Caron could always retreat to the strong arms, the calm voice and familiar sweaty-sweet smell of her mother's embrace.

Never in her adult life had she so longed to have Greta back.

Just for a minute . . . just to keep her from breaking apart.

Caron dropped her arms. The bathroom was hot and damp, but a chill descended on her where now there was no touch, not even her own. As if to underscore the hopeless, heartless permanence of her aloneness.

★ ★ ★

Caron waved down a taxi on First Avenue and directed the driver west and then north. When she saw the crowds out enjoying the warm night on upper Broadway, she and Josh got out.

The sick terror would be back, would dissolve her if she let it. But right now, there was one objective: to get away.

In the two years she had known him, she'd grown used to thinking of Harry's friends and associates as hers too. They, and Harry, had encouraged her to. But they weren't. One phone call after another to 'their' circle tonight had brought astonished incredulity.

She dared not go to her own friend Julie Gerstein in Massachusetts, or her colleagues and acquaintances in New York, and taint them with her danger.

The police hadn't protected her.

The shelter hadn't sheltered her at all.

I WILL kill you.

No one could help. It was up to her.

The busy street buzzed with conversation, with traffic noise, and the hot-air hum of an urban summer night. From an open-front pizza shop the smell of oregano descended, and Caron felt sick again, and held her stomach.

'Are you okay?' Josh asked shakily. His desperation colored each word. If she wasn't, then . . . what?

Caron squeezed his hand. She pulled him into a hug and nearly cried at Josh's trusting grip. Not the blasé teen now. He rested his head on her shoulder, and she could feel a tremor in his body, like when he'd had a stomach bug last June and she hadn't been able to stop his shivering even with her own body warmth.

'What are we going to do now? Where can we go?' Josh asked, his voice cracking.

'I'm thinking,' she said quietly before giving him a last squeeze and stepping back.

Caron's mind was clicking off what to do,

the way it did when she operated, six steps ahead, senses tuned to pick up an off note.

First, look more normal. The curious glances were dangerous.

Second, leave New York fast.

They crossed Broadway and went into a pharmacy. It didn't carry Dermablend, but there was an off-brand medical concealer. Caron bought that and led Josh to a coffee shop on the next block. In the ladies' room she cleaned her face better and used thick dabs of the cover cream to hide the areas that were red and darkening. After that she bought a thin beige cardigan at an evening-wear boutique, the only clothing store open. It had a strange, dressy metallic-gold weave, but it covered her bruised and scraped arms.

She stopped at cash machines, withdrawing from three accounts. When she had collected all the cash she could, the total in her wallet was $1,200. She scanned Broadway for a vacant cab.

'Now where?' Josh asked.

'The Port Authority bus terminal.'

'That's downtown from here.'

'Yes. But it's our best way out of New York. A bus is cheaper than a plane, and harder to trace —'

'That's not what I meant. Look.'

Caron followed Josh's pointing finger. Three blocks down Broadway a traffic snarl began. The taillights of the backed-up cars and taxis went on as far as was visible.

How could she have missed that?

Panic raced in. What else was she missing? She'd almost gotten them caught in a time-eating trap. Harry had a killer after them. Maybe more than one. Harry's resources were inexhaustible. People would do anything for him.

She remembered the black-sneakered foot, the knife . . .

She realized her hands were shaking where they held Josh. She clasped them together.

'Are — are we going to Cuba?' Josh asked. His eyes were wet again.

'No.' Caron gave him the answer her desperate brain had finally settled on. 'To Maryland. To a friend.'

'Not to Massachusetts? To Julie's?'

Caron shook her head. She realized as the stiff curls brushed her face that she hadn't cleaned her hair. 'Your dad would expect me to go to Julie's. He doesn't know Barbara, or even that I know anyone in Maryland. Barbara is an old college friend.'

'Will she help us?'

Good question, Caron thought, recalling the big-hearted but flighty roommate with whom she'd done little but exchange cards since college.

Her attention was suddenly caught by a car pulling up at the deli down the block. For an instant she thought it was the policeman's Buick, and horror jabbed her; but the driver got out, a slight, scruffy-looking young woman in painter's jeans, and went into the store.

Caron took another look at the car. It was even more banged up than the other one, with a bumper held on by wire, and rust on the doors.

She had an idea. 'Come on,' she said, taking Josh's hand.

She stopped the driver as the woman exited the deli with a steaming bag. 'I'm interested in buying your car,' Caron said. 'How much do you want for it?'

The woman took a step back. Caron saw her pallor, the unseasonable heavy clothing and other signals, and thought, Good choice.

'My car?'

'Yes. I'll pay five hundred.' She watched the woman slowly process the idea. 'Cash,' Caron said.

The woman looked from Caron to Josh. She clutched her bag of food. She turned toward the car, and then back to Caron.

'A thousand,' she said.

'It isn't worth that.'

The woman blinked. 'Seems like it is to you.'

'Six hundred.'

'Hey,' the woman said, 'I didn't start this.' She reached for the door handle.

Caron touched her shoulder, feeling its boniness. 'Wait. Seven hundred.'

'No. Get it, okay? I want to keep the car. I only paid attention to you because of a lot of cash maybe finding its way into my pocket. Otherwise, who needs the pain in the ass?'

Caron looked around. There didn't seem to be any other possibility, and she could hardly go parading up and down Broadway offering to buy people's old cars.

The woman watched her. 'You want it or not? A thousand.' She held out the key in a jittery hand.

Caron took the key and opened her purse, and hurriedly peeled off bills.

3

There were rips in the seats, and the car stank of old smoke. Josh hoped that was all the smell was, and not some dangerous fumes. He'd read about carbon monoxide, how it could creep in and make you unconscious before you knew anything.

If that happened, Caron could lose control of the car and they would crash.

But he'd be unconscious too, so he wouldn't know.

For a second the idea was nice.

That scared him. He sat up straighter in his seat and lowered the window more, and turned his hot face to the hot rush of air.

His eyes were sore from crying and he felt as if there were something in his veins other than blood, something heavy that kept him down and made his brain not function the way it usually did. He found himself thinking like his friend Nicholas's grandmother, who lived with Nicholas's family and would forget she had pans of food cooking, even when smoke darkened the room.

It was so hard to remember this day.

Not even the whole day; the last few hours of it.

He had woken early, still upset from last night. He'd dressed and met Nicholas at their baseball spot in Carl Schurz Park. They had batted until it grew too hot, then cooled their feet in the river, appreciating the sun after yesterday's storm, until a security guard made them stop.

They'd walked to Nicholas's and had sandwiches and Snapple and played chess.

Josh remembered ending a game, checking his watch, and deciding that there wasn't time to play another before dinner. He recalled helping Nicholas put the pieces in the box. He could picture himself saying goodbye to his friend's mother and grandmother, and joking with the doorman of his own building as he went in — his buddy Schlomo, who always had a new filthy joke that he would make Josh promise not to tell his dad.

He remembered going up in the elevator, ringing the bell, getting no answer, finally unlocking the apartment door with his key.

Hearing sounds . . .

The memory grew murky here.

His head had prickled, he remembered that, as he followed the noises to the other end of the apartment, his dad and Caron's

45

room. The TV? He knew it wasn't. He just wanted it to be.

Some blood on the wall. Yelling. Dad with his clothes half on, bouncing, flailing. Caron making a strangled noise, like what you think you do in a nightmare, the loudest that can come out. Something over her face.

From the moment Josh saw the blood, his deepest wish was to run back out. But he couldn't, because just then Caron's hand shot up, and there was more screaming, and his father turned and saw him.

He did remember that moment. A frozen picture. His dad with blood on his mouth, pants open, dick out. Caron wriggling to get free of sheets and her own tangled clothing, not yet knowing Josh was there.

After that it was cloudy again, racing-fast and yet very slow.

Josh had turned and gone into the kitchen, sat in a chair and covered his head with his arms. His heart slammed and thumped in his chest. His stomach burned. He sobbed like a little baby.

He remembered the cold table against his nose, bringing back the needles of pain from when it had been broken. That time his nose had felt as big as a car on his face. The hurt had been worse than anything ever before, the explosion right at the point of the bone such

46

an awful memory that, thereafter, he could never touch the point again without some of it flooding back.

His nose . . .

He should never have told Caron.

They wouldn't be here now if he hadn't.

He began to cry again.

★   ★   ★

The New Jersey Turnpike was still fairly crowded even at eleven p.m. Vans of families, and old cars like Caron's, with luggage and bikes tied on.

Maybe she should do that, for camouflage.

Josh was dozing, having cried himself to sleep earlier, his head jouncing against her shoulder. Caron was dangerously worn out herself; her eyes wanted to close.

She turned the radio louder and twisted the tuning knob, looking for music to keep her awake. But the radio was AM only, and all that came in was a local bible station and WCBS, the New York all-news station.

She listened to the sports and weather and politics and mayhem.

Shortly after she passed Camden, there was a change in tone. Voices perked up, there was background chatter and paper rustling.

'This just in,' the anchor said. 'Harry

Kravitz has scheduled a nationwide press conference tonight at eleven-thirty. Eight minutes from now. Newsradio eighty-eight will carry the conference live. TV star Harry Kravitz is expected to appeal for help in tracing his missing wife and son. Harry Kravitz, of course, was the star of *Scott*, the long-running weekly sitcom in which he played a smalltown lawyer. Harry has since become one of the world's major film and television stars.'

Acid burned in Caron's chest. Her foot shook on the gas pedal. She thought of pulling over to wait out the eight minutes and listen to her husband's lies, whatever they were going to be, but the danger of stopping panicked her.

She pressed harder on the gas to stop the tremor, speeded up, dropped back. A traffic stop would be tragic.

Then it was eleven-thirty and Harry's voice came on. Josh woke right up.

'My friends, all of you,' Harry said, 'I need your support. My wife, and my son, are missing.'

He sniffed back tears, coughed.

'Earlier this evening my wife, Dr Caron Alvarez, appeared at a police precinct here in New York. She was injured and not rational. She claimed that I — that I had . . . assaulted her.'

Harry's voice cracked on the last words. Caron felt desolate tears rise in her own throat.

He was so good.

She took Josh's hand and squeezed it, steering with her left.

'She further claimed that she has removed my son from my house for his protection. I have agreed to go on the air tonight in order to explain the facts of this matter to you — and to ask for your help.

'My wife — my wife was cut in the process of my attempt to take a scalpel from her. She was trying to kill herself with the scalpel.' Pause; cough. 'Earlier I said that Caron isn't rational. This condition is physically caused. Caron is — is . . . ' There was the sound of a hand muffling the microphone, then more sniffing. Then Harry continued in a strained voice, 'My wife is suffering from brain cancer.'

He finished by pleading with the public to help him find his precious wife and son.

'Many of you know my beautiful Caron from her wonderful achievements in the wake of Hurricane Andrew. My son is a charming thirteen-year-old. Your TV screens are showing their pictures now.

'I have adamantly refused to allow this act

to be pursued by the FBI as a kidnapping. My wife is not responsible for her actions. Her condition has been diagnosed by a blue-chip New York neurologist; she is a sick person, not a kidnapper. Instead, I appeal to you. Please, please watch for them. Help me get my family back — for the precious last months Caron will have with us. And Josh, if you can hear this, I love you, son. I *will* find you.'

Caron had to pull over. She eased the old car to the hard shoulder, cut the engine, and stumbled out.

'Caron?' Josh asked. 'Are you sick?'

'No. Just needed some fresh air.' Then, realizing what he meant, she got back in. 'I don't have brain cancer. I don't have any illness. Your dad made that up.'

They listened to the insects, and the cars whizzing past.

'I don't know why,' Caron went on. 'But I can guess. He has to put his explanation out there before people hear more about what really happened.'

'Offense instead of defense,' Josh said.

'Yes.'

'What are you going to do now? Will you contradict him?'

Caron turned to Josh in the dark car. 'We both have to contradict him.'

50

4

'You don't need to give me any CV, Dr Alvarez,' the WCBS Radio anchor said. 'You're one of the best-known doctors in the country.'

Caron closed her eyes. 'Thank you.'

'Thank *you* for calling us. Ready? We're taping. Go.'

Caron held the payphone tighter to stop it from sliding out of her sweaty hand. 'I just heard my husband's statement on your station. I don't have brain cancer. I don't have any physical problems, except for the ones caused by my husband when he attacked me tonight.' Caron stopped, gulped a shaky breath, and continued. 'Harry Kravitz beat me and raped me. He bit my mouth and my ears and my arms. He hit and kicked me in so many places I can only enumerate them by counting the swellings and bruises. He injured my vaginal and anal tissues by — by savage forced penetration.'

Caron clenched her teeth to stop their chattering. As with the police, she had to use every thread of control to tell her story without breaking down.

'My stepson came into the room where this was happening, or I probably would have been killed. Harry says he will do that. He will kill me. Someone has already come after me with a knife.'

Caron thought of explaining the meaning of Harry's supposed message to Josh — how 'I *will* find you' was really a reminder to Caron of 'I *will* kill you' — but realized, as she preplayed her own words of explanation, that she sounded paranoid.

She knew what Harry meant. But no one listening would. And the doubt would dilute the rest of what she was saying.

The anchor said, 'There was an attempt to kill you with a knife? Who did that?'

'I didn't know the man. But I know Harry sent him.'

After a moment the news anchor asked, 'Was Mr Kravitz ever violent before?'

'No. He has become loud and hostile, and there have been some so-called accidents . . .'

'What precipitated this fight?'

Fight? No. But Caron would gladly answer anyway. 'My stepson was concerned because Harry's temper's been worse and worse lately. He was worried that Harry would hurt him. When I asked Josh if that had ever happened, I found out that Harry — that he . . . broke

Josh's nose two years ago by pushing his face into a wall. The fracture was supposed to be from a fall, and I was . . . I was the surgeon who did the reduction.'

'You met Harry then.'

'Yes.'

'So your position is that your husband is lying.'

'He *is* lying.' Caron took in air to block tears. 'I love — loved Harry. We loved each other. I thought. He was the most wonder-ful . . .

'This isn't my doing. I don't have brain cancer and I'm not . . . making up accusa-tions for some sick reason. I confronted Harry with what Josh had revealed, and he attacked me. But it's not just my side of the story. It's mine and his son's. Josh will tell you. Hold on.'

With a wet hand Caron gave the phone to Josh. She listened to him explain what he'd seen. He stumbled over some words but told it scrupulously, no dramatic details. He said how confusing it was. He didn't mention the blood.

Caron tried to hear Josh from a neutral listener's position. Was he convincing? Or would people think she had coached him?

They loved Harry. They watched him whenever he was on, joked about having him in their bedrooms. They greeted him with smiles of delight on the street. Many still called him Scott.

They had little sense of Caron except as that Cuban doctor, Harry's wife, a face in *People* magazine.

But then Josh was relating the details about his nose, and his voice was stronger, his hurt clear.

'I never told anyone,' Josh said into the phone. 'My dad asked me not to. He cried. He said he would never hurt me again, and he didn't. But the way he's been lately . . . yelling and — throwing things sometimes . . . '

The anchor must have asked if he threw them at anyone.

'No,' Josh said. 'Just the wall or the floor.' He listened to the next question, then said, 'Yes, I miss my dad. I wish . . . ' The words trailed off and he sobbed into his hand.

After a moment Josh wiped his eyes and told Caron, 'He wants to know where we are.'

Caron took the phone. 'I can't tell you.' She tried to find words to say their lives depended on Harry not finding them, but the B-movie phrases that came to her were worse than no words at all.

She hung up.

'That was scary,' Josh said, sliding down in the car seat and bracing his knees against the dash. 'What if someone saw us at the phone, and was listening to the radio right then?'

'We haven't been on yet. They taped us.' Caron turned up the radio. A minute later, she heard herself, and then Josh.

'Plastic,' Josh groaned when it was over. 'It sounds so unreal. As if *we're* the ones making it up.'

Caron remembered a poster on the wall at the shelter, showing a man and woman each telling their side of a violent incident. The woman looked hysterical; the man was calm. The caption read, 'He lies better than she tells the truth.'

Caron realized the anchors were still talking about her, and turned the volume back up.

'We have on the line Dr Edwin Nusser in Boca Raton, Florida. Dr Nusser has asked to make a statement on the Harry Kravitz story. Go ahead, Doctor.'

'I worked with Dr Caron Alvarez here in Florida after Hurricane Andrew. Dr Alvarez was a hero, as hundreds of thousands of people know. If she says there is nothing organically wrong with her, then there is not.

If she says she is being victimized, she is. Dr Alvarez's integrity is beyond question. Let me be the first to say publicly that I am available for any help she needs, and I urge her to call me.' He gave a number.

Caron fished a pen from her handbag and wrote, glancing down from the road.

'Will you call?' Josh asked.

'Yes. But there's nothing he can do.'

Josh said, 'Maybe more people will come out on our side.'

'Don't hope for that. I'm not popular with many doctors. Your dad is popular with the whole world. Don't expect people to believe Harry Kravitz would hit his family.'

Josh gripped Caron's wrist. 'Why are we trying to explain, then? Why did we go on the radio? What's the point?'

'We had to respond to what your dad said because we couldn't not respond. But we can't expect much from it.' Caron accelerated to pass a pickup truck, and heard a dull rattle in the Buick. 'Thank you for backing me up on the radio. If anything helped, it was that.'

'I helped you?'

'Absolutely. Otherwise it would only be my word against your dad's.'

'Everyone loves Dad. They always have.'

'Not always. It can't be always. He must have hurt other people. You don't suddenly develop a violent personality disorder this late in life. Why did he split with your mother?'

'You know. She's crazy. She's never even wanted to see me.'

Caron looked at him, then back at the road. 'What if that's not true?'

Josh thought for a minute. 'You mean, maybe she's not crazy, and Dad lied about that? But then why would she reject a two-year-old? Why hasn't she contacted me?'

'I don't know. But if your dad wanted it that way, he'd arrange it.'

'You think he could?'

'He could do anything.'

Josh slid lower in the stained car seat. He rubbed his head as if it hurt. Tears ran down his cheeks. Caron patted his shoulder.

'If he can do anything,' Josh sobbed, 'then he can find us.'

5

'You found the shelter, and you *still* couldn't accomplish anything?' Harry demanded.

Ronald Brale leaned back against the park bench. 'It's a big 'anything', Harry.'

'Shit. Shit, shit, shit.'

Brale had changed out of what he called his 'cat burglar best' and was wearing a soft blue T-shirt and jeans. Conversing low on a hard bench in Carl Schurz Park, he and Harry could have been any two pals taking the air on a summer night. The fact that this particular bench was situated under a nonfunctioning streetlamp, and had been for eighteen months, Manhattan maintenance being what it was, kept passersby from recognizing Harry, or remembering the scene. Also, the number of passersby at three a.m. was limited, and confined to those who would not remember the Loch Ness Monster sitting on the bench eating an egg roll.

'What do you want me to do now?' Brale asked.

'What's your gut? Where would you guess she is? Could she have gone to another shelter?'

58

Brale rubbed his chin. 'Conceivable. But I used up a big chip and a lot of your cash finding that one. My gut . . . nah, I don't see her in another shelter. I spooked the ass off her, for one thing.' He ruminated for a while longer. 'I say she's taken off.'

'For . . . ?'

'I'm not Jeane Dixon. I don't know — family? Friends? Where do *you* think she'd go?'

'We know she's not at the hospital. She has no family except a sister back in Cuba. Caron lost touch with her years ago. There are a couple of people . . . a professor at Johns Hopkins we get Christmas cards from, and a friend in Boston. Woman named Julie, uh, Gerstein. An eye doctor.'

'How would she get to Baltimore or Boston?'

The dim moonlight outlined Harry's features — the jutting chin and perfect nose, the thick gloss of hair tumbling over his brow. But instead of the playful, inviting expression his face wore on television, Brale saw the tunnel-vision intensity Harry used to radiate in his stand-up days, when all his energy was beamed on the next set, the new club to breach, the performer to outdo for laughter and applause.

'Train, plane, automobile?' Harry said. 'I

59

don't know. If you had been back to me sooner, we could have set up something, had you watched the most likely route — '

'If I had been back to you sooner, it probably would have been in my one phone call from Central Booking. You can't just walk away from an attempted murder at a safe house and go on about your business. I had tracks to cover.'

'She and Josh would be too recognizable on public transportation,' Harry said. 'Unless she left Josh somewhere. Jesus, I wish I could talk to him now. I need time with him, to explain to him. He isn't sure what he saw.'

'He sounded pretty sure on the air.'

Harry had thought the same, but didn't dare admit that, to Brale or even entirely to himself. Josh's statement on the radio had shocked him. Didn't the boy understand he was hanging his father? How had the yearning, loving little boy at the hotel become the turncoat on the radio?

Down in his soul he was furious with Josh. But those feelings had to stay down — or Harry could end up in even worse trouble than now.

To Brale he said only, 'He's been with Caron all night.'

'Great touch about the FBI, by the way.

So,' Brale said, 'We have him with Caron as they talk to WCBS. Does she stash him somewhere and get on a train or plane or bus? I don't see it. Not *after* going on the air, *after* people know there's a scandal cooking. She's still recognizable; people remember the hurricane business. And you, Christ, you're candy. She's plenty interesting just as Mrs Harry. So we assume they're still together. What are their options? I get two. Hole up in New York somewhere and don't come out, or leave the area for a safer place, without using public transportation. Would she get a ride? Who would she call to pick her up?'

Harry shook his head. They were quiet for a minute. A slight black man walked slowly by, humming.

Brale said, 'Let's start from *what* instead of where or who. What is her objective now? How will she fight back?'

'Felhammer or Julie,' Harry said. 'She'll need a doctor to refute the brain cancer diagnosis, and she's not popular with doctors.'

Brale noticed the word *diagnosis*. Not *story* or *accusation*. Harry was already convinced he was the one telling the truth.

★ ★ ★

61

Harry had felt a stirring when the black man ambled past. The curled posture, the aimless walk, sent a signal.

Josh had come to mind again at that moment. Disloyal turncoat Josh, telling tales and revealing confidences.

Now, his meeting with Brale finished, he waited for Brale to be out of sight. When, looking south into the dark park, he could no longer see Brale, Harry set off to the north. With practised ease he refrained from walking fast enough to strike a wrong note for the hour, but set a pace that, if the man hadn't exited the park, should catch Harry up with him.

Harry's palms tingled. Josh's words banged around in his head: 'I never told . . . My dad asked me not to . . . He throws things . . . He hurt Caron . . . ' His arm muscles tensed and relaxed, tensed and relaxed, as if sucking in his anguish for release.

Suddenly Harry heard a rustle in a hedge, then a hiss. He stopped, listened hard. He peered around the foliage.

A man was urinating. But he was twentyish and shaggy-haired, with a big naked back, and Harry turned fast and left noiselessly.

Finally Harry found the black man. He was sitting on the edge of a bench with his hands folded almost demurely in his lap. There were sprinkles of gray in the tight curls. which shone in the slight glow from the nearest light.

Harry crooked an arm around the man's neck and dragged him back to the darkness behind the bench as the hands fluttered against him.

★   ★   ★

It wasn't Harry's oldest secret, or even his worst. But it was the only one that absolutely nobody knew.

The first beating had happened in the spring of 1967. He had a studio apartment on East 32nd Street, but spent most nights at his then-girlfriend Hermine's on West 10th. Hermine was biggish and comfortable and generous, and didn't mind frying up some burgers if Harry came in hungry at two a.m. after his night of stand-up.

'I'm awake,' Hermine would say when Harry hugged her in gratitude. 'What's the difference whether I'm awake in bed reading or at the stove cooking?'

One night, waiting at a sticky table off to the side of the stage at the Brooklyn comedy club Snickers, Harry had listened without smiling to an anti-Semitic routine by the comic ahead of him, a rising regular named

Darren Davies. The jokes had so offended Harry that he'd escaped to the men's room . . . and it was in there that the old feelings had returned.

Leaning against the locked door of the tiny bathroom, smelling the sewage-not-covered-by-PineSol odor, Harry had remembered that smell, and unendurable pain, from a childhood day back in Craig Head.

★ ★ ★

There were not many Jews in North Carolina, and Harry's father Aaron, having changed his name from Kravitz to Crane upon marrying a Christian girl, chose to keep the Jewish element confidential. But when Harry was in second grade, his newly widowed aunt, Darcy Levy, moved from New York to Craig Head. She made no secret of her religion, and the news was out.

One day Harry's two best friends, Sam MacArthur and George Beech, followed Harry into the boys' room after the three-fifteen bell.

'We're going fishing today, right?' Harry asked. 'I have to go home and get my pole.'

He realized Sam and George were just standing, watching him closely as he opened his fly and began to urinate.

'Don't you have to go?' Harry asked them.

'It doesn't look different,' Sam said to George.

George got down on one knee and peered closely at Harry's penis.

Suddenly Harry felt weird. 'What are you doing that for?' He finished up and zipped his fly.

Sam grinned. 'A report.'

'Everyone in the class wanted to know if yours was cut off at the end,' Sam said. 'Because of you being a Jew. They wanted George and me to find out.'

Harry felt a sharp twinge in his chest. 'Shut up,' he said, reddening.

'Take it back out,' Sam told Harry, 'so George and me can draw a picture of it. To go with the report.'

The weird feeling churned inside him. Harry wanted out of this bad dream and back into his fishing plans with his best buddies. He headed for the door to the corridor.

'Go to hell,' Harry said. 'Just forget all that stuff. We have to get our poles — '

Right then George and Sam grabbed Harry's arms.

It wasn't just George and Sam. Russ MacArthur, Sam's older brother, was waiting in the corridor with two other sixth-graders,

Melvin Clark and Jerry Albert. The five of them took Harry down to Mantle Beach, to the shaded opening in a stand of pines where Harry and George and Sam had spent a hundred afternoons fishing.

They shoved Harry to the sandy, needle-covered ground. His head hit a rock, just hard enough to cause a momentary spinning; and in that instant Harry saw himself and George and Sam as they had been right in this spot every other time, stretched out on the rocks, poles in the water. There would be a big can of Hawaiian Punch and a bag of potato chips.

One time Harry had been pulled to his feet by a monster tug on his line. The other two had leaped up and held his waist, yelling excitedly while he wrestled with the thing and finally reeled in a big, twisting bluefish.

'Look at that,' George had breathed.

'Great catch,' Sam had said, clapping Harry's back.

They had bragged all over school about Harry's accomplishment.

Now Harry was lying there with sand in his mouth and a terrible stomach ache where Sam had just kicked him, and the five boys were looking at him the way he and his two best friends had looked at the bluefish, debating whether to let it live.

'Take his pants off,' Russ said, pinning Harry's arms. Sam and Melvin stooped to comply.

There was the rasp of a match as Jerry lit a cigarette.

Melvin said, 'We going to burn him down there? Burn the hair first. It smells.'

'There's no hair on a second-grader,' Jerry said.

'Jews, there is. Hair all over 'em.'

'Not this one,' Russ said as Harry's trousers came off.

Harry let out a yell and kicked with both feet, but there wasn't a prayer. The boys were on him, pinning him back down.

'George,' Russ said, 'you just gonna watch?'

From his position on the ground, straining up to try to look beyond his feet, Harry could see his shrunken genitals quaking with the rest of him. His head and body ran with sweat.

George moved toward him. Harry watched in hypnotic horror as George lifted a bare foot and stomped his heel into Harry's scrotum.

He felt as if a sword had been stabbed into his bottom. He lost his breath, then caught it in a deep, groaning gasp that became a shriek as Jerry touched the cigarette to the head of his quivering penis.

* * *

Standing in the Snickers men's room, holding his ears against the venom booming from the stage, Harry felt tears on his face. The feelings were back, slamming him, the rage and the hurt.

The entire school had turned against him after that, replacing admiration and friend-ship with suspicion and contempt. Sam and George avoided him entirely. At least once a month Harry would fail in his attempts to avoid his three sixth-grade tormentors, and if the meeting happened to occur in circum-stances friendly to them, there would be a knee in his groin or a bang on the head with a school book. Once Russ MacArthur forced a live tadpole into Harry's throat, then called kids over to watch Harry retch his last two meals on to the sidewalk.

* * *

Discrimination had long since become a non-issue for Harry. He had changed his surname back to Kravitz and wore his heritage with proud defiance. He was in New

York. He had legions of friends who wouldn't have cared if he was a Muslim.

But the one thing he would not do was fuck up his own career. Darren Davies was way ahead of Harry in the pecking order, and a frequent emcee at Snickers. To take the man on would be comedic suicide.

Harry knew who the tears were for.

Not the long-ago lost friends.

They were for himself, for what he had lost tonight — his remaining principles, his self-respect.

By the end of the night Harry couldn't stand the emotions rolling in his gut. As the customers paid and left, and the other comics drifted to the bar to bull-shit, Harry headed for the door. At least he could leave without kissing Darren's ass. He could be proud of that much.

But Darren clutched Harry's shoulder warmly just as he was stepping outside. The clean smell of the spring night was in Harry's nostrils, he was almost gone from there with his one tidbit of pride left, when Darren said, 'Nice set tonight. Great job.' And Harry had to say, 'You too. Funny stuff.'

Sick in his heart, Harry had ridden the subway to Hermine's. But as he turned the corner on to her block, he found himself walking more and more slowly.

He realized that not only wasn't he hungry — he didn't have his usual desire to sit with Hermine, be with her, love her.

He wanted to hurt her.

What a suckass he was for chomping down those burgers, taking everything she offered. Hermine was trapping him. She obviously thought Harry was good for a heavy payback once he hit.

The more he thought about it, the more convinced Harry grew that Hermine was plotting to ensnare him, that all her seemingly sweet gestures were venal.

Harry passed Hermine's building and kept walking, around the block, around another. He got angrier, so angry he wanted to feel flesh in his fingers, wanted to hear her gasp and yell . . .

He was back near the subway now, but he could be at Hermine's door in under a minute if he ran . . .

Something told him not to.

He ran the other way instead, to the subway, down the steps and on to the platform, where he paced away three minutes until the train came.

He went to Prospect Park and walked some more. As he strode the cement pathway through the trees, a bum had asked for a match.

Reaching for it in his pocket, Harry had stopped, raised both hands, and clasped them around the man's neck. As the eyes opened in terror — wide, wider — Harry had felt elation flash through him.

Letting go, Harry had watched the man sag to the ground. His feet moving almost of their own accord, Harry had pounded the barely moving form with the heels of his leather shoes.

Soft whimpers, then no sound.

Harry gazed down for a minute, saw the chest move.

He got out of there.

Riding the subway back to Manhattan, Harry had felt an odd sensation which took him a while to identify: relief. The feeling stayed with him for weeks, overriding the cringing regret of the beating that often sneaked up.

★   ★   ★

Now, the black man's eyes were shut, not voluntarily. Blood dripped from his mouth and was smeared on his left hand, where Harry had stomped on it.

Harry checked his own hands, then his clothes, and hurried away.

This many years later, he felt the

71

self-loathing only briefly after he beat someone. He always chose an expendable sub-person, and he always left them alive, to be found and fixed up with his tax money.

What he still felt, every time, was the relief. He was grateful he could achieve it that way — that he could substitute the bums for the others: the kids . . . his own kid . . . and, usually, the women who loved him.

Usually.

But there was still the agonizing stretch before the relief kicked in, when he was consumed once again by the pain of being the one beaten — at the river by his former friends . . . and in the Snickers bathroom by his longing for the pinnacle.

6

Being accepted into the freshman class at Columbia University in New York was the most galvanizing thing that had ever happened to Harry. Once there, he worked every day at making the best of this chance to outrun his past, his already significant collection of secrets — both the ethnic one his father had attempted to keep, and his own less nobly motivated ones.

He became a force in Hillel, leading the movement to combat anti-Semitism. His campus radio program drew devoted listeners who compared his style to the zany humor of Ernie Kovacs.

After graduation Harry worked as a TV production assistant. At night he would take the subway to Snickers. Studying the regulars, putting together his observations with his radio experience and his personal lessons in self-control and group dynamics, Harry became a comic.

He began making money at it. He did guest spots on Mike Douglas and Merv Griffin, and on a Dinah Shore special. Audiences loved Harry; he wasn't mean, he worked clean, and he had a way of isolating that nugget of daily life and giving it a comedic spin that kept them wiping their eyes.

One night he was at the Improv, trying out new material. After his successful set another performer, a smart, up-and-coming prop comic named Ronald Brale, suggested they head over to the Copacabana. In the basement beneath the famous club was a lovely private lounge, with free liquor and cold sliced filet, for the big-ticket performers who dropped by. Harry and Ronald chatted with Steve Lawrence and Robert Goulet, then Myron Cohen.

Eventually the lounge was empty but for the two of them, and they poured a last brandy before moving out.

Ronald was just replacing the bottle when Boomer Picard, the club manager, rushed into the lounge. 'What the Christ do you two losers think you're doing in here?'

'Having a brandy,' Ronald said.

'Don't wiseass me.' Boomer shoved Ronald. 'I didn't see you come in, or I wouldn't have let you down here. This room isn't for showcase amateurs. Get the fuck out. Leave money for what you had.'

Ronald shoved back. 'Eat my wang.'

Harry watched the two square off. Ronald was brave; Boomer outweighed him, and everyone knew Boomer was a former boxer. But Ronald never took crap, onstage or off.

There was another shove exchanged, and Boomer went down, cracking his head on the cast-iron bar footing.

The noise resounded in the lush room. After a paralyzed moment, Ronald and Harry knelt, then stood.

Boomer was dead.

★　★　★

Harry was excellent with the police. Some of them knew who he was, and wanted his autograph. They were quite prepared to accept his explanation that Boomer had tripped on that loose corner of carpet and was beyond help the minute he fell.

It had come to Harry on impulse to cover Ronald. Later, analyzing the move as he lay back in his recliner at his apartment, Harry grasped the explanation.

He needed someone like Ronald owing him. He needed protection potential. Some old urges from his Craig Head days were returning. He swore he'd resist, but he'd sworn that in the past, and been helpless as the desire took him. The derelict beatings didn't always shower him down. And there was no longer a motivated police department to ice matters over, as had been the case in Craig Head.

Ronald was bright and neat and money-hungry. He liked to hurt people; Harry had seen that in his body language, his quickened breathing.

Harry didn't know what he'd need Ronald to do, and his better side dreaded needing him at all. But being a star mattered more than anything ever had or would, and Harry was on his way. Facing the probabilities honestly, he had to acknowledge that sooner or later, as he climbed, as he became better known, he'd need protection. At some point.

★   ★   ★

The following years were wonderful. Harry was picked up by the Paul Wundring Agency; there were gigs turned down; he was getting recognized on the street.

He maintained an active and healthy sex life. He succeeded at keeping his fantasies just fantasies. Brale wasn't needed, but Harry added regular payments to the pot, supposedly for comedy material, keeping Brale on retainer, as it were; you never knew. Nobody ever expected to make use of their flight insurance either.

Once in a while Harry had to protect

himself on his own. A television show changed producers, and the new person had her favorites and wouldn't book him; she blew off his calls, wouldn't go to lunch even at Crist Cella. So Harry leaked a made-up story of her heroin addiction and violent lesbian private life. A writer freelancing for *GQ* had written a nasty profile; Harry snooped around, found out the writer was selling cocaine to pay his overblown credit card bills, and reported him. Harry had also made sure there was enough evidence found to put the man away for a time.

But he had to stop that stuff. He loved show business too much to tarnish himself with the slimy side. And it was getting too dangerous. The risk wasn't justifiable. He'd only use Brale if he was in a really tight bind.

Harry was ecstatic when he got his first daily TV show. *Talkin' With Harry*, a celebrity interview show where everyone sat around on informal high stools and chatted, was a modest success, winning decent shares in its noon slot. Handsome, engaging, and easygoing, Harry could pull a laugh from anyone, but his real strength was the ability to make even the most dour personalities seem funny themselves. He would sift and dig until he knew what tickled them, then excise it, boost it, and play straight to it. All this took just minutes, and guests would leave feeling they'd been wonderful. They couldn't wait to be on again.

Eventually a hot soap went up against him in the slot. *Talkin' With Harry* sagged and was dropped. By now Harry had a penthouse and he holed up in it, trying to shake his overwhelming sense of failure. He even ordered his groceries by phone.

His sister Monica, newly divorced and relocating to Vermont, came north with her two children, eight-year-old Adam and ten-year-old Debbie, to spend two summer weeks in New York. She was keeping her married name, Wool, she sheepishly explained. She still felt guilty that she had not followed Harry's brave example in taking their father's original name.

Rising to the expected image, Harry swallowed his depression and played the successful television star, showing the family around the studios. Everyone there greeted him with kisses and handshakes, and there were several requests for autographs. It helped put his rejection in perspective. He began to sense an upcurve.

It wasn't long before Paul Wundring called Harry with a proposal for a new sitcom. The fact that the approach came from the agency head himself, and not the agent who usually took care of him, told Harry more clearly than any words could have what the significance level of this project was.

They made a pilot for *Scott*, with Harry acting the lead role of the lovably schleppy smalltown lawyer. Harry was able to fine-tune the dialogue for maximum laugh potential without pissing off any of the creative staff, an impossible feat. In Harry's interpretation, the character became less addled than country-smart, less silly than fun-loving. Harry's chesty build and sexy grin made a fine counterpoint to the ingenuousness. Adrienne Grunwald was perfectly cast as Scott's wife. Her cheerily sarcastic Greek-chorus persona only made the Scott character glow brighter.

★ ★ ★

Harry continued to pay Ronald Brale 'fees' for 'material' — though Ronald was long out of the comedy business, and they both understood what was being bought, even if it was never utilized.

Occasionally, as his own life and career rolled on in velvety good fortune, Harry considered cutting the man loose. But he came to be very glad he hadn't.

★ ★ ★

Sheila Dannenbring had the loveliest eyes Harry had ever seen, and he told her so.

'My only good feature,' she said, pouring champagne into the glass on his tray.

'They are *not*.' Harry took her free hand and turned it so the long smooth fingers rested gracefully along his wrist. 'Your hands are beautiful, and . . . I don't know you well enough to continue.'

They both laughed.

'Thank you for giving me the nerve to ask for your autograph,' Sheila said. 'We're not supposed to hassle the first-class passengers, but I can't resist 'Scott'.'

The show was in its first season, having been picked up by CBS, and Harry was not yet accustomed to the awe accorded a sitcom star. He blushed, stuttered, grinned, and blurted out, 'I can't resist you either.'

★ ★ ★

Harry and Sheila were married seven months later, and within a year they had a son. Sheila wanted to name him Robert, but Harry insisted on Joshua, out of loyalty to his heritage.

The marriage had its tensions. After an initial crackle, *Scott* suffered a wobbly two years in the ratings, and, though everyone

80

who ought to still took his calls, the insecurity was a constant burden. Sometimes Harry could feel stomach acid eating at him. When he grew that miserable, he was capable of releasing his anguish violently. Any annoying note at home could cause it.

He hated to see that side of himself emerge, and tried to prevent it. If he was tempted to slap Sheila, or throw an object, he yanked on his shorts, went out and ran in Central Park. Occasionally he required the release of a beating.

Josh was two when Harry's fail-safe system failed for the last time with Sheila. He had just dropped another smidgen in the ratings, making him body-sick with worry. That night, Sheila kept turning the television volume too loud when the last thing Harry needed to hear was others doing the job that might not be his much longer.

Harry broke Sheila's left arm in four places.

The marriage was over, of course, and Harry was furious at himself. But he would not relinquish his son, or his *Scott* image. He had to clean up.

He had Brale keep Josh and made pretend threats to Sheila along the line of what would happen to the child if she revealed their private business or tried for custody. Sheila had no idea he was pretending. He was able to convince her to go out of their lives forever.

Harry was determined to be a fine father. Josh would never need to wonder who he was.

Harry kept to that vow. He regaled Josh with the same tales he had heard as a boy, about bygone *mispocheh* and their feather-pillow business, but he didn't whisper them, as his own father had; he trumpeted them.

Scott regained its footing in the CBS lineup. It climbed into the top ten and copped Emmys every year. Harry and Adrienne were honored with solid gold gifts from William Paley, who called them 'the diamonds of CBS'.

Scott was Harry's life, but so was Josh. Harry structured his time to allow ample attention for his son. He enrolled Josh in Hebrew school, and practiced the lessons with him.

He didn't specifically discuss his own childhood. He evaded questions, lied when he had to. He invented an early life in Atlanta for details that had to be given. An internship he had actually done there while in college, rising from mailroom drone to production assistant, gave the CBS promotion unit enough to chew on when they wanted hometown publicity for *Scott*.

When Josh asked about his mother, Harry sadly explained how she was sick, sick in her mind, too sick to ever safely care for a child. She had gone off years before, and nobody knew where she was.

★　★　★

There came the horrible Sunday in February 1985 when Adrienne Grunwald's white Corvette slid across the Ventura Freeway in a slippery drizzle and was macerated by a dump truck. Adrienne died immediately. Her Airedale Sherman wasn't hurt.

It was William Paley himself who delivered the news of the *Scott* cancellation to Harry, not that it *was* news. Harry well knew that the American public could be taught to buy the fiction of a pretend family, but not the resurrection of a member mourned, and Adrienne was certainly that. Harry himself had shed real tears, hugging Sherman on his lap, as he narrated the favorite scenes and outtakes that had served as Adrienne's TV memorial.

That night Harry went down to the docks by the West Side Highway. He fixed on his target, a stumbling addict with filthy facial hair, and was readying to pounce, the fury

83

coursing through his arms, when the man suddenly ducked aside to light a cigarette. The body language metamorphosed instantly. Backing farther into the shadows himself, Harry watched in horror as the man efficiently performed the task and then slumped back into his role as he came out of hiding.

An undercover cop.

After him? No. The beatings attracted no attention in New York, derelicts bloodied one another all the time. The cop was probably watching for some kids who were getting press for setting fire to homeless people.

But Harry was shocked, appalled, livid. He could have tumbled right into the trap.

He quickly left the area and went to the Bowery. At the end of an alley he found a skeletal old guy who couldn't be an undercover anything. Harry began on the face, hitting the man's remaining teeth back into his mouth. He thought of all the wonderful joys of being Scott as he pounded the man's toes, and made noises under his breath.

* * *

There was a flurry of guest shots on network morning and late-night shows, and then a drought. Eating pancakes with Josh one morning, Harry thought about how the entertainment-world treatment of him paralleled the usual unfortunate reaction people had to a bereaved survivor: everyone flocked around at first, and then they all went back to their grocery lists and forgot about you.

But he put himself out there, and Paul worked the right people, and Harry's long love affair with the industry was still blazing. People adored him; not just the public, but producers and directors and other stars. His reputation as someone easy to work with, a performer who made other performers look good, was as strong as ever.

He did a couple of supporting roles in big-ticket features. He made network appearances. He substituted for Johnny.

There had been whispers for years that Carson was retiring. Certain names were rumored to be in line to replace him. David Letterman was mentioned, and Jay Leno, and Harry Kravitz.

'On a likelihood scale of ten,' Paul Wundring said one day in December of 1990, as they lunched among the pine boughs that decorated the banquettes at Le Cirque, 'you're eight. Letterman is nine, and Leno's six. That's how the talk is going.'

Harry's heart soared. He tried to continue

coolly with his meal, but Paul saw through it.

Paul clasped Harry's wrist. 'It's incredible, isn't it? You slog along and take the crap, and it's almost, almost, almost . . . and then it happens. You've broken out. You're on top.'

Harry eyes met Paul's He was overcome. 'I hope . . . God . . . '

The rumors continued. Nothing was decided. Harry came home one afternoon in the New Year and found Josh on the phone, using the wrong line, Harry's business line.

Harry was horrified. What if Paul had been trying to reach him?

He began to yell. Josh was *never* to use that line, Josh knew that.

As Josh was scrambling for words of apology, the line rang. It was Paul. Harry knew this was it, *the* call, at last. Harry was going to be the star of the world, he'd known it all along, and here was his notification. Nothing could hold it back, not Letterman nor Leno nor Carson himself, nor a busy signal.

But Paul was just calling to ask if Harry knew a good Kosher restaurant.

Harry finished the conversation and hung up. Josh went on with his apology. Harry wasn't hearing the words, just the buzz, the annoying insect cloud of noise vying for his attention with the pounding of his own blood.

When was he *ever* going to be able to relax and know he had the *Tonight Show?* The waiting was driving him insane. And Paul, how could Paul be so insensitive, *knowing* he was waiting?

Paul shouldn't have bothered him. Josh shouldn't be bothering him.

Harry's fury swelled, and the insect blather did too, and suddenly he did what you do to an insect. He smashed it against the wall.

7

Horace had organized Caron's entry into the States. She was enrolled at Johns Hopkins, which hadn't been difficult to arrange, as Caron's IQ and educational level were extraordinary.

Caron was scheduled to leave Cuba for Baltimore in August 1976 to start the semester. But in July word came from her father's associate Dr Felhammer that Horace was sick.

The late-day sun made orange pools on Caron's bedroom rug as she packed to leave Santa Conda. Valued possessions were cushioned in her clothing: family pictures and her mother's favorite figurines, including a bust of Vasco da Gama. This last Caron packed for her father, who had given it to Greta and loved it himself.

The bust was heavy and made the suitcase hard to carry. But an old voice of child-magic convinced Caron that if she brought it, her father would be well again and they could finally have the life together of parent and daughter.

Caron's sister Elisa and Elisa's husband

Reco went with her to the airport. The girls clutched each other and cried.

On the plane Caron looked out at the unending ocean and felt more alone than ever in her life — more even than at Greta's death. Because she hadn't known then that the pain of the empty place stays with you always.

But soon Caron would be with her father again, and maybe now, away from Santa Conda and its ghosts for all these years, he would want to be close to her.

★ ★ ★

Caron had always imagined Dr Felhammer to be a grizzled and gray mad-scientist sort of person. But the man who picked her out of the disembarking crowd was very tall and thin, with a full mustache.

He took her case and set it down. He held her hands tightly and kissed her on both cheeks. Then he told her Horace was dead.

Pneumonia, a devastating strain, it had come on fast and steamrolled through the antibiotics. The funeral was this afternoon; they had held it off for her.

★ ★ ★

The days after the funeral were a wet blur of agony. Caron spent them curled up under the covers of her father's big bed in the posh condominium unit that had been his home. She refused to stay with Dr Felhammer, or to eat the food he brought her. But he persevered, as if with a forest animal, and eventually Caron began to heal.

Dr Felhammer helped Caron sell the apartment and transfer to Smith College in Massachusetts, believing the nurturing smalltown warmth would help heal her further. Caron succeeded at Smith, and made a few friends, but she was lonely. She would wake before her alarm, an empty ache cramping her insides. She fell into the habit of phoning the weather recording early in the morning, because the forecast was given by a throaty, accented male voice that was exactly like her father's had been back in Santa Conda, when he had just awakened.

Caron went on to Harvard Medical School, distinguishing herself in surgery and pediatrics. She adored the babies and toddlers, spent her precious off-time with them, and was devastated every time they lost one. The pain convinced her to stick with surgery.

She graduated with honors in both areas.

Dr Felhammer was her only guest at both her Smith and Harvard graduations. Elisa had fallen completely out of touch.

* * *

Caron's roommate for her internship at Massachusetts General Hospital was Julie Gerstein — broad-shouldered, intense, honest, and determined to break through Caron's comfort zone.

'You think anyone you love will disappear,' Julie said one night as they walked back from a movie. 'You're afraid to put anything out to another person.'

'But that's my choice.'

'It's a choice that will make you a shitty doctor.'

Caron stopped. 'Not in surgery.'

'In anything. It limits the rest of your life too. Look, Caron, I know you've had awful breaks, but you're a grown-up now. It's time to come out of your cocoon and take some risks. Try, fly, jump.'

* * *

Caron pondered her friend's advice and began trying to put it into practice, beginning with Julie herself. How could you not feel love and gratitude for a person who insisted on struggling out of bed at five-thirty to walk her roommate to a six a.m. class so she wouldn't have to cross dark underground passages alone?

She became more aggressive in the operating room, asking to assist in procedures, making suggestions. Her ideas showed the beginnings of a sparkling surgical talent. She acquired a reputation among her fellow interns for a gutsy, maverick approach to surgery.

She caught the attention of her superiors at Mass General, and was offered a surgical residency.

★ ★ ★

One evening Caron was called to the pediatric ICU to evaluate a burn victim.

Wayne Snow was a nine-year-old with freckles and what had once been red hair. A can of charcoal lighter left too near a hibachi had exploded in front of him. He had part of one ear left, and no lower lip.

To keep from breaking into sobs, Caron immediately began making notes. She did it with her right hand. With her left she gripped Wayne's. As she wrote, she gave him encouraging squeezes. The one time he squeezed back, Caron brought his hand up and kissed it.

Wayne had surgery. During his recovery Caron saw him three or four times a day. She brought him Italian ice cream and videos. For a while he improved.

Caron sensed the downturn almost before it was quantifiable. The physical signs weren't even significant when she began to feel the letting go.

She wanted to grab Wayne from where he rested and pump him full of blood and medication and breath. She wished she could scream at him not to give in. It tormented her that regardless of education and training and skill and passion it was not in her or anyone's power to save Wayne.

He died three weeks later. At his funeral Caron was so overcome, she had to leave the church.

* * *

She kept dreaming about the boy. He would appear whole and healthy in a picket-fence scene, or ride past her on a bike.

One afternoon after two night stints, when Caron was supposed to be sleeping, she couldn't shut the dreams off. She got up and went walking at Boston Harbor, fighting the blustery November wind. She decided to take a few days and wear herself out at tennis camp. Maybe that would ease her sorrow, interrupt her compulsive replaying of the surgery and aftermath.

Caron stopped by the hospital to check her upcoming schedule before making the camp reservation.

Another surgeon was reading the posted sheet when she got there, an Argentinian resident named Pier Natillo.

'How are you doing?' Pier asked Caron.

She started to give a rote answer, but saw his face and understood that it was a genuine question.

'A little better, I guess. I still think about Wayne all the time, dream about him. I have to let go of this.'

'Why?'

Caron looked at him.

'It is appropriate for us to mourn our lost patients,' Pier said. 'There is something very wrong with doctors who don't. Would you want your child forgotten by his doctor?'

Away for her long weekend on the courts, Caron found some solace in the constant whacking of the ball . . . and in Pier's words, which echoed with kindness, humanness. She was too often appalled by the distance maintained in medicine. Here was a doctor with warmth.

'Call him,' Julie said after Caron had been home a week and not run into Pier again. 'We can do that now.'

'No.'

'Then at least manipulate him into calling you.'

So Caron watched the surgical schedules and made sure to bump into Pier.

'Hello again,' he said, touching her arm. 'You are looking better.'

She had forgotten how attractive he was, with his satiny black hair and big square hands. She tried to think of a way to achieve Julie's suggestion, but Pier saved her the trouble.

'I hoped I would see you around,' he said. 'I wanted to ask you to have dinner with me.'

★ ★ ★

On a snowy Friday night the next week Pier picked her up in his Jeep. They had seafood platters at a dark, woody restaurant that sat on a loop of the harbor.

'Are you still dreaming about Wayne?' Pier asked Caron.

'Not as much, but — yes. He haunts me.'

'It's terrible, isn't it, the pain of these losses? I've had four.'

Caron shook her head. She could see in his eyes that he reacted to pediatric deaths with the same black hopelessness she had experienced after Wayne. 'How do you get through that? Sometimes I wish I could be like other doctors — '

Pier held up his hand. 'I will finish the thought for you. You wish you could neutralize the deaths as they do, by consigning them to some faraway intellectual bin of surgical averages and mortality rates.'

Caron blinked. 'Exactly.'

Pier took her hands across the table and held them tight.

* * *

The following weekend, they went to a Spanish movie and laughed at the jokes before the rest of the audience, who had to wait for the subtitles — which made them laugh harder. The weekend after that, Pier invited Caron to his house for Sunday brunch.

He lived in a rented cottage on an estate in a rural pocket of Lexington, three rooms with an attached greenhouse. The greenhouse had panes missing and was overgrown, but the constant sun kept it warm, and it was earthy and damply fragrant.

'Do you mind if we eat in there?' Pier asked, dishing out chicken salad.

'I was hoping we could,' Caron said.

They sat on a blanket on the dirt floor. A piano sonata played in the background. After the meal, Pier brought out a plate of cut-up fruit, which they ate with what was left of a bottle of Riesling.

He fed her a slice of cantaloupe, and she reciprocated with a strawberry. But he kept her hand and kissed it instead of letting her pull it back. Then he used it to draw her over close to him. He folded her in his arms and they kissed.

They made love on the blanket, and afterward lay for hours talking and listening to the winter birds squabble over seed in a feeder just outside.

★ ★ ★

Caron had always reacted with vague discomfort to the phrase *in love*, as if it were some foreign term she was supposed to understand but didn't.

After the day in the greenhouse, it began to creep into her thoughts when Pier came to mind, which was more and more often.

They loved being together. Were learning the minutiae of each other's lives. Cared about each other's cares.

For the first time since childhood, her baseline loneliness was beginning to shrink.

In April Pier asked her to marry him.

'We make an excellent couple. You know we do,' he said. 'We both want a home and children. Why wait any longer?'

* * *

As the moon rose on their wedding night, they were walking the beach in Bermuda when Pier said, 'You'll go off the Pill now?'

'Not yet.'

'When?'

'When my residency ends in September. We discussed that.'

'Can't it be sooner?'

Caron laughed. 'Be patient, Pier. We'll have our brood soon enough.'

But Pier brought it up again and again. He wanted children so badly. He just couldn't wait. It might take a few months to conceive. They should begin trying.

Caron put her pills away. Pier had studied the techniques for improving the chance of conception — waiting forty-eight hours between acts of intercourse, lying with knees raised afterward — and they waited expectantly for a missed period. But it came each month.

'We're probably trying too hard,' Caron said one day in August, damming back tears, as they stood in the bedroom of the cottage. 'Maybe we should stop thinking about making a baby and just make love.'

Pier glared at the Tampax box in her hand. 'I don't understand this.'

'I don't either.'

She reached for him, needing the comfort, wanting to give it. She ached to hold their child, to share that indescribable creation. Her unresponsive, unchanging body was bewildering. Twice she had dreamed of an exquisitely furnished but dusty and cob-webbed room inside herself.

But Pier simply left, muttering that he had patients to see.

* * *

Still working on the hypothesis that they needed to relax, Caron made several attempts to set the stage for the rich lovemaking they had enjoyed so often before the wedding. She bought new underthings, new music. Instead of waiting for bedtime, she approached Pier at times she thought would pleasantly surprise him.

But Pier criticized the music and seemed

99

uninterested in her initiations.

Caron tried not to be over sensitive, but Pier's responses hurt badly. He had always been exacting, but now that they both seemed to consider her a failure anyway, each new rebuff crushed her.

One afternoon after work, as she hurriedly changed clothes so she wouldn't have to greet Pier in her scrubs, Caron decided to insist on a fertility workup. Pier hadn't wanted one; they were complicated and degrading.

But anything was better than this limbo.

★　★　★

They had the tests. The morning of their appointment to discuss the results, Caron stood at the kitchen counter and drank three cups of coffee, but couldn't eat.

Pier came up behind her and hugged her around the waist. He was so rarely demonstrative now that the touch was a lovely warm blanket. Caron snuggled back against him, emotion bursting within.

The waiting room of the infertility office was separated by a clear glass partition from an OB/GYN waiting area. Chairs were arranged back-to-back from one area to the next, but Caron was very aware of all the pregnant bellies behind her.

100

After a while she turned in her seat and looked.

She realized she had already nearly decided she would never be able to be one of them.

Some of the women were lovely, especially a petite Latina with a big gleaming smile. Her violet maternity blouse enhanced her huge brown eyes. A toddler nestled in her lap against what would be his new sibling in two months or so.

Caron's throat burned with unspilled tears as she stared at the perfect replacement for herself in Pier's life.

In her imagination she saw the woman in a short night-dress, her breasts ripe beneath, slipping into the big bed in the cottage. Pier came into the scene and lay beside her, and reached to stroke her hair . . .

The scene was so real that Caron felt ill with the pain of it. Her morning coffee was bitter in her throat.

She had to dart a glance at Pier, to see if he was looking at the woman.

He wasn't, of course. He was reading a surgical journal.

Caron forced herself to face forward in her chair. They didn't have the test results yet. There was no proof she had a problem. Sometimes normal women took months to conceive. She might be just as beautifully pregnant as that any day.

As soon as Caron and Pier entered the infertility specialist's office, he came around his big desk to join them in a grouping of soft chairs. Caron's hands went to her chest. She knew what that meant. It was exactly what surgeons did when there was bad news. They made the family comfortable and pretended to be comfortable themselves, and then told them the person was dead.

'I'm sorry,' the man said. 'The sperm count is quite sufficiently high. Your tubes are not functional, Caron. We can try the usual procedure, but I don't promise much result.'

The woman in the violet blouse popped back into Caron's mind as the tears dripped into her flat lap. Pier got up and put his arms around her and laid his cheek against hers.

'We'll get through this,' he said, his breath warming her ear.

★ ★ ★

Caron had her fallopian tubes blown out. It hurt like hell and didn't change anything. She was advised against taking fertility drugs; they wouldn't help.

But, miraculously, the chill was gone now from the marriage. Pier seemed to need her comfort as much as she needed his.

One night they went to a movie that had a wrenching birth scene. Caron reached for Pier's hand at the exact moment he reached for hers. He brought hers to his mouth and kissed it. 'We have each other to love and care for,' he said quietly.

'Yes,' she whispered back. 'But I can't stop wishing — '

'Yes, you can. We're stopping together. The past is gone. We two are the family. I love you with everything I have.'

★ ★ ★

Despite Pier's brave words, Caron couldn't let go entirely of the idea of raising a baby. As the weeks passed, she watched her co-workers head home to their families each night, and she ached for a child to touch.

The pediatric unit became a tough place to be. Once there, Caron wanted to cuddle all the little ones instead of working.

Without telling Pier, she went to an adoption meeting.

It was so hard to shift from longing for a child of your own to welcoming someone else's. You had to give up a big piece of the picture. But she and Pier could choose adoption or no child.

The meeting was at a church in Waltham.

103

Too-cheerful people pasted on name tags and poured juice. But Caron learned what she had come for. There were children available, especially if you were willing to adopt older ones.

She left the church with an envelope full of literature, but wasn't ready to go home yet. She drove to the village green in Lexington and got out and sat on a bench in the dark, clutching her envelope.

Hot tears wet Caron's face as she thought of all the baby things hopefully collected. So often she had dreamed of her pregnancy — the first signs, the test, telling Pier. The months of joyous waiting. Even the bloating and sickness; their favorite OB at the hospital was always saying how healthy a harbinger that was, that there was nothing he liked to see more than a pregnant woman throwing up all over the place.

Caron had pictured their baby at birth, moist and crinkled. The guessing games about who he or she looked like. The names: Greta. Elisa. Pier Junior. Horace.

The labor, the delivery. Lying in Pier's arms as she nursed, Pier whispering sweetly to her.

There was never going to be any of that.

Her chance was gone, dead, stolen from her with the same awful finality as Wayne

Snow's future had been stolen from him.

So once again Caron mourned, not for one child this time but for all the children who would never be hers.

★ ★ ★

When Caron told Pier about the adoption meeting and her thoughts and feelings, he was the one who cried.

Caron put her arms around him and rested her head on his shoulder. 'It's so hard,' she said. 'So sad.'

Gently Pier held her away. His kind eyes looked into hers. 'I can't do this. I'm so sorry,' he said.

Caron swallowed. She prayed that this would not be Pier's final decision. She had to find a way to make him reconsider the idea of adoption. Never having any child to hold and raise would be terrible for her.

Then the real shock came. 'I do love you, Caron. It is horrible to leave you. But I have thought and thought. To give up on having my own child is more horrible.'

★ ★ ★

Caron didn't wait to find a new place before moving out. It was too excruciating to be around Pier and all the broken hopes and feelings. She packed a suitcase and went to a hotel in downtown Boston, and got into bed.

For the entire first day she simply lay there, too miserable to sleep or even to cry. The sun went down. The night brought swarming pictures of dilated birth canals and enormous toothy smiles. She dreamed that a scalpel cut her open from scalp to toes, and all that was inside was dust; it billowed out of her head and body in dry clouds.

When morning came, Caron walked to the window. She located the release levers and ran her fingers over them. She raised the window and sat on the sill.

All she had to do next was duck and shift her weight, and in a few seconds her lead blanket of pain would be gone.

She pictured herself hitting the sidewalk below, scattering the lines of hurrying pedestrians, knocking people down. Dust spilling out of her, covering the concrete.

She sat there until rush hour was over and the sidewalk was much less crowded. She could do it now without hurting anyone.

No.

People below wouldn't get hurt. But what about those who cared about her, the big remaining two, Julie Gerstein and Dr Felhammer?

This might be the most pathetic fact of all, Caron thought as she watched a fly bounce against the outside of the glass. Her suicide would affect exactly two people in the world. There was no one else left to care. Her mother and father were tragically gone; Elisa and Reco had moved from Santa Conda, and none of Caron's attempts to locate her sister had produced a hint of her whereabouts.

But . . . no bounty meant less pain. Less to lose: no parents or husband or unconceived children to mourn.

She should have kept her life the way it had been before Pier.

If she never had anyone again, she would never have to go through this again.

She couldn't lose what she didn't have.

Caron lowered the window and went back to bed.

★ ★ ★

She finished her Mass General residency in solitude, turning down the dates she was offered, spending what emotion she was willing to risk on the children she now mostly treated. There was safety in the volume. If you didn't beam yourself to just one man, woman, or child, then the loss of that person could not be so devastating.

Caron's next residency was at Johns Hopkins, where Dr Felhammer, though their schedules prevented frequent contact, was always there.

That completed, she had to decide what was next. She could essentially take her pick of top facilities. Back to Mass General, and Julie? Stay at Hopkins?

Neither felt right.

She was alone, and that was that. She truly had no one to rely on totally but herself. Perhaps by accepting that truth she could begin to achieve the internal peace that always seemed just another connection away.

Caron applied to the New York Hospital/Cornell Medical Center for a position as a full-timer — an on-staff plastic and reconstructive surgeon — and was welcomed with the same enthusiasm as she had been throughout her academic life. Her reputation was growing. She attacked surgical challenges with the passion that had no other channel, turned down nothing, embraced the impossible. Cases that no other doctor would touch were her specialty.

She settled into the city. In her few leisure moments, she enjoyed long walks, during which she sometimes felt she was the only person walking alone not by choice.

She spent time in the city's libraries. She

had loved libraries since childhood, knew their systems and sounds and smells. Comfort could be eked from the feel of a straight wooden chair, the rustle of a magazine against the tabletop.

Ironically it was at a library that she received a final devastating blow. Leafing through a surgery journal, Caron caught a hauntingly familiar smile. Pier — with a wife and baby son. Not the actual woman in the violet blouse, but close. The picture caption said they were leaving the United States to practice medicine in Argentina.

Caron let out an agonized groan before she could silence herself.

8

Seeing the picture of Pier's wholeness was more disturbing than Caron could ever have imagined. Though the lonely path she had chosen after the break-up had been healing, she had really only postponed an issue that would have to be confronted eventually. No matter how much she wanted intellectually to spend her emotional life in a vacuum, the emotions themselves wouldn't have it. Inside her shield a human was imprisoned, and it was beginning to struggle against its bonds.

The picture brought echoes of another way — of trying and discovering instead of closing and avoiding.

But it also brought the horror, the unendurable hurt of rejection and loss.

Part of her wanted to try again.

And the other part was terrified.

★ ★ ★

Harry took Caron to Elaine's on their first date. People stared, and a couple asked for his autograph, glowered on by Elaine as they did so.

'I've been reading about this place since before I came to New York,' Caron said. 'I can't believe I'm really here — with a celebrity.'

'Card-carrying,' Harry said.

Caron smiled. She had exquisite teeth, Harry noticed, as if polished and trimmed by a lapidary. 'Can I see the card?' she asked.

Harry looked perplexed for only a second. He pulled out his wallet and flipped her a gold AmEx, his AFTRA card, and his SAG.

Elaine trolled by, whispered in Harry's ear, kept going. Harry smirked.

Caron asked, 'Am I allowed to know what she said?'

'Just that, uh, she's never seen me work so hard to impress someone.'

Caron laughed. '*That* impresses me.'

* * *

After the parsimonious, compartmentalized emotion of Pier, Harry's love was a sunbath. Caron felt its rays the way she had once experienced the Santa Conda sunshine, when it could heat her distress away as she lay in its force.

Her own feelings were too untried and too long boxed in for her even to approach giving back the way Harry gave, but he seemed

111

patient. And if she could have resisted Harry, she couldn't resist his son.

The young boy who had been so sweet in the emergency room was a wonderful child. Josh was smart and compassionate. He had a way of narrowing his eyes as he listened to you or studied something you were showing him, and you knew he was totally with you. He liked baseball, chess, and cooking, and was good at all three.

Occasionally Harry apologized when a change in his plans or Josh's meant Josh would be joining them for a day or an evening, but Caron was delighted.

Harry wanted to see Caron operate, and she arranged for him to observe a breast reconstruction on a mastectomy site. The pride of using her skill, doing what she did best, while her famous lover watched raptly, beaming, was intoxicating.

Harry was invited to countless social events. Everyone wanted him. Caron began to accompany him. Television or school commitments sometimes meant they couldn't go to one they'd looked forward to, but these were not problems in Caron's view. Dedication to profession and family were glowing points in Harry's favor.

★ ★ ★

The night Harry proposed, Caron had spent half her day in surgery on a lung cancer patient who was probably going to die. She had dragged herself home and found the message inviting her to dinner, and called Harry to say no.

'I'm depressed and wiped out,' she said. 'I'm going to make a sandwich and go to sleep.'

'Not tonight.' Harry lowered his voice. The delicious rumbly whisper always melted her. 'I won't take no. Tonight is important. Historic.'

They met at a dark little Spanish place. Harry ordered hors d'oeuvres and a bottle of wine, and when she had relaxed somewhat, he put a ring box on the table.

'Harry!'

He pushed the box toward her. 'Open it.'

Everyone in the restaurant was watching and listening. Caron felt their interest and excitement and envy. She said, 'I have to think. I don't know if I — '

'You don't need to know now. Think all you want. Take a day. Take two. But meanwhile' — he opened the box, took out an emerald-cut topaz surrounded by diamonds, and put it on her finger — 'wear it and enjoy it.'

They were married at the Plaza on a Saturday night in May 1991. Rabbi Manfred Rosenstein officiated. Ten-year-old Josh was best man; Julie Gerstein attended Caron. Dr Felhammer was recovering from prostate surgery, and couldn't attend. Paul Wundring gave Caron away.

'You're getting a lovely husband,' Paul said quietly as he walked her along the flower-lined runner to the *chuppa*. 'Harry is one of the megatalents of our lifetime. He's lucky too, to have found you. I hope you stay happy together forever.'

Caron told Harry about Paul's wish as they lay together in their suite at the Dorchester Hotel in London. Harry kissed her and held her and felt the words as a blessing. They *would* stay happy together forever.

His life had permanently changed that January day in the New York Hospital emergency room.

As he had watched Caron work on Josh's nose, her slim fingers pushing and probing, he had been conscious of an aura that was nearly religious. It bathed all three of them. Everything was suddenly acutely felt: the dried tears on Harry's face, the remnant of his excruciating remorse; his shining love for his beautiful son, this splendid small human who was real and good through and through; his sense of Caron as the healer.

Harry hadn't known her for even an hour, but he was overwhelmed by her. He had to have her in his life. Her clean, healthy goodness would erase the final shreds of his other life, his other self, that was dead as of now, as of what he had done to his child.

And he would give to her as well. He would get the *Tonight Show*, and be the premier personality, wealthier and more famous and better loved than ever. All this would be his gift to Caron. He would show her a magnificent life at 114 East End, unsullied by his old problems. Fulfil dreams she hadn't dreamed yet.

* * *

Caron had never lacked money. Having plenty now was nothing new. But Harry taught her unimagined new ways to use and enjoy it.

She had always dressed in a manner her mother had termed 'smart' — trimly cut jackets, collegiate sweaters . . . small pieces of real jewelry. Her skin tended to be rough and dry from the washing and the harshly laundered garments necessitated by surgical routine. She wore make-up when she thought of it.

But under Harry's influence Caron began to wear her thick golden hair lighter and curlier, the look fashioned for her by Enzo of the Eastside Salon. Sabrina Valin, the wife of Harry's lawyer Tomas, recommended a make-up adviser and also a dresser, who regularly scouted the boutiques for Caron's clothes, creating color combinations that highlighted her exotic quality and styles that showcased her pleasing figure. For the first time in her life, Caron owned a wardrobe of glittery evening outfits, which she wore to all the events Harry was called upon to host or participate in, or simply attend with his now striking young wife.

She loved the fact that he cared enough to want this for her, to so appreciate the effect.

Johnny Carson was still hanging on to the *Tonight Show*, and Harry was still in top contention to replace him. Meanwhile, his popularity was higher than ever. He guest-hosted for Johnny regularly. Paul Wundring had to turn down all but the best TV and concert bookings, or Harry wouldn't have had time to shave.

The social invitations were, as always, a constant blizzard as well, and many were accepted. But Harry kept pockets of time for family and friends.

These were some of Caron's favorite days — especially those spent with Harry and Josh together. To have a family that she belonged to and that counted her as a vital member was a dream realized. She kept waiting for Josh to decide that he was too grown-up to go places with his father and stepmother, but he seemed to enjoy the outings as much as Caron did.

She had to monitor her tendency to overprotect the boy. On a boat trip to watch whales off Cape Cod, Caron had been so anxious about Josh leaning over the railing that she planted herself next to him and kept her arm around him until his exasperated sigh made her remove it.

Her medical detachment disappeared if it was Josh who was sick. She nearly became ill herself with worry if it looked like anything serious. A pediatrician friend told her she was behaving like a brand-new mother.

'But I am one,' Caron had responded.

Sometimes Harry seemed to need more protecting than his son did.

On a Sunday in April 1992 Harry and Caron were at brunch at the Valins' beach house in Westport, Connecticut, an annual event that marked the start of the season. Looking around at the sprouting flowers, smiling at the catlike cries of the gulls, Caron thought about her first time here, in 1991, a month before the wedding.

Nervous among the celebrities — Tomas represented many — and self-conscious in her khakis and loafers, Caron had been grateful for Sabrina's kindness, as the woman introduced her around the yard with a motherly arm at her waist while Harry socialized indoors. Tomas had been less solicitous, but Caron had learned eventually that Tomas was never that — and certainly not with Hispanic women, she had discovered, as she attempted to strike a common-ground note that had merely made him icier.

Now, though, married nearly a year and comfortable in her new role and its trappings, Caron was occasionally graced by Tomas's attention, as she was today.

He sat down next to her on the white wrought-iron bench that overlooked the sound below the rise on which the house was perched. He discussed the grass and the sunshine, both unusually robust for April. Then he said, 'You're working hard, I hear.'

'Yes.'

'You don't have to, of course. You could abbreviate your surgical schedule, or go into a multi-partner private practice.'

Thinking they were still having smalltalk,

118

Caron said, 'One day I might. Not soon, though. I like my full schedule.'

Tomas drummed his fingers on his thigh. He wore tennis shorts, and his legs were lean from his daily post-dawn games.

'This is a high-stress period for Harry,' Tomas said. 'He's been in abeyance waiting for the *Tonight Show* decision. As you know.'

'Of course.'

'If he gets the show, the stress won't diminish. Quite the opposite. And if he doesn't — well, we're just talking another type of tension, aren't we? Which is why,' Tomas went on, making eye contact now, 'you ought to consider rebalancing your work and your personal life.'

Caron looked back. 'Are you saying I should be there for Harry more?' she asked with her customary directness.

'I'm saying he's devoted to you. He needs you. And, yes, you should.'

Caron studied Tomas's small dark eyes, his tanned face and neck. A mole near his collarbone looked like a nascent basal cell. She would remember to mention it, but first she wanted to understand this conversation.

'Is Harry upset?' she asked anxiously. 'Why didn't he tell me?'

'He might not want to upset *you*.'

'Do you think he's really hurt?'

Tomas shook his head. 'He's simply mentioned that he wants you home more. He misses you.'

On the way back to the city, Caron left her seatbelt off so she could sit close to Harry, shoulders touching, as she formulated a gentle way to mention what Tomas had said. She hated the idea of Harry being secretly unhappy with her.

Finally she took his free hand and softly said her piece.

Harry grinned uncomfortably and admitted it was true.

'But,' Caron said, 'you know I need to be at the hospital.'

'I know. I just don't like unlocking the apartment and finding you not in it.'

⋆ ⋆ ⋆

Harry couldn't admit to himself that the empty apartment wasn't all he didn't like.

There had been a Parents' Night at Dalton, a so-called potluck dinner; of course, all the pots had been filled by maids. Many Dalton parents were prominent, but Josh had always been the kid with the most famous father. Harry approached school functions enthusiastically, for that reason among others. All the kids wanted his autograph. Even the coolest

120

of the cool moms and dads tended to redden and suck up.

But at the potluck, Caron was the magnet. Sleek in a fiery coral pants outfit, her honey hair in ringlets, Caron accepted thanks and compliments for a recent Career Day appearance at which she had described with photographs how she'd fashioned a new nose for a dog-bite victim.

A couple of the people actually bypassed Harry to shake her hand and smile adoringly at *her*.

The next morning, Harry called Paul and asked him to sound out the Carson people: *was* the man retiring, or not?

Harry, Caron and Josh were watching a video that evening when Paul called back to say that none of his contacts knew anything. The Carson camp was stonewalling. The movie ended while Harry was still talking to Paul. Josh went off to bed. Caron put on the eleven o'clock news.

'You finished the tape?' Harry asked when he came back.

'Yes,' Caron said. 'There wasn't much left. Do you want to see it? I'll rewind.' She picked up the remote.

'I don't remember where it was up to,' Harry said irritably.

'I'll roll back until you spot it.' Caron

pressed the Rewind/Search button.

'No!' Harry grabbed the remote. 'I don't want to see the end.'

'It wasn't a surprise — '

'Don't *tell* me!' He stood glaring down at Caron.

The force of his anger was like a shove. Involuntarily she moved aside on the couch.

'Maybe you don't like to be surprised,' Harry said, 'but I do. Normal people do. Everyone but the kind of anal robot who has to prethink every step — '

'I'm not — '

'Don't interrupt me!' He flung the remote to the floor. 'I leave to take a call and come back to find that nobody gives a shit that I was watching this tape too. *You're* done, so who cares that I was still interested in seeing how it ends? You have no goddamn consideration — '

The phone rang. Harry went to answer. Shaking, Caron washed and brushed her teeth. She was sitting up in bed, reading the *Times* uncomprehendingly, when Harry came in and sat on the mattress at her feet.

'I'm sorry,' he said. 'I apologize for the outburst. I was wrong.'

'But what — '

'I don't know. I guess I was letting off steam. I've been so uptight about this

Tonight Show business. Paul just called back — he heard Carson has prostate cancer.'

Caron winced. 'How awful.'

Harry wanted to ask her about that, get the answers to the questions Paul hadn't had. But he restrained himself. It would be better to wait with the medical questions. He didn't want to seem like a self-absorbed vulture when the poor guy had cancer.

9

For Harry's forty-fifth birthday Caron got the entire Rainbow Room closed to the public on a Saturday night. It wasn't even that difficult. They were happy to do it for Harry.

She and Josh planned and huddled and made lists, and Harry never suspected. Josh was excited to be part of the secret. He guarded it passionately, not even letting Nicholas know. Caron took him to Churchill's for his tux, and waited patiently without voicing a syllable of opinion as he picked out his tie and cummerbund in a South Seas blue. She hugged him and said how gorgeous he looked.

The party was a huge success. Absolutely nobody had declined. Every celebrity in New York, and many from Europe and the West Coast, toasted a stupefied and thrilled Harry with nothing-spared champagne.

Leno and Letterman were there, and Johnny Carson, looking very healthy.

★　★　★

An hour before dawn Harry and Caron lay sweaty and happy on their king-size bed after two vigorous bouts of lovemaking. Caron's head rested on Harry's chest. Stroking the thick muscle there, she thought about the party, and about her magnetic and mercurial husband.

She loved him ferociously.

His mean episodes hurt her. His drive was a live, pulsing entity that could push Caron aside, as well as everyone and everything else. But she hadn't signed on for a fairy story. Half her life had been fairy stories, and they always ended with the princess falling off her turret.

Caron knew what a poor marriage was. Her sister Elisa had all but written the textbook.

Harry didn't abuse her. Harry didn't disrespect her. He didn't hit or kick her, or reduce her to sobbing helplessness with vicious insults. Harry got nasty when he was particularly tense or angry. And in his rarefied situation, tension and anger couldn't be helped.

Harry was special. Harry was the diamond in the gravel heap. And he returned the passion. He adored her and Josh. He gave and gave.

How many times had Harry put his own work aside to spend a day at the movies or the zoo when Caron felt down? How many mornings had she awakened to Harry's breakfast treat of the week, some ambitious specialty he'd risen early to surprise Josh and Caron with? How many holidays had he determinedly made extra-lovely, to fill the emptiness of her past?

Caron slid nearer to Harry, as close as she could, and covered his leg with hers.

You heap your love on me, she told him silently. *All this passionate unconditional love. You have opened me and let it flow in and warm my old cold spaces.*

She thought of Pier, of the affection that was sometimes there and sometimes not. She'd had to keep watching for it, checking to see if it had gone. Pier's passion went unconditionally only to his patients.

Having experienced only that, Caron had thought her love with Pier was *it.* Now, with Harry, she knew. She had been afraid to care again, for Harry and for Josh — but the risk had paid off beyond her wildest hopes.

How much easier it is, Caron thought, to *return love that's real.*

Before Harry, so many of Caron's resources had gone to fighting her chronic lonely sadness. What a difference now. She was so lucky.

Nuzzling Caron's head with his chin, Harry felt emotion barrel through him. Glad tears welled.

He was boundlessly lucky.

What a wonderful surprise the party was — all the greats, come to pay homage to one of their coterie.

He couldn't stop remembering the famous faces, the brand names. Barbara Walters. Jack Nicholson. Shirley MacLaine. Stephen King had worn a monster mask with his tux, then taken the mask off and presented it to Harry. Demi Moore had smacked a big kiss on his mouth.

And who had arranged this mind-blowing event? His cherished wife and son. His beloved family.

He truly could not believe his luck.

How tragic his life could have been, left to steam along its original track. Harry thanked every higher power that had ever been conceived of for his second chance — for all his second chances.

At least he was giving back. At least he had proven his worthiness for those chances. His gifts had been allowed to flower, to become his reimbursement to the universe.

He covered Caron's hand with his and

stroked her fingers, her surgeon's hands, the nails short, the bones tiny. He remembered when he had first seen this woman, these hands, that aura. He'd been so right to campaign for her. She was great for him and for Josh.

Except for some regrettable lapses, Harry had kept his self-promise about Caron. He had supported and nurtured her, had changed her life. This chance, too, he had met and merited.

He was proud of his new self. The old Harry was buried. No one would be able to dig up the parts if they wanted to; with vagueness and quasi-lies Harry had dissolved every clue to his origins. People he'd known as a kid back in Craig Head had no notion that schmucky Harry Crane was now princely Harry Kravitz. Those who did know couldn't say so without admitting complicity in some extremely dirty stuff or risking embarrassment; who would believe their word against his? Who had more credibility than Harry? Hadn't the entire entertainment and media world just honored him?

Harry drew Caron closer and kissed her hair. He closed his eyes, but was too excited to sleep.

10

'I'm really going to miss you,' Harry said for the fourth time as Caron set her packed suitcase next to her briefcase and began filling her carry-on bag. He leaned over the bag as she put in a bathing suit. 'What's that for?'

'Essentials. In case the suitcase gets lost.'

'You're so structured.' He frowned. 'Why is that an essential at a surgeons' convention?'

Caron turned to face him. Half jokingly she said, 'Do I stand over you and comment on what you pack?'

'Okay, I'm sorry.'

'I know you don't want me to go — '

'You're right. But *I* know I'm being a jerk.' Harry put his arms around her and pulled her head to his shoulder. 'Pay no attention to me. Have a great time.'

'Just don't have it for long.'

'That too.'

★ ★ ★

Boca Raton was luxurious, and hot. All the doctors complained; Caron did too, but secretly she felt something she never felt any more, homesick for Cuba. The palms and the dank heat, and the people . . . everyone who waited on her or cleaned or carried seemed to be Cuban. Once Caron spoke Spanish to a maid, and the woman looked at her in confusion and replied in accented English.

Late on the second day of the convention it began to rain, the sort of deluge she remembered from childhood, surging curtains of water. The forecasts took on a note of alarm, and by the next morning hurricane warnings were in effect.

Hurricane Andrew wrecked Florida. Emergency vehicles were dispatched to fetch any nearby medical personnel who could work. Caron joined a group of other out-of-state surgeons at Shore Point General Hospital. The emergency room was bursting, the waiting room so packed patients couldn't sit. Triage was performed in hallways. Blood was everywhere. Workers trying to deal with broken hospital windows could barely move through the waves of people.

Hurrying back from a trip to the bathroom, Caron passed a triage nurse checking over a group of new arrivals. The nurse had selected out two people with bad cuts from glass shards, but seemed to have missed a head injury in another: a teenage boy stumbling away to wait was bleeding from the nose and an ear.

Caron brought him to the nurse's attention. The red-headed nurse looked from Caron to the boy and back again, her face set.

Suddenly Caron understood. The boy was Cuban.

Caron brought him into an examining room and admitted him. She swallowed her outrage, told herself she might have been mistaken, or it could have been an isolated instance of ignorance. She went back to work at a fierce pace. But she watched.

As the day wore on, and the stream of injured hewed to a profile, Caron's stomach tightened. She wasn't wrong. The preferred patients — and, in the feverish crowding, the *only* patients to get attention — were white and non-ethnic.

In a fast meal break, Caron tried to explain the situation to some of her fellow northern surgeons. She got lip service, but they were over-adrenalined and had other concerns. A couple of local doctors made it clear that the discrimination was business as usual.

After grabbing three hours' sleep back at her hotel, Caron discovered some phone service had been restored. She called Harry in New York.

'I was frantic,' Harry said. 'Thank God you're all right. All those dead and injured. Where are you? I had the AP trying to contact you, everyone — '

'I've been treating victims. But listen . . .' Caron told Harry about the discriminatory medical care, the untreated Hispanics. 'I can't ignore this. People are exsanguinating. They're having seizures, and not being cared for. A fourteen-year-old Cuban girl choked to death on her vomit. I'm going to make some noise. Prepare yourself.'

★ ★ ★

La Clinica Gratis para Victimas Cubano del Huracán Andrew was operating by that afternoon. Caron and a growing stream of nurses, plus a few sympathetic doctors, worked out of a storefront medical office hastily rented for a big handful of cash.

By evening the patient load swelled as word spread. But there were more personnel too, and Caron expanded into the next two empty storefronts. Patients with immediately treatable injuries were recruited after treatment to help.

The Spanish-language media pestered her for interviews. Except to publicize the service, Caron said little. She refused to take

132

time away from seeing patients to answer questions.

★ ★ ★

It was morning, Caron knew, because light came through the glass, but otherwise she had no sense of how long she'd been running from fracture to gash to rupture. She couldn't remember when she'd last slept.

A four-year-old boy sat on his father's lap while Caron examined him. The father crooned reassuringly, but it wasn't necessary; the child was barely responsive to Caron's probing.

'Has he vomited?' Caron asked. '*Ha vomitado el?*'

'*Sí. Muchos veces.*' He explained that General Hospital had sent the child home, saying he was all right, but the father had grown worried when the boy simply lay wherever he was placed.

Caron asked if the hospital knew about the vomiting, if they had checked the boy's eyes, what else had been done.

He had every sign of a profound concussion. A first-year medical student would have known. The boy shouldn't have been raised from a stretcher, let alone sent home.

'Dr Alvarez?' a nurse said.

It was outrageous.

'Doctor, just five minutes?'

Caron felt a strong light. She looked up to see a woman with a microphone, and behind her a camera that said *CNN*.

★ ★ ★

A UPI photographer won a Pulitzer for the shot he got at that moment of Caron, furious tears streaming, as she struggled to explain the situation. Her hair hung in lank loops, there was blood on her jacket, and one hand rested caressingly on the cheek of an unconscious child.

By the time she flew back to New York three weeks later, she was famous. *People* magazine dubbed her the 'Heroine of Hurricane Andrew'. There were overtures from book publishers and film producers.

'You really don't want to pursue any of this?' Paul Wundring asked her as she and Harry held hands on a banquette at Le Cirque. 'I've sorted through the proposals. Some are quite dignified.'

'No,' Caron said firmly. 'I did what someone had to do, that's all.' She smiled. 'I can't even say anything that isn't trite. I have no insights to share. People needed help, and

I gave it, and that's that.'

Later Paul called Caron at her office. 'Last chance to change your mind. You sure you won't consider *60 Minutes*?'

'No.'

'Are you . . . are these your real feelings? Or are you afraid Harry would feel threatened?'

'Harry is bigger than that. He was totally supportive of what I did. He *paid* for a lot of it. No, Paul, we have no jealousy problem. I just want to keep on being a doctor, and nothing else. Now I'm going back to work.'

11

In the year after Hurricane Andrew, there were more attempts to seduce Caron on to the movie or television screens or into print, but she declined. When asked why she didn't want to go on treating impoverished Cubans, she expressed satisfaction with having made a modest change in the nature of medical care in Florida, but said she preferred to continue her work in New York.

Harry was tapped to emcee the 1993 Academy Awards. The day the deal was made, Harry had his assistant Graceann book a table at the Four Seasons for the following Saturday night. A special seven-course meal was prepared, every element a departure from even the usual unique and creative menu. Harry and Caron and Josh, plus Paul and Tomas and their wives, feasted on skate, sweetbreads, and the contents of a miniature dessert trolley fashioned exclusively for their table.

Harry wore a dove-gray silk-and-linen suit with a hand-stitched shirt of pearl pink. Caron was breathtaking in metallic gold, with diamond butterfly earrings.

136

Several newspapers subsequently featured a picture of the festive group.

The following week a series of infuriated letters appeared on the *New York Times* Op Ed page. The writers, all doctors, lambasted Dr Caron Alvarez for publicly accusing them of being money-grubbing bigots lacking in social conscience (a direct quote from her CNN interview) when she herself was clearly too busy enjoying the riches from her instant fame to even pretend to still embrace her very temporary and convenient commitment to the medical problems of poor Hispanics.

* * *

The furore mushroomed. Caron was called a celebrity doctor with a celebrity husband who was nothing but a publicity opportunist. There was a demonstration outside New York Hospital.

The Los Angeles *Times* reported that a militant Hispanic group had pledged to disrupt the Oscars as a protest against the 'heartless and obscene use of poor Hispanics by grand-standing celebrities'. The story was picked up nationally.

A week before the Oscar telecast, Tomas and Paul met with Harry and the telecast producers, and network representatives. That afternoon Harry announced that, for the good of a fine American tradition, he was declining to emcee the ceremony.

Billy Crystal replaced Harry. He built his monologue, and much of his transitional material, around the fact that he'd had no time to prepare material. The Hispanic issue was not mentioned. There was no disruption. Billy was wonderful.

★ ★ ★

For the first time in over two years Harry took a late walk in Central Park. Near the reservoir he spotted a drunk slumped at the base of a tree. He stood for a minute, screened by a bush, looking at the man, making sure he was still alive. The man moved slightly.

Harry wanted him conscious. If he wasn't, the search would continue.

Deliberately Harry cracked a branch. The man raised his head and looked blearily around.

Harry pounced on him like a panther, from the side. He pushed the man's face into the dirt and heard mews of pain. He punched the man's back again and again, and then stood and used his feet.

138

★ ★ ★

Harry seemed to wear his disappointment with grace. The fuss over Caron waned. She and Harry had bought back credibility with his willing abdication from the limelight.

Johnny Carson finally announced his intention to retire. He didn't seem to have cancer. He joked about golf and girls in teddies.

Jay Leno was named as Carson's replacement.

Harry nearly threw up when he heard. He went in and sat cross-legged on the bathroom floor, replaying the conversation with Paul, feeling the contents of his stomach bubble and jump. He felt dizzy, and rested his head on the rim.

The cool porcelain was refreshing, but that wasn't good. Refreshed was extra-conscious. Harry craved numbness. He ached to take a vacation from the misery of his loss.

★ ★ ★

Graceann booked a villa on a tiny West Indian island called Patty Pig Tail for Harry, Caron and Josh.

'Just a week,' Graceann said. 'A healing week with your family. There's nothing I can't handle or stall while you're gone. Not,' she went on, watching Harry's face, 'that I won't be swamped with stuff for you. But you need time out. Go. Enjoy.'

★ ★ ★

The island was full of birds. As they got off the launch on arrival, they were given hats to wear at all times, to deflect the droppings.

'Bless Graceann,' Harry said as they sat down to dinner the second night on their veranda. The cook brought a platter of grouper and cho-cho, and Harry served Caron and Josh, and then himself. 'I didn't think I'd be able to get away mentally at all. I thought I'd just go through the motions. But I am actually starting to relax a bit.'

Josh said, 'Can we snorkel tomorrow?'

'Sure,' said Harry.

'You two go.' Caron rubbed her eyes. 'I need a day to charge my batteries.'

Harry looked up from the fish. 'You all right, love?'

'Yes. Just tired.'

They ate without talking for a while. Then Harry said, 'We came here to do things together as a family.'

Caron looked up. 'Yes. And we are. I'm only saying I need a day to — '

'You explained. To charge your batteries.'

The edge in his voice was obvious. Suddenly the atmosphere was electrified as if before a thunderstorm. Josh was looking from Caron to Harry. Under his 'Jamaica' T-shirt his narrow chest lifted and fell rapidly.

'If you'd like me to go with you,' Caron began quietly, 'I can — '

'But your batteries. You can't neglect your *batteries*! And far be it from me to force you — '

The maid appeared with a pot of tea on a tray. Harry swept his hand in an unthinking gesture and struck the tray, sending the pot sailing into Caron's lap.

She jumped up, gasping. 'Ice! Please!'

Harry dumped out his water glass, catching the ice in his hand. Caron yanked up her skirt. Harry put the ice on her red-splotched thighs.

'I'm so sorry,' he said. 'I'm a clumsy jerk.'

★ ★ ★

As they were getting ready for bed in the spacious master room that was open to the outside, Harry looked at Caron's thighs, which still showed small spots of red. 'Does it still hurt?' he asked.

'No,' Caron said, but she winced when she

climbed up to the platform bed.

Harry watched her settle the sheet gingerly over herself. 'Is it possible you did that subconsciously?'

'Did what?'

'Spilled the tea on yourself.'

Caron frowned. 'I didn't spill it. You did.'

'I gestured in response to what you were saying. Thinking back, I'm wondering if you more or less made that happen.'

'Of course not. Why would I?'

'To get out of snorkeling.'

'That's ridiculous.' Caron shut off her lamp.

Harry walked around to face her. Her eyes were shut. He said, 'Don't call me ridiculous and then go off to sleep.'

Caron opened her eyes and sat up. 'I said the statement was ridiculous, not you. I'm *tired*, Harry. And *I'm* the one who was burned. Just let's put it behind us and go to sleep.' She lay back down.

Harry made a fist and hit the headboard right next to Caron, a hard, jarring *boom*, and strode from the room.

★ ★ ★

The next morning, Harry behaved as though nothing had happened. Josh was wide-eyed,

142

trying to take the temperature of the situation, and Caron could see him physically relax as Harry collected snorkeling supplies and joked with the maid about their box lunches.

When they were set to go, Harry kissed Caron's cheek and said, so only she could hear, 'Forgive me?'

For which? Caron wanted to ask, but she wasn't even sure she understood the question herself. So she assigned the craziness to the stress, hers and Harry's. She kissed him back and nodded.

It was a tough time for both of them. It wasn't fair to judge only Harry. For all she knew, he might have been right about her provoking him.

12

Jay Leno's ratings weren't great. Some heavy-handed maneuverings by Jay's manager didn't help, nor did his letting her go.

'He's in the toilet,' Paul told Harry. 'Maybe he'll pull it out, and maybe not. NBC is watching very closely.'

'What if he doesn't make it? Would they offer it to me?'

Paul stirred his vodka with a finger. 'Maybe. And maybe' — he looked straight at Harry, his striking jade eyes shining — 'you might turn it down.'

'Turn it down? Why?' But a suspicion was building, a feeling Harry hadn't had in a while, of what might be waiting for him over the rainbow. Paul wouldn't toy with him for any negative reason.

Paul leaned toward him over the table. 'I got a call this morning from Sam Saloubian at CBS. You know the late-night show they're developing to go up against Leno and *Nightline*?'

'Sure,' Harry said. 'Letterman's doing it.'

Paul shook his head. 'They're changing their minds about Letterman. Even Dave doesn't know yet. They want to talk to you.'

Harry was quiet, taking it in.

'They weren't just feeling me out,' Paul said. 'They were practically asking for your hand in marriage.'

Harry leaned back in the padded armchair, his heart pounding. He looked at the water spots from melted ice bits on the dark wooden table. He looked at Paul, dear Paul, who always underplayed . . . who wouldn't have used the words he just did unless this was a shrink-wrapped, bow-tied, done deal.

He lifted the swizzlestick from his drink and looked at the Hyatt logo and took a mental photo of the glasses and napkins. Then he dollied back and up and shot the whole scene, with himself and Paul and the anonymous hard-ticket suits at the surrounding tables.

Little did they know they were witnessing television history.

* * *

The meetings with CBS went wonderfully. Sam and his people treated Harry like the star of stars. The show was to be called, simply, *Harry*.

'They'll debut me a few weeks after the start of the fall season,' Harry told Caron and

Josh. 'To catch the wave just as people are getting bored with the new shows that aren't going to survive. You should see the promotion plans. Ads up the wazoo. And the spots are brilliant.'

★ ★ ★

Harry spent a week taping the promos. There was a different celebrity with him for each one, begging to be on the show: Tom Cruise, Bruce Willis, Michelle Pfeiffer, Tom Brokaw. CBS called in due bills on both coasts to get the people.

The day they were done taping was the hottest on record for an August 14. Harry went home to his air-conditioned apartment to wait for word on what the network guns thought of the spots. If they loved them, the campaign was launched; the spots would start airing immediately, and the October debut was set. If the response was mixed, they might retape or rethink, and the schedule could be delayed.

Harry made himself a turkey sandwich and iced tea. He tried to eat out on the front terrace, but the heat was choking. He watched a Povich rerun and a soap, and waited, and waited.

The phone didn't ring at all.

The sky grayed. Lightning blinked every few minutes. There was a smash of thunder, and rain began. Giant drops splattered the terraces and mixed with soot, then grew to a torrent.

Josh came in, his hair dripping, squooshing across the floor. He took a towel and dried off, then reached for the phone.

'Don't use my line,' Harry said, jumping to look.

'It doesn't matter. They're all out. The whole neighborhood has no phones. Schlomo told me.'

'Shit. Why?'

Josh looked at him. 'The storm.'

'Don't be sarcastic with me!'

'I wasn't.'

'And don't talk back!'

The house phone buzzed. Harry hurried to answer. It was an antique and never used, but perhaps CBS, not getting through on the phone, had messengered a letter.

But it was just that idiot doorman, saying Josh had left his bike in the lobby, and did Josh want it put down in the bike room?

'Yes,' Harry snapped, not bothering to point out that Josh would hardly be going out to ride it now.

Caron came home at six-thirty. There was still no phone service.

'It's been out four fucking hours,' Harry said. 'There's no news. I know because I went to the corner and called Paul. But if there *is*, I won't get it.'

Taking lettuce from the refrigerator, Caron asked, 'How important can this news be? You know you have the show. They're not going to give it back to Letterman. Whether they do or don't approve the ads doesn't affect that.'

'True. Maybe the start date, but . . . '

'You're so used to almosts, you're putting this in the category and getting all upset for nothing.'

'Am I? Maybe you're right.'

They had chicken salad, which Josh had made, and vichyssoise. Caron and Harry watched TV while Josh cleaned up.

'Thank you, sweetheart,' Caron told Josh, patting his back as he rinsed out the sink. 'And the chicken salad was delicious. The water chestnuts were a really different touch.' She opened a cabinet and reached for teabags.

Harry called from the living room, 'Bring me a brownie, love, would you?'

'None left,' Josh answered.

Harry came into the kitchen. 'That's impossible. There was a whole box yesterday.'

'I didn't know you wanted them. I took them to Nick's.'

'Jesus Christ.' Harry clapped his hands hard, right in Josh's face. 'You see a fresh box of bakery goods in here and you don't know we want them?'

'I'm sorry. I'll get you more. Is the bakery still open?'

'Harry,' Caron said, 'calm down. This is no big deal.'

'It is to me! I felt like having a brownie!'

Harry left the kitchen, started into the living room, then spun around and came back. He pointed a finger at Josh, nearly touching his nose. 'You watch that sarcasm. I do not like it. Don't pull that crap with me again.'

Josh made a sound of bewilderment that came out like a choked guffaw. 'Dad — '

'Don't you fucking *laugh*!' Harry shrieked.

'Harry!' Caron grabbed his arm. 'Stop this. Leave him alone.'

Harry glared fiercely at her, then left the room, not looking at Josh.

★   ★   ★

Caron stayed up late. Harry slept, but she was disturbed, replaying the scene with Josh.

Harry had to learn to make a distinction between the tensions of his career and his treatment of his son. He could expect just so

149

much understanding from the boy, and he was getting more than the legal limit already.

It wasn't fair. It had to stop, before Harry left a lasting emotional gash in Josh. Being sensitive, vulnerable, and thirteen . . . and the son of a star . . .

She had to have a proper talk with Harry.

★ ★ ★

Harry left early the next morning. Caron had the day off. She showered and put on black leggings and a T-shirt. Josh came into the kitchen as she was pouring juice. He was in his pajamas, rumpled and unhappy.

'I wasn't being sarcastic to Dad last night.' He stood and watched her pour a second glass. 'He was mean to me for no reason.'

Caron put her arms around him. The pajamas were soft and had a child smell. Just another year or so, and the hormones would buzz around, and he'd smell like a teenager.

'He was mean,' Caron agreed. 'He owes you an apology.'

'I'm afraid.'

'Of what?'

'Of Dad. I'm afraid he'll hurt me.'

Caron stepped away and held Josh by the shoulders. 'You know, sweetheart, your dad is strung tight right now. It's no excuse for being mean, but try not to let his temper scare you.' She gave him his juice. 'You know your dad wouldn't hurt you.'

'Caron.' Josh put the glass down. 'I have to tell you something.'

★ ★ ★

While she waited for Harry to come home, Caron tried to find chores to do around the apartment, but nothing held her for long.

She went out to the supermarket, but was too distracted to buy anything.

The phone service was back on, and she tried to call Julie Gerstein. They hadn't talked in a few months. She reached Julie's machine at home, and her voice mail at Mass General. She left messages to call as soon as possible.

She finally heard Harry's key in the lock just before four.

'They loved the spots,' Harry called before the door was shut after him. 'Creamed over them. They couldn't say enough — Sam Saloubian came in to tell me himself. Stayed in my office for twenty minutes, shooting the breeze about how great the show is going to be. Guess which spot he liked best?'

Caron was waiting for him in the living room, sitting stiffly on the couch. 'I'm in here.'

Harry came in. 'Guess.'

'Harry,' Caron said, 'I have to talk to you.'

'About what?'

'About Josh.'

'What's he done?'

'He told me,' Caron said, 'how his nose was really broken.'

Harry didn't speak, but his breathing quickened. He sat in a wing chair facing Caron, his elbows on his knees. He held her eyes. 'You're upset,' he said.

'I'm more than upset. I'm sick.'

'I know it was unspeakable — '

'Your *child*! You broke your child's nose, and lied about it, and made him lie!'

Harry slid down in the chair and gave an enormous shuddering sigh. 'I've carried this around all this time. A cement block in my stomach. I'd give anything for it never to have happened. I'd give my life.'

Caron stood and went to the window. Haze drifted high over the river. Heat penetrated the window glass. She stayed there with her arms wrapped around herself, shivering.

She wasn't hearing anything she hadn't expected. Was she? Or had she hoped in the back of her mind that there would be some magical explanation that would take the horror away? Some verbal lifeboat to climb into?

But there wasn't. The marriage was over.

Behind them were the rooms where their family intimacy had been a force on its own, the daily naked details of three lives blended.

To give this up, the only real belonging she had known, was impossible.

But the impossible had to be done, because she couldn't stay.

Behind her Harry said, 'If you knew how desperately I love Josh . . . how sorry I've felt . . . I swore to myself and to Josh that it would never happen again, and it didn't. I never touched him.'

Caron walked back toward him, not looking at him, and he went on, 'I hope Josh told you that too.'

'Yes.'

Harry watched his wife pace the living room. Her strong legs in the black pants showed muscle motion. She held her head rigidly, the way she did when she was tense about one of her cases. He thought of reminding her of her own assessment of Josh's fracture, how relatively innocuous it was, but didn't feel she'd receive that well.

It was possible that some good could come out of this. At least the truth was exposed. He no longer had to carry that burden. The three of them could have open communication about this past tragedy, and healing would begin. He could continue to build on the trust he had promised Josh that awful night he would always honor. And with Caron knowing, they could all work in tandem to tighten the bond of their family unit on a base of mutual honesty.

'Where is Josh?' Harry asked.

'At Nicholas's.'

Harry got up. 'I'm going to call and ask him to come home. We can all talk.'

'Why, Harry?'

He stopped and turned to her. His eyes were red. 'I can't stand to have us like this, pieces all over the place. I wish we could have all talked it out when he brought it up. I'm sorry Josh felt he couldn't tell you in front of me. When *did* he tell you?'

'This morning. And, Harry, if you wish it had been brought up another way, you' — Caron coughed, sniffing back tears — 'you could have done that.'

'I know.'

'Making Josh keep the secret compounds what you did.'

Harry rubbed his eyes. 'I was afraid you'd leave me if you knew. And I kept my promise. From that day on, I never raised a hand — '

'*Is that what you really believe, Harry?*'

'What do you mean? Of course I — '

'Do you tell yourself you had one bad moment, and you've been a loving dad ever since? You threaten that child all the time! I see you do it! You did it last night! Knowing you *have* been violent, knowing you broke his face, puts your behavior in a whole different category. Think how it seems to Josh: when you shake a fist in his face, you're not just making a gesture. You're implying you'd smash him again!'

'It wasn't a fist. I just pointed — '

'Last night it wasn't. But I've seen you send Josh threatening messages many times. I just never understood there were teeth in the threats.'

Harry let out his breath. 'This is getting out of hand. You're analyzing it into an *Oprah* segment. I gave Josh my word I wouldn't ever hurt him again. I cried to him. Josh knows it was a one-time tragedy. He trusts me.'

'No. He doesn't.' Caron moved close to Harry. Hands on hips, she faced him. 'That's why Josh told me about your attack. Because he's afraid of you, Harry! Your son is afraid you'll attack him again!'

'Quit using that word. *Attack.*'

She shook her head. 'I've backed away from using a lot of words, but I won't any more. There was so much I should have seen.

Harry, you're a child beater!'

He snorted. 'Give me a break.'

Caron wiped tears from her face. Her voice shook with anger. 'You could have hit Josh again last night. I happened to be there to defuse you. But you can't have another chance to do that to him.'

Harry blinked. 'What? What do you mean?'

'You know what I mean. We are not going to live together any more.'

Harry's insides lurched. 'You want to leave me?'

'How could I stay with you? How could Josh?'

'Josh?' Harry shook his head. 'I could never lose Josh.'

Caron started to answer, but couldn't find words to penetrate Harry's defensive screen. She stared at him for another minute, then turned and went into the bedroom.

'What we need,' Harry said, following her, 'is a family meeting. A chance to get it all out — '

'You're wrong. What we need is to be away from one another.'

'Temporarily.'

'Permanently.'

She watched his face crumple. The word reverberated around her, and her chin trembled and tears slid down.

156

'For Josh's sake, Harry. Think of your child!'

'I am! Josh needs me! *ME!*'

Through a sob, Caron said, '*If* Josh wants to stay with you, I want a professional to okay it. I need to hear a child psychiatrist say you and Josh are all right together.'

Harry's mouth opened. He gaped at Caron. 'You'd blab our private business to an outsider?'

'Not if you say no. But if you want to keep Josh — '

'That's extortion!'

'*I can't leave him here like this, Harry!* And no matter what we decide, do you think people won't find out why we're splitting up? You can't keep these things secret!'

Harry's hands were trembling. He stuck them in his pockets. There was a crackle in one, a note from Bruce Pettibone of CBS about the Tom Brokaw promo; Harry had kept it there in his pocket all afternoon, touching it now and then, loving the words: 'Fantastic spot for a fantastic talent — this means you, Harry.'

He brought out the paper, looked at it, and crumpled it in his hand.

'*You can't keep these things secret . . .* '

Harry had a sudden picture of Bruce stepping into Sam Saloubian's office. Bruce

157

walked across the heavy carpet to Sam's desk, rested his hands on it, and leaned over.

'Harry Kravitz is a child beater,' Bruce said.

Sam stood. His eyes widened. 'Are you sure?'

'Everybody's talking about it.'

The picture flipped, and now Harry saw a videotape being carried down to a basement workroom at CBS. A gofer held it at arm's length. The new logo for his show was on the box: it was the promo reel.

'Reuse this?' the gofer asked, holding the tape over a pile of tapes already there.

'Nah,' said the Igor tape technician who inhabited the workroom. 'Burn the sucker. Guy's a child beater.'

Something in Harry's chest dropped. He felt as if the breath had been sucked out of him by a giant machine.

He looked at the note again, and then back at Caron. She was staring, gaping at him, as if he were some animal. As he watched, her face took on a disgusted look: the animal drooling, the animal pitiful.

On top of everything else, the look was too much.

With both hands Harry shoved Caron. She fell backward on to the bed.

The disgusted look changed to fear.

That gave Harry strength. She was right to be fearful. She wasn't right about one goddamn other thing, but she was right about that.

Caron struggled to get up. Harry jumped on top of her with his full weight.

* * *

Caron felt the impact of Harry's knees in her stomach, and lost her breath. She hadn't had an instant to tense her muscles.

She tried to shout, but there was no place for her voice to begin.

Harry pounded her chest with his fists. She reached to pull his hands away, but couldn't grip them.

'You can't stop me! You can't stop me!' Harry said, pounding in rhythm with the words.

Caron stopped struggling. Her heart was slamming against Harry's blows. But she still had no breath, and with the crush of his bulk she couldn't get it back.

'Self-righteous,' Harry was muttering. He mimicked her: ' 'If you want to keep Josh . . . *If* Josh wants to stay with you' . . . He's *my son*, you self-righteous bitch!'

* * *

159

How wrong he had been to think Caron was the completion of the family circle. She was the broken link.

He hated, hated, hated her.

Harry grabbed a handful of Caron's hair and jerked it, watching her face, and was rewarded with a grimace of pain. But then the bitch got a hand free and batted at his eyes, and he had to bite it. he sank his teeth into her thumb, and she yelped, and he bit harder.

Caron slackened suddenly. Her face was all screwed up. But Harry wasn't ready for her to give up. He needed to show her some more. He owed her.

He owed her for the mess she'd made of his life.

He'd picked her out of the slag heap, a foreign doctor with a two-by-nothing hospital office, and given her glamor and diamonds, champagne every night. He'd trusted her to be a second parent to his son. He'd given and given and given. And what had he received?

A looting. She'd looted his life.

She'd pretended to be worthy of his trust, but she wasn't. She was a bottom-feeder.

She'd screwed him.

Harry looked down at Caron, lying beneath him. She opened her eyes and seemed about to speak, but there was nothing Caron would have to say that Harry needed to put up with, and he silenced her before the words could form, by chopping his fist into her mouth.

There was blood, it covered his hand, and he wiped the hand on her shirt, felt the softness of a breast, and pounded that too. Caron groaned and tried to curl away from him. He let her for a minute, the way she had let him think *he* was safe with *her* — then he turned on her the way she had turned on him.

Harry kicked off his trousers and shorts. He pulled himself up and straddled Caron, rose on his knees, grabbed his stiff penis, and jammed it into her mouth.

★ ★ ★

Caron tried to wrench her head aside, but Harry held it there. Blood and saliva, and the pushing down her throat, nearly made her black out. She had to raise her head to have any breath at all, and that just worsened the invasion. She tried to bite down, to injure, to make Harry stop — but her jaw had no power.

Suddenly Harry shouted, and the taste of semen joined the metallic bite of her own blood. Caron gagged and tried to spit, but

Harry's knee was on her neck, and she could only spit on herself.

* * *

Harry wasn't finished. Jesus, did he owe her.

He rested a minute, sitting back on top of her. Her face was full of glop.

It was a start.

She was talking to him; he saw her lips move and strained to listen, for her voice was low and whispery.

'You're hurting me,' she moaned. 'You have to stop.'

Harry bounced on her chest. 'You're half right.'

'Oh! Harry — '

Rather than waste his breath telling her to shut up, Harry hit her again.

His strength was zooming back. He felt it running and filling him. Power in every moving part.

What teaching tool should he use on her next?

* * *

Blood drops hit her eyes. Caron blinked them away through a red wall. Oh, God! She couldn't move or speak — would she now be prevented from seeing too?

Caron tried to capture a strong breath. She focused on it, her lungs, her diaphragm, her windpipe. That was what they did in the ER when they were losing a patient: they tried to remind the body's system how to survive.

She knew she was in physical shock, clinical trauma. She felt the fluctuating signals from within, could key them to what she usually saw from the other side.

She had a sudden picture of how she would look now from there — the patient. The victim. But she couldn't summon any next steps. What was the victim supposed to do?

She thought of the beaten women who passed through the emergency room, whose husbands or boyfriends had put them there. Caron had always seen the poor things as being like Elisa, their inertia acting as tacit permission.

Now she was being beaten and assaulted by her own husband, and she was helpless, and she was hurt and might die.

Caron felt Harry's weight leave her chest, but an instant later her black pants were being yanked off. She arched to heave herself off the bed, but Harry jumped on her again. He jammed one knee into her solar plexus and the other between her legs.

What Caron felt next was Harry's penis,

ripping its way inside, sending waves of agony that swamped her.

★ ★ ★

Was he getting his message across? Was the statement clear?

It beats hiring a skywriter, Harry thought, pounding Caron's body.

After a few minutes he grew tired of the view, and of the pitiful sounds coming wetly from Caron's bloody mouth. He stopped and rolled off, and found to his satisfaction that his river of strength wasn't confined to his sex. With a good yank on one leg and one arm, he was able to flip Caron on to her front. To stanch the noise, he pushed her face into the bed before he positioned himself to enter her anally.

★ ★ ★

Caron moaned with the pain in her mouth and jaw as they were pressed against the bedspread. But she was breathing again, her oxygenated tissues gaining capacity, and for this blessed moment there was no weight on her.

She threw herself sideways, off the bed.

She landed on her knees on the carpet and

164

didn't dare stop moving, despite showers of pain from her head to her crotch. Scrambling, using her knees and elbows, she propelled herself toward the doorway.

* * *

Knocked briefly off balance, Harry needed just a second to recover — but he waited before continuing, impressed by Caron's idiotic attempt to get away from him. Like watching a spider in the sink before blasting the water at it.

Harry let the spider reach the door before grabbing its leg and throwing it back on the bed, stomach down. He gave it a good stomp in the back, to remind it who was on top.

Then he gave it the screwing of its life.

* * *

The explosion of misery, the racking horror, broke through Caron's terrified stupor, and suddenly there was breath enough to yell. She screamed and punched backward with her fists, and thrashed. The pain worsened, making her shriek louder. Harry was yelling too, trying to shut her up, but she didn't stop, and neither did he.

The phone rang next to the bed. Harry

paused for a fraction, and with a giant lunge Caron knocked him sideways and yanked herself out from under him.

She heard a new sound and turned.

Josh stood in the bedroom doorway.

13

Josh hurried away, but the sight of him immobilized Harry momentarily.

Caron paused only long enough to grab her purse and her pants. She yanked those on, yelled for Josh, found him in a kitchen chair looking chalky.

'Don't leave,' Harry called from the bedroom.

Caron pulled Josh out of the apartment into the corridor. 'If you leave,' Harry called, 'I will kill you. I *will* kill you.' She heard him shout her name again at the sound of the apartment door closing, and ran faster.

In the lobby, Schlomo the doorman stepped back in astonishment at the sight of Caron, bloody and filthy, dragging Josh. She thought to ask his help, but heard one of the other elevators open, and Harry call her name.

* * *

'Where are we going?' Josh kept asking as Caron hurried him along Eighty-first Street.

She didn't answer at first, concentrating on

taking enough turns to evade Harry. Finally she said, 'To find a phone.'

'What does — What happened?'

They came to a Chinese restaurant that was grimy and neighborhoody, and went in. Caron sat Josh on a torn maroon banquette out of sight of the street. 'Your dad . . . lost control. You were right to be afraid. He hurt me badly. I'm sorry we had to run like this, but we do, and . . . that's about all I can explain for now. Let me make a call. Let me try to get help for us.'

She called Paul Wundring. She tried to control her shaky voice, but couldn't. He listened in silence to her story.

'I'm . . . shocked,' Paul said when she was done. 'I can't assimilate it. Where did you say you are now?'

'At a payphone. Josh and I have nowhere to go. I'm terrified Harry will find us.'

'Give me the number,' Paul said. 'I want to call Harry and call you back.'

There was no number on the phone. 'I'll call you in ten minutes,' Caron said.

She reached Tomas in Westport. At first he listened without interrupting, but made clipped, rushed noises as she described the details of the attack.

'You're calling from where?' he asked.

'A payphone.'

'Where, exactly?'

'I — I don't want to say.'

'How can I help you if you won't say where you are?'

'Tomas, I told you, Harry says he will kill me! I'm not telling anyone where I am!'

'This is — quite an amazing tale, Caron. You're accusing one of the most respected personalities in the world of despicable criminal acts. I don't feel I can take the conversation further without hearing Harry's side.'

The words and the tone told Caron that Thomas would be no help at all. She hung up.

* * *

She got Paul's machine when she called back, and his answering service at the office number. She waited, tried again, but with the same result.

She had to pause for a minute to force her shuddering breaths to a slower rhythm before she hyperventilated. She sagged, holding on to the wallphone for support. Josh was watching her, his mouth open, like a small horrified child.

Caron dialed Julie Gerstein at home. She answered on the first ring.

'I got your messages,' Julie said. 'But there was no answer at your apartment when I tried to call. Is something wrong?'

Where do I start? Caron asked herself. 'I left Harry. Ran away, literally. I'm at a restaurant phone. I have Josh with me. Harry beat me up and raped me. Sodomized me —'

'Caron!'

'It came out of nowhere. Well, it didn't, but I failed to see the signs . . . That's all I have time to tell you now.'

'How badly injured are you?'

Caron tried again to slow her breathing. 'I'm a mess. But I can get around.'

'Have you called the police?'

'Not yet,' Caron said, peering through the grimy restaurant window. There was no way Harry could know where they were, but that was logic, and her fear didn't respond to logic. Harry could, would, be here any minute. He could drop through the roof, slip through the cloudy glass.

'Go to your office,' Julie urged. 'You need to have the rape exam anyway. Can't they protect you there at the hospital?'

'That's the first place Harry would look for me.'

'Well, what are you going to do? What can I do?'

'I don't think you can do anything.'

'Come to Boston, Caron. Stay at my apartment. Get on a plane — '

'I'm not going anywhere Harry could find me.'

'Then you have to go to the police. You're a rape victim. You're a battered woman, Caron. That's what they have secret shelters for. Get yourself and Josh to a safe house and then blow the whistle on your husband the great TV star. Tell the world about the freak.'

14

'Hello?' Barbara Wrenn said, her voice musty with sleep.

'Barbara, it's Caron Alvarez. I'm sorry to call so late.'

'Caron?'

'Have you been listening to the radio?' Caron asked, and knew from the silence that she would have to start way further back.

'Wow,' Barbara said, 'could I call you tomorrow, hon? I was up late, and I'm really wiped out — '

'No.' Caron rubbed her own aching eyes. 'I have to talk to you now, Barbara. I need help.'

★   ★   ★

It was nearly four a.m., but Ocean City, Maryland was still lively.

Barbara's apartment house was a homey low-rise with a strip of sandy garden in front. After the raucous down-town, the quiet street was a frightening showcase for the loud old car, and Caron shut off the ignition gratefully.

She patted Josh's shoulder to wake him. 'Let's go in, and you can sleep in a real bed.'

Barbara met them at the door. Caron hadn't seen her in fifteen years, and they had been tough ones, apparently: Barbara's large stomach protruded beneath her sweatshirt and leggings; metallic auburn hair showed an inch of dark roots.

Caron had cleaned up in New York, but the bruising and swelling made Barbara step back in shock. She pulled Caron and Josh inside.

Caron began, 'I'm so sorry to burst in on you in the middle of the night — '

'Well, I can see you had to.' Barbara looked closer at Caron's face. 'Does that hurt as much as it looks like it does? What happened? Were you beaten up?'

Tears came, stinging the open wounds by her mouth, and Caron wiped them away. Her head hurt so much. 'Can Josh lie down before I start?'

★   ★   ★

'Holy hell,' Barbara said for the fourth or fifth time. 'No wonder you had to leave New York. How do you hide from a TV star?'

The question hung there like the steam from their cups of tea. Caron couldn't begin to address it, any more than she could seem to function beyond tucking Josh in and telling Barbara what had happened.

173

Pain knifed her everywhere, inside and out. Her head felt as if it had been slammed with a baseball bat. She hadn't tried the tea, but her lips were so sore, she couldn't imagine drinking anything but the iced water she'd had earlier.

The internal agony that the Darvocet had kept tolerable for all those hours of driving was intense now. Her vagina and rectum felt shredded. There had been blood when she urinated.

She took ointment and peroxide from Barbara's medicine chest, dressed her wounds as best she could, and fell into a dead sleep on the couch.

Josh was still sleeping when Caron woke at ten.

Barbara's apartment was a godsend. She owed Barbara a chunk of her life — and now she had to impose on this casual Hallmark relationship still further.

'I need some clothes,' Caron told Barbara. 'I need to change my hair and whatever else I can. I need cash, any you can give me. And — I would like to leave Josh with you for a little while.'

Barbara blinked. 'You want him to stay here?'

Caron nodded. 'I'm sorry. But together Josh and I are too recognizable. I hope it will only be for a couple of days. Until I can find a way to fight Harry.'

'Clothes, no problem. I don't have much money . . . '

* * *

'Without you?' Josh asked, his eyes filling.

Caron squeezed him tight. 'Just for a few days. So I can . . . work on this.'

He couldn't let go of her. She was holding his head against her shoulder, and he snuggled in as close as he could. He saw a green and purple welt on her neck, and shut his eyes.

'Where are you going?'

'To try to find people who used to know your dad.'

* * *

'Dr Nusser, this is Caron Alvarez.'

'Dr Alvarez! Are you all right? What can I do?'

Caron sighed. 'Nothing. You're wonderful to offer, but . . . there's nothing.'

'Are you in Florida now? You could stay here with me and my wife, get your injuries treated — '

'I'm not in Florida. And I'd never endanger

175

you by coming there.'

'What about that cancer claim of your husband's? You can refute that in black-and-white. I'll arrange a CT scan, blood work — '

'No one cares about the facts. The world thinks Harry is God and Santa Claus rolled into one. No, Dr Nusser, I won't bring my poison your way. I can't stay in any one place. Harry will find me. He already found me in a safe house. It only took him two hours.'

★　★　★

'You have reached Harry Kravitz's office at CBS-TV in New York. I have established this special number for information regarding the disappearance of my wife and son. Please leave your name and number, your location, and any information you have. This is Harry Kravitz saying thank you and bless you.'

'I am Farah Dikta, in Ithaca, New York. I just saw your wife at Wegman's Supermarket . . . '

'Mr Kravitz, my name is Robert. I'm calling from Tucson. I might be wrong, but I just got off a plane from Dallas, and I think your wife and son were on it . . . '

★　★　★

Caron was two hours out of Ocean City.

Lying on Barbara's couch this morning before getting up, fighting back panic, she had assessed her physical state and pronounced herself able to proceed, not that there could have been a choice. Then she had sifted through her so-called options, in case she had missed one in her frantic ruminations the night before, as she and Josh barreled through the night to Maryland.

She couldn't stay in New York. There was no one there who wasn't more a connection of Harry's than of hers. Every attempt to save herself in New York had only brought more danger.

She couldn't go to Julie in Boston, or to Herbert Felhammer in Baltimore. That was just what Harry would expect. She had even considered Cuba, but there was no way to achieve that without smugglers' money, and what would she do to save herself once she got there? What about Josh?

There was no place she could stay, period, because in order to have a hope of fighting Harry, she had to get to people — and first she had to find them.

She had scant resources to search: a last-legs car, two changes of clothes, and $174.

She should have seen long ago that Harry

had the potential for violence. The clues were right in front of her once she knew to look back for them. She had been so delighted to be a charter member of a family at last that she had deleted and denied, missed the layers of control, the dependencies building, the adjustments in Josh's behavior, in hers.

And now that she did know what Harry could do, she had to follow that thread back as far as it would take her.

She couldn't be the first. She might not even be the worst. Harry's furious mutterings during the attack, as best she could recall now, confirmed that: bits of curses about the family circle, about what they had done to him and what they deserved, just as Caron did.

Harry had so many adoring friends and associates, so many eager invitations, that the absence of family hadn't sounded the alarm it should have. Not to Caron, to whom having no family was the norm.

There had to be reasons why none of Harry's family were in his life. Reasons why Harry never mentioned them, gave no clue as to where they were . . . until yesterday, until the hate had erupted.

She didn't know where to look, except to start in Harry's home town of Atlanta. She wasn't even sure who she was looking for.

But they had the only bullets that would stop her monster.

★ ★ ★

Josh couldn't stop thinking about his mother.

'*She's never even wanted to see me,*' he had told Caron.

'*What if that's not true?*' she had asked.

What if it wasn't?

He sat on the bed, looking at the TV without seeing it. He felt shaky and sick to his stomach, but hungry too, even though he had just finished a big hamburger that Barbara had made for him.

She had been the one who put the TV on. Adults always did that when Josh was around — if he went to his dad's office at the network, he wouldn't be there two minutes before someone plunked him into a chair facing a TV. As if kids needed some essential nutrient they could only absorb from a moving screen.

Caron had made him promise not to watch his dad. She had said that in the way she always brought up matters she thought Josh would object to, with her sideways look like a cat's, but Josh had been glad to agree.

He couldn't even think of his dad without

recalling the blood and the screaming, and the nightmare whirl-wind after.

Josh pulled his knees up and locked his arms around them and tried to remember his mother. He had a dim mental picture of a tall thin lady with big cool hands. In the mind-picture she had a crazy expression.

Josh couldn't remember any specific times with his two parents together. His dad had always said not to try. Don't think about her, his dad had said. There's no reason to. She's not like us. She's sick in her mind.

'What if that's not true?'

Could his mother be around somewhere, living a life?

What would she be like? Would she want to see Josh now?

Some instinct, mercifully nonspecific, told him that if she hadn't wanted to so far, whatever had caused her to make that choice would not have gone away or ended, and she would, or would have to, make it again.

He grabbed the two pillows from the head of the bed and hugged them to himself.

★   ★   ★

Caron reached a town called Brazel, near the bottom of the DelMarVa Peninsula. It was busy and honky tonk, full of vacationing

180

families spilling out of cramped motels. She bought a map of the area, and located the Brazel Library.

With Barbara's help she had altered herself as much as possible. Her long honey curls were now a brief dark brown shag cut. Her bruises were layered over with Dermablend. Buying the hair color and make-up, Barbara had also picked up tortoiseshell glasses with clear round lenses.

But Caron still felt nakedly exposed.

The morning's *USA Today*, under the headline 'Son Confirms Kravitz Assault', had pictures of Harry, Josh, and herself. Every newspaper had something. That would only get worse.

The librarian didn't give any extra notice to her hair or glasses, as strange as they felt to Caron. She directed Caron to the reference area.

Caron waited until the woman was gone before locating the out-of-area telephone books. It wasn't a huge grouping; thank God there was only one for Atlanta.

She turned to the Ks, and saw four Kravitzes. She took out a notebook and copied them all.

Caron left the library and found a luncheonette with an old brown phone booth, the type she hadn't seen since first coming to

181

the States. Pumping in Barbara's laundromat quarters, Caron dialed the first of the Atlanta Kravitzes, Carla F.

'I'm calling from Harry Kravitz's office at CBS-TV in New York,' she told the woman who answered. 'Harry is attempting to locate distant relatives there in Atlanta for invitations to a reception celebrating his new program, and I'm phoning to ask if you are related to him.'

'No,' the woman said. 'Our branch is from up in Ohio. But give him my sympathy, would you? I saw him on TV this morning, the poor man. I hope they find that wife and child of his, so he can enjoy his party . . . '

Caron called David, Stephanie, and Steven Kravitz, each time hoping someone would hesitate or stumble, or give her some reason to continue on down to Atlanta and talk face-to-face.

But there was no hint of recognition from any of them.

Should she go to Atlanta anyway?

What for?

No money, no one to contact, no hint that Harry had any family there.

A dead end.

It was boiling hot in the booth. Caron creaked open the door. She wanted a cold drink, but no one in the restaurant was paying attention to her, and she didn't dare change that.

She couldn't think what to do next.

What other thread did she have, that she could pull on?

Dizziness came, overwhelming her. She had to grip the door handle to stay upright on the seat. Her breakfast rose in her chest, and she stumbled from the booth to the ladies' room, and vomited for long, burning minutes.

She sat on the floor of the stall, her hand over her chest, as if to quiet her knocking heart.

The memories came back. Harry's face over hers, the snarling contorted face. Daggers of pain inside; the bloody taste.

She vomited again.

Trauma. The word blinked and blinked behind her eyes.

She'd been running on adrenaline, thinking she was holding on emotionally. But for all her emergency room training, she hadn't done what victims needed to in order to move past their experience: face it. Know it. Own it.

The recollections had come in flashes through the long night and in her sleep, but driving her, not driven by her.

So she did now what a rape crisis counselor

would have gently helped her do if she had been able to avail herself of that luxury.

Sitting on the damp tile floor, her trembling hands gripping the toilet seat, Caron explained to herself what had happened.

She had a husband with hidden rotten spots. Cancer of the soul. Unwittingly she had touched those spots, and the boils had burst on her. The man whom she had shared with and trusted, whose child she loved, had turned the spigot of his poison full on her.

This wasn't a bad stretch that would be over soon. Harry wanted her dead. He was already manipulating his associates, the media, and his millions of fans to achieve Caron's death and his survival.

The man with the knife had found her easily, and would again if she stopped anywhere. She could hear his breathing now, see the knife. She could feel the punches as it stabbed her.

She had no safe place, no resources, no idea how to save herself, nobody on her side who could help.

No wonder she had just crashed to a stop.

There was a small, sparkling mirror above the single sink in the ladies' room, and Caron gazed into it. She had cleaned herself up and repaired the sweat damage to her make-up and cover cream.

She looked at her eyes behind the glasses, and tried to find some vestige of strength there.

She repeated phrases to herself, trying to tease out to the surface what comfort and confidence existed in her own hidden places.

She thought of the homeless, hopeless people she saw at the hospital, who somehow survived in New York. She remembered the Florida Cubans, their tenacity and courage. And the people at home — not the rich and well-fed neighbors of the Isla, but the Cubans of now, the average citizens who routinely stand in line to receive rationed potatoes at a store that has nothing else.

She concentrated on the strength of those who had no choice but to be strong, and, studying the person in the mirror, acknowledged that she was one of them.

★ ★ ★

Back in the phone booth, Caron dialed Barbara, brought her quickly up to date, and asked for Josh.

Hoarseness indicated he had been crying.

She said, 'This is so hard, isn't it?'

He did cry then. She listened and tried not to do the same. She concentrated on what she

185

needed to ask, as soon as Josh was ready, and how best to access whatever he remembered.

When he seemed to be running down, she said, 'Your mother's name is Sheila, isn't it? What was her last name before she married?'

'Dannenbring.'

'That's on your birth certificate?'

'Yes.'

'Do you know what it says her birthplace was?'

'Allemar, New Jersey.'

'Do you remember her at all, Josh?'

He sniffled. 'Just little bits.'

'But your dad said she was in a mental hospital? Did he ever say the name?'

'He said he didn't know where she was now.'

Listening to the scared small voice, Caron wished she could be there, sitting beside him, holding him. It had to be torture for him, alone and distraught in an unfamiliar state, no parent or even quasi-parent nearby . . . the sick reality of what his father was, roiling in him.

He'd been a brave kid that first night she met him, trustingly submitting to her treatment.

He had to be more brave now than any thirteen-year-old should need to be.

Thank God he was out of the apartment.

She'd heard their statements replayed on radio news-casts, and Josh's voice sounded shaky, but clear and honest. His statement lent validity to hers. Without it, she would be merely a hysterical woman claiming rape, with no evidence and no corroboration.

'Why do you want to know about my mother?' Josh asked.

'I'm going to look for her. The town hall in Allemar might have information about where she lives now.'

'What can a crazy person do?'

'Remember what we were saying last night? What if she isn't a crazy person? What if she's a scared person?'

15

It was terrifying to head north.

Getting on to the interstate, Caron pushed her foot firmly down on the accelerator. Sweat wetted her scalp, and trickled down her neck. The big car seemed to sense her reluctance like an old savvy horse; it coughed and bucked.

Allemar was in South Jersey, fortunately. Having to go anywhere near New York would have paralyzed Caron.

The trip could be useless. Maiden name, town of birth — these got lost as lives unfolded. And Sheila might not be anywhere in this part of the country. Harry might tell the truth sometimes.

But there was nothing else. She had to try.

A blue-red flash filled the car. To Caron's horror, there was a police car behind her, the driver motioning her to the side of the turnpike. She pulled over, her hands quaking.

In a second he was at her window. The gun at his hip looked huge. His hand rested on it. He held the other hand out.

'License and registration, please.'

Caron sucked in air. 'I don't have them with me.'

The policeman was silent. Then, 'Step out of the vehicle, please.'

Caron got out. The man took a long look at her. His hand was still on his weapon.

'Wait here,' he said, and went to his car.

Panic slammed her. Had the trooper recognized her? Was he getting on his radio right now?

He was going to draw the gun and hold it on her, make her come with him, capture her for Harry, for death.

* * *

In the downstairs banquet room of Trattoria dell'Arte, the editor-in-chief of *Parents* magazine stood at the center of the dais unfolding her welcoming notes for the Parent in Public Life Award luncheon. TV cameras were covering the event, thanks to the high profile of the honoree, Harry Kravitz.

The room was jammed. Last year's winner, Susan Sarandon, hadn't drawn nearly this many people, the editor reflected as she finished her opening talk and picked up the award plaque.

'And now, it is my pleasure,' she said, 'to present this award to a man who has set an

189

outstanding example in parenting. We're grateful that he could be with us today; as you all know, he is embroiled at this time in the most painful situation a parent can face. So let's give him all our support. Please welcome Public Parent of the Year Harry Kravitz.'

The applause boomed out. Harry got up and made his way to the lectern. He hugged the editor and kissed her on both cheeks.

The applause continued. Harry tapped the mike and tried to speak, but the crowd wouldn't let him. They got to their feet and clapped louder.

Harry had to turn away and wipe his eyes.

★ ★ ★

The ophthalmologists in Julie Gerstein's group took turns working Mondays, and today had been hers. But the afternoon appointments were light, and Julie was done by two.

Driving home along the Charles, she kept turning to enjoy the sun dapples, and finally pulled over to take a walk.

She passed a man on a bench reading a *Globe*, and peered to see if there was any mention of Caron. The morning papers and television news had said she was missing.

Thank God.

All morning Julie had been distracted during her appointments, one ear on the phone. Caron had insisted she wouldn't come to Boston. But Julie thought she might call.

Julie felt sick thinking of Caron, sweet and serene Caron, hurt and traumatized and desperate. She longed to jump into the pit and fight alongside her. Now that Harry's strategy was evident, she wanted to attack it on medical grounds, mount a posse of doctors to refute the brain cancer crap.

But without Caron, there was no way. 'Because Caron wouldn't lie' wasn't a clinical explanation.

She saw a man watching a Red Sox game on a mini TV and walked over to him. 'Hi,' she said. 'Could I ask a favor?'

The man grinned. 'You can.'

'When the next commercial comes on, could I see CNN?'

'You can see it now.' He changed the channel.

Together they watched a national weather report and the start of a feature on bacteria in chicken.

'Looking for something in particular?' the man asked.

'News about Harry Kravitz and his wife.'

'It is some story, isn't it? Best show since Burt and Loni.'

'No,' Julie said harshly, but then realized his view was predictable. He didn't know Caron. He wouldn't understand that this was an obscene travesty, and not some celebrity dog act.

Which, she thought with a sick pang, was the problem in general.

She said, 'I can't help feeling sorry for someone in that position — '

'Yeah. He's a sitting duck. His wife yells rape, and all he can do — '

'I meant *her*. How does an innocent victim escape from a household name? Harry Kravitz is obviously a sociopath, and yet he has the credibility to get the world on his side, while his poor wife tries to make people listen — people who don't know her, but think of him as family.'

Julie wanted to say much more, to explain how well she knew Caron. But she had to be discreet in case Caron came to Boston to hide.

'Well,' the man said, 'the truth should come out as soon as the wife is located.'

'I hope she isn't. I hope she turns the heat way up. I hope she pelts him with specimens and pathology and hair samples and DNA until he can't deny it any more.'

Caron touched her door handle, but realized immediately she didn't dare take off.

The trooper was back, his face hostile. 'Is that the real thing? Or fake?' he asked, pointing.

She hid a gasp. 'What do you mean?'

'Your inspection sticker. This heap shouldn't have passed.'

'It's . . . not my car. My girlfriend — '

The trooper rolled his eyes. 'Save it.' He knelt by her rear bumper, which Caron now saw was hanging. With a pair of pliers he had apparently just taken from his car, he snipped and retied the wire that held the bumper on. When it was secure, he stood.

'Drive this thing back to New York. Have it fixed, and get a real sticker. And find yourself a new boyfriend,' he finished, pointing at Caron's damaged face that the cover cream didn't thoroughly hide.

★ ★ ★

'But Julie didn't say Caron was going to do that. She just said she hoped. Right?' Harry asked.

Ronald Brale smiled into the cellular phone. For Harry, denial was a river in Egypt.

'That's what she said,' Brale confirmed.

'And Caron probably never had an examination. There wasn't time before she went to the place downtown, and after you got there, she must have run in panic.'

'She could still have an examination,' Brale said.

'How?' Harry demanded. 'Where's she gonna go that she's not taking a big chance of exposing herself?'

'I don't know. But she's not here with Gerstein, I can tell you that. I know every move Gerstein has made, and Caron hasn't contacted her. She obviously thinks that might happen, though. She wouldn't even admit she knew Caron. She was stepping all over herself to avoid it.'

Harry let out his breath. 'You'd better stick with Gerstein. What can we do about Felhammer? Have you got someone else to watch him?'

Brale stretched in the car seat. He was parked in an apartment complex next to Julie's, watching for her to come home. The receiver for her phone tap was on the floor of the passenger side, next to the mini TV.

'Not a good idea, Harry. Too many cooks.'

'But he's wide open. Caron could be there now, while you're tracking Julie.'

'I'm going to keep working them both.

That's what we planned.'

'I know we planned it, but that leaves holes.'

'Not really. Bugs in Baltimore, bugs here, me going back and forth — we're covered. Better this than bringing another person into the equation.'

In his kitchen, the day's newspaper coverage spread out on the table, Harry pondered that. Putting someone on Felhammer would sew up the net, but Brale had a point: the person wouldn't have Brale's pedigree, and could be corruptible. What if he trotted himself to *Hard Copy* and made a half-million-dollar deal to expose Harry?

'Unless,' Brale said, 'the other person wasn't given the program. Just a bounty hunter with orders to find her and bring her home.'

'You know one?'

'Yeah.'

'How much would you have to tell him?'

'Very little. They work alone. Finding people is all they do. They have their methods — all clean.'

Harry listened to Brale's description. It made sense. He told Brale to go ahead.

Meanwhile, Caron was almost certain to wind up with Felhammer or Julie very soon, or at least contact them for money that would have to be sent to an address. Harry knew exactly what she'd drawn from their accounts, and how long it wouldn't last, what with transportation and her other expenses. She couldn't go to another cash machine without revealing her location. There was simply no other option for her but her friends.

And then Brale could do his job, and Harry and the nation would mourn together the tragic suicide of the brilliant young surgeon, and he and Josh could go back to normal.

*　*　*

The Allemar Town Hall had a secluded parking lot in the rear. Caron used the privacy to apply more Dermablend. Then she sat for a minute to force back the breathless fright that came in waves each time she had to get out of the car and expose herself.

But this was a necessary stop. With luck there would be birth or property records or other documentation about the Dannenbring family, with first names, and maybe the most recent forwarding addresses. Even though the data would probably be many years old, it would be something to go on.

She climbed the steps, passing two teenage girls in shorts with their legs stretched out to catch the last rays. She reached to open the glass door of the building, and couldn't.

The sign filled her vision suddenly: *Tuesday through Friday 9:00 — 4:00; Monday and Saturday 9:00 — 2:00.*

It was three-thirty on Monday.

'*Damn* it,' Caron bit off almost silently. One of the teens looked up. Caron turned and walked slowly back to the car. She thought she could feel the girl's stare, but when she sneaked a look, the girl was lying back in the sun again.

In the stifling car, Caron closed her eyes as discouragement enveloped her. Harry would be stepping up the pressure as she remained missing. The pitch of coverage would galvanize every passerby to watch for her.

She couldn't go back to Barbara's; it was too dangerous, with Josh there, and the two of them on every television screen and in every paper. She could not put Barbara and Josh at risk. Staying on the move was her only protection, and thus the protection for all three of them.

For she had no illusion that Harry would spare Barbara or any innocent person in his effort to incinerate her, his wife, his new nemesis, the concrete barrier to the continuation of the sleight-of-hand mirage that was Harry Kravitz. The more the events of the last two days burned their truths into her, the clearer Harry's pathology became.

She should have suspected. It was so logical now. She should have questioned.

But she had built defenses, had helped Harry build them, rather than see even an edge of the unthinkable reality.

16

'. . . no further information on the disappearance of Dr Caron Alvarez and her stepson, thirteen-year-old Joshua Kravitz . . . the family, as you know, of Harry Kravitz. There are reports from California to Maryland of the two being seen, but a spokeswoman for Harry Kravitz says they are still very much missing, and that concern is increasing for their safety, as Dr Alvarez is said to be in poor health . . . '

Caron thumped the car seat. Was this falling into the category of fact now, this evil fiction about her health? And had she really been reported in Maryland? Was she more identifiable than she realized, even disguised?

Was she being watched now?

Would the man with the knife find her?

She tried to push the terrifying thoughts down and find a cheap place to stop for the night.

She located a Motel Six near the interstate and counted out forty-seven precious dollars. She let herself gratefully into the stale smoke-smelling room that looked out on an industrial park, washed her face and hands, and found a phone book.

Luck at last.

Three Dannenbrings: Kenneth, Maura P., and S.

Was it possible that Allemar would prove to be more than just a starting point? Could Sheila still live here?

It was very hard not to reach for the phone, but Caron knew better.

★　★　★

Following the section of the Allemar street map she had copied out of the phone book, Caron found Pear Terrace. Number 15 was a small Cape, overgrown and needing paint, with three cats snoozing on the grass in the dusky light.

With a thrumming heart Caron walked to the front door and rang the bell. The cats looked up with bored eyes.

Nobody answered.

Caron peered through a window into the one-car garage. A small white Ford sat inside.

There were no lights on in the house, but the car was shiny and the cats were fed. Wherever S. Dannenbring was, she seemed to live here.

Caron checked the mailbox, but it was empty. Then she noticed a Lillian Vernon catalog half buried in the dirt by her feet. She read the label.

Sheila Dannenbring, 15 Pear Terrace.

'Hello,' someone said coolly behind her. Caron jumped, turned to find a rangy ponytailed woman coming up the walk in sweats and Reeboks.

★ ★ ★

The New York Association of Scholars of Ancient Hebrew had its headquarters in a storefront on West Forty-third Street. For crime-prevention reasons, there was a sliding gate over the façade on evenings and weekends, but the gate slid back and forth with regularity every Monday evening as the scholars collected for their weekly activities.

Schlomo Bendagin looked forward to Monday all week. It was well known at 114 East End that he was available to fill in outside his regular doorman shift any time except Monday, and he saw the day as a holy commitment.

On this day, as Schlomo fitted his key in the gate, one shoulder bending under the weight of his book bag, he was startled to see a tall, broad-chested man with thick reddish-brown hair step from the next doorway and approach him.

This too was someone with a holy commitment.

★ ★ ★

The woman who had to be Sheila Dannenbring looked evenly at Caron. The cats were stirring expectantly. Caron took a breath to introduce herself, but kept quiet as she watched the beginning of recognition on Sheila's face.

Recognition, then dread.

'Get out of here,' Sheila said.

Caron shook her head. 'Harry told that story about brain cancer so no one will be surprised if I die. I'm in terrible danger. Josh is too,' Caron said. 'Please let me come in.'

Sheila stared hard at her, and Caron saw the old eyes in the still-young face. I've made my compromises, the eyes said, and I'm in hell, but I'm in it alone.

'Why Josh?' Sheila asked.

'Will you let me in?'

Sheila stepped aside and held the door open. She led Caron into a country-smelling living room with a bay window that faced colorful back gardens. A wheelbarrow and an open bag of fertilizer sat there, as if part of an ongoing and not faithfully tended project.

Caron sat on a loveseat. Sheila took the one

202

opposite. The fabric was slightly damp; Sheila seemed to be someone who didn't remember to shut windows.

The moisture and the earthy smells reminded Caron suddenly of the greenhouse in the cottage in Lexington, the early happiness . . . and the subsequent losses that she had thought were so awful.

How naive . . .

Sheila asked, 'Why did you say Josh is in danger?'

Caron leaned forward. She tried to hold Sheila's eyes. 'Josh saw what Harry did. The beating and the rape. He publicly supported my statement — '

'I know. I heard you on the radio. But Josh . . . even Harry wouldn't — '

'No?'

Caron let the question shimmer there. She went on, 'I know you love Josh. I love him too. He's out of Harry's way for now, but he's not safe, Sheila. Please tell me anything you can about Harry's past. Is his family still in Atlanta? What names can you give me? The only chance we have to beat him is with facts, and people who can expose the truth of what Harry is really like.'

'Beat him? You're dreaming.' Tears rolled down Sheila's face. 'Would I have given up my child if there had been a chance of beating Harry? Would I have promised never to contact Josh, let my son believe whatever lies Harry fed him?

'There are no other facts or people,' Sheila said. 'Harry guarantees that. You are alone, just as I am. Don't let Josh speak against Harry again. I don't care what *you* do, but I haven't hibernated all these years, doing just as Harry demanded, for Josh's sake, so that you can ruin it.'

Sheila was crying hard now. The one cat that had followed them in climbed into her lap and settled there uncomfortably.

Caron asked softly, 'What did Harry do to you?'

Sheila took off her sweatshirt and held out her left arm. The short T-shirt sleeve revealed an odd bumpy look, too many bony bends.

'I waited too long to have it set. Then I didn't go back for the operations they wanted to do. I was afraid there would be questions, and Harry had said he would kill me if I told.'

Caron stared. 'So there's nothing on record about Harry being responsible for this?'

Sheila dropped her arm. 'Nothing at all.'

'Harry likes to break bones,' Caron said. Then, deliberately, 'He broke Josh's nose.'

Sheila gasped. 'Yesterday? But I thought it was just you — '

'Not yesterday. Almost three years ago.

That's how I met Harry. I treated Josh in the New York Hospital emergency room. Both Harry and Josh lied. They said he fell on the ice.' Caron leaned close again. She took Sheila's hands, seeing the smaller left one, the bones and muscles that couldn't bear much use. 'Now do you see why Josh isn't safe? You have to help us. Please, Sheila. Say what he did to you. Tell it all. Let me call WCBS.'

Sheila's chin trembled. 'I can't do that. But . . . '

'What? *Please*.'

'I shouldn't tell you this. Monica made me swear I wouldn't. But maybe it will help . . . '

★ ★ ★

'You sure it isn't hokey to be doing this from here?' Harry asked Graceann.

She moved salt and pepper shakers to the other end of Harry's kitchen table. A pool TV crew were completing their setup nearby in the foyer.

'Absolutely not,' she said. 'You're striking a familiar family note with a message to America. What are they all doing at this time of night but sitting around the kitchen table? *Their* families are intact, not kidnapping each other's kids and telling

205

awful lies about their spouses. You're communicating from your kitchen to theirs.'

Harry rubbed his eyes. Graceann squeezed his shoulder. 'Steady as she goes,' she said.

'When I proposed to Caron,' Harry told the camera, 'I promised I would take care of her forever. 'In sickness and in health' is not a phrase I regard lightly. Nor do I separate physical health from emotional. The cancer cells that are eating away at Caron's neurological system are making her sick in every way, and all of you have to help me find her so I can keep my promise.'

Harry's voice began to fail. There was an empathetic silence among the crew in the apartment, and in most of the thirty million homes around the country with televisions tuned to the program, while Harry regained his composure.

'Your screen is showing you the 800 number to call if you have any information about Caron,' Harry continued huskily. 'Many of you kind people have already phoned, and I bless you for your help. Don't stop watching for Caron and Josh. Watch harder than ever.'

★ ★ ★

Russell Moorpath felt privileged to be working the Kravitz case. Bounty hunters never had their names in the paper, and he couldn't even tell anyone he'd been hired to find the wife and son, but it was an honor just the same.

He carried no weapon and used no more sophisticated devices than payphones, but he had a superb informational network. As usual, it was giving him what he needed. Through a trooper friend Russell had learned of a traffic stop that looked promising. He was also checking out bits and pieces from a couple of motels and convenience stores.

A pattern was emerging.

He was excellent at his work.

Another two days at most, and he would have the lady and the boy delivered safely home.

17

Herbert Felhammer wanted to throw a shoe at the television. Not eight a.m., and already his day was ruined.

It wasn't enough that Harry Kravitz had had the freedom of the airwaves last night — now all the network morning shows were rerunning the man's sniveling lies.

He felt sickeningly helpless.

It wasn't just his deteriorating body, though that was depressing enough, with the malignancy popping up in a new place every second minute. It wasn't even the cruel contrast between his wasted vessel and his pristine brain, the mind keener than ever, as if fueled by the exhaust of the process below.

It was that he saw Caron's nightmare so clearly, and he couldn't help her, couldn't make her come to him despite prayer and meditation and every thought-message technique he tried.

Stepping haltingly back to his chair after shutting off the TV — he refused to own a remote, the damn things, he wouldn't have any reason to get up and walk at all if he gave in to that — Dr Felhammer asked himself a new question.

Why did it have to be a thought message?

He'd been lying low for Caron's sake. In case she decided to call or come to him for help, he shouldn't announce himself.

But Harry knew he was there, and Harry was the point. So why did he have to keep quiet? Why couldn't he call up Katie Couric and tell her a thing or two?

★ ★ ★

Now Caron knew that Harry had a sister and an aunt in Virginia. She knew the sister's name: Monica Wool.

Once Caron had made sense to Sheila Dannenbring, the information she sought had come. The problem wasn't Sheila not telling; it was Sheila not knowing.

But how naive of Caron to have expected otherwise. You don't reweave the fabric of your life with holes in it. Harry had lied and smokescreened with brilliant precision.

And what a lot he had to lie about.

Sheila had received a terrified, cryptic phone call from Monica, when Sheila and Harry had divorced, that hinted strongly at another unspeakable secret of Harry's.

Monica wouldn't say it right out, but Sheila

felt the bottom line was that Harry had sexually abused his niece, Monica's daughter Debbie.

So it appeared that Harry wasn't only violent. He was a molester of little girls.

Sheila also knew that Monica had lived in Vermont and most recently Virginia, but never Atlanta.

Now Caron knew where to look, and what she was looking for.

All she had to do was find it.

She was too tired to make it all the way to Virginia on Tuesday night. She stopped at a neon-sign motel on a busy strip along the mid-Delaware coast. The area was sleepy and redneck. Deep, dank water ran in a drainage ditch behind the parking lot.

A family was moving out of the room next to hers. There were three bouncing, laughing kids, the oldest a girl about Josh's age. They were outside, tossing a small box of cereal back and forth, playing catch with it, as the parents packed their car. Caron watched them through her window blinds: five people who belonged to one another.

For her entire life that had been the ideal. Then she had found it, and lost it, and found it again — a comfortable, enveloping family of which she was a piece, like three cushions on a sofa.

Harry, Josh and Caron.

She turned from the window, futilely massaging the ache in her chest.

She checked in with Josh from a payphone. His first question was whether she had found his mother, and she said no, feeling the truth would hurt him more than the lie.

Leaving the phone, she glanced at a rack of newspapers — and got her daily view of her own face on three of them.

It was her old light and curly look, no glasses, but her stomach hurt nonetheless.

To add another disguise element, she bought liquid tanner, took it back to the motel, and slathered it on.

Later, hungry, she left the room to drive down the road for food. Unlocking the car, nervously scanning the dark parking lot, she was just thinking gratefully that the unnerving darkness was also a blessing when a man suddenly appeared next to her.

'Dr Alvarez?'

Caron gasped. She spun to face him.

★ ★ ★

The lady looked scared to death, Russell thought. People usually were spooked when he found them, but she seemed petrified. He wondered if the illness did that, mixed her up so bad her emotions were all out of whack.

She jumped away and ran around to the back of the car. He followed, grabbed her arm, and was just about to identify himself, try to calm her down, and ask where the boy was, when she lurched out of his grasp and fell against the car.

A chunk of the bumper hit the ground with a clang, and she landed on top of it.

★ ★ ★

The man was reaching for her. Grabbing the piece of bumper, Caron scrambled away and stood. She hit his outstretched arm with it.

He winced. 'Doctor, listen — '

'Get away!' she said hoarsely. 'Leave me alone!'

But he wouldn't, he kept coming for her, and Caron reacted. With all her strength, she swung the bumper in a two-handed backhand at his head, instinctually aiming for the vulnerable temple.

He went down, but was still breathing.

Panting, gasping, praying no one would come out, Caron dragged the man to the ditch. She held him there, his head and shoulders under the black water, until he died, then pushed him all the way in.

Before the body was totally gone from sight, Caron was driving out of the lot.

* * *

Josh's right ear hurt so much, it had woken him up. He had turned to lie on the left, which helped a little.

But he couldn't fall back to sleep.

When the wind came up at night, sometimes it threw sand from Barbara's yard against the windows, which made Josh jump, worrying about someone out there.

He was afraid all the time.

He wished like crazy that he could be back in New York. Even the burning smell in Nicholas's apartment called sweetly in his longing.

If he could be back playing Scrabble with Nicholas, he'd even ask the grandmother to play too. He'd do anything.

He missed home. He missed Caron. He missed his father — or who he'd thought his father was.

Josh thought about Caron a lot. He couldn't stand to remember her as hurt as she was, so he always pictured her, when she called, the way she'd been before any of this happened, with her curly hair and plain eyes and undamaged skin.

213

This morning he had made pancakes, big and fluffy the way Caron liked them . . . as if they would bring her back.

Josh turned over on his pillow, then said a soft 'Ouch' at the pressure on his ear. Tears came, rolling hot and burning down his face on to the pillow. He felt hot all over.

★ ★ ★

By seven a.m. Caron was in Virginia. It had taken her hours to stop shaking.

She needed nourishment, but hadn't dared leave the road. She kept waiting to be caught. For it to be the end.

But she hadn't been.

She didn't know how the man had found her. But it was possible that, in eliminating him, she was loose again.

Finally she pulled in at a crowded rest stop in Spencerville to find breakfast.

Washing up in the ladies' room, she was slightly encouraged to see that her dark skin not only camouflaged her bruising better than the Dermablend alone, but changed her whole look. With the hair and the glasses, and the heavy lipstick penciled to change her mouth shape, she was truly different from the Caron people saw in her photos. Women milled around the room, in and out of the long line of stalls, and no one glanced her way.

She sat at the restaurant counter and ordered eggs and coffee. Just under sixty dollars left; the once-comforting lump of cash got smaller every time she looked at it.

A television mounted on the wall had the *Today Show*. She watched Bryant Gumbel finish interviewing an astronomer.

Then a commercial, then her breakfast came. Buttering the toast, Caron saw the screen suddenly fill with Katie Couric — and a very familiar face on a screen next to Katie.

Dr Felhammer.

Caron stopped, her hands remaining in midair.

Katie was asking him about bruises.

'I have seen lacerations and bruises on Caron,' he said. 'Once, a hematoma on her hand. She always claimed accidents, but when the same person hurts you repeatedly by accident, you must suspect subconscious volition. About this brain cancer — '

'You confirm that Caron Alvarez does have brain cancer, then?' Katie asked.

'No!' Dr Felhammer exploded. He was worse, Caron could see. His shoulders were frail and curled, and his hands trembled. But his voice was strong. 'Caron does not have cancer. Period. End of tale. I'm a doctor, and a cancer sufferer. I know. She no more has cancer than you do. It's a vile lie.'

Caron made herself finish the eggs. She paid and put the change in her wallet and made her way to the ladies' room without rushing, though it was hard.

Wonderful, loving, brave Dr Felhammer, who hadn't bought the fiction that Caron was accident-prone, even when she herself had. Caron's impulse was to phone him and insist he leave Baltimore, but she knew he'd never listen. She would be bringing greater danger to herself and to him if she called.

He had created enough danger for himself already. What would Harry do to him? Was it possible he wouldn't dare? Would Harry be smart enough to save his destruction only for Caron?

The bathroom was even more crowded than before. Every stall was filled. Then one opened right next to Caron, and she gratefully took the door from the smooth-faced blonde teenager coming out.

'It doesn't lock,' the girl said. 'Want me to hold it for you?'

Her stomach rolling, Caron nodded, not trusting her mouth to open and emit only words. She hung her purse on the door hook and got down to the floor just in time before her breakfast came up.

Her head swam with pictures of what could happen to her friend . . . and what she herself had made happen to the man at the motel. Now it was Dr Felhammer whose temple Caron struck. His semiconscious body she forced into the ditch.

Dr Felhammer sinking under the dark water, gone.

Caron Alvarez, doctor, saver of lives. Not now. Angel of death.

How could she?

Finally, trembling, she sat, gripping the toilet, until her stomach began to settle. She wiped her eyes and mouth and got to her feet.

She reached for her purse.

It was gone.

Caron ran from the stall, looking wildly around for the bag or the girl. She wanted to knock on the adjacent stalls, but didn't dare.

She stood for a minute, breathing hard, panicked. She had absolutely no money except what was in the purse. All the elements of her disguise were in there, the tanner and Dermablend, and the cosmetics that altered her look. Her car keys, thank God, were in her pocket. But her notes . . .

Were they in the purse? Harry's sister's name, the other pieces of information from Sheila?

217

Pretending to look for an earring, Caron stooped to the floor. She searched the floors of the stalls adjacent to hers, in case the purse had simply fallen.

But Caron knew it hadn't. The purse, and the ingenuous girl, were long gone.

'What did you lose, hon?' a woman in a gray sweatsuit asked.

Everything. I've lost everything.

Caron looked at the woman, and for a disconnected moment wasn't sure whether she'd said the words out loud. But she must not have, because the bland smile didn't change.

'My earring. But I found it. Thanks.'

Shaking again, Caron ran cold water and washed her hands. She was about to splash her face when she realized she could do no such thing. She had no way to replace anything she washed off.

Not for the first time, it occurred to her that, automatically, she was waiting for support in her time of trouble.

Support from Harry.

The sweatsuited woman finished at the sink next to Caron's and went to the hand blower. Her open handbag sat on the sink counter, close enough to touch.

A lipstick was peeking out of a zipper compartment.

Caron grabbed it and stuck it in her pocket.

★ ★ ★

Caron's notes were in the car. She fell across the seat in relief, reading them over and over, as if to commit to memory what had nearly been lost in every way.

She locked the car back up, thinking with anguish of how cavalierly she had thrown away precious money on it, and went to the line of payphones.

She didn't dare risk a call to Julie or Dr Felhammer now, any more than she could before.

She called Barbara collect.

'I'm empty pockets, Caron. Worse than empty. And Josh . . . poor kiddo, he has an ear infection.'

'Oh, no. Are you sure that's what it is?'

'I took him over to the clinic. They gave us Erythromycin.'

Another reason Barbara didn't have any money. She'd probably spent her last hundred on the doctor and the pills. Caron felt awful.

Barbara said, 'I get paid Friday. My check gets deposited right into my bank account, so at noon I can go to the cash machine and draw money out and wire it to you.'

Caron rubbed her neck. 'How is that done?'

'It's easy. I just go to the drugstore. It only takes an hour or so to reach you. But you have to pick it up down there at an address they give me, and you have to prove who you are.'

'Prove it how?'

'Some usual ID.'

Caron thought a minute. 'I'll call you right back.'

Caron had not had any reason to sort carefully through the debris already in the car when she bought it. But now she sifted quickly through the glove box. Papers, matchbooks, a Mace spray — then a treasure: the car registration.

'Ramona Cruces.' Caron spelled the name for Barbara. 'Find out where I'll have to pick the money up. I'll call you tomorrow.'

'What will you do for the next two days? Do you have food?'

'No.'

'Caron, listen. Go into a busy diner at the lunchtime rush. Check your watch, be waiting for someone. Go to the back of the place to call the person or use the head. On your way out, there should be tip money on tables they haven't cleaned yet. Just scoop it up.'

Caron collected nearly twenty-eight dollars. It wounded her to look around the diner at the thin-faced waitresses whose day she was ruining, but the money saved her.

She spent seven dollars on gas and a Virginia map. The map told her there was a major library twenty miles south of Spencerville.

★ ★ ★

Dialing around the daytime talk shows while he signed correspondence at his desk, Tomas Valin stopped at *Donahue* when he caught the end of a film clip of Harry's.

He listened to the discussion as he moved paper. It wasn't great for Harry. On his side was the fact that Caron had offered no rape examination results as yet. But the busybodies on the screen made much of Josh choosing to leave his biological father and go with his stepmother; and they questioned why there was no medical evidence to support Harry's claim about Caron's brain cancer.

'I don't understand,' an audience member said into Phil's mike, 'why the media aren't looking into it. That doctor in Baltimore says it's not true. Where are her doctors? Where are her tests? Why isn't anyone demanding some proof?'

Tomas wondered the same.

★ ★ ★

Julie Gerstein loved parties, but she wasn't loving this one.

Fifty-odd doctors popping crudités and beer-can tabs around a long blue pool at someone's house in Wellesley — she had looked forward to the evening. But that was before she had known that her best friend would be beaten and raped and missing.

Julie had seen the *Today Show* this morning, with Caron's old friend and mentor defending her. She had never thought about bruises on Caron, but hearing what Felhammer had said, Julie could remember subliminally noticing a few too many minor injuries — and only since her marriage to Harry.

Julie had anguished all morning over whether to call the media herself, and finally decided to wait.

There were so many things she wanted to do. Scream Caron's innocence into microphones; go to wherever Caron and the boy were and rescue them; jump on Harry Kravitz and maim the perverted bastard, kill him with the most painful of weapons.

But it was Caron she had to put first, and Caron still might need to come to Boston. If she did, Julie would have to hide her, and public screaming didn't go with hiding.

★ ★ ★

By Friday morning Caron had a list of thirty-seven people named Wool, of which four were M. Wool, one was M.I., and one M.C. The latter two were not likely to be Monica; if Monica had a maiden-name initial, it would be K. But Caron included them anyway.

She was on her way to pick up her cash at the location Barbara had given her, the Flagg Market in Spencerville.

Then, she hoped to God, she would locate Monica and convince the woman to tell her what Harry had done to Debbie — and then to tell the world.

But Sheila had been fiercely resistant. The only way Caron had broken through was to show her the danger to Josh. She had no such leverage for Monica. The opposite; Monica would fight to keep her secret. Harry would have made sure of that.

Caron folded her list and went out to the car. She opened the windows to release the furnace-like heat, and it billowed over her. She felt the beginnings of a swell of discouragement.

But as she climbed into the car and set her bag on the seat, her hand brushed the list of Wools, and she remembered what she had accomplished so far.

She had survived with no money. She hadn't been recognized. She'd made progress. Harry had tried twice to have her killed, and had failed, and didn't know where she and Josh were now.

She had beaten him for this long.

18

'Spencerville, Virginia!' Harry shouted into the phone. 'She's there now. Her wallet just came in the mail. 'Found in Spencerville, Virginia', it says. And you're still wandering around in all the wrong places while an old wreck of a doctor has the gall to contradict me on national television! That schmuck you hired hasn't even reported in!'

Ronald Brale leaned back in his car and held the phone away from his ear as Harry ranted. When the noise began to die down, he brought it back.

'Shut up, Harry,' he said conversationally. 'If you want me to keep helping you, stop being a lunatic. You know we can't touch Felhammer now. You might as well open your fly and show the teeth marks on your dick.'

Harry wanted to throw the phone, but settled for kicking the coat closet door instead. His leather boot only made a small dent, so he kept kicking until there was a satisfying hole.

'What the hell are you doing?' Brale asked. 'It sounds like a cannon going off.'

'Never mind me. You have to get to Virginia.'

'I'm on the way.'

★ ★ ★

Harry had to go to his office, but he didn't like the thunderous face the mirror showed. He took a fast, very hot shower to try to calm himself.

Toweling his lush hair, he caught himself in the mirror again, and wasn't reassured. He looked like crap.

How the hell had Caron managed to reach Virginia with the entire country watching for her? Some of the media coverage was starting to veer away from his side. Could it be that people doubted him, and looked the other way when they spotted her? What was she doing there?

He didn't like the fact that she was in the South at all. Too many ghosts. Not that she knew enough to exhume them.

Ron would just have to make goddamn sure Caron was found, and that she finally succeeded in killing herself.

Then Josh would be back, and he and Harry could heal and grow and be a family again.

Harry looked at the mirror some more.

He appeared younger with his hair still wet. Like he used to look, back in his freedom-fighter days.

Back when he was really a genuine good guy.

He dropped the towel and leaned into the mirror. He studied the molded chin, the compassionate eyes, the famous hair.

He truly had been good then, not just the cartoon of good.

Suddenly it all hit him in a downpour. Here he was, sending a man to kill his wife with her own scalpel — the wife he had unspeakably attacked when she called Harry on his treatment of Josh.

He had the whole movie coolly planned: Josh back, the new show a smash, himself the devastated widower. Not a movie, however; a crime. His crime. One of his crimes.

What the hell had happened to him? How had the Jewish patriot become the homicidal devil?

How could he begin to crawl his way back?

Harry went into the bedroom and lay on the bed. He was naked and cold in the air-conditioning, but he was immobile, his thoughts churning and crashing like storm surf.

He lay there, listening to the voices fuming inside him. Remembering the voices above him, long ago at Mantle Beach, when he was so horribly trapped.

He was trapped now. The fact was, he had traveled beyond the point of no return with Caron. He couldn't crawl back from there. She had made it impossible. She had announced her intention to destroy him.

So he had no alternative but to prevent her from doing that. To escape from his trap by the only means possible. Then he could begin in his own way to grow back into the person he was supposed to be.

He'd been dragging his feet on some of his current plans for Caron, assuming that she would surface any minute and be solved by Ron. But Harry understood now that he had to mount additional action.

For starters, he had to erase any doubt among the public that his facts were right. He had to prove Caron was the one lying.

It was time for the audiotape.

He rose and dressed, and went to the office.

★ ★ ★

' . . . This is Harry Kravitz saying thank you and bless you.'

'Hello? I'm a train ticket agent in Muncie, Indiana, and there is a passenger with a

228

young boy who might be Dr Alvarez . . . '

'The morgue, that's where she is. Pussy-
face sinner . . . '

'Mr Kravitz, please call Mrs Semper. I saw
your wife this morning. She was at the
Framingham Mall. I'm in Massachusetts . . . '

★ ★ ★

Leaving the office of the foot doctor,
Schlomo looked worriedly at his pocket
watch. The mail didn't usually come until
after one, but that could only be relied on
early in the week. From Wednesday on the
mail boys tended to hustle, especially when
the weather was warm.

He had to get back to 114 East End. He
wished his mother didn't move so slowly.

He put her in a taxi, repeated her address
twice to the driver, who appeared to think as
slowly as his mother walked, and hurried
back to take over from the relief man.

★ ★ ★

'The mail came already? Is it still in the box?'
Jack Dodge demanded.

'No,' Schlomo said. 'Mr Kravitz took it up
with him. I'm sorry. I thought I would be
back in time.'

229

Jack ground his teeth. They were clean and straight and even, and covered by a large, sexy mouth that motivated women to want to listen to him all night. His six-foot-one massive-shouldered frame added to the package, as did his penchant for blade-creased clothes that fitted as if he wore them for a living.

'Is Kravitz still up there?'

'No.'

'You have to let me into the apartment.'

Schlomo gasped. 'The hell.'

'You have to,' Jack repeated. 'Look, don't make me convince you all over again. You know the story. I have to know everything that goes on here. I have to see what came in the mail. I have to find Caron first.'

Part Two

Friday to Monday
August 20 – 23, 1993

19

Straightening Harry's desk, Graceann Geroka held up a rope of connected paperclips. 'What is this?' she muttered to herself.

Her eleven-year-old daughter Lilly thought the question was for her. 'A necklace?'

Graceann looked over. 'I meant, why is he hooking paperclips when he has so much going on? In the length of time this took, he could have given another interview.'

Lilly Geroka watched her mother drop the chain into the wastebasket. She understood that her mother's job was to get exasperated about such matters, but she also thought it was cool of Harry to play with paperclips.

Harry was so nice. Lilly didn't even mind having a sore throat, razor-sore, if it meant staying home from day camp and going to work with Mom.

The buzzer on Harry's desk sounded, and Graceann pressed the speakerphone button. 'Yes?'

'It's me,' Harry said. 'I'd like you out here. We need to go over some points before the news conference.'

'I'll be there.' Graceann gathered her notes.

'Can I go?' Lilly asked.

'You stay in my office and rest. You're sick. You can watch on the monitor.'

'Can't I watch in the studio?'

Graceann took a long look at her daughter. Worriedly she touched a sprinkling of pimples on the child's forehead. 'This needs a cortisone shot,' she said, thinking aloud as she had with the clip chain. Then, to Lilly, 'All right. Fluff your hair and put on some blush. When we go into the studio, just sit and watch quietly. Don't say anything.'

'I never do,' Lilly said.

* * *

Waiting to board his flight at LaGuardia, Jack Dodge scanned the newspapers at the stand near his gate. Every one, *Galaxy* included, had pictures of Harry and his wife.

Jack couldn't stand to look at the guy.

The world was shocked and unbelieving at Harry's wife's accusations.

Jack was neither.

In a way he was surprised that it had taken this long for Harry to trip over himself. And in another way, Jack had feared it might never happen.

People bought the Harry they were fed.

Jack had waited and waited for his chance

234

to feed them another one.

He had to find the wife. She was his chance.

★ ★ ★

M.C. Wool in the town of Iolanthe was a Monica.

Still confused by the C, Caron hoped she had the right person. But something in the woman's voice had told Caron, *Hurry and see her.*

The Wool home was a trim pink stucco box with a groomed lawn. As she parked, Caron saw someone pass a front window. She went up the walk and rang the bell.

The door opened right away.

Caron knew immediately that this was Monica. The jutting chin, the eyes . . . the dark-blonde hair that was the same thick glossy texture as Harry's.

And Monica knew her.

'You can't come in,' she said. 'You have to leave.'

'Please let me talk to you,' Caron pleaded. 'There are lives at stake — '

'I know that. And I refuse to let mine be one of them.'

'You have a daughter.' Caron leaned closer to Monica. 'I think I know what Harry — '

'Leave. *Now.*'

Caron stood on the doorstep, her heart thumping, looking at the eyes which were so like Harry's.

'My stepson and I are in terrible danger. He's only *thirteen*. He saw what Harry did to me — '

'I'm closing the door,' Monica said.

This was hopeless.

Caron sighed. 'I'll be at the motel by the shopping center. The Knights Inn. I'm registered as Ramona Cruces. *Please* think about what I said — '

She was facing the closed door.

⋆ ⋆ ⋆

'She left Spencerville alone in a car with New York tags,' Brale said. 'Going southeast.'

'Southeast? *Fuck.* Are you sure?'

'Sure as I can be without a Triptik. She bought a bag of stuff at a convenience store and was heading for the interstate when the clerk had to run out with a turkey sandwich she forgot.'

'Darcy,' Harry muttered.

'Who?'

'Darcy Levy. Old aunt of mine. She lives in Center Beach. Caron must have found out about her. I don't know how, because nobody but my sister would know, and even *I* don't know where my sister is. Look, you have to get there first. Grab Caron before they can talk. Darcy could hurt me.'

'What's her address?'

'I have it at home. Red something . . . Ruby. Ruby Lane. And Ron, if you have to let Darcy know you're there, don't waste it. Make her tell you where to find Monica. We might really need to.'

20

Harry's father Aaron Kravitz was a New York boy who changed his surname to Crane after he was rejected by four excellent colleges, and was then promptly welcomed by Duke.

He studied sociology and business. An accounting firm in Craig Head, North Carolina, snapped him up before graduation. Within the year he was engaged to Selma Sarah Poll, a stenographer at the firm who loved his jokes.

Selma and her parents held a summit and decided that, for the welfare of future children, the fact that Aaron was, as they viewed it, previously Jewish, was best kept confidential. So the wedding took place at the United Lutheran Church. When Harry came along, and Monica a year later, the babies were baptized.

But Aaron had his deceased parents and ancestors to answer to. While the Polls could decide about their friends and family — Craig Head was their town — Aaron wanted his children to know their history.

Each evening, while Selma took her walk to the duck pond at the end of their dead-end street, Aaron would regale Harry and Monica with descriptions of their grandparents and great-grandparents. He told stories of how they earned their living in the feather pillow business. He talked about how Jews were discriminated against, and how he had agreed to pass for the sake of keeping the peace, but his children needed to know who they were.

In 1952, Aaron's brother-in-law, Bradley Levy, was killed in a Jeep crash in Korea. Three years later his widow Darcy relocated to Craig Head and began teaching at Dune Elementary School.

Darcy didn't hide her religion. It was then that the Polls' pre-wedding concerns for their grandchildren were realized.

In the diner where he bought lunch most days, Aaron was looked at. Monica learned to walk quickly past groups of teasing children.

Harry stepped into hell.

His aunt Darcy tried to find out why he was so pale and shaky-looking all the time, but Harry simply would not tell.

Darcy phoned Selma, but Selma did not want to hear about any problem with Harry.

'He's going through an adjustment,' Selma said, trying not to sound accusing. 'Just let him alone. He'll manage for himself.'

★   ★   ★

At the Knights Inn Caron sat on the misshapen double bed with her arms wrapped around herself as Harry played for America the audiotape that proved she was lying.

On the tape, a phone conversation, Caron was demanding a divorce. She was shrill and vicious and threatening. If Harry refused, she told him, she would claim he raped and beat her.

Harry was hurt and outraged on the tape, but treated her irrationality with caring concern.

'It's driving me crazy to air this tape,' Harry told the camera. 'My family's private business should be private. The conversation wasn't even meant to be recorded — it just happened to take place on a phone line of mine that has taping capability so I can do business without making notes, and I didn't realize the tape was rolling. I certainly never had any intention of playing this for anyone, let alone for all of you. But I am desperate.'

He turned away for a second. Caron could see Graceann Geroka, on the sidelines, crane worriedly. When he turned back, his eyes were red.

'I aired the tape,' Harry continued, 'to clear up any confusion about my wife's condition. Some of you, meaning well, might have seen

Caron and chosen not to notify me. Well, now that I have shown you how disturbed Caron has become from this illness, I know you will understand. As I have said, her cancer was diagnosed by a top neurologist at a blue-chip hospital, so there is no doubt. In consideration of this doctor's privacy, I am honoring his request not to divulge his name.

'All I want is Caron found, so we can care for her properly — and my precious boy returned home to safety. God knows where they are now — or in what condition.'

A sob escaped, and Harry covered his face.

Caron was crying too. The horror overwhelmed her. Harry had pieced together bits of old phone conversations she hadn't known were being recorded — and had not only presented the result as genuine, but *actually seemed to believe it was*.

She sat back against the headboard, her teeth beginning to chatter.

Thank God she and Josh had escaped from this maniac.

It was the only positive thought she could muster. She had never felt so hopeless. The 'evidence' against her was mushrooming. Dr Felhammer, Dr Nusser and some of her more vocal colleagues, plus certain news commentators who were carefully neutral, constituted Caron's only support besides Josh.

Josh . . . his courage was transcendent. They were still playing parts of his WCBS statement, along with hers, in the news stories. Without Josh's corroboration her claims would have no credibility at all.

She prayed he wasn't watching the television right now, wouldn't have to see this new phase of his father's psychosis.

Beside her the phone rang. Caron froze.

Then she remembered she had told Monica the name of the motel.

'Hello?' Caron said in a gasp.

'Dr Alvarez?'

'Monica?'

'No. My name is Darcy Levy. I'm Monica's aunt. And Harry's.'

* * *

One of Sheila Dannenbring's cats was sick, and she stroked its warm head as she watched her former husband skewer another wife.

Over the years Harry had only grown better. It was easy to see why his fans adored him, how Harry was their hero no matter what. The humanness, the sincerity that flowed in his every motion, seemed so real.

Sheila had no idea how Harry had managed to create a phony tape in Caron's voice. But she knew he had.

The psychic pain Sheila felt every day of her life, the bare air where her son should have lived, was so much worse after talking with Caron. The baby she hadn't seen since he was two now had individual form and identity. Sheila felt his absence fiercely. She wanted to know what he looked like, how his voice sounded, how he walked, what he snacked on after school.

The cat mewed, and Sheila realized she had stroked too hard. Cradling him gently, she reached for the remote and shut the television off.

Yet again she thought about doing as Caron had asked, publicly revealing how Harry had destroyed her.

And again she knew she couldn't.

Not because of the danger to herself. She couldn't feel much more dead now anyway.

It was Josh. She didn't dare risk Harry taking his revenge out on Josh.

★   ★   ★

It surprised Paul Wundring to learn that Harry was in the habit of recording phone conversations. Not that Paul had ever said anything he wouldn't want on tape; the idea of your words being recorded without your knowledge was just awkward. Jarring.

243

He was also surprised that a woman as intelligent as Caron hadn't known better than to make threats on the phone. But maybe that poor judgment was part of her illness.

And most surprising of all, of course, was the look inside a woman he had thought he knew. Amazing what showed when you heard a person talking to someone other than you, when they didn't know you were listening. He learned more about his clients from their conversations with other people, at parties or business conferences or whatever, than from hours of one-on-one talk.

Paul shut off the TV as Harry's news conference was ending and went into the bathroom to wash and brush his teeth.

His face in the mirror was sad. *He* was sad, profoundly so.

The situation was simply a tragedy. Paul ached for the whole family.

★ ★ ★

There were three Western Union outlets in Spencerville, and Jack Dodge had already done his act at two of them.

If this Flagg Market didn't bite, he'd have to float a whole new scenario.

He'd been so sure of this one. Where else do you go but Western Union when you suddenly run out of money? There's always a person buried in your life who will wire you cash.

He pushed open the screen door of the store and heard it thwack shut behind him. No air-conditioning; how could they sell cold cuts with the stuff sitting out in the heat? He went to the counter and smiled at the twentysomething Ivory girl with long straight seventies hair.

She smiled back. They always did. 'He'p you?' she asked.

Jack pulled the pictures from his pocket. They were all of Caron, the same head shot, but each was hand-changed: dark hair, upswept hair, much more make-up, very light hair, two styles of glasses.

'I'm looking for this lady,' Jack said, laying them out on the counter as if for Solitaire. 'She could look like any one picture, or like a combination. Or different from all of them.'

The girl bent and slowly studied the display. At the dark-haired one she stopped, pointed. 'This. But with a bigger mouth — and, I think, glasses. Yes. But not like these or these. Brown ones.' The girl straightened. 'She picked up money here.'

Jack kept his face neutral. His hand itched to grab his wallet, to warm her with a twenty or two, but something said no.

245

He looked deep into the girl's blue eyes, the first intelligent eyes he'd seen since he got off the plane. 'You're very observant. Mind if I test your memory a little further?'

'All right.'

'When was she here?'

'Yesterday.'

'Did you see her come in? Was she in a car?'

The girl took a step back. 'Maybe I — Why do you want to know? Are you her husband? Did she run away from you?'

Smart face, mini-series mind, Jack thought, but promptly revised that when the girl said, 'No, I can see you're really worried about her.' She searched his face a minute longer. 'There was a car. I saw it.'

'Can you describe it?'

The girl gave a small smile and went into an office at the end of the counter. She returned with a photocopy.

Now Jack couldn't contain his grin. A New York State car registration, 1984 Olds, to Ramona Cruces. Address in upper Manhattan, Harlemish. Ramona's signature on a receipt-of-cash form.

Memorizing in case she said no, Jack asked, 'Can I have a copy of this?'

'This is a copy. Take it.'

'Bless you.' He leaned on his hands on the

counter, putting his face closer to hers. His shirt was open; a chain bisected a curl of brown hair before disappearing. The girl pinked slightly. 'One last question,' he said.

'Yes?'

'Do you have a record of where the cash came from?'

'Yes.'

She seemed about to go on, so he waited.

'We're told never to reveal that. We're not supposed to reveal anything at all, of course, but — '

'Of course not,' Jack said. Again he wanted to give her money, and again he resisted. Abruptly he asked, 'Do you know who the woman is?'

She shook her silky head.

Hoping to Christ there was a feminist core along with the unlikely eyes, Jack took his shot. 'It's Caron Alvarez. Dr Caron Alvarez. Wife of Harry Kravitz.'

She gasped. 'I didn't recognize — '

'No, because you weren't supposed to. She disguised herself.

'Forget what you've read and seen,' Jack went on. 'Kravitz did everything she says. She is running, but not from me. From him. I'm on her side. She needs all the help she can get.' Jack leaned toward her again, fixing her eyes with his big intense ones, his most genuine gaze. 'If I could get you to take that record of who sent the cash and destroy it, you would be helping enormously. You might be saving a life or two. Don't show it to me. Just burn it.'

The girl held his gaze. He watched her deciding. Finally she went back into the office, and a minute later Jack smelled the match.

She came back out. 'I don't know if this matters, but she had a map, and there were notes on it. All I remember is Iolanthe, circled.'

'Iolanthe? What's that?'

'A town.'

'Where?'

'A few hours southeast of here. Near Marwick.'

'Was that where the money was wired from?'

She hesitated at this change in the rules. 'No. That's all I'll say.'

'What's the best way to get there?'

'Go south on the interstate. When you get near Marwick, look for Route Four east. I don't know exactly what the exit sign says. You know, you're not the first one in town asking for her today.'

Jack stiffened. 'Who else?'

'My aunt is the cashier at the Exxon station. She told me a man was in there asking about Caron Alvarez. I should have put that together with what you — '

'What did he look like? Where did he go?' Jack squeezed the girl's hand. 'If your aunt is half as bright as you, I have to talk to her.'

* * *

'Thin. Ratty-looking face. Or maybe that was just my feeling.'

Jack could see the family resemblance, the thoughtful face like her niece, the airy gestures.

'Tall?'

'About like you. Long legs; I saw him unfolding 'em when he climbed out of the car. Had one of those little flap-up phones in his hand. *Real* little one. Must cost a bunch.'

'Notice the car?'

'Always. A red Camry.'

'Were you able to tell the guy anything?'

'No,' the woman said. 'I didn't realize until I saw your pictures that it was Dr Alvarez I sold some gas and a state map to yesterday. The picture they keep showing on TV is different. But,' she went on before

Jack's encouragement could blossom, 'somebody must have told him something, because I saw that Camry fly on to the southbound interstate about an hour before you got here.'

21

On her way to Center Beach, Caron listened to the Olds growl and clank. Every sound brought a pang of dread that the car would break down miles from help.

But the worry paled next to the awful jumble in her head, the processing of what Darcy Levy had revealed to her.

Harry raped that little Debbie. Right in his apartment in New York. Harry knows it, Monica knows it, and I know it. She was only eight. And she wasn't the first, either. He raped another poor little girl back home. He was still in high school. Imagine, a big football player attacking a tiny child . . .

Caron couldn't stop thinking about the little legs flailing as her own had, the invasion, the tearing torture.

She tried to force the picture back, but it replayed, a tape loop rolling over and over.

Harry's savage face, gusts of breath in hers . . . Debbie's . . .

Thank God Darcy had agreed to see her.

Darcy was afraid of Harry, just as they all were. Not for herself, but for Monica and Debbie. And now it was clear why Monica

251

had so passionately rejected Caron's pleas.

But there was no way to help any of them without someone like Debbie to tell her story.

Caron couldn't wait to reach Center Beach. There was so much that Darcy could contribute. Caron hadn't needed to convince her the audiotape was faked. There was a nobility about the woman that shone through even over the phone.

Thanks to Darcy, Caron now knew for certain that Harry had raped Debbie. The information clanged something deep in her memory, but the harder she tried to remember why, the more elusive the reason became.

She also knew from Darcy that Harry's Atlanta roots were a total lie: he was from the Outer Banks of North Carolina, a little town called Craig Head. The fact that Harry had hidden that meant there must be invaluable information to be gained down there.

★ ★ ★

Josh was wholly sick of frozen lasagna, the only dinner food Barbara seemed to have. But she made such a ceremony of setting the table and folding napkins and everything that he didn't have the heart to say so, or to offer to cook something instead.

He was cutting cucumbers to make a Greek salad when tears just suddenly started rolling from his eyes. Barbara saw him rubbing them with a fist, and squeezed his shoulder.

'What is it, Josh? The tape?'

'No. I don't know.'

'I guess when it's your own father, it's tough to believe the thing is phony.'

Josh put down the knife. 'What if it isn't? What if that's true?'

'It isn't true. It's a pasted-together line of snips of other tapes. They have audio computers that blend all the sound together so the background is even. I know about this. I used to work in a recording studio, where they made commercials. You wouldn't believe some of the tapes they made, fooling around. Dirty ones, like the President, uh, making love with a chicken.'

Josh took a napkin and wiped his wet face. He remembered his dad crying on TV, his face red, his hair rumpled, and started to cry again himself.

★ ★ ★

He should have gassed up in Spencerville, Jack told himself. He'd been in such a goddamn rush to gallop off to Iolanthe, he'd

253

left the Exxon station with his rented Nissan three-quarters down.

What in hell's name was Caron doing down here? If her objective was to hide, why poke around in bumfuck-nowhere southern towns whose citizens had nothing better to do than scrutinize every spider that ever wandered over their border? Why not pick an anonymous big city and disappear into it?

Could there be someone Caron was heading for who would protect her? Provide money?

Or, Jack wondered, could her agenda possibly be the same as his own?

Why hadn't she lost her New York tags? How smart were doctors?

He was so busy cursing her, he almost missed the New York tag on the red Camry in the service area he was passing.

Tall. Ratty-looking. Bingo.

You could see the menace in the man, in the way he interacted with the mechanic. There was no overt sign that the gentle-spoken, gangly, fiftyish guy was anything but a northern schlub with car trouble, but years of watching for people to show themselves sideways had conditioned Jack to spot the nuances before the proof appeared.

Who the Christ was this?

Did he know where Caron was?

Jack waited for the man to finish up and leave, then started the Nissan. He eased on to the interstate three cars behind the Camry and settled in to follow it, presumably to Iolanthe.

* ★ ★

There was an exit sign for Route Four to Iolanthe. Jack had cut the Camry a lot of slack, knowing where it was probably headed, and so was unprepared, as he moved right to exit, to see the Camry still in the far left lane, not far ahead.

What the hell?

Jack sat straight up. Get off and head for Iolanthe and maybe find Caron but lose Bozo? Or stay and play Simon Says?

He decided to stay.

22

The Camry was starting to sputter ever so slightly once again as Ronald Brale left the turnpike for Center Beach.

Fucking car.

He should make Harry spring for a Lexus right now, before he had to drive any further.

Well, he'd have one soon enough. Harry already owed him the national debt, and it was only going to get worse.

He pulled into a South King station, lifted the Camry hood, and tightened the wire that had just been replaced.

Then he looked up Darcy Levy in the public phone book, checked the local street map in it, and headed for Ruby Lane.

★　★　★

Darcy Levy stood at the front window, watching for Caron Alvarez. She hadn't been able to force down any lunch, and she felt nauseated and hungry at once. The gastroenterologist always insisted she not let her stomach be empty, it was the worst thing for her ulcer, but today there was no

256

choice. The lump in her throat wouldn't let food pass.

Harry, anything to do with Harry, produced that effect.

Part of Darcy felt sorry for her tortured nephew, for the born courage that circumstances had turned to something else, something aggressive and sick.

But primarily it was the others who had her sympathy — the people whose lives intersected with Harry's, and who suffered for that.

She had hoped Harry's fame and success would eliminate his dark needs. For several years her hopes had risen. She would watch him on TV, as Scott or as himself, and try not to let the horrible secret about Debbie poison everything. She tried hard to respond simply to the affable person presented.

But that had been useless. Clearly Harry was more dangerous than ever. This poor wife, his son . . . Monica terrified again for Debbie, for all of them . . .

Except for the ulcer, Darcy was strong and healthy for her age. Her arms were wiry from caring for the climbing clematis along her front fence. She walked on the beach every day, even in rain, and, though not much of a cook, ate well. She was a regular at several Center Beach restaurants.

She liked her life the way it was. The notion of opening it to admit a battered and raped spouse of her nephew, with all the ramifications involving herself and Monica and Monica's children and numerous ghosts, was agonizing.

But how could she not? Caron Alvarez was afraid of being killed — and from Darcy's point of view, it was a very reasonable fear. Caron's only hope lay in exposing Harry. Nobody knew better than Darcy how little cooperation Caron would find in that objective. So few people knew about Harry. Those who did had long since been motivated to shut up.

The clematis shook as a car pulled into the driveway, a small red sedan. Darcy craned to see Caron. But it was a man who got out on the driver's side — and there was no one else in sight.

The lump in Darcy's throat grew.

★ ★ ★

Caron pulled in behind Darcy's red Toyota. Smoothing the sweaty creases in her skirt, she went to the door. She rang the bell; no answer.

Had Darcy changed her mind, and left the house?

258

She rang again and waited. She felt chilled, dejected, her hope bubbling away. Hours of driving, overwhelming tension, and she had fixed her hopes on getting some information, some direction, from this strong-sounding woman who seemed to know perfectly well the Harry that was so patently unbelievable to the rest of the world.

Caron rang once more, then tried the knob. The door opened, and Caron stepped into a cool small foyer with a staircase to her right.

'Darcy?' she called.

A man materialized at the top of the stairs. He stared at Caron for an instant, then leaped down, but Caron was already racing back out of the door, her blood pounding in her head with the two realizations that had just slammed her:

The red car had New York plates.

This man was the one who had broken into the shelter.

Her fingers were inches from her door handle when the man tackled her.

★ ★ ★

Jack tried to follow the Camry on the local streets, but it was too risky. He drove back to the South King station. The Camry would have to pass there on its way back from

259

wherever it was going; there were few roads between that corner and the shoreline. Jack hated to let the man go, and possibly lose a chance at Caron, but he couldn't risk being spotted.

He parked behind a pickup truck and sat back to wait.

* * *

Caron's face was in the sandy dirt, the grit in her mouth. The man held her down with a knee on her back. She tried to scream, but only succeeded in inhaling more dirt.

Her pulse thumping, she waited to feel agony — or nothing.

Suddenly the knee lifted a fraction; the man seemed to be struggling to get a weapon in place.

Caron snatched the moment. She lunged her body sideways and drove her elbow as hard as she could into the man's genitals.

With a husky roar the man rolled away, balling himself up. Caron grabbed open the car door, fumbled for the Mace can in the glove box, aimed it in the approximate direction of his head, and sprayed.

* * *

Again Jack almost missed the catch of the day, so intent was he on his new primary target.

No red Camry, but the white 1984 Olds with New York tags — and behind the wheel the Caron the Western Union clerk had picked out, with straight hair instead of curls, and dark skin.

He put the Nissan in Drive, scooted around the pickup, and headed out after her.

★ ★ ★

Caron could barely see to drive. Her terror was a fog surrounding her. Her foot shook on the accelerator.

From somewhere she had pulled the courage to stop at the first outdoor phone after Ruby Lane to call the emergency number on it, and give Darcy's address and the urgent message that the woman needed help. But Caron very much feared Darcy was beyond help already — as she herself could be.

Had Harry traced her to Virginia, and then assumed she was there to approach Darcy? Or was Harry systematically sending a killer to any stop he thought she might make — and then erasing whoever was there?

That made Caron's stomach lurch.

What tragedy was she bringing on these innocent people by needing them?

And what could she do now to save herself from the man from New York, who would be speeding after her at any moment if he wasn't already?

She pressed the pedal harder, felt the car gather speed. It wasn't much further to the interstate. But once on it, what could she do? Where could she go? What would happen when the Camry caught up? Would she be murdered right there on the turnpike?

Caron thought of Josh, waiting for her at Barbara's, trustingly doing what she asked. She had promised him she would be back soon, and they'd be safe.

It was possible no one would even know she was dead, depending on how it was done. Or her death would be a big story, and Josh would hear the news on TV.

Abused by his father, witness to the horror in the apartment, yanked out of his life to run for hers . . . and then he would find out on television that his one protector was gone?

Immediately she felt Josh's anguished desperation, so much worse even than when Harry had broken his nose, that unspeakable betrayal.

Caron began to cry, choking gasps that made her stomach worse. Josh was waiting for her to fix things, and she would probably die instead, and leave him stranded, and even be responsible for more deaths. Maybe Darcy's already. Monica and her children would be killed . . . and Sheila? Would Harry know Caron had been there?

Suddenly Caron realized she had an alternative to a suicidal trip on the interstate. She was about to pass a shopping center with a giant supermarket, a Rite Aid, and several other stores, and endless parking. She cut her wheel sharply to make the entrance, drove to the back of the lot, and parked in a line of cars that couldn't be seen from the road.

The Toyota was nowhere around.

Caron rested her head on her hands on the steering wheel and tried to stop trembling.

After a while she looked up, like a turtle raising its head from the shell, and scanned again for the red car, and didn't see it.

Her stomach was on fire. She had to have some antacid.

She hurried into Rite Aid.

★   ★   ★

After two near-misses in a day, Jack was careful to stick close to Caron, but still she surprised him by copping that turn into the shopping center.

What the *Christ* was going on?

He drove slowly to where she had parked. She was still in the car, just opening the door.

She got out.

★ ★ ★

Taking cash from her wallet for the Tempo tablets, Caron glanced at the newspapers on the rack by the cashier, and nearly collapsed.

KRAVITZ WIFE SEEN HERE. FUGITIVE WIFE IN VA.

Every muscle wanted to drop the tablets and run, run, and not stop. But Caron made herself stay very still, prepare each motion, seem normal. Sweat ran on her face. She paid, took her change, slowly left the store with her purchase, walked to the car, got in, and locked the doors.

The tablets were plaster in her dry mouth. The closed-up car was baking hot. But she couldn't go back out for a drink; the headlines made her feel like she glowed radioactively.

She had to get out of here, out of Virginia, once she had given the man in the red car a chance to leave Center Beach behind.

Should she go to Craig Head? What other choice was there? It seemed to be the beginning of Harry and of everything.

She cracked open the windows slightly.

Suddenly there was a shadow across the passenger side. A hand reached in through the small space above the window and pulled up the door lock. The door opened and a man got in.

All Caron's remaining control dissolved. She screamed and scrambled with both hands for her door handle — but the man grabbed her and covered her mouth.

23

'Stay still. Hear me out,' Jack Dodge said. It was like gripping a wet trout. 'I'm all you have, Doctor.'

She struggled ferociously. He held her pinned with one hand, the other over her mouth.

'My name is Jack Dodge. I'm with *Galaxy*. I'm working on a story about you. *You*, not that demonic psycho you're married to. I'm here to stick with you, listen to you, keep you safe, and tell your side. Are you *hearing me*?'

He waited for the words to penetrate. Suddenly, amazingly, they did. He felt her slacken under his hands. He risked letting go.

She dived out through her door.

He scrambled across the seat after her.

She had a spray can in her hand.

*   *   *

Caron pointed the nozzle at the man's face. She jammed her thumb down on the pump, but no spray came out.

Sand must have clogged it.

Terror moved her feet. She took off across

the parking lot. But she was exhausted, and within moments the man had caught up and was holding her by the shoulders.

'If you yell,' he said quietly, his chest heaving, 'we'll have an audience. Listen to me. Just *listen*.

'I used to know Harry, back in his early TV days,' the man said. 'He was angry about a *GQ* story I wrote, so he tried to ruin me. He was responsible for me spending two years in Attica.

'I consider Harry Kravitz vicious, out of his tree, and capable of anything up to and including murder. If there's a sin beyond murder, he'll do that too, as soon as he discovers it exists. Am I describing a persona that's familiar to you?'

★　★　★

Now Brale had no choice but to get rid of the car.

He was not, however, in a position to hit Harry up for a Lexus — not when he had to tell him that he'd found Caron and lost her — and that he'd had to kill Darcy Levy.

'Jesus,' Harry said. 'That's lousy news, Ron.'

'I couldn't avoid it, Harry. She was wild. She would have killed me.'

'What did you . . . do with the body?'

'Don't ask. Just be glad I got there before Caron did.'

'Lousy news,' Harry said again.

Brale wanted to shoot Harry through the phone. *He sits in his network office and intones his lines as if he really has a heart, while I chase a woman who should never have been able to avoid me this long, finding more problems as I go — problems that should be entirely Harry's.*

But he only said, 'That's the breaks, Harry. And I'm getting rid of the Camry. Caron knows it now. I don't want her to see me coming.'

'Fine, Ron, but just *get* her, will you? Cut her good with that scalpel. I'm waiting to hear from you that it's done.'

'You will. Just as soon as I change cars.'

'You have an anonymous way to pay for the new one, I assume.'

'You can count to ten, I assume.'

Harry hung up on him.

There was a picture of Darcy from an old Radcliffe alumni magazine in Harry's desk. He wasn't sure why he'd kept it, but he took it out now and propped it against his clock.

The face was kind and intelligent, and that had been Darcy. Harry recalled how she had tried to help him survive in grade school, not

268

understanding how useless it was. Darcy had that built-in sense of right and wrong and never understood that not everyone was the same.

Darcy had been an achiever when that was tough for a Jew and a woman. She hadn't let widowhood become her job. She had lived her years independently and productively.

Harry sat for a time with the picture. His eyes hurt.

He didn't know where Josh was. Caron was a loose cannon. He wanted his career and his life to return to what they had been — not this crisis-center maelstrom.

He wished the whole situation could be obliterated.

Finally he took the picture into the bathroom, struck a match, burned it, and flushed the last black scraps away.

There was another picture he had to take care of. He had to incorporate Brale's description of the alterations Caron had made in her appearance, and get the new likeness on the tube.

★ ★ ★

Caron stared at Jack. She felt shaky and sick and alone. Her stomach had devoured the Tempo and was screaming for more after this new assault on her nerves.

He could be anybody.

Someone on Harry's side with a more diabolically subtle approach than the man in the Toyota. Or a true reporter, but a lying one, who would leave her stranded and exposed once he had some personal material from her.

But Jack might be telling the truth. An old grudge? With Harry, very likely. A *Galaxy* story? Again, it could fit, Caron knew the tabloids had far more money to chase scandals than the conventional media. *Galaxy*, the *Enquirer*, and the *Star* had enough credibility to be quoted as sources of new details on this or that sleazy story. Harry was always grousing about it.

Could it be? Could this be a lifeline?

She got back into her car, and he got in on the passenger side.

'Question,' Jack said, resting his arm along the back of her seat. 'What are you doing here?'

'Here in Virginia?'

'That'll do to start, yes.'

She might as well answer. Harry would know what she was trying to achieve as soon as he found out she was down here.

She gave an exhausted sigh. 'I'm looking for — for who my husband really is. For proof. It's the only way I can fight him.'

'He isn't easy to discredit. I've dug and dug.'

'You have?'

'I didn't start working on this story just this second, Doctor. I've talked to half of Atlanta. What did you get so far?'

'I'm not going to say.'

'Where's your stepson? You have him taken care of somewhere?'

'Yes.'

'What do you know about a tall guy in a red Toyota?'

'No comment,' Caron said. 'I have questions too. How did you find me?'

'Your wallet was found in Spencerville and mailed to your apartment from there. I was watching your mail. I flew down and got lucky tracing you. Probably the guy in the Toyota started from there too. Does that jibe with when you first became aware of him?'

She was silent.

He knew he needed to be patient, that she'd be an idiot to give him answers just because he was asking questions. But his own acute sense of being closed in on made him push.

'You need me, Dr Alvarez. Right now you stand out, no matter what color you are or how much paint you wear, but with me you're part of a couple. You need another car, money, my criminal mind, and my newspaper. But,' he said as she started to answer, 'you have to realize that for yourself. So I'll give you ten or twenty minutes to come to your senses. Meanwhile, we have to get the hell out of here.'

'I know. I just saw a newspaper in the drugstore,' Caron said. 'It's out that I'm in Virginia.'

'Not exactly. Every newspaper in every cheesestraw town in the country has you seen in their area. Harry has the entire nation treasure hunting, and when you tell them to look, they find. See this?' He took a *People* magazine from his jacket.

HARRY VS CARON was the cover story, with a jagged line separating pictures of the two of them, and an inset of Josh across the line.

'My God,' Caron breathed, turning to the article.

'It has a poll. They all have polls. America is behind Harry. You're in the toilet. But don't read it now. You have to get out of this *car* is what I meant. I'm driving a rental,' he said, pointing. 'I want you to come with me while I find Virginia plates to put on your car. That'll get us out of state, where I can get you another car. I don't want you in the rental any more than necessary. These are stopped too often. And an overjuiced cop is just the kind of good-soldier jerk who would race to his two-way and contact Harry.'

Caron looked at the Nissan. As dangerous as her own car was, the Olds represented a degree of safety, in that she owned it and controlled it. Transferring to Jack's car and Jack's control was a horrifying idea.

Way at the front corner of the parking lot there was a flash of the garnet red of the Camry. Caron rose in her seat and stretched to look.

In her mind she could suddenly see the knife, its point against her neck. She could hear the man breathing, smell his hair.

The red car came into view. It wasn't the Camry. But the terror still thundered through her.

If Jack Dodge had found her, the man in the Camry could too.

Obviously there were damning facts to be learned in Craig Head. Darcy had confirmed a devastating one. If Harry found out Caron was headed there, he would be even more determined to have her killed.

Jack made it sound as if his mission was to keep Caron safe. She didn't buy it. She didn't believe Jack was going to all this trouble to write a story about her.

He was using her.

But he was right. She had no resources. He did. She needed them.

Jack wasn't just her only chance for a motel room and a hot shower. He just might be her only chance to live.

She didn't have to trust him, any more than she trusted any man except Dr Felhammer. All she had to trust was that he wouldn't leave her in worse trouble than she already was.

So let him use her. She would use him too.

24

At WNXX-AM, All-News Radio 1010 in South Bend, Indiana, Don Aprile was finishing a banana and watching the wall clock tick toward the start of his next thirty-minute air shift. His copy was on the desk. He'd finished writing it ten minutes ago.

He was sick of the Kravitz story. But the damn thing had been nothing less than a third lead since it broke a week ago, and the *People* piece seemed to have pushed it back to first place.

Not that there was a lot new on it. Sightings of the wife everywhere but Uranus. Celebrities saying how true-blue Harry was. Public opinion polls leaning overwhelmingly his way. A couple of ragtag people defending the wife.

That in itself invited Don's sympathy.

And curiosity.

'Why the hell isn't everybody slicing this story to bits?' he asked out loud. 'Why aren't we seeing Diane Sawyer waylaying doctors and demanding medical data? How come Morley Safer isn't digging back to prove or disprove what that poor old guy in Maryland said about seeing bruises on Alvarez?'

'What?' the writer at the next desk muttered.

'Never mind,' Don said. He picked up his copy and walked toward the studio.

★　★　★

Caron's senses noted the new-car smell of the Nissan, the sweet blast of cool air from the vents. Though the Olds was her means of escape, and the only semblance of control she had, it had come to represent dread and discomfort. It was always hot and smelly and discouraging. She feared breaking down in it. Now it was recognizable.

Jack punched in a number on his cellular phone. Caron listened to him trade seductive quips with a woman in his office named Robin. Then, 'What's the nearest international airport to Center Beach? One with a long-term lot. I'm guessing Norfolk.' He waited, playing absently with the silver dollar on a chain around his neck. 'Even better. Thanks, love.' He clicked off.

'Four long-term lots,' Jack told Caron. 'Two with a thirty-day max, two more thirty to sixty. We'll go play in one of the second group.'

'I'm not potchkying around any more, Ron,' Harry said. 'You have to bring in another man. This has to be done with.'

Brale knew that tone. 'I'll do my best, Harry.'

'Do it today. Did you change cars?'

'Yes.'

'And have you — '

'Don't nag me, Harry. I know what I have to do. I'll get back to you.'

Brale tapped the phone with a fingernail, pondering. Aside from Moorpath, who didn't know the full agenda and who seemed to have disappeared into space, Brale had held off bringing in anyone else because his judgment had been that he alone could take care of Caron — and he still wasn't convinced he couldn't.

There was a man named Peter Torres in Bridgeport, Connecticut, who was tied to Brale the way Brale was tied to Harry — by means of incriminating information held. Brale had hidden the man after he had killed a woman for money — and, for posterity's sake, had then detailed the matter on paper and put it in a safe deposit box.

Peter was a very vicious dog on a very tight leash.

He could always bring in Peter. But not yet. The fewer cooks, the better. Harry himself knew that; Harry was panicking.

It was Brale's job not to panic.

* ★ ★ ★

Jack cruised along the aisle of the long-term lot as if seeking just the right space. He passed a black Saab, gave it a long look, continued on down the row, and stopped.

'Sit in the driver's seat,' he told Caron. 'If anyone official comes by, look ditzy and drive off. Circle back in five minutes and I'll jump in.'

He was back before anyone at all came along. Caron moved over as he slid two license plates under his seat.

'Excellent choice of car,' Jack said with no nod to modesty. 'There was a *Washington Post* from last week in it, so those folks are gone till late September. Now we'll go back and put these on your car and run the hell out of this state. While we're doing that, you might want to consider sharing with me what you've found out about Harry. Let me put that another way. If you don't, I can't do you any goddamn good at all.'

★ ★ ★

Caron did feel less like a lighted target riding next to Jack. She would have no matter who was in the driver's seat; it was simply the change from being alone, the illusion of couplehood.

All she had now that was valuable were the secrets she had learned. Nobody even knew Caron was aware of Craig Head, except Darcy Levy. She could only pray Darcy hadn't been made to tell the man in the Camry.

From the little she knew of the woman, Caron bet she wouldn't reveal anything she didn't want to.

Of course, *want* wasn't the issue.

But Caron couldn't bear to think about what might have happened to Darcy. The possibilities were too awful. If she let them in, they would swamp her, and she would be beaten.

Darcy had trusted her. Or had been willing to.

What would be her own fate if she trusted Jack?

Abruptly she asked, 'What did Harry do to you?'

'I told you.'

'Only an outline. Tell me again. In detail.'

He was quiet for a minute. 'In 1978 I was an entertainment writer with great by-lines — *Playboy*, the LA *Times*, all the hot markets. *GQ* assigned me to do a profile of Harry.

'He sat still for a couple of interviews, but he didn't like being asked anything deeper than what brand of seltzer he drank. I thought I saw a black edge in Harry, and I tried to provoke it. Nice guy, TV idol . . . I didn't buy it, and I went looking for the downside. He didn't show me much, but what he did, I put in the piece. I quoted every rude thing he said to me.

'I never heard directly from Harry. But three weeks later I was arrested for dealing coke. I had sold to a couple of friends, small quantities, but somehow two big bags were found in my apartment. Enough to put me down for two years. Two years in Attica.'

Jack turned to Caron. 'I swear those bags were put there.'

Caron said, 'I want documentation on everything you just said.'

★ ★ ★

'What's going on, Ron?'

'You shouldn't call me, Harry, you should wait for me to call you. I don't need the phone ringing at the wrong time. What's going on is, I found her car. I'm waiting for her to come back to it.'

'Where are you?'

'I'll tell you the details later.'

'Call me as soon as — '

Brale clicked off.

He was parked in a row of cars, but with a clear view of the Olds, which sat by itself. He assumed it had been hidden by other cars when she left it. His good break; if the row hadn't emptied out, the car would have been much harder to spot when he finally doubled back to search after making sure Caron didn't get on to the interstate.

He didn't think Caron had left the car for good. There were clothes and a small bag still in it.

Brale had traded the Camry for a dark green Mazda. He didn't feel at home in it yet, but he could function.

The scalpel was within easy reach.

He could believe that Caron would finally give up and end her life in her old car, out of money and options.

All he had to do was wait.

★ ★ ★

Jack said, 'My editor knows my whole background. Hand me the phone. I'll put him on with you.'

281

Caron shook her head. 'Your editor would lie.'

Jack rolled his eyes. 'Do you know who my editor is? Evan Heller. You've heard of him. He's an award winner. He's been quoted on *60 Minutes*.'

'Do you have a clipping or anything about your arrest?'

'Not on me.' He let out his breath. 'We'll stop at a library. If they have any interactive computer service at all, I should be able to pull up clips and my GQ article.'

'It's almost nine. There won't be one open.'

They were quiet. Then Caron said, 'If we call Attica, and you authorize them to release the information, maybe they'll confirm that you were there.'

'Not over the phone. I'd have grounds for a lawsuit if they did that. But look, if you'd be satisfied hearing confirmation of my Attica time on the phone, there's another way. Grab the cellular. Dial Crescent, Ohio, Directory Assistance. Area Code 216. Ask for Ho's Service. H-O-apostrophe-S.'

'Why?'

'Ho is Horatio Plimpton, my old cellmate. He'll be at his gas station. He always is. If I tell him it's okay, he'll confirm everything I'm saying.'

Caron thought. Jack could have had this

whole tale planned, and the man, whoever he really might be, prepared.

But it had been her idea to talk to someone on the phone.

Maybe she should wait for a library.

But that would be tomorrow at the earliest.

She could be dead by then.

She was an idiot not to insist on something she could hold in her hand and read.

But it was all about time, and about deciding. That was how it had been so far on this horrible journey — work fast, stay ahead, choose the least-awful risk.

Jack was rude and boundaryless, and Caron wasn't sure how bright. And he was only going to tell her what he needed to.

But to be no longer alone . . . to have money, help, resources . . . a glimmer of light for herself and Josh, some reason to hope that the monster might not macerate them both . . .

She dialed Ohio.

25

The minute office of Ho's Service contained a wooden desk with one leg substituted for by a can of rust remover; a heavily nicked school chair; two file cabinets with fishing gear in them; and a three-line, microchip-programmed phone system that was considerably more sophisticated than the highest-tech hardware currently available from Ohio Bell.

There was no need for more than one line, and that one not often. Though the service station was busy, the business was drop-in. But the owner had been a telephone installer before landing in Attica for grand theft, and had used his incarceration time for obsessive study of the technology that had become his passion.

On Saturday evening, August 21, the gleaming black phone rang at ten past nine. Ho Plimpton, a heavy-shouldered black man with short hair graying at the front, touched the button to answer.

'Ho's.'

'Is this Horatio Plimpton?' a woman asked.

'Yep.'

'I'm calling about Jack Dodge.'

'About what about Jack Dodge?'

'I'm with him now. He made certain claims about himself that he says you can verify. When and where did you meet Jack?'

Ho made a face at the phone. 'Who are you?'

'Hold on, please.' Caron covered the mouthpiece and said to Jack, 'He wants to know who I am. Don't tell him. Just ask him to answer me.'

'You can tell him who you are. He's a con. We keep secrets.'

'No.'

'Jesus.' Jack took the phone. 'Honey? Tell her, will you? Answer whatever she asks.'

'You okay, Jack?'

'Fine. Just showing my credentials.' He gave the phone back to Caron.

She repeated the question.

'Attica State Prison,' Ho said. 'We shared a cell fifteen years ago.'

'What was Jack jailed for?'

'Selling nose candy.'

Caron said, 'Do you know how he came to be arrested?'

A husky chuckle. 'He was set up. But who wasn't?'

Jack whispered to her, 'I never told about Harry.'

She covered the phone. 'Why not?'

'Why bother?'

Caron looked at him. He looked straight back.

She uncovered the phone. 'What does Jack do now?'

'He's a reporter for the *Enquirer*. No — *Galaxy*.'

Caron took a breath and let it out. 'What's on his neck chain?'

'He didn't have one. You can't wear them in prison, except religious ones.'

She sat for a minute, holding the sweaty phone. Finally she said, 'All right. Thank you,' and handed it to Jack.

'I'll be in touch,' Jack said, and clicked off. He turned to Caron. 'Okay?'

As okay as it was going to get. 'Yes.'

'That was an interesting question about the neck chain. What were you going for?'

'Nothing in particular. Just any wrong note.'

They had parked at a busy McDonald's to make the call. A mile down the road was the shopping center where the Olds waited for its new plates.

'So?' Jack said. 'Talk to me. What have you found?'

'Harry's not from Atlanta. He was born in Craig Head, North Carolina, the Outer

Banks. He lived there until college.'

'Ha.'

'He raped a little girl when he was in high school. That wasn't the only time. He also raped his niece, his sister's daughter, when they visited him in New York years ago.'

A police car moved slowly through the McDonald's lot, and exited. Jack watched it leave and then started the Nissan. He drove out in the direction of the shopping center.

'Where did you get all that?'

'From Harry's aunt, Darcy Levy. First I found Sheila Dannenbring, Harry's first wife, from Josh's birth certificate. Sheila told me Harry had family living in Virginia.'

Jack glanced sideways. 'Good work. What else did the aunt say?'

'He had a history of violence and vandalism. He used to break up the town after losing football games. That's all she told me. She — I'm afraid she might be dead.'

Without warning, Caron was crying, hot tears spilling into her already grimy lap. 'I talked to Darcy on the phone. She agreed to see me. But the man in — in the Camry was at her house when I got there. This man already tried to kill me in New York.

'I didn't see Darcy at all. The man came after me, and I barely got away. I called the police and sent them to her address.'

She's running for it and she stops to call the police on what is probably a DB, Jack thought. Yet another reason to be astonished she's still alive.

And confirmation he himself had been expecting: Harry had someone killing anyone who could reveal his true nature.

No surprise. Still, you can smell the other guy's sweat on your wife and see the motel matchbook peeking out of her purse, and it's a shock anyway to catch them doing it.

'Amazing you weren't found sooner,' Jack said.

'I was. At a motel in Delaware. A man accosted me in the parking lot. I killed him.'

'You *killed* him? How?'

'I brained him with a hunk of metal and pushed him into a ditch full of water.'

Jack shook his head. From tears over a nice old lady to a dispassionate confession of offing a guy.

She was a surgeon, all right.

But when Jack glanced sideways a moment later, Caron's cool doctor mask had slipped to reveal the same anguish as when she'd spoken of Darcy. Tears rolled from agonized eyes and her fingers curled tightly around one another.

Jack pulled into the shopping center. All the stores were still open, but potential shoppers were home watching TV; the lot was way less crowded than before.

He took a space near the road, a few hundred yards from where the Olds was parked at the back.

Caron wiped her face. 'Let's get this over with.'

'Not yet.'

She looked at him.

'Just being careful,' Jack said.

He kept his eyes on the Olds. There was absolutely no activity around it, just a few other unoccupied cars. No red Toyota. He didn't know what was prickling at him.

He watched it a while longer, and then made a decision.

He started the car. 'We're leaving.'

'In this car? But we — '

'Yeah. But I don't feel right.'

'My things are in there. What do you mean, you don't feel right?' Then, 'Never mind. I get it.'

He meant the gut judgment she had come to depend on in surgery. All the facts pointed one way, instinct another.

This wasn't surgery, but she would have to learn very fast to be as alert as if it were.

★　★　★

Brale was expert at watching out of a car without revealing that the car was occupied.

From the Mazda he had seen the comings and goings in the shopping center lot for several hours. He had tensed when an open truck with a passenger resembling Caron had driven in. He had trained his binoculars on numerous women of every description who were alone in vehicles.

Just because he watched everyone, he had scoped out the rented Nissan carrying the couple, and watched it park just inside the shopping center, and sit there.

And had realized after a minute that the people weren't getting out.

He began to breathe faster. They weren't arguing or talking or anything, just sitting. He focused the glasses as sharply as he could and studied the woman in the passenger seat.

It was dark, but some light from a pole fixture spilled into the car. A black woman . . .

No.

A dark-skinned woman with straight black hair and glasses. Caron, as he had seen her in Center Beach.

Brale's fingers gripped the binoculars. He studied the face until he was sure. He shifted to the driver.

Smooth-faced, fortyish, thick hair. Nobody

290

he had seen or Harry had described. Some mystery friend or lover? A pro bodyguard or detective? Why the rental?

Brale had a sinking feeling. There should have been some move involving the Olds by now. The man with Caron either suspected Brale was here waiting for her, or was just being cautious.

Either way, if the guy was any good, this was as close as Brale was going to get to Caron this time.

As that realization hit, Brale saw the Nissan's headlights go on, and the car quickly leave the lot.

He slammed the binoculars against the dash.

★ ★ ★

'I saw the article in *People*,' Barbara whispered. 'I read it at work. Josh doesn't know about it.'

'Thank God,' Caron said.

'Well, but he watches television, Caron. I can't stop him. You and Harry are all over it. Poor thing, he gets so teary. That tape — you know about the audiotape?'

'I saw Harry play it. Josh was watching?'

'Yes.'

Caron groaned.

'I explained to Josh about faking tapes,' Barbara said, 'but I don't know how much he understood. He thought he was hearing you . . . '

'I know.' Caron leaned wearily against the plastic phone shelter outside a diner in West Virginia. They were out of range of a cell, and Jack's phone wasn't usable. It was three in the morning and the last sleep she had had was the abbreviated period she had forced on herself before driving to Center Beach. Her body ached and her stomach burned. She alternated between gratitude for Jack's help, and terror that she was making a fatal error by accepting it.

But with money from Jack she had been able to buy scissors and bleach and new make-up and new glasses. And they were on their way to Ohio to get a car from Ho's Service — one that would take them to Craig Head.

'Could you wake him, Barbara?'

'Sure, hon.'

Caron heard Josh's sleepy mumble. It brought back all the mornings when she had coaxed him up for school or sports, with juice and a kiss. She had to cover her mouth to keep from breaking into tears again.

'I'm sorry to wake you, sweetheart. I just wanted to talk to you. Barbara told me you saw your dad play that audiotape on TV.'

'Yeah.'

'Josh, it's not true, not a second of it — '

'Barbara told me.'

'But do you believe her?'

A beat. 'I guess.'

Caron felt a cold ripple down her back. 'Sweetheart, I swear I never said what you heard. I never threatened your dad . . . '

Caron went on and Josh listened, but there were no words to counter what he thought he had heard with his own ears, presented by his own dad.

Josh had witnessed the attack, but only for a moment. His preadolescent mind would have been busy revising that, and Harry was helping.

Harry's credibility was riding far above her own. Nobody in the whole damn world believed Harry had beaten and raped her.

What was his own child supposed to think?

For the first time Caron saw the nauseating possibility that she might not be able to keep Josh from Harry.

★   ★   ★

Josh made a stop at the bathroom before going back to bed. He saw Barbara's pink razor on the sink. He thought how good it had always made him feel to see his dad's shaving gear around the bathroom at home.

He missed his dad more and more.

Josh got back into bed. It was warm in the room, but he tunneled down under the blanket and folded himself around the extra pillow, and still felt chilly.

After a while he slept. He dreamed of his father in a jail cell, with the bars separating him from Josh. His father kept reaching, trying to caress him, but the spaces were shrinking, until his dad couldn't even get his fingers through.

26

Twenty minutes after sunrise Caron and Jack crossed from West Virginia into Ohio. They stopped for coffee and bought a *New York Times* and a Cleveland *Plain Dealer*.

Her face, altered by the straight dark hair and dark skin and glasses, was on the front page of both.

Dr Felhammer's picture was there too.

He was furious about Harry's 'tape'. He tore it apart. It didn't sound like Caron. That wasn't how she structured her sentences. The law enforcement people should demand the thing and analyze it. Dr Felhammer wanted to know when this charade would end, and this dangerous man be arrested.

Caron traced the picture with her finger. The sweet, brave man.

She was petrified for him.

Caron pulled down the mirror on the visor. The new picture of her was amazingly accurate. Panic began to churn. With the bleach and scissors and new make-up she could change again substantially, but not until she had a bathroom and a place to spread out.

With every article, every radio and television story, she felt more exposed.

Soon she would run out of new looks.

What she needed was a plastic surgeon.

She made a sound of irony that was frighteningly unlike a laugh.

★ ★ ★

'Thought it might be her,' Ho Plimpton said to Jack by way of greeting. 'Only a brouhaha this big would have you using me for ID.' Then, to Caron, 'You look like your picture in the paper. That's no good.'

Jack was pulling his duffel bag out of the Nissan. 'She's only been in the paper with that look since this morning. She's about to change it. Where's your bathroom?'

'Around to the left there. Your car's next to it. White Century. Old-fart-mobile. You can't drive a Century over twenty-five, and you have to be so short in the seat you almost can't see over the wheel.'

'Thanks.'

'Don't ask me for anything more. I'm staying shiny clean.'

'I'll need you to return the Nissan.'

Ho snorted. 'You don't want much.'

'I want more than that. I want you to return it in Virginia. What good is it to sweep away tracks by not getting another car in Virginia, and then ditch the rental where *Galaxy* and I could be traced?'

'That's *all* now?'

'Almost.' Jack reached into the Nissan once more and handed Ho the Virginia plates from the Saab. 'Get rid of these, will you?'

★　★　★

A tractor buzzed back behind the service station somewhere, and the big bathroom smelled of just-cut grass. Caron stared into the mirror. Black hair fell as she shagged bangs across her forehead. The bleach solution was in a squeeze bottle, waiting.

Her bruises were gone. The laceration on her lip from Harry's bite was healing, but still tender, and there were two canker sores around it. Marks remained on her thighs. It was still uncomfortable to urinate, and occasionally she felt sore inside after hours of sitting in the car.

On a *Primetime Live* she had watched in a motel room when there was a story about herself and Harry, Caron had seen a piece about battered wives. ABC apparently didn't think Caron was one, however, because the pieces were clearly considered unrelated.

But she was, she knew that now. She had

been one long before Harry attacked her. She should have realized so much sooner. Especially after all she had tried to do for Elisa, her poor sister ... getting Elisa pamphlets on domestic violence and making her read them.

Caron met her own wide eyes in the mirror. *I knew it all when Elisa was the one. I knew she was abused, and I was angry because she didn't know. I cried because I couldn't make her listen. I hated how she denied it.*

★ ★ ★

In the two years of her marriage, Caron had done as much denying as Elisa had. Harry was simply a high-strung celebrity. Harry was under pressure. Harry had a temper.

What nonsense.

The three stages of battering she had first read about in the pamphlets applied to her marriage as surely as they had to Elisa's.

Caron had always been nervous as the tension built; stage one. Stage two was the battering episode. Stage three was the contrition and renewal, what the pamphlets had called 'El Período de Luna de Miel', the 'Honeymoon Period'.

Now she was completing the cycle by

blaming herself, taking the responsibility for the suffering of everyone involved in trying to save her.

It was vital to resist that. If she didn't, she'd follow the whole path and keep seeing Harry as omnipotent.

A batterer had to keep up his image. He had to be admired by everyone. That was why most batterers confined their rage to their families. You didn't need a famous husband to be caught in that trap.

But having one made the trap a thousand times worse.

He lies better than she tells the truth.

She had to be more proactive. Not spend all her time just trying to evade. Hammer Harry back. Use Jack, use whatever she could.

Otherwise, she was simply handing over to Harry the power to destroy her.

★　★　★

Josh was tired of hearing himself complain, tired of the tears that always wanted to burst out. Tired of feeling in trouble and in danger, and not sure, when he asked himself, exactly what the trouble or danger was.

In the long days, when the television got too boring, or when his mind overrode it,

Josh would revisit old times. Down in the financial district with his dad on a hushed Sunday, Dad pointing out façades and doors and telling histories. Caron and Dad and Josh out on the apartment terrace eating ribs, his favorite meat to barbecue, with that coleslaw that bit; Dad giving a sip of his dark beer.

It was so impossible to match up that Harry and Caron with the ones he saw now.

So more and more, he stayed with the old ones.

He missed them so badly.

27

It was Don Aprile's lucky day.

The world was fairly quiet.

The Kravitz story was one of the few that people woke up for even in the unbreathable heat that stifled most of the country.

Which was why his piece not only got enormous play in South Bend, but AP pickup.

'We phoned every neurologist in New York City,' Aprile was quoted in the wire story that ran in hundreds of newspapers, and found its way on to another several hundred radio and television newscasts. 'Nowhere could we locate the so-called top blue-chip neurologist at the unnamed New York hospital. Not even a stonewall. Zilch. We found Dr Alvarez's gynecologist, her dermatologist, even the physical therapist who treated her tennis elbow. None of them would tell us anything, of course, but there was no neurologist's office to even blow us off.'

Squinting at the small TV in the kitchen of Ho's tiny house, Jack Dodge said, 'We did that already.'

'Did what? Made those calls? *Galaxy* did?'

Caron asked. 'Why wasn't it in the paper?'

'It was caca. Not finding the doctor doesn't prove anything.'

'But it suggests something.' Suddenly Caron stood. Excitedly she ran her hand through her newly cropped blonde hair. 'This is getting a lot of play. How can I keep it going?'

She paced the kitchen. 'I could have had a CT scan in Florida a week ago. I didn't think there was any point, and I didn't dare go down there. But why not now, in Ohio, if there's a way to find a trustworthy neurologist? We have an anonymous car. You could drive while I hide. It would be ammunition. And it would keep attention focused on wherever the doctor is while we get down to Craig Head.'

★ ★ ★

Watching Jack on the phone with his office, Caron felt the shakiness in her fingers that had begun to appear each time her connection to him gained yet another link.

She had been able to accomplish so much less when alone, but at least she had been alone. There wasn't the added terror of possible betrayal.

With all he knew and had seen and heard,

302

he could put her in Harry's grip in a pulse-beat, if he wanted to. Or could throw her into the shark tank simply by pulling out and stranding her.

Once again she reminded herself that she had made the choice to 'trust' him. She always saw the word in quotation marks in her mind, the concept being such a temporary interpretation.

It was the best call. The proof was in the reality. She was alive. Josh was alive. Two of Harry's men had found her, and she had defended herself and broken free and was still free.

Listening to Jack confer with a *Galaxy* colleague about pinning down the right neurologist, she felt something new: pride. For the first time, she wasn't just dodging Harry's bullets. She was shooting back.

★ ★ ★

Russell Moorpath's bloated and partially decomposed remains were found wedged against the side of the drainage ditch by a motel guest out for a twilight walk. Police determined that the body had been trapped by debris at the mouth of the underwater drainpipe, had finally been dislodged and floated to the surface.

The cause of death was drowning. There was evidence of a blow to the head. It was not an accident.

The contents of his wallet were soaked but readable.

* * *

Ho was right, Jack thought, goosing the Century as best he could along I-77 north. Goddamn thing drove like a forklift. They'd been on the road almost three hours already.

But it would get them to this doctor in Cleveland, with no company.

He didn't feel wonderful about the doctor. There hadn't been enough time; the man was the best the *Galaxy* researchers could find for now, with CT scan capability on his premises, and it was someone's cousin's uncle or whatever who knew him, had made the contact and arranged the secrecy.

But Caron wanted a CT scan, and she was getting one.

Jack had showered and shaved in Ho's one john, amid hair-bleach fumes, but he still felt scratchy. It was the one way in which he would never fit the swashbuckling journalist persona: he liked a sparkling marble bathroom to pull himself together in, with fifty-dollar towels and designer shampoo. He did not do well soaping up in creeks, into which category he placed Ho's facility.

In fact, there was a lot about this gig he didn't like.

Mostly that there were too many blocks in the way of his objective.

What Jack really craved was to race down to Craig Head. He was foaming to begin, to ask and press and pay, and collect what fell out, and mold it into a club that would split Harry Kravitz's head open.

Jack hadn't much patience with this doctor idea of Caron's, or with any time-waster that kept them from the Outer Banks — except for the car switch, which had been a necessity.

But neither could he stomp on the woman to do everything his way.

She wouldn't, for one thing. She might have been a bit of a wuss so far, accustomed as she was to taking crap from her psychotic husband, but she was starting to show some testes.

For another, he guessed she was entitled to view the situation as having other elements than Jack Dodge's chance to bring Harry down.

★　★　★

Riding beside Jack, thinking ahead to the appointment, Caron suddenly remembered why Darcy's description of Harry raping his niece had prickled at her subconscious.

On a bright June Saturday just over a year ago, Caron and Harry had played doubles with the Valins at a tennis club in Westport. A family of four on the next court — mother, father, son, young daughter — had seemed to catch Harry's attention; Caron had noticed him glancing over there. She had delayed her serve a couple of times until he looked back.

Caron had assumed he was distracted by the father, whose groundstrokes were outstanding; Harry always loved to see fine tennis.

But that explanation hadn't quite computed. Caron had dismissed the matter at the time, but it jumped back now, and she saw why.

To be studying the father, Harry would have had to direct his gaze slightly more to the left. The little girl was on the near-half of the court. Her tennis skirt flapped up every time she darted for a shot, revealing a plump behind in brief panties.

Harry wasn't watching the man. He was looking at her.

★ ★ ★

'Mr Kravitz?'

'Yes. Who is this?'

'Dr Francis Hollenburg. I am a neurologist in Cleveland, Ohio.'

Harry clenched his teeth at the slow voice. Away from New York everybody talked slowly. They had plenty of time. He kept ending up on the phone with these people. But there was nothing he could do. He had to take the calls, any that Graceann couldn't weed out. You never knew who might have the gold key.

'And?' Harry said as courteously as he could.

'I have heard your statements about your situation with your wife. They are credible. And, sadly, I am acquainted with the dementia that can accompany malignancies such as hers.'

'I appreciate your input, Doctor —'

'I remember her irrational claims from a year ago. Her remarks constituted a wholesale condemnation of the medical community. It was in all the papers. Her statements were quite strange; she has apparently been ill for some time, and is failing now. For that reason, I would be remiss if I failed to inform you of her whereabouts. She is in Ohio. I expect her in my office approximately five hours from now.'

* * *

A nurse hurried Caron down the corridor of the medical building, away from the usual patient entrance to the doctor's office. Jack followed them.

'I'm the only one besides Dr Hollenburg who knows your identity,' the woman said. She was tall and bottom-heavy, and wore a white pants uniform. She brought Caron into the CT scan room. It had a closet and two exit doors. Diplomas and certificates covered the walls, plus several photos of a multi-dog-and-child family group.

'I'll need you to step outside,' the woman told Jack.

'Sorry,' he said. 'No.'

'Dr Hollenburg can't perform the examination with another person here.'

'Pretend I'm her Siamese twin.'

Caron said, 'Let's just proceed. You can wait outside, Jack. Your story won't suffer. I'll tell you every detail.'

He thought about making a case for being there to protect her, but she was on target: the story was the point. He knew when he was aced. He went out.

'Relax, now,' the nurse told Caron. 'The doctor will be right in.'

She left, and Caron sat in a chair. She was

trembling all over. It was frightening to be around so many people. Her current look was the most misleading yet, she even jarred herself when she glanced in mirrors, but two people in this office knew who she was, and that was two more than usual . . .

The second door opened, and the doctor came in. He was bone-thin, with lustrous gray hair and a matching mustache.

'Dr Alvarez,' he said.

Caron winced at hearing her name. She didn't like being seated and having to look up at him, so she stood. Male doctors always wanted to loom over everyone.

'I want a CT scan, please,' she told him. 'Then, this evening, I'd like you to notify WCBS Newsradio in New York, and the *New York Times*. Here are their numbers.' Caron held out a slip of paper. 'Thank you for helping. Of course, you have my word that there is nothing physically wrong with me. As you'll see.'

The doctor nodded once. 'I'll see what's there to see. How are you feeling? Any headaches? Dizziness? Blurred vision?'

'Nothing at all.'

'You're certain?'

'Yes.'

'Mood swings? Has this edginess become more pronounced? Often, with this disease,' the doctor said almost conversationally, 'the emotions are the bellwether. Adults, especially, may present with bizarre behavior and odd talk long before the physical symptoms appear.'

'I'm not presenting with any of that. I'm not sick.'

Caron was growing cold.

The doctor moved closer to her. 'Think what your husband is going through. All he wants is to have you and the child home, where you can be helped.'

Behind Caron the closet door squeaked. She spun around and gasped, the sound nearly a groan.

The man in the Camry.

'He'll be taking you back to New York,' the doctor said.

He didn't say anything further, because the other man was on him, burying a scalpel in his chest. Caron saw the scalpel hand suddenly slick with blood. Flecks spotted the doctor's mustache and coat.

The man pulled the scalpel out and faced her. Impassive pointed face, hard, intent.

Caron's insides boiled with horror. She screamed, took a step back, then another.

The man lunged at her just as the door opened. He half turned toward it, and his heel caught the line of blood escaping from the pool under Dr Hollenburg. He slid as Jack Dodge watched open-mouthed.

Caron leaped for the scalpel, but the man grabbed at her with his free hand, and the momentum of his slide forced her hand up, pulling the blade across his eye.

Howling, he went down, his blood streaming, joining the mess on the floor.

Jack grabbed Caron's hand and pulled her through the door and down the corridor.

She crouched under the dashboard while Jack drove and cursed, and sirens blared past them.

'Fucking idiots. One fucking doctor with integrity they have to find, and they can't.' He punched numbers on the cellular.

'You told me I could trust you!' Caron said.

'You can. You'd be dead now if you hadn't. You would have walked right into that trap in Virginia. Now at least the guy who was after you is out of service, until Harry disinters some other goon to take his place. If there aren't more around as it is. And the CT scan was your idea. *I* shouldn't have gone along with *that*.'

He spoke into the phone. 'No, it did not go well,' he said, and explained what had happened.

There was a flurry of talk in a woman's

voice that Caron couldn't make out.

'Look, Robin,' Jack said, 'it isn't enough to just be beautiful and good at what you do. You have to be *not wrong*! You can't send a hunted fugitive to someone who will betray her! Caron almost got killed just now! That, she can do without our help!'

Listening as Jack ended the conversation, Caron hugged herself tighter into the space, feeling the hard frame around her, as if she might just float off without it. She felt out of range, beyond herself. She kept imagining a sticky, wet sensation on her arms, and she had to keep looking to be sure it wasn't blood.

'Harry wants it to look like I killed myself with a scalpel,' Caron said. 'I thought the man had a knife, but it must have been a scalpel all along.'

She watched Jack's foot on the accelerator, the bones moving under his sock, and told herself that was real, a real object to fasten on, to keep her right here.

Otherwise, all or part of her might take off and not come back.

28

Harry was genuinely haggard-looking, and there hadn't been much they could do in make-up.

At the podium, his hands shook. That was genuine too.

A CNN reporter raised her hand. 'Harry, you have consistently referred to Caron today as a murderer — when, in fact, there doesn't seem to be solid evidence. That scalpel could have been anyone's. Why would she murder the doctor?'

Harry spread his hands. 'My wife is not in her right mind. I can only guess. Maybe it was so frightening to her to actually see her test results that — '

'That she killed the doctor.'

There were titters at the clearly sarcastic words, but Harry only winced in pain.

'What about the man with the eye wound?' another reporter asked. 'Who is he?'

'An associate of mine who was attempting to help my wife.'

'Where is he? Will he make a statement?'

'He's at a hospital. I'm sorry, but I can't let him be disturbed. It's bad enough he had to get hurt because of my wife's problems. I can at least spare him the indignity of questions.'

There were shouts from reporters wanting his attention, but Harry silenced them with a gesture. 'I have more sad news to report,' he said. 'My wife has, I'm afraid, killed someone else.'

There was a hushed murmur from the crowd. Harry went on, 'A man I hired to locate Caron apparently found her — and has not lived to bring her safely home. The man's name is Russell Moorpath. He had no weapon. He meant Caron no harm. His body was just found in a sewage ditch. The police there are saying Caron hit him in the head with a heavy object.'

There were more shouts, louder now, but Harry stepped back and raised his hands. 'That's it. Thank you all. I'm too upset to continue.'

★ ★ ★

'I didn't kill the doctor,' Caron told Josh. 'The other man did. Then he was hurt when he tried to kill me and I defended myself.'

Josh was sobbing on the phone. He didn't try to hide it any more. Caron squeezed her eyes shut in an effort to let the pain roll over her, past her.

She said, 'It's true that I killed the man they found in the ditch. I would be dead now if I hadn't.'

'You did that?'

'Yes.'

'I heard that he — he didn't have a gun or anything. Maybe he just wanted to talk to you.'

'No. Your dad wouldn't have sent him just to talk. Josh . . . I'm so sorry about all this. I won't say it will be over soon, because I can only hope; I can't know. I wish I could be there with you.'

'I wish too.'

* * *

The cellular rang and Jack answered. He listened.

'Excellent,' he said. 'Make triple sure we keep that quiet. Let's hope it takes a while for anyone else to find him.'

Jack glanced at Caron. 'Our rat friend is at Catholic Medical Center in Massillon, Ohio. The Catholics there are close-mouthed. My guys had to cross every palm but the Pope's. He was admitted as Gerald Morris. The eye will be okay.'

'I'd like to go back there and stab his other one,' Caron said.

Jack clicked off his call and dialed another.
'Who are you calling now?'
'Ho,' he said.

★ ★ ★

Caron and Jack covered more than half the distance to the Outer Banks, and spent the night in a motel near Winston-Salem, sharing a room. The Cleveland story was on every channel. The picture of Caron showed her in her last disguise; the nurse was apparently not in a fit state to recall how Caron looked now.

The Hollenburg family mourned their loss. There was speculation about the injured man, but no suggestion that he had been the one to kill the doctor. Nobody questioned whether Caron had killed him. The best anyone had to say in her defense was that the facts weren't in, so who could know her reasons?

With two murders tied to Caron, her remaining credibility, what there was of it, hinged on Josh. Josh leaving New York with her. Josh supporting her version of events. Josh rejecting his father to be with his stepmother.

'They know who to trust. Kids know,' said one of the legions of psychologists tapped by the networks to explain the unexplainable to America.

* * *

Caron and Jack had shared a regular full-size bed, not even a queen or king, rather than ask for something else.

Caron woke cocooned in numbness before the facts crashed back. There was a blessed moment of haze, and then a physical shock as the pictures of yesterday blazed to life.

The doctor she was supposed to trust. The scalpel, meant for her.

Her new name: double murderer.

Her stomach rocked, and she jumped from the bed and ran to the bathroom.

* * *

Listening to the retching, Jack rolled his eyes and then clapped his hand over them to fight the pain in his sinuses.

The pollen down here was ferocious.

Another reason he'd love to have this project over with.

He rose on his elbows to try to clear his head, and looked at the empty space next to him. He had spent nights with women he adored, or was hot for, or just liked and had

317

gotten drunk with.

It was an odd experience to share a bed with someone he was profoundly indifferent to.

He did feel sorry for Caron, knowing Harry as he did, the relentless viciousness. But he himself was so fixated on his long-awaited chance to carve Harry into little pieces that he had little energy left for her.

And it was tough to like someone who thought you were stupid.

★ ★ ★

Caron wiped her mouth and rested back against the tiled wall. Her short hair was soaked.

After a few minutes she pulled herself up, turned the shower on, and stepped in.

She was soaping her hair when she saw movement through the translucent curtain.

'*Jack?*'

'I need to pee. I think that's your old doctor friend on *Good Morning America*.'

Caron grabbed a towel and ran to the TV. She watched the close-up of the old, sweet face, the pained, lined eyes. Her heart began to pound.

'He's sick,' she said. 'I wish he'd just back down. I'm terrified of what Harry will do if he doesn't stop speaking out. I would call him, but I don't dare.'

'We can get a message to him.'

'Can you?'

'Yeah. Better than we can pick doctors. Tell me some private thing he'll recognize. Something for the person to mention, so he'll know the message really is from you.'

Caron paused. 'The Vasco da Gama statue. I brought it from home when I came to the States. It's probably still in his guest room.'

'Okay,' Jack said, scribbling in his notebook. 'And there's something else you ought to do. Get Josh back out there.'

'How do you mean?'

Jack buttoned his shirt. 'Josh made an impression. He's your only eyewitness, and a tremendous one. Dissing Dad and defending Stepmom — people heard that. It's a big plus for you. He should have more to say.'

'But he's hidden, and I want him to be safe. If I let him call attention to himself . . .'

'Where is he?'

Caron looked at Jack. 'I won't say.'

He made a sound of disgust.

'You can be as annoyed as you want,' Caron said. 'You don't need to know.'

29

'You want me to call for a massage for you?'
Graceann asked Harry.

'No.'

'You look like garbage.'

'Thank you.'

They were in Harry's office, with a tape on
the screen that they were watching sporadi-
cally: child psychologists on an *Oprah* show.

'The blonde on the right,' Graceann said.
'She's very trustworthy-looking. And I like
the man with the big belly.'

'Not him. Get the guy in the suit. He
radiates officialness.'

'You think so? He's a stiff.'

'Officials are stiff.'

Graceann clicked the sound down. 'I have
an idea. Something I've been thinking about
suggesting to you.'

'What?'

'How about if Lilly and I move in with you
temporarily? To show our support for you.'

Harry patted her shoulder. 'I know I have
your support. I'm okay by myself. But
thanks.'

Graceann shook her head. 'You're not

getting it. This isn't about taking care of you. It's about making a statement.'

Harry looked up.

'If you were such a devil,' Graceann said, 'would I feel safe under your roof, me and my child? Lilly and I will act as representatives of the millions of fans who know you could never do what you're accused of.'

'My God, Graceann.' He rubbed his eyes. 'I don't know what to say.'

'Why don't you say you'd like us with you?' Her voice softened. 'I see the torture you're going through. I see you getting worse and worse. I'm afraid you'll become ill. At least let us help keep it straight in people's minds what a sweetie you are.'

★ ★ ★

Harry said quietly, 'You shouldn't be allowed to live, Ron.'

'Fuck you.' With his healthy eye Brale stared with hostility at the now-hated cellular phone, the instrument of all his bad fortune.

'You'd better have news for me,' Harry said.

Brale swallowed. The painkillers made his mouth so dry. 'I talked to Peter. He's set. He has the doctor tape. He'll take care of that, and then pick up Caron.'

321

'God help you if it doesn't happen exactly that way. I'm sick of hearing neat little plans that blow up into incompetent fiascoes. We're out of time, that's all. I can't have Caron running around one day longer trying to destroy me. Did you find out who the man with her is?'

'Not yet.'

'Jesus Christ, Ron. What if he's a professional? How will you get to her?'

'Leave that to me and Peter. He's much more of a prick than I am. He's a sick bastard. He'll have just what's needed.'

★ ★ ★

Even with every window open it was hot in Barbara's apartment this morning, the hottest since Josh had arrived. The sun was super-bright. Noise drifted in of fun being had. Everyone was going to or returning from the beach.

Josh hadn't been outside in daylight in a week. Every couple of nights Barbara would take him for a drive, which he thought was really nice of her, but he missed the sun and his freedom and Nicholas, and even Nicholas's forgetful grandmother.

And Schlomo.

And Caron and his dad.

Barbara had hard-boiled some eggs. Josh took two, and a glass of milk, spread paper towels on the bed, and turned on the TV to watch while he ate breakfast.

He found a movie with cars doing flips. As he was starting on the second egg, a commercial came on, and he changed the channel. He watched the end of a talk show. Then Josh heard, 'Next on NBC, we will go live to Harry Kravitz's latest statement, just getting under way.'

Josh put the egg down. He reached for the clicker. Each time Caron called, she told him again not to watch his dad, and Barbara said it every day.

But Caron wasn't on the phone, and Barbara wasn't there. He could watch his dad for a minute. Then he'd change the channel.

His father came on, standing, his hands in his pockets. Josh had only seen brief moments of Harry on newscasts. He looked shockingly bad. His mouth was pinched and his eyes seemed deeper in his face.

Josh leaned closer to the television. The remote was still in his hand, and he didn't realize he was squeezing the unit tighter and tighter — until the Off button clicked and the screen went dark.

He scrambled to bring it back. The *live* slug was on, this was his dad live, so different in just a week, but still him.

Harry said, 'This message is about Josh. My son. Any parent can empathize with the agony I feel, not knowing where my child is. And with Caron's judgment in serious question . . . well, that doesn't help. I can't even reassure myself that she has made responsible arrangements for Josh's wellbeing.'

Harry turned away. Then there was another camera angle that showed a portion of the seated press, and Josh saw a familiar face: Lilly Geroka, his father's assistant's daughter.

What was Lilly doing there?

'More than ever now,' Harry said, 'I need all of you to do everything possible to help bring my family safely home. I have two people here today, child psychotherapists, experts who will say a few words about the danger to a child who is kept from his parent.'

Josh listened to the experts, a man and a woman, explain about the confused and lonely feelings he indeed had. He heard them describe his father pretty well too, as a controlling and high-strung man who was usually a fair and loving father.

The bulletin ended and Josh switched back to the car-chase movie, but it didn't hold him.

Now he understood why Caron and

Barbara didn't want him to watch his father.

It made his feelings explode. It made him want to reach through the screen and touch. See the smile. Feel the fierce hugs.

Josh turned off the set. He went to the kitchen and did the dishes from last night and this morning.

The Disposall was still echoing as he went back into the bedroom and turned on the set again. Without thinking about what he was after, he flipped channels on the remote, looking for Harry. Finally he found him, on a CNN recap of the press conference.

That was followed by an interview with a Cleveland police detective about how they were no closer to locating Dr Alvarez for questioning on the Hollenburg killing. Then Caron's picture, with her hair short and weird.

Josh looked hard at the picture, and at his father in the other half of the split screen.

For the first time, he asked himself whether he should believe his dad more.

His dad was too strict, and yelled a lot. Harry admitted that. But did it make him the crazy man Caron said he was — especially when Caron was acting crazy herself?

Should he believe his stepmother over his blood father?

Asleep and awake, Josh had been over and

over the wrestling-type scene on his father and stepmother's bed that he had walked in on. Till now he had accepted Caron's explanation, her accusations of his dad.

But wasn't it, with all those thrashing arms and legs, like the Playboy Channel shows he sneaked a look at sometimes? Caron *was* injured, but Josh hadn't seen his father doing the injuring.

His dad had seemed teary on the television just now. Harry was hurting, that was clear. Crying with missing him.

It made Josh cry too.

He lay face down on the bed, wetting the spread. Harry had looked as if it was all he could do just to get words out.

Josh remembered his dad swimming with him at Mr Valin's pool in Connecticut, towing him around by the feet, both of them laughing so loud.

He didn't know what to do.

He wished Barbara would come home, or Caron would call.

He wished he could talk to his dad.

Finally that wish was stronger than the others.

Josh thought of his dad's voice, the difference he'd always loved between how it sounded for everyone on TV, and how it was for Josh alone.

He longed to hear the just-for-him voice again.

Josh got up. He washed his face. As he was toweling, it came to him that he no longer wanted Barbara to come home.

She would stop him.

Anxiously he ran to the front window, but there was no sign of her. He hurried back to the kitchen, grabbed cash, stuffed it in his pocket, and went out into the tangy air and the sunshine.

* * *

Peter Torres moved toward the videotape on the television screen, closer and closer, until he could see the separate eyebrow hairs on Herbert Felhammer's wasted face. He watched the wormlike mouth move, the little curved lines like snake scales on the lips.

'I do not know why this travesty is allowed to continue,' Felhammer said. 'Dr Alvarez is running for her life. No one is dead at her hand. This is another diabolical element of the lie Harry Kravitz has created to cover his own evil.'

Joan Lunden said, 'I understand you have plans to examine Dr Alvarez.'

Peter watched the lips tremble, the scales vibrate, with the man's intensity.

'My plan,' Felhammer said, 'is to convene a group of impeccable physicians to examine her and certify her excellent health.'

'And then?'

'We will keep her safe while this terrible situation is resolved.'

'So you are now asking Dr Alvarez to contact you?' the anchor summed up in her serene voice.

'Yes.'

'Dr Felhammer, your own health isn't the best right now, isn't that true? How is this tension affecting you?'

Felhammer grinned slightly. 'It keeps me breathing.'

★ ★ ★

This was the worst Harry could remember, this sensation of being at the dead end of his tether. The pressure was merciless.

Keeping all the parts of himself contained right now was like holding firecrackers back from going off after they've been lit.

He took long walks in the park, because he couldn't go unrecognized on the street. He'd always been highly visible, but now he was unable to proceed one block without being stopped and wished well and asked for an autograph or given advice.

He hurried along the walkway, his trade-mark hair covered by a Yankees cap, quickening his pace, chasing the tinge of relief he sometimes got from the motion.

Today he just felt worse no matter what.

He hadn't craved a child in a while, but he wanted one now. For days that pull had been building. It was at his toughest points that the need came, so it was no surprise . . . but there wasn't the option. He couldn't give in now. Someone seemed to be watching his every breath every minute.

The park was fairly populated. That was fortunate, because he was tempted to do what he had sworn off, find a derelict and let the pin out on some of this awful pressure.

He kept walking, feeling sweat on his chest. A breeze came and went.

Every time he tried to close his eyes at night, Caron appeared behind them. Caron down south. Caron talking, asking, hearing. All his vile secrets. Caron behind a bank of mikes, the way he himself was, nearly every day now.

People listening to her and turning to him with revulsion. The people of his audience. Everyone at CBS. Camera operators rushing him with their monster gear. All his celebrity friends stepping over one another to jump on screen and disown him.

Where the hell was Caron? How close was she getting? If she actually made it to Craig Head, would his closets stay shut? All the money spread around back then, favors traded, pressure put on . . . Would it hold?

Who was the man with her? Darcy dead, and the Cleveland doctor, Felhammer on deck, Brale hurt. With the grace of God, Caron and, necessarily, her companion, would join the body count. How would that affect Harry's credibility? How many corpses could he get away with?

The public seemed to have a very high tolerance for unacceptable circumstances if you were a top celebrity. Harry simply had to hope for that dispensation. He had no choice. He couldn't leave Caron alive.

And what about this new man, this temp of Ron's? The first hire had gotten himself killed. Would this guy fuck up?

That chilled the skin where Harry's sweat ran.

Or would he simply be more efficient? Find Caron, find Josh, sweep up.

Harry wiped his face and thought how he should have used Ron and Peter from the start. Then this would be over.

Longingly he pictured that, his sobbing press conference as he clutched Josh to himself, mourning his wife. Then the new show, the publicity, the send-off it all provided, that irresistible human-interest spin, giving his fans the opportunity to segue from their slice of his real life right into enjoying Harry the talent.

Harry's eyes burned with frustration at how close the picture seemed, and how distant it was right now, the horrifying potential for the scenario he'd run first, with himself as object of hate.

Behind him there was a gurgling sound. Harry turned. A drunk, not feeble, just black-bombed. Hard muscles under his T-shirt, but dragging his hi-topped feet in a baby shuffle. Eyes on nothing.

He would be simple.

Harry watched him shag past. His own hands pulsed, the fingers contracting. He could feel the points of impact along his own body, the gratifying invasion of limbs as the victim thrashed.

And the end, the slump, the capitulation.

Then the man was out of sight in the sun-bright park, and Harry took a big breath and let it shakily out.

★　★　★

Herbert Felhammer hated the chemotherapy more than he hated having cancer.

331

He had seriously considered rejecting the treatment.

But in the end he had given in. They always do, the technician had told him, making him feel like even more of a tired old grandstanding fart.

So twice each week he had to take a taxi to the Martin L. Dusenheim Memorial Pavilion of the hospital, and walk through the double doors, through the cheerily flower-lined vestibule, and into the sunny waiting area of the treatment center. There he would pick up a crisp new magazine and not read it while Esme, his technician, prepared to insert the poison into his vein.

Later today the taxi would take him there. Right now he waited on his porch steps for it to take him to the urologist. He was outside fifteen minutes early, since it was so nice and hot. They told you to stay out of the sun with the medication, but fifteen minutes wasn't going to hurt. By the time any damage showed, he'd be checked out of the world anyway.

A white compact car pulled to the curb, and a girlish redhead got out. She approached the steps.

'Dr Felhammer? I have a message for you. From Dr Caron Alvarez.'

He stiffened. 'Caron?'

'She's okay.' The woman reached into her purse and gave him her press ID. 'She wants you to stop talking to the media. She said to tell you it's terribly dangerous — '

'Her husband isn't dangerous? She's not in danger? And who the hell are you?'

'I'm from *Galaxy*. My picture is on the card there. One of our reporters is with Dr Alvarez, and we're in touch with him. Dr Alvarez asked us to tell you — '

He moved his hands agitatedly. 'How do I know Caron has had anything to do with you? You're a reporter — '

'The *statue*,' the woman said, outshouting him. 'Vasco da Gama. Dr Alvarez said to mention that if you had any doubts. She brought it from Cuba. She remembers it being in your guest room.'

Felhammer gazed at her.

'All right?' she asked.

He nodded. He closed his eyes. 'She wants me not to help.'

The redhead was, at thirty-two, an experienced tabloid journalist whose emotions were kept packed in a musty trunk. But she felt bad for this ill old man doing his noble best.

'It's not about helping,' the redhead said. 'It's about adding to her worry. She's afraid for you. And she's scared enough as it is.'

'She needs the help. I know many doctors. I — '

'I'll see that she hears what you said. But my job was to tell you her part. Be careful. Keep your door locked. I or someone else from *Galaxy* will be back in touch if there is another message for you from Dr Alvarez. Meanwhile, can I pass the word back to her that you understand?'

The taxi had come. Dr Felhammer pulled himself up. 'Yes.'

* * *

Sitting at his home desk, absently scraping his knuckles back and forth over the wooden edge, Harry only hoped Josh was staying somewhere with a television set.

Or if not, that people in his vicinity would be more on the alert now, after the press conference, and call with information that would enable Harry to send someone for Josh.

It would strengthen his position enormously to have Josh leave Caron and come home. And it was his best chance to learn where Caron was. His son would tell him.

The phone rang.

'Dad?'

'Josh!'

The boy exploded into sobs. The phone shook in Harry's trembling hand.

'Josh, son, where are you?'

* * *

More than breath, Josh wanted to be with his father without waiting another minute. Now that he could hear the special voice, it was as if all the elements of his father were coming through the phone, making him feel the way he had as a little kid, when he'd been waiting somewhere for his dad to come and get him, and he'd been late, and then had arrived, to Josh's enormous relief. And then, in the car on the way home, Josh would gather up everything about his dad, the whole feel of being with him, to save in case some day he never came.

But he had known as his finger touched the dial buttons that there was one thing he could not do for his dad — and that was to give away Caron's secrets of Barbara and Ocean City. Whatever Josh did or didn't believe, he had sworn not to tell, and that was the end of it.

'I can't tell you,' he answered Harry. 'But I'm coming home.'

'Thank God! Are you hurt? Are you all right?'

'I'm fine.' He sniffed. 'I miss you.'

'Josh, tell me where you are. I'll come for you.'

'I can't. I'm taking a bus to New York. Dad, I miss you so much — '

'Don't take a bus. I'll arrange a limo for you. You can leave immediately. Just tell me — '

'No, Dad. I have to hang up now. I'll call you as soon as I get to New York.'

★ ★ ★

The connection was broken. Harry nearly heaved the phone.

Having Josh back was a real break, but he was no closer to knowing where Caron was.

He'd make sure to notice what time Josh reached New York, which would at least eliminate all parts of the country outside a certain radius.

He dearly wished he could send someone to the Port Authority Terminal to check where the bus came in from. But Brale was convalescing and Torres was busy in Baltimore. And even though it would be legitimate to want to know about the bus's point of departure, Harry didn't dare leave that particular clue, should something subsequently happen to Caron in that same place.

Assuming she was near where Josh had been. But you couldn't trust any assumptions about Caron. She didn't give a shit about taking care of Josh. She was only interested in herself, her own protection.

He put the phone back in its cradle, glaring malevolently at it.

* * *

'Dad! I'm here. I'm at Port Authority.'

'Stay there, Josh. Tell me where to find you.'

'The Hebrew National hot dog place.'

Harry's eyes were wet. 'Don't move. I'll be there before you can finish your first one.'

30

Stuck in the single line of vehicles waiting to cross the Wright Memorial Bridge to the Outer Banks, Caron looked around at the normal-life signs, the campers and vans and cars packed full of vacationing families, their gear tied on roofs or protruding from trunks. She had a straw hat on, and sunglasses, with her spiky light hair showing on her forehead.

Traffic jams were dangerous. Everything was more dangerous now. She was a double murderer. Harry said so, therefore she was. Harry wanted the world to look harder for her, therefore they were.

How many times had she and Harry and Josh begun vacations in this steamy sunshine, gazing out at a water vista, eager to reach their destination and put their swimsuits on?

Just days ago that was a normal memory. A pleasant experience, to be repeated. The close, happy, successful family of three enjoying life.

Now they were three units, as separate as could be. Josh shut up in an apartment with someone he barely knew, traumatized, miserable, with no relief he could be honestly promised. Harry in some terrible fiction born of his delusions, a rabid wolf pretending to be Father Goose. Her husband, lover, partner . . . pursuer.

Caron on the run, switching disguises and strategies not quite fast enough, closed in on, losing ground she never had . . .

Desperate to destroy Harry . . . before he could destroy her.

★　★　★

I'm finally here, Jack thought. Kitty Hawk, Nags Head, Craig Head . . . the signs had brought him closer and closer.

What was evil in Harry Kravitz had begun here somehow. The beginning had to be shown to dovetail with the end, with Harry's massacre of his wife.

It was the only way to rip the blindfolds off.

Now Jack's real work could start.

★　★　★

Caron dialed Barbara's number on the cellular. She answered on the first ring.

'Oh Lord, Caron,' Barbara said, 'Josh is gone. He left while I was at work. I've driven all over, looking — '

Caron's moan came from way inside. 'Could someone have — have taken him? Is there any sign that — '

Jack looked sharply at her.

'No,' Barbara said. 'Nothing out of place. One of my neighbors saw him leave, by himself. She doesn't know who he is, of course. I'm so upset.'

'He must have seen Harry on TV,' Jack said.

Caron told Barbara, 'There was another news conference. Apparently Harry made a strong case that Josh responded to. Don't blame yourself. Thank you for everything you've done. It was . . . you're a hero.'

'Oh, Caron. I tried to keep him from watching Harry — '

'I know you did. You did the most anyone could. I have to go, honey. I'll call you. Bye.'

Tears streamed as Caron choked out the story for Jack. 'Barbara's neighbor saw him leave, by himself. I'm terrified!'

'It has to be because of the news conference. You know the kid. What's your take?'

Caron gave a sigh that was more a groan. The tears ran harder. 'He loves his dad. What he saw with us happened very fast. It's not as if he saw Harry take a hammer and hit me over the head. I should probably be glad he trusted me as long as he did.'

She wiped her eyes, digging her fingers in against the anguish. 'But if he left, that means he trusts Harry more now. And I can't leave him in that delusion. It's too dangerous.'

She turned the cellular phone back on.

* * *

'Caron.' Harry whispered the name in a rasp that froze her scalp. 'You're done. It's over. Josh is home with me. Where the fuck are you?'

'Far away, Harry. I want to speak to Josh.'

'No.'

'Put him on!'

Harry took a breath at this unfamiliar tone. Then, 'I decide who Josh speaks to. Forget it, Caron. Just forget this whole act and get back here. Do I have to spell out how I'm going to make you do that?'

Caron put a hand to her chest. Jack saw the gesture and narrowed his eyes.

'Yes,' she said, the word catching in her throat.

'It's simple. You run yourself home and go on the air and cancel all your false alarms. Or Josh will get hurt.'

Caron rose up in the car seat. Jack watched her whole body tense. Her face got tighter, harder. There were no tears now.

'Harry,' she said in a near-croak, 'don't touch Josh. Don't touch him. Or I *will* go on the air, and I'll tell about Harry Kravitz the baby raper!'

Harry gripped the phone with aching fingers. Darcy? Had Darcy told? It had to be. There would have been a phone conversation before Caron went there. So he was safe; Darcy was fish bait.

But if Caron yanked on that thread, who would she pull out? How far would she go? Would she find her way to Craig Head? She was starting to surprise him.

Harry wouldn't harm Josh. But Caron didn't know he wouldn't.

It would be helpful to point that out to her.

'You don't have a clue what I'll do, Caron. Josh is accident prone. You treated one of his accidents yourself. If you're not here to prevent it, he might have another.'

Harry hung up.

Caron started to dial Harry back, then stopped. She raised raw eyes to Jack.

'He threatened to hurt Josh. He means it.'

'If . . .?'

'If I don't go home and give up, deny everything publicly.'

'You won't, will you?'

'No.'

She dialed.

Harry said, 'Hel —'

'Don't think you can manipulate me into doing what you want. You can't, Harry. Not now. *You are the dead one if you hurt that child.*'

★ ★ ★

There was immediate work to do. The pressure had just been upped a thousand percent. But for a time, all Caron could do was sit and quake.

She thought of Harry and Josh together in the apartment: a small animal in a cage, and a monster circling it.

Everyone was watching Harry, but what security could that be, when Harry had managed to torture his wife with the entire world looking on?

Images tumbled in Caron's head of Josh bleeding, Josh crying, a broken doll under a giant's foot . . .

But she had to stop thinking of Harry, and even of Josh. Now she was Harry's captive, as certainly as if she was still there pinned beneath him. To have any chance at all against him, she had to not only function, but fly.

She said, 'Now Harry will figure out that I

know about Craig Head. But he doesn't know we're here now. We have to move fast and leave fast.'

'Three hours,' Jack said. 'We should have that long.'

Caron insisted on going to the library.

'Don't,' Jack said. 'Why take the chance? Keep yourself under wraps.'

'We have so little time. There's only so much you can do alone.'

'But the library makes no sense.'

'How can a reporter say that? It makes perfect sense.'

Jack said, 'Harry has erased his origins here. He won't be in the paper.'

'I'm not so sure.'

Jack shook his head. He started the car. 'Don't forget what I told you about blending in. Watch the people, get a fix on their attitude, and wear it. If they're bored or provincial, you be too. Don't hurry, even if you're scared. *Especially* if you are.' He palmed his hair off his damp forehead. 'I'm going to get a haircut.'

★ ★ ★

Jack left Caron at the Craig Head Library and went to Edson's, a barbershop he had seen when they drove in. It was in Purcell, just over the line from Craig Head.

He stood a minute looking in the window before going inside. There were four chairs and three barbers that he could see. All the chairs were occupied. Magazines and Coke cans sat around.

The signals were good.

Again he ran a hand through his plentiful hair. Its most recent trim had cost $85.00 plus a killer tip at the Regency; Paolo would wince and frown when Jack went back there to have the damage from this job cleaned up, and maybe add on to the tab.

But there were sacrifices you had to make.

He pushed the door open. There was an actual bell.

The oldest barber by quite a bit had the first chair, which held a sales type in a pale suit. The barber nodded to Jack. 'Rolly at the end is free in a minute.'

'I'd rather wait for you,' Jack said.

'One ahead of you after this.'

'No problem.'

Jack settled into a chair and watched the abortion being performed on the salesman. Mouse-brown hair was buzzed straight across at the neck and ears. The top was Buster-Brown-short over the brow.

The man left and another took his place, with similar results. Jack watched with a

345

ripple of dread as the barber finished up with a brushful of powder on the second man's neck.

Jack sat down in the barber chair. 'Just a very light trim,' he said.

Jack managed to cover his dismay as the barber picked up old-fashioned hook-handled scissors. But instead of cutting, the man used them to gently separate sections of Jack's hair, whispering to himself as he did.

'Pardon me?' Jack said.

'Just looking.' He moved around to the front and studied Jack's bang. He moved the hair between his fingers. 'Paniko oil?'

'Yes,' Jack said, not hiding his surprise.

The barber smiled slightly. He tightened the cape around Jack's neck and went to work.

From the first motions it was clear the barber was on a par with Paolo, all the Paolos. Jack watched him feel angles with his fingers, then follow with the scissors as if it were all one instrument.

'Very good,' Jack said.

'A treat for me. I don't have too many chances since I've been down here to work with real style.'

Jack's disappointment stung. The cut was great, but that wasn't why he was here. He wanted a long-time fixture to chat with.

'How long have you been in the area?' Jack asked.

'Four years.'

Shit.

'This time. I lived up in DC a while.'

'So,' Jack said, 'you lived on the Outer Banks before?'

'Born and bred in Kitty Hawk. Only a little after the Wrights.'

Jack laughed dutifully. 'Beautiful spot. I can see why you couldn't stay away.'

'Mm-hm.' The barber stepped back to assess his work at Jack's collar line. 'You like it straight across, or shagged a little?'

'Shagged. But not too much. You must get celebrities down here on vacation. People at the hotel said they saw Heather Locklear.'

'Really? I didn't hear that.'

'Some other TV personality too. Geraldo Rivera, I think. Might have been Harry Kravitz. Isn't he originally from around here?'

'Don't think so.'

'The talk at the hotel,' Jack said, 'is that Harry Kravitz grew up in Craig Head. Graduated from the high school there in the mid-sixties. He was a football player.'

'News to me. Around here, anyway, football is nothing to be proud of if you played back then. Those kids really roughed it up after the games.'

347

Jack was vibrating inside, trying to formulate his next move. He made himself sound sleepily casual.

'I can understand that. I was a hell raiser.'

The barber shook his head. 'Not like them you weren't. Bad stuff. A man like Harry Kravitz wouldn't have been mixed up in it.'

Jack wanted to pounce. Instead, he laughed. 'Football players are stars. They can get away with anything.'

'You said it. Gel? Or spray?'

★ ★ ★

'That was all I got,' Jack told Caron over the cellular. 'Interesting guy. Can cut hair *either* like a rube or like an artiste. Picked up on a hair oil I use that's rarely even available outside the Orient. Finishes conversing when he finishes cutting, and that is bloody *it*.'

Caron was using the library payphone. 'So you learned what, exactly? That Harry might have done some kind of misbehaving with other football players?'

'He didn't place Harry here at all. And he was vague about the misbehaving. It could have been anything from egg throwing to serial murder. There was no way I could ask if it included raping little girls. Damn it, why wouldn't a native his age know Harry grew up here?'

'You'd better go check births,' Caron said. 'I'm going back to the microfilm.'

'What the hell *for*? You got nothing from the newspapers.'

'I didn't know I should check the football schedule to see where to look.'

★　★　★

The Purcell Library had a Wright Brothers motif that extended even to the ladies' room; the sink faucets were little airplanes.

Caron ran her wrists under the cold water, a technique from medical school, when the surgeons were always sleep-deprived. But it was panic she was trying to chase, not sleepiness. She had to focus fiercely on what she was doing, because the thought of Josh pushed it all aside if she dropped her concentration for a moment.

Back in New York when she had first known Josh, she had needed to keep a hand on him when they crossed the street, for fear he would move the wrong way and get hit. Irrational; he was a city boy. But the worry was always with her out on the street with him.

What she was enduring now was like a

continuously running tape loop of Josh stepping into traffic.

Panic blackened whatever she thought about. Now that Harry knew where to look for her, how much could she hope to learn in the short time left before they had to leave Craig Head? Who had replaced the man in the Camry? How close was he? Did Harry even now have her watched, and would she be killed as soon as an opportunity was created? Or would she be given away by some upstanding citizen who saw through her disguise?

Caron forced away the terror and went back to her microfilm.

She had been through issues of the *Banks Tribune* and the *Craig Head Review* earlier, without finding any Kravitzes at all. This time she concentrated on Craig Head High School football news, noting game dates and who won.

Suddenly she came upon a football team picture.

Her pulse thumping in her ears, she rolled in tight on the boys, scanned from face to face. Passed a big-necked blond, felt a shock of recognition, zipped back.

Yes. It could be.

Down to the caption, roll back and forth to focus.

No Kravitz.

Caron followed the list of names, moving from player to player with her finger to find the blond's name.

Harry Crane.

She gasped and sat back, her hands to her face, breathing hard. She could feel her cheeks flaming. She looked around with only her eyes to see whether anyone had noticed her reaction, but the three other reference room occupants were absorbed in their work.

She didn't know why Harry's name had been different then, but any doubt that she had the right Harry dissolved as she continued to study the picture. The young face was fleshier, the hairline lower, but the handsome features and extroverted body language were Harry's.

Now she had a name to go hunting for.

★ ★ ★

The town hall clerk was as impressed with Jack as he wanted her to be, but it didn't matter. There was nothing for him to see. Not one Kravitz as far back as the records went, and that was a lot further than Harry did.

Jack kissed the clerk's cheek on his way out, absently, his brain slicing for what to do next. What was the missing chunk? A better history-obliterating machine than he'd ever seen? A name change?

He could hardly go showing Harry's picture around.

But he could go looking for it.

⋆ ⋆ ⋆

In the hot building cleaners were busy preparing for the opening of school, and only too pleased to stop for a second and exchange greetings and weather complaints with this friendly new coach finding his way to the gym.

In an office next to it were team pictures from wartime to the present. Jack found what he needed fast.

After his second pass at the town hall, Jack picked Caron up at the library.

'Harry Crane was his name before Kravitz,' Jack said as she got into the car. 'I have their address, but there's no family left here. *But* I know where we can find Harry's football coach. His name is Francis Hoag.' He turned to accept her congratulations.

'I got the coach's name too,' Caron said. 'And, I'm pretty sure . . . the name of a girl Harry raped.'

Jack blinked. 'You're kidding.'

Caron unfolded notes. 'The Craig Head

paper is a weekly. It has extensive sports coverage and recitations of local goings-on. I made a chart of football games won and lost, and police reports after the losses. I tried to keep track of which players seemed to be kept out of games. Sometimes I found a correlation, when the kid appeared in the police column for fighting or vandalism, or drunkenness — as if he was sidelined for disciplinary reasons.'

She looked slowly around, as she always did now, for trouble. 'Back in the fifties and sixties, local papers often carried a column of who went to the ER of the hospital. It was called the accident room in those days; one of my professors used to joke that the reason those columns don't exist any more is that they'd be breakfast food for lawyers.

'I took that listing and factored it into the chart. One night, the night after they lost a home game in which two passes of Harry's were intercepted, there was a Gaynelle Rimby, age eight, treated for 'injury and contusions'. That week Harry missed the only two games of his senior year.'

'Jesus.'

'I don't know how he could have gone on playing that season, and entered Colum-bia — '

'Sure you do,' Jack said with a bitter

chuckle. 'The same way he beat me and, so far, you. By not giving a damn what he has to do to cover his mistakes and get his way.'

They were about to pass a gas station. Jack saw a phone booth. 'Pull in here. There's a phone book. Let's see if we can find this Gaynelle.'

'I did. She's an OR nurse at the hospital in Kill Devil Hills.'

31

Gaynelle Rimby was a milk-skinned blonde with beautiful long eyelashes. It took Jack Dodge about forty-five seconds to understand that she would be no more vulnerable to his quick-thaw technique than would a bear.

'You can't be serious,' Gaynelle said quietly. They were in one of the OR lounges, which Caron had located by striding up to the floor in her doctor mode and coaching Jack to do the same. 'Have you noticed how well received women are when they claim rape by celebrities even when it just *happened*? How much credibility do you fantasize I would have after twenty-eight years?'

Caron said, 'But there must be others around here who were victims of Harry, at least of his violence. Or who knew about it. The football coach, for one. If several of you could speak out — '

'Forget it,' Gaynelle said. 'Just don't even dream that dream. What do you think you're dealing with here, reality?' She stood and began to pace the lounge. There was a fierce

355

energy in her step. She was a fighter, but one who knew when the count was up. 'Fran Hoag is senile as a stone, and he wouldn't have anything to say if he wasn't. People in Craig Head don't even realize Harry Kravitz was Harry Crane. I might not have either, except that his disgusting face and his voice are burned into me.'

Jack said, 'Harry wants Caron dead. He's already tried three times to kill her. He beat his first wife so badly she has permanent injuries, and he managed to ensure she'd never see their child again. Besides you, he raped his little niece, and possibly others — '

'And killed his own aunt, I'm guessing,' Gaynelle said. 'Or was it just a very convenient accidental drowning?'

Caron gasped. 'Darcy? She is dead?'

'It was in yesterday's *Review*. Her body washed up in Center Beach, Virginia. She'd been living there. They're not sure yet whether she was alive when she hit the water.'

Jack squeezed Caron's wrist. To Gaynelle he said, 'The only way to destroy Harry is for people to be honest, to have the courage — '

'Don't you dare say courage to me.' Gaynelle leaned over to look Jack closely in the face. 'I was eight years old, and Harry screwed me everywhere he could. My insides were in shreds. His family bought everyone

356

off, and he was never punished. I cried every day and night, and there was no formal help for rape victims then, and I had the *courage* to survive anyway. I had the *courage* to watch Harry become the idol of America, and not drive myself insane over it. I had the *courage* not to let the guy ruin my life.'

She turned to Caron. 'Let me tell you something, Doctor. I could *speak out* until the cows come home, and it wouldn't help you, because *nobody is listening*. They didn't to me, or to whoever else Harry chewed up, and they're not listening to you. Give it up. You won't win with him. Leave the country. There's nothing else you can do.'

Caron pleaded with her. Gaynelle was the person they had come to Craig Head to find, and it was unthinkable to walk away still helpless. But the scars were profound, and scar tissue is protective. Gaynelle would not budge.

Leaving the OR floor, Caron felt dejection in every limb.

'Get a grip,' Jack said low in her ear. 'You look like the walking dead.'

Caron pulled herself upright and tried to project her doctor status. On the elevator she stood extra-straight next to Jack. Her head was pounding and she could barely squeeze back hysteria. Part of her wanted to lie down

357

on the floor and never get up.

Blindly she hurried from the elevator, along the hallway toward the main door, Jack following. But they had to stop at the next corridor intersection to let a stretcher and an ambulance crew through.

A flurry of agitated Spanish reached Caron's ears. She found herself automatically listening. The stretcher moved through and the traffic jam of people dissolved, but still Caron listened, trailing behind the stretcher.

'Wrong way,' Jack hissed.

'Wait a second.'

The stretcher held a man with bloody injuries. An IV was in place. He didn't look responsive. His wife was trying to explain that he had a rare and serious heart condition, but nobody understood the Spanish, so she kept pointing to her husband's neck, indicating his missing Medic-Alert necklace. She held a tiny baby, who wailed softly.

'What is she saying?' one of the ER nurses asked the crew.

'I don't know,' a paramedic said. 'They were in an MVA. The car was flipped, and a bunch of people pulled her husband out of the driver's seat. One of the guys helping took all the jewelry off him and then bugged out. That must be what she's upset about.'

The nurse said, 'One of the orderlies

speaks Spanish. Can we get him?'

'Reynaldo?' someone else said. 'I don't think he's on.'

'Well, we'll just have to cope.'

The wife kept talking, her voice rising as she saw she wasn't being understood.

Caron listened harder to the Spanish. Suddenly she heard a term that chilled her all through:

Wolfe-Parkinson-White Syndrome.

The trauma team was working to slow the man's heart rate. Standard procedure was to inject Adenosine, and if that didn't work, then Verapamil, which would do the job in seconds.

But there was one condition in the presence of which Verapamil would have the opposite effect. It would accelerate the heart rate and very likely kill the patient.

Wolfe-Parkinson-White.

Caron switched her attention to the trauma team. She listened to the orders and assessments.

'Adenosine, six milligrams rapid IV push,' the doctor said.

A nurse watching the monitor said, 'Still too fast. No break in the tachycardia.'

'All right — administer twelve milligrams Adenosine rapid IV push.'

'Narrow complex,' the nurse said.

'Verapamil,' the doctor said, 'five milligrams IV.'

There was a sitting area a few yards away. Caron hurried that way, grabbing around in her handbag for a pen.

'What the hell are you doing?' Jack said. 'We have to . . . oh, bloody goddamn.'

Caron followed his eyes. On a table was a newspaper with a large head shot of her . . . complete with blonde spiky hair.

Jack grabbed it and read the caption. 'The woman in Hollenburg's office,' he summed up for Caron. 'After recovering from her shock, she was able to describe you. Look, we have *got* to take off.'

Caron glanced back at the team. A nurse was readying the syringe containing Verapamil. Caron tore off a corner of a magazine and scribbled, 'Wolfe-Parkinson-White'. She ran over to the Spanish woman and explained in her language what to do with the note.

The woman looked at her, then at the scrap, then snapped her head back up. Caron watched recognition enter her expression.

Oh, God, Caron thought. My picture must be all over the place.

She walked away.

The Spanish woman held the note up to the ER doctor's eyes.

'*Shit!* Hold that med!' the doctor said,

grabbing the syringe of Verapamil from the nurse who was about to inject it into the IV tube. 'This guy has WPW. He needs Digoxin.'

'Not a second too soon,' someone said.

'How did she write that?' someone else asked.

The noise and conversation never stopped, but there was suddenly a charged moment when Caron knew she was out of time. These people would take a good look, and would recognize her.

Forcing herself not to fly out of there, she turned, scanning for her best escape route.

Jack reached for her arm.

Suddenly the Spanish woman was holding her arm instead. She pushed Caron into one of the chairs in the waiting area. She nestled her baby in Caron's lap, lifted Caron's blouse, and said, 'Dale comida al niño.'

Caron looked up. The woman locked eyes with her, and then, with a gentle hand, pushed Caron's head so that her face was hidden as she appeared to nurse.

'Okay,' Jack said very quietly. 'Okay.'

Caron stayed there, stroking the baby to keep it quiet. It made sucking motions, eager to really nurse, and she was afraid her terror would frighten it. Her heart thundered as people milled about near her; the newspaper Jack had tossed under the table seemed neon-lit. Pain from the tension flamed low in her abdomen.

Caron willed the place to clear so that they could leave. The three-hour mark had been passed twenty minutes before.

The baby yowled, and she stuck a knuckle in its mouth and felt the tickle of its sucking gums and wondered with an awful pang of anguish if she would ever again be able to appreciate such simple joys as holding a baby.

At last the area emptied out. The man was being treated, and the ambulance crew had left. The Spanish woman returned, smiled, retrieved the baby.

'*Gracias,*' Caron said.

'*Muchas gracias a usted.*'

'*Su esposo estara bien,*' Caron reassured her. '*Estoy segura. Yo soy un doctor.*'

The woman smiled. '*Yo se.*' She knew.

Her smile faded. In Spanish she told Caron, 'Go immediately to change yourself. You look just like your picture. I hope God will keep you safe. I knew you were a good woman. Go now.'

★ ★ ★

As soon as they crossed the bridge back to the mainland, Jack stopped to buy a new hairpiece for Caron.

Waiting in the car, Caron dialed the apartment, listened to the ringing, prayed Josh would be the one to answer. Visualized him getting to the phone, picking it up.

'Hello?'

'Josh! I'm so glad to hear you, sweetheart.'

'Are you mad at me, Caron?'

'No.' She took in air until her chest hurt. Now she knew he had reached home safely. But she could hear his fear. His sweet voice trembled with it.

'I love you, Josh. I understand that you needed to go home. Are you all right?'

'I'm . . .'

'Where's your dad now?'

'Taking a shower.'

'Is *he* mad at you?'

'He says he's not, but he . . . seems like he is.'

Caron gripped the cellular with a chilled hand. 'How? What's he doing?'

Josh wasn't sure what to say. He was very afraid of his dad, but couldn't give any proof, to Caron or to himself, of why he should be. This change had happened very quickly. One minute his dad was teary and happy and hugging him close as the reporters watched; the next, he was like a storm cloud, moving heavily through the apartment, his steps a rhythmic threat.

'Let me talk to him, Josh. Is he out of the shower?'

'Yes.' Then, in a whisper, 'Don't tell him what I said.'

Harry came on. 'Hi, Caron.'

'You will not touch Josh, Harry. Do you *hear me?*'

'You're coming home, then. Great. Josh and I look forward to seeing you.'

It might have been the infuriating fake-calm tone — or Caron's own volcanic build-up. The days of rage and frustration funneled up and she shrieked into the phone, her voice resounding in the empty car.

'*You are a devil! You're a sick monster! You don't deserve to live, Harry!*'

When her own noise had stopped, she heard its echo mingling with a dial tone.

★ ★ ★

'Your picture is everywhere,' Jack said, getting back into the car. 'Every paper. CNN has a nice montage of each of your looks, in order. There was a TV on in the store. I got you an auburn wig and wire-rim glasses. Also padding material to beef up your shape.'

He started the engine and pulled out of the parking space.

Caron said, 'Josh got home. I just talked to

him. He sounded . . . like a mouse in a trap. Harry is toying with him and making sure I know.'

Her voice was raspy with dammed-back emotion.

Jack asked, 'Has he hurt the kid?'

'Not yet. All that will stop him is for me to come home and cancel everything I said.'

Jack braked too hard, cursed, and reached to steady Caron. 'Sorry. These people are oblivious. So you'll just go hand yourself over to Harry now?'

'Don't be a moron.'

He let out his breath in a hiss. 'I'm aware you haven't much respect for my brain power. That is too bad, because you are wrong. But I won't try to change your mind. I'll just offer as evidence the fact that you are still alive and more or less undiscovered. You and I know you would be dogmeat by now without me. So think whatever *you're* stupid enough to, but leave me out of it. *Don't* call me a moron again, Caron.'

After a minute she sighed. 'All right. I apologize.' Then, 'I didn't mean I would do what Harry wants. I won't give up. I was talking about what Gaynelle said. Getting Josh and leaving the country.'

'That's giving up.'

It is for you, Caron wanted to say. It

doesn't work for your story. No lights-and-whistles ending.

She rubbed her lower belly where her tension seemed to have settled in with knifelike little pains.

'How can I leave Josh with Harry? *Harry is going to hurt him!*'

'But that will happen no matter what, unless we *stop Harry!*' Jack ran a hand through his hair. 'I agree there's nothing more for us here. Gaynelle has gone her distance with what happened to her. She is cemented to her path. That's her right. But I say we head back north and break through some silences. Harry's niece. His sister. His ex.'

'I've already —— '

'I haven't.'

* * *

On the northbound turnpike the air-conditioning was off in the car and Jack was sweating beside her, but Caron couldn't get rid of her chill. She listened to Jack talk on the phone to the woman called Robin who always seemed to be on the other end.

'When was Felhammer contacted? And he agreed to throttle down? Good. Who talked to him? Uh huh. Maureen was the perfect choice. No, love, I don't think she's superior to you. Just different.'

Robin made some reply that elicited a wide grin and mischievous laugh from Jack.

Finally he said, 'Okay, enough foreplay. Put Evan on, will you?'

He passed pleasantries with the editor, then said, 'The kid is back home. Caron called Harry, and he's basically saying he'll hurt his son if she doesn't play on his team. Yeah. Unbelievable, isn't it? The guy is more malignant than any street skel, and dangerous as Hitler because he has the masses convinced he's a prince.'

Listening, Caron felt colder still. She had nearly been killed, could be any time. Josh was a bug under a dragon's claw. And here sat her protector, chattering happily away, as if admiring the protagonist of a screenplay.

I'm here to stick with you, listen to you, keep you safe, and tell your side . . .

Okay. And her father was just away on a vacation, and Pier had really loved her, and her brother-in-law Reco was taking great care of Elisa somewhere.

But whatever Jack's program actually was, he had succeeded in keeping Dr Felhammer safe, and Caron was more than grateful for that.

★　★　★

367

Herbert Felhammer always felt terrible after his treatments. You weren't supposed to until hours later, but he did.

He answered Esme's goodbye with a limp wave and walked slowly out. His stomach was shaky, his footing unsure.

He'd get in the cab and go home and scramble some eggs. Then he'd eat by the radio — a Mozart hour was scheduled — rest, and clean up the dishes.

A hot evening.

The taxi driver walked Dr Felhammer to the door as always. He was a retiree himself, and not exactly an ox, but he was, thank God, healthy, and he prided himself on giving extra assistance to those who required it while preserving their dignity.

'Have a good evening, Doctor,' the driver said as Dr Felhammer unlocked his door. 'Anything I can give you a hand with before I go? Meal preparation?'

'No, thank you,' Felhammer said, though it would have saved him fifteen minutes of bending and reaching and lifting, with rests, if he had asked for help starting dinner.

The driver left, and Felhammer locked and chained the door. He had taken the *Galaxy* woman's warning seriously, though he wasn't quite trembling in his boots. He would do a certain amount of cooperating just to save Caron stress, but his priority was still to stand up to the piranha she was married to, and clear her reputation however he could.

He was taking eggs from the refrigerator when the doorbell rang. He went to the door, reached for the knob, remembered his promise, and looked through the peephole instead.

A man was there, neatly dressed in a short-sleeved shirt and tie, with a briefcase. He looked alert and bright, like the red-haired woman.

★   ★   ★

Peter Torres had watched the taxi leave. Now he waited for the old man to come to the door. The sun was hypnotically hot, even this late in the day, and his shirt was damp.

But he'd be out of here shortly, he was confident of that, and back in his air-conditioned car, having earned the bonus for this phase. Then he'd be off to hunt.

Felhammer opened the door on the chain. Peter ordinarily was prepared for such eventualities, but the bonus here rode on the naturalness of the effect of his work, and a broken chain would tend to interrupt that impression.

369

'Good evening,' Torres said. 'I guess you're expecting me?'

Felhammer said, 'You're from *Galaxy*?'

'That's right.'

Felhammer closed the door, slid off the chain, and opened it. 'I thought this conversation was finished. I agreed to what I was asked. Do you have further news of Caron?'

Torres came in. 'Do you mean about the man traveling with her?'

Felhammer waved a spatula. 'I thought he was another *Galaxy* reporter. That's what your colleague gave me to understand. Don't you people ever talk to one another?'

Torres wasn't quite sure of the significance of what he had just seduced out of Felhammer, but he had a strong feeling there was some. Ron and his boss hadn't seemed to know who the man with Alvarez was. So they should be very interested. Bonus-bonus-interested.

Now he would do what he had come for.

He set his briefcase on a chair. He walked into the kitchen, which seemed to be where Felhammer had been when he came in.

'Please!' Felhammer said, following him, panting between quick little steps. 'You are not welcome in my house. Simply because I spoke to your colleague doesn't give you the right to come in here and go where you like.'

He was still talking, but Torres was getting the feel of the kitchen, the smooth floor, the cooking equipment around. An egg . . . dropped on the tiles . . .

He took two, let them drop, and in the next motion turned and grabbed the slight man. He swung him into the egg, getting it on the shoes, and then gave a good heave.

Without a sound but for the impact, Herbert Felhammer slammed into the counter.

Torres watched the blood mingling with the egg, reached fast and neatly for a pulse, felt none. He walked quickly back to the front, took the briefcase, turned the latch to lock the door behind him, and went out.

★ ★ ★

'Fuck,' Harry said quietly.

'You know who he is?' Brale asked.

Harry sat back on the sofa, the phone resting limply on his shoulder. He rubbed his burning eyes. His stomach burned as well, despite the Maalox he had been pouring into it.

'I think so,' Harry said. 'Tell me again what he looks like.'

'I only saw him through binoculars and a

windshield, remember. Square jaw, straight hair long in front. Late thirties, early forties. Well built, from the top half I could see.'

Jack Dodge.

Harry wanted to throw up. Just when he'd rid himself of the old doctor . . . Something worse, much worse.

He finished with Brale and lay back on the sofa, holding his boiling belly.

The sonofabitch *pisher*. Wait all these years until Harry was tipping over just a little bit, and then jump on the chance to push him all the way down.

The guy must be obsessed with having his revenge on Harry.

So how had this happened? Dodge must have managed to track Caron down. How was that possible, when Harry's own man couldn't?

Dodge had cards. Currency to offer Caron. Protection, money, and, most vitally, investigative resources and a media megaphone.

Investigative resources. Harry's stomach twisted good now, making him groan and lift his knees. He could no longer keep his mushrooming panic at bay with the reassurance that it was just Caron snooping around his private past, Caron who had to stay hidden and therefore was limited.

She had a jackal with her, a carnivore

sniffing and macerating whatever tidbits of Harry's life he was able to paw from the dirt.

And Harry's own child hadn't said anything. Josh must have known Jack Dodge was with Caron, but hadn't had the decency to warn his own father of this danger.

Harry heard a key in the front door. With a huge effort, he pulled himself upright on the sofa and got ready to welcome Josh, Graceann and Lilly home as if his life hadn't just crashed to bits.

Part Three

Tuesday to Sunday
August 24 – 29, 1993

32

In Eggar, North Carolina, Jack and Caron stopped for gas and food, buying cans of tuna and crackers, all that seemed safe in the ceiling-fanned grocery. Caron didn't feel like eating, but Jack insisted.

'No food means no strength. You've come this far. Don't let Harry bludgeon you with his threats. He has passion on his side. All truly insane people are driven by their passion. Get yours back fast.'

The cellular phone rang. Jack put his tuna can on the dashboard and picked it up with oily fingers.

'Yes?' A pause. 'When?' He listened, his face grim. 'Any indication at all that it wasn't an accident?'

Caron spun toward him. 'What has happened?'

He gripped her arm to quieten her. When he finished the conversation and beeped off, he held it tighter to tell her, 'That was Robin. Dr Felhammer was found dead in his house this morning.'

'No!' The word trailed into a sob that shook her body. She covered her face.

She felt as if her last standing wall had been blown up.

Wonderful Dr Felhammer, who had let a squirrel live in his attic because he couldn't bear to call an exterminator.

Dr Felhammer, who knew and worked with her father, who treated Caron as his valued and respected favorite daughter, who had become her surrogate family. Who had bravely and selflessly ignored the spears flying past him on their way to Caron, in his zeal to correct a terrible wrong.

And had finally been impaled on one anyway.

Caron cried, tears dripping through her fingers.

She remembered crying like this when her father died, and how Dr Felhammer had petted and crooned to her and finally left her alone when she insisted. But he had been there still, then and after, just to be there, to be a wall for her.

She had been devastated to learn that he was dying. But it hadn't had to be this soon.

And if not for Caron, it wouldn't have been.

* * *

Turned away from her, looking out of the car window at nothing, Jack listened to Caron cry.

He had been briefed with coils of print-out and knew what the old man meant to her. He also knew what he had seen for himself on TV, and through Caron's perspective: a great old maverick, nobody's baby. Taught what and how he liked to. Hooked up with other backboned people, like he'd been about to do with this team of doctors who were supposed to certify Caron's health.

Jack wondered if that could still be done, but immediately saw the why nots. Already they had trusted one doctor, and that had been worse than a fiasco. There were certain to be other doctors around who remembered Caron as a troublemaker and wouldn't mind making some trouble for her.

Plus, it was dangerous to try to coordinate such an effort, as had just been so convincingly proven.

* * *

Usually, when Harry held a press conference or was pounced on by reporters as he left 114 East End or the network, Lilly Geroka had to content herself with bits on the news later, since she was either at day camp, or she just wasn't allowed to go to watch.

She was so excited that this time she could see the press conference live, as she had done just once before.

Her mother hadn't wanted Lilly to go; she never did. But Lilly had jumped around and begged like a terrier, and reminded Graceann that she had lost four pounds and her face was clearing up with the new diet, and Graceann had given in.

Lilly had on her new pink jeans with the matching ballet shoes. Like last time, she was allowed to sit in one of the press seats, off to the side.

It was exciting, but sad too.

Harry looked more and more unhappy, with Caron still gone. It didn't seem to help him much that Josh was back.

From the little time Lilly had spent with Josh, she thought he was very nice. She had great trouble putting herself in the place of someone who would leave home, so maybe he wasn't as nice as she thought, but Josh was far more polite than some of the boys at school.

Lilly had been afraid that if Josh came home, she and her mother would have to move back to their own apartment. She was glad they were staying on with Harry. There was all that space, and the closets as big as rooms, and the kitchen like the open-plan restaurants. Harry had pictures of his TV and movie star friends all around. There was a treadmill right in front of a TV, which was how Lilly had lost the weight. It was so much easier to exercise when you could lose yourself, plan your treadmill time by what was on.

Lilly knew they'd move when Caron came back. But with Harry so sad all the time, Lilly would be a terrible person if her first wish wasn't for that to happen.

She watched her mother moving around the set. Harry wasn't there yet.

There was something about this point in the setup, when she'd been present for Harry's TV shows, that always made Lilly catch her breath. It had the same feel as a home before the party starts — with all the napkins in straight piles and the rooms clean and hushed.

Just then Lilly saw Harry come on to the set. He was reading some papers as he walked. His face was tight and unhappy, but he was wearing a gray suit, a soft gray like cat fur, instead of the shorts he'd had on at home this morning. He seemed more like himself — not so glowery.

She preferred being around Harry when he

was dressed in a suit. He acted different. He was the Harry she saw on TV and on the phone and in discussions with her mother, where her mother was always writing as they talked.

In shorts or in his pajamas, Harry was sometimes like the boys at school. He would bump into her as they passed in the kitchen or in the hall, and grab her to keep her from falling. But the places he grabbed weren't her arm or hand. Once when she was in the kitchen getting some chips, he had stood behind her and reached for something way up in a cabinet, and she had felt his thing poking her. That truly must have been an accident, though, because Harry never noticed, just went on making his salad, though Lilly was sweaty with embarrassment.

She was embarrassed now, just thinking about those incidents.

And it was silly to think about them at all, because she owed Harry her support. He needed the two of them, as her mother was always reminding her.

The reporters were coming in and taking seats. The party is starting, Lilly thought, and then felt really ashamed.

★ ★ ★

Harry couldn't believe what he was reading. The god-damn polls, even the stupid man-on-the-street articles, were starting to turn against him. Graceann had just given him a roundup of press response to Felhammer's death, and all these fucking idiots who had been falling over themselves to adore Harry now 'had doubts'.

Well, not all. He still had plenty of support. But Harry didn't like the trend.

Even his own troops were not there for him. Paul should have reported this downturn personally; Harry shouldn't need to depend on his personal assistant to monitor pulse. And why the hell wasn't Tomas jumping in with advice?

And Josh . . . Harry couldn't get over his son not telling him about Dodge. Traitorous behavior on the boy's part. Even if Josh hadn't been with Caron every minute, he must have known. To see his father galloping toward a cliff and not say a word of warning . . .

That was Caron's influence. Rotten bitch Caron. She'd never beat him. She was going to be in little pieces first.

It made Harry burn all over to think that Caron and Dodge could be in Craig Head. But if they were, then Peter Torres had a clear shot.

'First,' Harry said, 'I want to express my heartfelt sympathy to my wife, if she is watching, on the passing of her great friend Dr Herbert Felhammer. I know this tragedy will add to the anguish she is experiencing with her own illness, and I feel for her.

'I would like to share with all of you some very upsetting news. I have just learned that my wife is not alone.'

There was a stirring of voices, and Harry went on, 'At some point before the murder of Dr Hollenburg in Cleveland, Caron was joined by a reporter for the tabloid newspaper *Galaxy*. She has apparently allowed this person to remain with her, and is traveling with him. Where, we still don't know.'

Harry coughed. He paused and appeared to pull himself together. 'I am becoming more and more anguished myself over my wife's bizarre behavior. This is still more disturbing evidence . . . '

★ ★ ★

This felt so different from the last time Josh had seen his father on television.

Then, Josh had longed to be home with

Dad. Now he was home, and he wished he weren't.

He felt like a stupid confused wuss. Why couldn't he just find a way to be, and be it? Why did his head keep changing everything around, making him glad to be with Dad one moment, and sick to his stomach the next . . . until the sick part was there more and more?

His dad seemed to change every minute. Sometimes his face or voice was like something from a nightmarish movie. He *looked* like Dad, but as if someone hadn't sculpted him quite right.

He wished he could talk to Caron.

He was really afraid.

★ ★ ★

It drove Julie Gerstein insane to feel so helpless.

Why couldn't everyone see that Harry Kravitz was a lying snake? It was so obvious.

She longed to make noise. She had promised Caron she wouldn't.

But she hadn't promised not to let Harry know what she thought of him.

385

33

The doorman opened the taxi door. Harry paid and tipped the driver and got out, and went quickly into his building before he could attract the attention of passersby.

He followed a girl of about ten through the lobby. She had round little buns in white shorts. She carried a tiny purse with a shoulder strap. He watched the rear end move as she walked, and the little thighs, and his mouth became dry.

For no reason he thought of Goldfish crackers. Salty treats you could enjoy by the mouthful.

Harry wanted a mouthful of what was walking in front of him.

He followed the girl on to the elevator. Apparently she was the one kid remaining in New York City who hadn't been told not to be alone in an elevator with a strange man.

But the kid was lucky, Harry thought, because he had to be extra-super careful right now.

They rode up. Her floor came before his. He took a good long look as she exited the elevator; he could look, at least.

Inside the apartment, Harry went and got a ginger ale and crackers. He was thin, his face was thin; he wasn't eating enough. The gauntness helped convey his distraught condition, but he felt his lack of strength, and if there was one commodity he needed now, it was that.

Chewing the dry crackers, he thought again of the girl in the elevator.

The news conference had gone well. Graceann had said so, but she always did. No, the proof was in the response of the attendees, the respectful questions — or, if not quite that, at least not the bluff-calling rudeness. But they all wanted to talk to Josh. And that could be good. Josh could add his voice to Harry's, begging Caron to come home, convincing their audience to find her. Tomas didn't like the idea of Josh being interviewed. But Tomas couldn't tell him what to do.

Harry put the ginger ale away and poured milk. It was nourishment, and it would soothe his constantly troubled gut.

He had not slept last night, thinking of Jack Dodge out to crush him. Vindictive *momser*. It drove Harry over the line to picture Dodge tearing at the barbed wire that protected his secrets.

At least the wire was there. At least Harry

had taken out insurance every time.

He'd like to take that wire and rake Jack Dodge's skin with it, right up his back and down his front.

Again the girl in the elevator came to mind. Harry thought about the shorts coming off, the perfect skin exposed to his view, and his hands and teeth.

He could smell her, taste her.

* * *

Schlomo Bendagin thought Harry Kravitz had probably done exactly what his wife had said. He was fairly sure it was his own presence in the lobby that had stopped Mr Kravitz from following his wife and son any further on that Sunday night. If Mr Kravitz had really been worried instead of guilty, wouldn't he have chased her all the way out of the building, called to Schlomo to help?

So often in these last days Schlomo had considered revealing exactly that to the reporters. They badgered him all the time; it would be easy.

But something kept telling him no.

In a way he couldn't explain, he feared that would make things more dangerous for Josh.

So Schlomo had to content himself with

the one way in which he had helped: letting Mr Dodge see the Kravitzes' mail.

From the latest news, it seemed that his actions had been useful. Mr Dodge had located Dr Alvarez.

Schlomo had noticed tonight how Mr Kravitz walked to the elevator right behind the little Malik girl. Very close behind.

Close enough to make Schlomo focus the security camera inside their elevator.

But there had been nothing to see.

Probably Schlomo was overreacting.

He couldn't help it; he was so upset over the whole business. He had to try to keep his worry from running away with him.

Mr Kravitz was enough of a real-life SOB without Schlomo imagining him to be a child molester as well.

★ ★ ★

The phone rang. Harry snatched it up. 'Yes?'

'Harry? This is Julie Gerstein.'

He stopped breathing. 'Hi, Julie,' he said as naturally as he could.

'I saw you on TV today. I've seen you a lot. You're a lying scumbag, Harry.'

'I don't have to listen —— '

'Yes, you do. You're a liar and a batterer and a rapist — and, I'm sure, a murderer. You just haven't been caught yet, or caught good enough. But you will be.'

* * *

'Don't let the press near Josh,' Tomas said, 'until you know how he's going to answer their questions. His statements were supportive of Caron earlier on. What about now?'

'Obviously,' Harry said, 'he's fine now that he's out from under her influence. I know who he supports. I don't have to ask him.'

'Every goddamn reporter he gets near will pounce with that question. You don't want Josh in the same hemisphere with the press without knowing exactly what will be said. Ask him.'

* * *

'You *do* want Caron to come home, don't you?' Harry asked Josh.

'I — yes. I guess.'

'You can't guess. You have to know. You're going on TV.'

'Why do I have to go on TV?'

' *'Why do I have to go on TV?'* ' Harry mimicked in a nasty high voice. 'How about to help your dad? Is that such a foreign concept to you? Don't bother answering. I know where your loyalty is. Or where it isn't.'

Josh moved around to the other side of the kitchen table, away from Harry. There was a bowl of apples on the table, and for a crazy second they looked like solid steel, like weapons for his father to throw one by one.

In his imagination he saw Harry lift one and wind up to throw it at him.

'No,' Josh said, shrinking away.

Harry made a noise of disgust. He reached across the table and gave Josh a shove that sent him hurtling sideways against the refrigerator.

The *snap* of one of Josh's forearm bones echoed in the room.

★ ★ ★

'Harry knows I'm with you,' Jack Dodge said, clicking off the cellular phone. 'And so does the world now. He just announced it at a press conference.'

Caron thumped the steering wheel. 'How did he find out?'

'I don't know. But he's using it for all it's worth. They put up both our pictures. He said it's further evidence of how unbalanced you are. He also expressed his condolences to you, his dear wife, on the death of Dr Felhammer.'

391

Caron felt panic climbing up from her stomach. The sick fear burst over her. It was the same as the man breaking into the New York shelter . . . the motel ambush . . . the horror in the Cleveland neurologist's office . . . the knives Harry was twisting in her insides with his taunts about Josh. Harry had power and knowledge and he was using them to surprise and then destroy her.

Her hands were slippery on the wheel.

★ ★ ★

Caron swerved out of the way of a car in the next lane and slowed down.

Jack thought of telling her to pull off the road and let him drive, but didn't. He might not live very far past the Virginia state line, but Caron needed the distraction of driving. The pressure on her was boom-boom-boom, one blow after another.

Caron had guts. The least he could do to match them was keep his butt in the suicide seat.

He said, 'Something we have to talk about. With both our pictures on parade out there, I no longer function as a disguise for you. Every Mattel bounty hunter is now looking for the two of us together. They don't have your current look, and I'll change mine, but they're watching for a couple now. You have to decide whether you still want me along.'

Days ago, it was not a choice Caron would have hesitated over. She would have grabbed the opportunity to jettison her annoying companion, reclaim her autonomy, make her own decisions in this nightmare, now that the disguise factor was obsolete.

But days ago, Harry hadn't had Josh in his possession.

Days ago, she wasn't living with the vision of the boy in hell, so many different kinds of hell, they deviled her waking and sleeping.

Days ago, it hadn't been her stepson's life that would be lost unless she convinced someone from a rancid pocket of Harry's past to stand up to Harry with her . . . to the Harry the world thought it knew.

So much bothered her about Jack. His insensitivity, his doubtful intellect, his tendency to treat her and the emotional issues in the case simply as recalcitrant story elements that might endanger his shot at whatever the tabloid equivalent of a Pulitzer was . . .

But he deserved credit too.

He was using her, but he was helping her. If she let him go, there weren't other helpers to choose from. To be alone with her mind-pictures of Josh and Harry would be unendurable.

Jack hadn't had to point out that Caron no longer needed him. And he hadn't had to leave the choice of whether he stayed to her. He could have simply decided to leave; to find another way to settle his personal score with Harry.

To stay was to expose himself to Caron's dangers.

To be with her, and become a fellow victim, when the next ambush came . . .

To meet the same fate as Darcy Levy and Herbert Felhammer.

Caron wiped her face. The tears had stopped. The abdominal pains she had been feeling off and on were very on now, her stomach rebelling against the intolerable stress.

'I'd like you to stay with me,' she said.

There was a beat of silence. Caron glanced over and saw something pass across Jack's face; then it rearranged itself into its usual half-amused smirk.

'Then,' he said, 'I will. Iolanthe, here we come.'

34

'They were in Craig Head,' Ronald Brale told Harry. 'Peter's positive. Several sightings. But they left. No way of telling with what — except that if it was anything they could use, we would probably have heard it by now.'

'Where's Peter?'

'Still there. Awaiting orders.'

'Have him call me directly,' Harry said.

In his leather chair in his New York living room, Brale rubbed the bandage that still covered his eye. It was coming off later today, thank God. He was expected to be able to see fine.

'Sure you don't want me to talk to him?' Brale asked. 'As of tonight I'll be ready to work.'

'There's no time left for passing messages. Have him call me. And I'm going to be needing you both.'

Harry hung up.

He had to know if they had located Gaynelle. If so, he would need to decide what to do. He couldn't have another body. But he couldn't have Gaynelle damning him, either.

The phone rang and Harry dashed to get it.

'This is Peter Torres.'

'You're in Craig Head?'

'Yes. They were here, but they're gone now.'

Harry loosened his grip on the receiver. If they had found something worth staying for, wouldn't they have? Wouldn't there be a press conference down there, especially with that fucking publicity ringmaster at Caron's side, panting to string Harry up? If they had what they needed, wouldn't they be shooting off fireworks instead of sneaking out of town?

But where were they sneaking off *to*?

'Where to now?' Torres asked.

'Stick there for the moment. Find out where they went.'

* * *

'Whoever did the doctor,' Ho told Jack over the cellular, 'it wasn't the boy from the Cleveland deal. He went from Massillon to New York by limo with the eye still covered.'

Jack said, 'He couldn't have detoured?'

'Could have, but he didn't. I never lost him.'

'Where exactly is he now?'

'At an eye doctor's office on East Sixty-second Street.'

396

'So maybe Dr Felhammer's death was really an accident.'

'Maybe,' Ho said.

Clicking off, Jack turned to Caron's anxious face. 'The rat guy is in New York. You heard the rest. Maybe it was an accident — and maybe not. But I've been meaning to give you this. Here.' He reached into his bag and took out a small revolver. He stuffed it in Caron's purse.

She looked down at it, and then back to the road.

Her hands were cold. Her stomach felt awful.

★ ★ ★

'Graceann? This is Caron.'

'Caron, hello. How — '

'I want Josh. Please, Graceann, put him on.'

'I can't do that.'

Caron felt encased in ice. 'Why not?'

'Harry feels . . . Josh shouldn't talk to anyone just now.'

'*Josh is my child! Put him on!*'

Graceann was silent. Caron said, 'Let me talk to Harry.'

'He's not in.'

'Look, Graceann — '

'Caron, I empathize. I really do.' She paused, thinking of the call from Caron that Harry had taped yesterday, with her calling him a monster and saying she hoped he died. The woman was truly frightening.

But it was only the phone. Caron wasn't here. Graceann said, 'Harry would really like the opportunity to sit down with you and hash things out — '

'Listen to me,' Caron said hoarsely. Her throat was raw with the effort to speak over her panic. 'I know you believe Harry. I know you think I'm nuts. The fact is that Harry is a violent maniac, but I won't try to convince you. Just, please, as a mother' — Caron breathed back a sob — 'tell me how Josh is. Tell me he's okay.'

'Well . . . yes. His arm will heal all right . . . '

'His arm? *What happened to his arm?*'

'It's fractured. He fell — '

'*Like he fell three years ago? LET ME TALK TO JOSH!*'

Graceann hung up on her.

Caron squirmed around on the car seat like an animal in a box.

'Call again later. Keep calling,' Jack said. 'Drive them crazy.' He was driving now.

Her head played through all the awful ways Harry could have hurt Josh. One of them was real. His arm was broken.

She knew without a hair of a doubt that Harry had done it.

He had to show Caron he could.

And what else could Harry do? What was going to happen to *her*?

Every car that passed seemed to hold a killer. Imprisoned in the Century, helpless behind clear glass, Caron waited for a crash or a shot. Twice she thought she saw the man with the scalpel, and had to walk herself back through the facts: he was in New York, Ho had said that definitely.

But neither Ho nor anyone knew who had killed Dr Felhammer, and how soon that man would find Caron.

It hadn't been an accident. He was looking for her now, she was sure.

Watching her twist in her seat, sweaty and pale, Jack found his own nerves thrumming.

'I know what we both need,' he said suddenly, exiting the interstate for a small shopping complex.

He parked, went into a general store, and picked up a pint of Gordon's vodka.

Back in the car, he held out the vodka to Caron.

No, she thought, but reached for the bottle anyway.

Within a half hour Caron knew that the abdominal pain that had been building wasn't stress; it was a urinary tract infection. The two swallows of vodka proved it, burning her urethra like liquid flame as soon as she urinated.

'What's wrong?' Jack demanded, helping her back into the car as she stumbled, doubled over, from the stand of trees she had used as a latrine.

'An infection from the rape. It's a common enough consequence; I don't know why I didn't spot it sooner. God, the pain.'

She bent over on the seat.

Jack put an arm around her shoulders. They had done a lot of talking in the forced closeness of the car and whatever they could arrange for sleeping, but Caron had never revealed the details of Harry's attack. Typical; she was so much braver than he had understood at first. It had happened; it was unspeakable; that's that.

'What will help?' he asked her.

'Septra or Bactrim, but there's no way to get a prescription drug. Cranberry juice. We have to find cranberry juice.'

Jack had to watch her suffer for another hour, until they came to a store that sold

400

cranberry juice. Caron was stoic, keeping as quiet as she could, but he knew she was on fire. He'd had that crud a time or two in his life. Peeing through a molten straw was what it felt like.

In the dusty little way station in Salvona, Virginia, that served as market, post office, and gas station, Jack found a big bottle of Ocean Spray. Despite the Orioles cap and jacket and scruffy unshaven face that turned him convincingly local, the young blond-mustached clerk looked carefully at him. Jack's famous calm was disappearing, the longer this trip became; he wanted to run out, jump in the car, and gun it.

But he stayed still, paid, ambled away as if he had all day.

★ ★ ★

As soon as she could function again, Caron called the apartment.

Harry answered.

'What happened to Josh's arm?' she demanded.

'He slipped in the kitchen and broke it.'

'Put him on.'

'I can't do that, Caron.'

She had been very afraid that her last conversation with Josh was a lucky break that

401

would not happen again — that Harry would withhold Josh to entice her back.

'You hurt him, didn't you? You broke your son's arm!'

Harry's voice dropped to a teasing whisper. 'You have no way of knowing, Caron. He slipped. Or he didn't. Nothing else might happen. Or something worse might. The only way you can assess the situation, or affect it, is to come home.'

Sweat poured from her body. Her shirt was soaked. She was in hell now. This was hell.

'Harry, I swear to you, if that child is not all right, I will cut your heart out myself. The world is going to know what a demon you are. I have all the details.'

'You don't have shit.'

She forced her voice into the same teasing rasp Harry had used.

'You have no way of knowing. I might not have anything. Or I might have dates and witnesses and proof, just waiting for the right moment. *Make sure Josh stays healthy, Harry!*'

★   ★   ★

Monica's house felt different as soon as they drove up.

'Monica's not there,' Caron said as they sat

402

in the car on the dark street, looking at the house. Lights were on in two rooms, but there was no sense of her presence. *Please don't let this be a dead end. Please make her help.*

'Somebody is,' Jack said, squinting at a shadow passing inside a window. 'Let's go see who.'

They went to the door and rang the bell. For a long minute there was nothing. Then a man's voice: 'Who is it?'

Jack pointed to Caron. She said, 'I'm looking for Monica.'

The man kept the door closed. 'She's not here.'

'Could you open the door? I have to talk to you.'

Another long pause. Then the door opened and a man of about twenty-five stood glaring. He had soft light hair and features that slightly resembled Harry's. He looked back and forth from Caron to Jack. His eyes were hostile.

'I know who you are,' the man said. 'Do you have any idea what you've done to my mother? That's why she went away. Her aunt is dead because of you. She's shaking in her boots. What does it take to convince you people not to involve her in something she can't help you with anyway?'

'You're Adam,' Caron said.

'Yes, I'm Adam. And what else I am is sick of the whole deal about Harry Kravitz sticking pins in all of you. My mother can't help it; she was born his sister. But *you* picked him — '

'She didn't,' Jack said quietly, 'pick to be raped and beaten. Any more than your sister — '

'How do you — '

' — picked to be raped. But she was, and Harry is the kind of freak who just gets worse if he's not stopped. Stopping him is what we're going to do. And your family's help is vital. Could we come in, just for a minute? We've been on the road all day. Caron is ill. We could use a bathroom and some water.'

'There's a diner in the town.' He moved to shut the door.

'Please,' Caron said, the word ending as a hoarse plea.

Adam looked at her. The angry eyes were so like Harry's. She searched for some extra quality Harry's didn't have, some sign of a warm core, and saw a glimmer of it. But Harry could project humanness himself. He could project whatever he needed to.

Finally Adam stepped back and opened the door all the way.

★ ★ ★

404

The cast felt so heavy on Josh's arm. And not just the cast; there was a cloud in the apartment that was as heavy as nuclear radiation.

He sat on his bed turning the pages of one of his baseball books, but not seeing them.

He shouldn't have come home.

Josh had never seen his dad like this. Not just a bad mood, or even a terrible one; there had been those before, but when they were over, Dad would be great again, his real dad. Even when he'd smashed Josh's nose, Dad was brokenhearted after, hugging him and apologizing and swearing never again.

Josh had waited after the kitchen argument for Dad to change back into that mood, waited in mind-pain that was bad but that would be gone soon, like waiting for a stubbed toe to stop throbbing.

But the change hadn't come. His father had just pretended nothing had happened.

The cloud was around all the time now. Dad was Non-Dad.

* * *

By ten forty-five on Wednesday night, Jack Dodge and Adam Wool were in a wooden high-backed booth at the Cockscomb in Iolanthe, with beers in front of them, having

405

already emptied three bottles between them. Caron was at the Days Inn.

The bartender set down their dinners, ham steak with fries, the best the kitchen could do this late. The ham was starting to curl and the fries were limp, but it was hot food, and Jack had had more than enough of meals in wrappers.

His persuasive skills had accomplished much tonight: nourishment, and Adam here sucking down beers. Two more and Jack could go to work.

'You don't need to tell me where your mother is,' Jack said. 'I won't push on that. I know you want her to stay as protected as she can.'

'You have that right.'

'I have a few things right.' Jack grinned at Adam. He suspected friendly-father would be the best approach, but he wasn't ruling out fellow maverick.

He continued on his current course. He asked innocuous open-ended questions about Adam's lifestyle and plans, his views and opinions.

When Adam's fourth beer came, Jack said, 'You know, I don't blame you one bit for being a pit bull where your mother and sister are concerned. I'd be the same way. When was Debbie molested?'

'Where did you get that information? My mother didn't tell you. Debbie didn't. You haven't even met her.'

'Darcy Levy told Caron.'

Jack could see Adam examining the hinges of that, finding the precariousness of a third-hand claim from a person now dead, realizing he could still deny and stonewall.

But the tension and the alcohol were playing into the equation Jack had set up, meeting the inviting paternal ear. He watched Adam's thought process, the temptation of unburdening beginning to pull at the boy. It had to be a fierce load for a twentysomething kid to be the only protector of his two best-loved females from their murderous brother/uncle.

For a fleeting minute Jack felt dismayed and guilty. Watching himself play Adam like a harp, he asked himself whether he was actually increasing the danger for the guy and his family.

He reflected how uncharacteristic that thought was for him, and wondered what the hell was happening.

While he was wondering, he got a big surprise.

'It wasn't only Debbie,' Adam said. The eyes that had been so hostile earlier were big and shiny now, and as Jack watched, they narrowed and began to spill out tears. 'He did me too. I was ten. He fucked me in the ass.'

★ ★ ★

'Jesus God,' Caron said. 'Poor Adam. Poor Josh. He could do that to Josh.'

Jack watched her tears start, as he had watched Adam's earlier, and felt lousy again.

He wanted to tell her that it wasn't likely, Harry wouldn't dare right now, Josh was safe from that at least.

But he believed there was nothing Harry wouldn't dare do, and that Josh was no more safe than Caron had been.

She had had the whole evening alone to think about Josh and Harry together in the apartment, with Josh already hurt. Now, after the news from Jack's long, wet dinner with Adam, she was more distraught than he had seen her.

She paced the carpet, wiping her face, fresh tears coming right after. Her hands moved helplessly, as if people were drowning in front of her and she was reaching for them and not getting a grip.

Her husband was torturing her, torturing Josh, butting them against each other. Harry knew Caron loved his son more than he himself did, and he used that. Harry was an obscenity, a Jim Jones, a David Koresh, but worse: everyone adored him. Image versus evil, with image winning easily.

Jack had hand-fed that package to his editor, deliberately exaggerating, simply to buy some extra time and space for his series on Harry.

But he was realizing it wasn't exaggeration.

Harry was abusing his wife and child in front of the entire world, and getting away with it.

Harry was exquisitely dangerous, brilliant at destruction in the name of glory.

'Caron,' Jack said, 'Try to calm down.'

She didn't answer for a minute. She seemed deep in her own misery. Then she turned to him. 'I want to talk to Adam. I want to tell him how desperately we need him. If he realizes that he could actually save Josh — '

'He realizes. I banged him over the head with it. There's no chance. Harry is the person who destroyed his family. You can't begin to convince him Harry wouldn't kill them all.'

Caron stopped pacing. She rubbed her eyes. In her mind she saw a spiderweb, a giant one made with Krazy Glue, and Josh heading for it.

Sweet, soft Josh. Harry's fists and teeth and penis.

Another of her darkest terrors confirmed. Her abnormal psych text come to life. Harry wasn't only a pedophile, but the most sadistic type of victimizer. The more acute Harry's own stress, the more helpless and vulnerable the victim had to be. Probably adult victims to start, then a child. Then not just any child. Then not just a female. His niece and nephew. And . . .

When she could get the words out, she said, 'I'm going to call Harry's agent and his lawyer. I'm going to tell them that I have first-hand evidence that Harry raped a young boy, and that they must use any means possible to keep Josh safe. It's a risk — '

'It's not just a risk. It's idiotic. Do you want to remove any *doubt* in the minds of those people that you're insane? How can you even consider telling Harry's two closest associates that you're certain Harry intends to fuck his own son?'

Caron hugged herself. She knew that, of course. The desperate moment of wishful thinking was gone already. She might as well have decided to fly.

Her abdominal pains were back. She poured more cranberry juice and gulped it down, glancing out of the window, as she couldn't stop doing every minute now.

Every time she heard a car, she heard the instrument of her death. The swish of a scalpel, the boom of a bullet. She no longer even had the advantage of knowing what her killer looked like.

Adam . . . she burned to reach him. She felt the excruciating distance between the promise and the loss in every case — Sheila, Darcy, Gaynelle, Monica. Darcy lost by murder, the others because of fear, the same fear as Caron's: Harry had savaged them. They knew he would again if they spoke out.

The spiderweb was back behind Caron's eyes. Josh was closer to it. The strands waved, beckoning. The killer glue glistened.

Caron forced back sick terror.

She couldn't lose again.

She faced Jack, her eyes hard. 'We have to break through to someone. We're out of time.'

Jack let out his breath. 'We're out of *people*. All we can do is go back. Try again with someone who said no. Who should it be? Where's the hole in the fence? What's your gut feeling?'

Caron's mind had been racing along the same path, sifting and sorting and probing.

'Sheila Dannenbring,' she said. 'Josh's mother.'

411

35

Lilly Geroka sat at the mirrored dressing table in the bedroom she now shared with her mother, since Josh had come home. Her complexion was a little better, but she didn't look good. Her face was droopy. Her stomach quivered.

Her mother would be home in a few minutes. Graceann would be in this bedroom in a few minutes.

Lilly still wasn't sure she had the nerve to tell her.

She got up and turned on the radio. She loved it loud, but always restrained herself. It wasn't worth her mother or anyone having a cat fit. Her girlfriends simply turned it up when their parents weren't around, but Lilly was always afraid someone in the building, whichever building, would tell.

Usually music was good at taking away whatever happened to be chewing at Lilly's feelings, but not today.

Today all she could think of, as Gloria Estefan pounded out her salsa-beat lyrics, was her mother walking into the bedroom, and what would or would not happen then.

412

The minutes went by and still Lilly kept her eyes on the mirror, as if this other person with the improved complexion and no smile would make the decision for them both.

Then Lilly heard the door open and saw her mother in the glass. And the other person must indeed have made the call, because Lilly saw the mouth in the mirror move, and heard the words come out, before Graceann could even say hello.

'Harry was touching me. He did it three different times.'

'What?' Graceann said, as if Lilly had stated that there were wolverines under the bed.

Lilly didn't know what to say to that, and her stomach was quivering like crazy, so she kept quiet and waited.

The silence stretched on. Graceann was out of sight of the mirror, so Lilly turned. Her mother was sitting on the edge of the bed, her high heels on the floor, massaging a foot.

'Did you hear me?' Lilly asked.

'I heard you say Harry touched you.'

Lilly waited for a question. When none came, she said, 'It wasn't an accident, and it wasn't, you know, like a father or something being nice. He had his hands on my top and my rear, and . . . tried to push one inside. In my legs.'

Lilly's voice was shaking along with her stomach now. Liquids rolled around down there. Her mouth was tissue-dry. She wanted to tell her mother everything, about seeing Harry's wiener and getting poked by it, but she just couldn't.

Finally Graceann said, to herself it seemed, 'He doesn't know which end is up.'

Lilly had no idea what to do with that.

Her mother looked over at her. 'We have to make allowances for Harry. He doesn't mean to upset you, Lilly. He's just so upset himself right now.'

'I know that. But he doesn't have to — '

'And we won't be here much longer. We'll be moving home as soon as the situation is resolved. So just don't worry.'

Lilly didn't see how the 'situation' could be 'resolved' soon, since if Harry was telling the truth, then Caron was dying, and if Caron was telling it, then Harry was going to jail.

Lilly said, 'Could you ask Harry to stop?'

'Stop *what?*' The wolverine tone again.

Lilly's eyes filled. She turned back to the mirror. 'Never mind.'

Graceann finished changing and left the room without saying anything more. Looking at the other face, Lilly realized she had never before considered the possibility that Caron might be the truthful one, and not Harry.

414

She started to follow that notion, but screeched to a halt.

★ ★ ★

'He's back in action,' Ho told Jack.

'Still in New York?'

'Yes. But the bandage is off, and he's moving like a dude with places to go.'

'Do whatever you can to find out what the place will be, huh?'

'Try my best.'

'Stick with him — '

'I know.'

★ ★ ★

' . . . This is Harry Kravitz saying thank you and bless you.'

'This is Marv's Quik Stop in Salvona. Salvona, Virginia. The fellow was here, looked a lot like him. The reporter guy? He bought cranberry juice . . . '

★ ★ ★

Virginia. Caron and Dodge were in Virginia. Between the store clerk's description of them, and the pattern of calls to the station, that was the probability. So Harry was right; they hadn't found dick in Craig Head, or there would be bells and whistles by now.

Harry shifted on the park bench. He *had* to gain control of the situation. If Caron spewed her venom, and was taken seriously . . .

Where the fuck was Caron on her way to? The obvious answer was Monica — she might live there, near Darcy — but you had to be careful of obvious answers. If Monica lived in Virginia, and Caron knew that, wouldn't she have gone to Monica while she was in Virginia before? Or had Brale scared her out of the state?

Harry still couldn't get anything from Josh about Caron's whereabouts, current or former. The little Judas was closed tight.

Had Caron learned something in Craig Head that was propelling her to Monica?

The night was warm, but not as tropic-hot as some had been. There was a hint of change in the smell of the park tonight. Even the derelicts seemed to feel it, Harry thought. They moved differently.

He tried not to watch them.

Besides everything else, he had had another call from that vicious man-hater Julie Gerstein. Harry had hung up on her, but she had gotten in some name-calling first.

His insides were jumping with the pressure.

He and Josh would face the cameras and

mikes together tomorrow. Tomas didn't like it, wanted Josh kept as low-profile as possible, but Harry disagreed. A little practice questioning would shape Josh up. It was important for Harry to be seen with his son by his side. The world needed to know who was the *mensch*.

Harry got up and brushed off his pants. He headed back to the apartment at an easy pace, purposefully ignoring the occasional other strollers.

It was nearly two a.m. He was scheduled to talk to Torres, and then Brale, within the hour. He had taken the walk to let his thoughts jell, to decide the next move without the hysteria of his desperation creating rash, dangerous decisions.

Harry felt no less frantic. He was swimming a wide river, a dangerous river, and he was closer to the opposite shore than the one he'd left, and the nice safe land sat invitingly, soon to be within reach. But the distance still to cover, though narrow, was the deadliest part, because he was depleted and the traps were the most grave. Plus, the prospect of safe relief, *vis-à-vis* the stakes if he failed, brought his emotions to a peak of hysteria.

He ached to get rid of them all, the whole bunch who would stand in the way of where he was going — just shoot and keep firing, clear the path.

But with what reason he had left, he needed to decide his course, and that decision seemed to have made itself while he was out here.

Monica was a pussy. She was congenitally scared, irrevocably scared, and her kids too; Harry had made sure that wouldn't change. Caron and Jack Dodge and fistfuls of tabloid dollars would not break them open, he was quite certain.

But knowing Caron and Jack were probably in Virginia was reason enough for Harry to send his firepower there — all of it.

Caron should never have stayed alive this long. He wanted her dead so badly, he had sleeping and waking dreams about her empty, helpless body. Void of its power to affect him.

He would send Torres and Brale to Virginia and charge them with one task: to find Caron and kill her immediately. No alternative was acceptable. Ideally Jack Dodge should be left alive, so as not to inflate the body count any further; but they could kill him if they had to.

The public was enough on Harry's side for him to get away with it. There were ways of explaining. People heard what they wanted to hear — and they wanted to hear that Harry was a good guy.

36

On Wednesday, August 25, *Hard Copy* devoted its entire half hour, as it had done twice before, to the Kravitz case. But this time, rather than simply rehashing and recapping and livening the footage with new but not very newsworthy interviews with minor characters tweezered from the woodwork, the show uncovered a significant detail.

The *Hard Copy* reporter sat with a neatly dressed older man. He held himself straight in his seat. His face was intelligent and compassionate.

'On the last day of Herbert Felhammer's life, you drove him home in your cab,' the reporter said.

'That's right. I drove him often. He was a sweet man. Those chemotherapy sessions drained him.'

'And for that reason, you gave him extra help.'

'I try to for everyone. But, yes, Dr Felhammer was quite weak.'

'You helped him walk into the house?'

'Yes. I offered to help him start his dinner, but he said no.'

419

'So you left?'

'Yes,' the driver said.

'You locked the door on your way out?'

'I always did. And I listened to make sure Dr Felhammer put both chains on.'

'Both chains. The front door had two chains on the inside.'

'Right. One at eye level, and one low down. He didn't like to use that one, because it was hard for him to stoop. But I always insisted.'

Suddenly the screen showed a blow-up of a portion of the police report on Dr Felhammer's death. One paragraph was circled and highlighted: 'All doors to the premises were locked when victim found. Chains at inside front door not in use.'

Once again the screen showed the reporter.

'Clearly,' she said, 'a major inconsistency.' She turned to the driver. 'You're certain the chains were on?'

'Absolutely.'

'You left the house at what time?'

'I noted it on my sheet. Five twenty-two.'

The police report filled the screen, with another section highlighted.

'Dr Felhammer's pocket watch was broken at five twenty-seven,' the reporter said. 'In that five minutes, could he have gone outside for some reason?'

'I can't see how,' the driver said. 'He moved like a snail.'

To the camera, the reporter said, 'The late Dr Felhammer, who was so vocal in his condemnation of Harry Kravitz, evidently died as the result of a kitchen fall. But that conclusion has suddenly become open to question, with the revelation that a door chained minutes before his death was found unchained when no one else is supposed to have been there — and no one has admitted they were . . .'

★ ★ ★

'It will probably not take root anywhere,' Tomas said. 'These people just like to see themselves on TV, and you know the tabs make a big deal out of nothing. There's no point in responding unless we have to. If so, I'll respond for you.'

'Bullshit,' Harry said. 'I'm the one the innuendo was directed at, and I should address it.'

'No,' Tomas said with more vehemence than he ever showed in such discussions. 'You give weight to the matter if you address it. The point is that it is not worth your attention. Are you hearing me, Harry?'

* ★ ★

Caron answered a call on the cellular. It was the woman named Robin whom Jack always joked and flirted with.

Robin told her about *Hard Copy*. 'Jack wanted to be kept informed of any interesting press. Tell him, okay?'

'Yes,' Caron said.

'You won't forget?'

Caron replied in her most abrupt professional tone, 'Of course not.'

The woman chatted on, and Caron cut her short. Afterward, she wished she hadn't. Robin was inane, but didn't deserve to have the exhaust of Caron's desperation blown in her face.

Her emotions were wild animals now. Everywhere she turned was a trap.

★ ★ ★

Marie D'Ambrosio's favorite program was not *Hard Copy*. She favored quiz shows and the more intelligent sitcoms. But occasionally, while escaping commercials during whatever she was watching, she landed on a tabloid show and stayed for a minute.

Wednesday night's *Hard Copy* was about the Kravitz case, no surprise. Nobody could get enough of that. Her reference section at the library was busy with people reading the magazine and newspaper accounts of it.

Marie went to click on to something else, but a series of pictures of the wife caught her attention for some reason.

She moved closer to the screen.

One of the pictures was so familiar.

Then there came a commercial break on *Hard Copy*, but Marie didn't change the channel. She sat and pondered why she had had that feeling.

She thought about it through the break. She watched the reporter discuss the background of the case. The pictures came on again. On impulse Marie picked up the VCR remote and pushed Record.

The feeling faded, and Marie stopped the taping after a while and went on with her evening.

The next day was warm and bright in Allemar, New Jersey, and Marie had to be at her reference room desk when the library opened at nine. Too bad; if it had been a Tuesday, her late day, she could have spent the morning at the pool.

To compensate, she took a walk at lunchtime, stopping to pick up a sandwich at Vero's Deli.

Marie was walking out with her bag of

lunch when she noticed a car parked at the curb with a woman in the passenger seat.

Again the funny feeling, like last night . . .

But Marie was staring, and that was rude, so she went on her way.

Near the end of a busy afternoon in the reference room it hit her. The picture was familiar, all of them were, because the woman had been in here, on her reference floor, a week or so back.

And she had been in the car outside Vero's today.

She looked different. But she was the same person. Dr Caron Alvarez, Harry Kravitz's sick wife, with various alterations in her appearance.

Marie could barely wait to race home and look at her tape, and make sure she was right.

★ ★ ★

The Josh-is-home news conference took place with Harry and Josh standing together behind the microphones, Harry gripping Josh's good hand and doing almost all the talking.

There were sympathetic murmurs when Harry explained how Josh had slipped in the shower, one of the stress effects the boy was showing.

Later Graceann brought tea for Harry and

424

Josh to Harry's office. When she had left, Harry clicked the video cassette of the news conference into the VCR. He and Josh watched it in silence.

'See?' Harry said at the end. 'You had nothing to be nervous about. You were fine.'

Josh frowned. 'I hardly said anything.'

'You stood there and showed your support for me. That was all you needed to do.'

Josh shrugged. He sat curled over, not looking at his father.

'I know you're unhappy,' Harry said. 'I know you hate this whole business — '

'I do.'

'Well, we all want to see it over with. That's why — '

'You're not going to ask me again where I was, are you?'

Harry drank the inch of cold tea in his cup. He was simply not getting the facts across to Josh. 'It's not morbid curiosity. You know how sick Caron is. She needs medicine, she needs treatment. Her head is sick. She's not rational enough to understand that I'm trying to help her.'

The intercom buzzer sounded. Harry pressed the Talk button, said, 'Not now, Graceann,' and released it. 'It's great that you want to honor people's secrets,' Harry continued to Josh. 'I'm glad you have that principle. But in this case, you are doing harm. You're hurting Caron.'

'I'm not hurting her — '

'You are. You're preventing her from getting the treatment she needs to prolong her life.'

Harry paused to let that penetrate. The boy was so stubborn. What a goddamn infuriating trait to have to deal with right now.

Josh was looking at him with a face that made him even angrier. Harry knew that face. It appeared on people at a point in a discussion where they knew they were no match for Harry verbally, and so they fed all their venom into their look.

Harry met the face with one of his own that would brook no garbage. He leaned forward in his chair. 'If you're not part of the solution,' he said, 'you're part of the problem. Do you know what I'm saying, Josh? And you are for sure part of the problem on this. It would be so simple for you to help, yet you insist — '

'You *said* you wouldn't keep asking me!'

'Stop harping, goddamn you!' Harry roared. He didn't plan it, but his hand shot out and slapped Josh's cheek hard.

He heard a rustle behind him and turned. Paul Wundring stood there.

'Graceann tried to tell you I was here,' Paul said. 'I only have a minute; I didn't think you'd mind if I came in.'

'Not at all. Sit down.'

'I can't. I just came to bring you the deal memo for UK rights to the new show. It seemed nicer than faxing it. Milestone that this is.'

He handed Harry the papers.

Harry read the treasured words, the United Kingdom's commitment to *Harry*, the proof of how he was regarded not only by his own network, but by a large chunk of the world. With this deal people would be watching *Harry* in Great Britain, Australia, New Zealand, Egypt, India, Hong Kong, and fifty other countries. His hands shook a little.

It was incredible to have this. Fantastic that Paul had hand-delivered it.

What a moment.

It worsened the burning in his stomach.

So, so close.

Harry prayed Caron was dead already.

How long had Paul been there? How much had he heard of the argument? There was Josh, sitting and holding his face and pulling an expression as if the bomb had dropped. Would Paul get the wrong idea, without the context?

That had been happening more and more lately, with Paul *and* Tomas. They seemed to see small matters out of proportion.

'God, thank you,' Harry said. 'I'm — Can't you sit just a second and visit with us?'

'No time.' Paul blew a kiss to Josh and shook Harry's hand, and was out through the door.

Josh stood. 'Can I leave now?'

Suddenly the juxtaposition was too clear: the deal memo, the latest shimmering coin in Harry's pot of gold, and Joshua Samuel Kravitz, Harry's immediate obstacle to it.

He looked from the papers to his son, and felt his heart rate leap with the fury of it.

Then the buzzer went, and Harry reached to silence the intercom, but Graceann was faster.

'There's a call on line five you should take. A librarian in New Jersey.'

37

One of Sheila Dannenbring's cats lolled on a square of noontime sun on the doorstep, blinking at Caron. It didn't move when she tried the door.

Not surprisingly, it was locked. Caron knew Sheila wasn't home. She and Jack had been a block from the turn into Pear Terrace when Caron had spotted Sheila driving off in the other direction.

Caron leaned tiredly against the door. It was too risky to use a motel any longer, so they had slept in the car, badly, and she felt dirty and sore and despairing. Abdominal pain stabbed her; the cranberry juice only did so much.

The plea to Sheila had to be made by her alone, she and Jack agreed on that. For Sheila to see Jack would throw everything off.

From somewhere Caron had to find the resources to reach inside the woman.

Jack had dropped Caron off and followed Sheila. They needed to know where she went. If she took too long getting home, Caron would have to approach her wherever she was.

They couldn't wait any longer. Every minute that passed with Josh in Harry's web was a stomach-churning horror for Caron.

Caron went around to the back of the house to find a hidden spot to wait. Bushes along the garage were too summer-dry to hide her totally, but there was no other screening in the yard.

She eased behind them and settled on the ground, drawing her knees up and clasping them to make herself as compact as she could.

★   ★   ★

There was a nice fat feeler from Germany about *Harry* that would have made Paul Wundring extremely happy if he hadn't been so worried about the personal situation with his friend and client.

Paul shifted bunches of paper on his desk. His thoughts swirled and collided. Shards flew, and he couldn't put them back together in any pattern that felt innocent.

What he'd seen in Harry's office had shocked him. He hadn't had a good view, but was quite sure Harry had hit the boy. Harry had never done such a thing before as far as Paul knew. And the way Harry had

430

talked to Josh — the vitriol, the obvious manipulation . . .

Maybe it was simply the tension of this horrendous ordeal.

But . . .

This was not the first time Paul had doubted Harry since Caron had left. The first time had been just after one of Harry's own press conferences, when Paul had seen Harry follow Graceann's young daughter with his eyes, when no one else had seemed to be around.

Screened by a file cabinet as he was dialing his office, Paul had watched Harry's eyes lock on to Lilly . . . then track her as he would a fashion model in a bikini, following every move as she powdered her face and brushed her hair.

Paul had finally decided he must have misread the situation. Harry was preoccupied, staring at nothing, Lilly was just in the way.

But Harry's expression today had been the same as with Lilly. The intensity, the . . . *heat* . . .

Paul dropped the papers he had been busying himself with and closed his eyes.

★ ★ ★

431

Ho Plimpton couldn't reach Jack's cellular from his own, and it was making him crazy.

He called and called, and got only the singsong circuits-busy tone.

He had lost the ratman, lost him in a Jersey cloverleaf jungle. Jack was counting on Ho knowing if the guy so much as coughed, and here he was loose, and Ho couldn't even tell Jack that.

He drove with one hand, the other dialing every other way he could think of, but nothing did it.

★ ★ ★

There was a red mark on Josh's cheek that didn't go away.

It was joined by another one on the same side when Harry hit him for leaving dirty suds on the bathroom soap.

Josh was afraid most of the time now. He was so sorry he hadn't listened to Caron. He should never have left Barbara's.

But he couldn't think of anything to do. Who would believe Josh was being hit by his dad? Caron was right about that too. Even Mr Wundring had seen Dad hit him, and hadn't said a word.

His feelings were settling into a straight line — he was still afraid, but didn't care so much about the fear. It reminded Josh of a television show he had seen about POWs, how all their feelings got worn down at the tips.

He must be as much of a wuss as Dad thought, if he was already like a POW. It took them years to feel this way.

★   ★   ★

Sheila didn't have the stomach for the Stop & Shop. But she had barely been able to move from the house lately, and she was out of food and everything else.

She loaded bags into her trunk and was closing the lid when she realized she had forgotten fertilizer. She stood a minute, debating; she was so tired.

But she was always tired, and the only lift she experienced most days was from her flowers. She couldn't stay on and on inside, thinking about Harry, thinking about Josh, running the picture of the boy with the cast on his arm back and forth across her mind like a serrated knife.

So she relocked the car and went back into the store.

★   ★   ★

Everybody should be so easy to tail, Peter Torres thought. That arm ... he could recognize this gal in pitch dark. People walked differently when they had something permanently wrong with a limb, even if it wasn't a leg.

He had followed Sheila into the supermarket, in case she was meeting Caron there. He would have given them both points for that. But no; Sheila just did the gal thing, buying juice and chicken and whatnot.

He watched her pile her bags into her car and was about to head for his own when he saw her hesitate with the trunk lid halfway down.

She looked back at the store. Torres resumed his inspection of the half-price grills displayed all around the store entrance. Without watching her directly, he tracked her back inside, then went in after her.

★ ★ ★

Jack studied yet another row of Hallmark cards. He had discovered this trick while tailing celebrities, the infamous kind *Galaxy* readers adored: if you found yourself a card shop in view of wherever your target was spending time, you could hang out forever, reading the cards. That was what

434

people did in card shops.

Finally he saw Sheila wheel a cart out to her car and load it. Quite a few bags; he himself lived alone, and never needed more than one or two to be fully supplied. What the hell was she buying? What were all the women buying who dragged six or seven grocery bags into their single apartments? He saw them all the time in his building in New York, and the puzzle was as confounding as why they could never go and pee by themselves.

Jack saw Sheila start to close the trunk, then stop. She stood there, holding the lid, probably wondering what other two bags of stuff she had forgotten.

Watching her, Jack became aware that someone else was watching too. A tall, balding guy standing by a bunch of barbecues in front of the store.

Then Sheila closed the trunk and headed back to the store, and the guy looked away.

Jack watched through the card store window as Sheila entered the supermarket. The balding man didn't look up. But a moment later, he wandered into the market himself.

Jack picked up a card and pretended to study it while he pondered. He rolled the last three minutes back in his mind, trying to decide whether he needed to worry about the guy. He probed his memory for what the balding man had been doing earlier, before Jack had consciously noticed him.

After a few minutes, Sheila came out with another bag, a big one. She added it to the storm-center provisions already in her trunk, got into the car, and left.

Jack watched for the balding man, but he didn't appear.

False alarm. The guy had been downtrodden-looking anyway, kind of a typical shopping center denizen.

Obviously Sheila was going home. Jack would wait, as he and Caron had planned, for Caron to call him on the cellular after she and Sheila had talked.

* * *

Inside the Stop & Shop, Peter Torres watched Sheila Dannenbring drive away. No need to follow this instant; there was ice cream in her load. Only one place she was going now.

He gave her a couple of minutes to get completely out of the shopping center and then left the market and scanned the storefronts for lunch possibilities. There was time for a fast bite before he went to the house.

Caron heard the noise on the gravel, peeked out, and saw Sheila's car. She listened to the garage door opening and closing. When she saw Sheila go into the house, she went to the front door.

'No,' Sheila said softly when she opened it and saw Caron. 'Why are you back? I don't *want you here.*'

Caron groaned, the sound escaping before she could restrain it. Sheila clasped her arm and pulled her inside.

'You can't stay,' Sheila said. 'Sit down a minute, pull yourself together. Then you have to leave.'

Holding on to the backs of furniture, Caron made her way to the loveseat, the same one she had sat in over a week ago. Sinking down, she thought how the time had been full of promises and almosts, but ultimately worthless.

Harry was still the beloved national treasure, using the airwaves as he always had, to anchor himself in that image. Josh was out of his safe hiding place and in the shark tank, hurting and trapped, in terrible danger from his famous dad. Caron had nothing — nothing to war with, to give her hope . . . nothing but the probability of more loss, more pain, more death.

Caron had rehearsed ideas and phrases for Sheila, seeking the words that would penetrate, unlock, convince. But those were gone now; she couldn't recall a single one. The contrast forced on her by this seat, this room, this house, this woman, was crushing: Caron had been desperate on her first visit too, traumatized and beaten, but she was still at the beginning, and her spirit kept her in motion.

Now it was hard not to stop.

Caron said, 'Harry has Josh. You probably know that. But there's something you don't know.' Caron gave an enormous sigh. 'Do you remember Harry's nephew Adam?'

Sheila nodded.

'Harry raped him when Adam was younger than Josh. Adam said so himself. He never told.'

Sheila gasped.

Caron went on, 'Harry has already beaten Josh. His arm is broken. There will be more. Harry's at his worst when his own stress is high, when there are roadblocks in his way. He'll — he'll molest Josh and intimidate him into keeping quiet. He'll beat him again. I know just what Harry will do to him. He did it to me.'

Caron gazed straight at Sheila, her dark

eyes drilling. 'You know it will happen. And you know no one but you can stop it. There are records left somewhere, X-rays, *proof* that he's a wife beater. You know where to look for it. He can't lie his way around his history with you.'

Sheila was crying into her hands. Caron had willed back her own tears but they fell now.

'Please,' Caron moaned, and Sheila nodded.

* * *

Jack was starving. He was bloody tired of sandwiches. And he needed something to take his mind off the frantic wait.

After days on the road with few culinary choices except fried everything, he was glad to see on the shopping center directory that it contained several food places. *Restaurants* would have been an overstatement.

He decided on the Chicken Shack. He located it on the directory diagram and started toward it.

He was just passing the Fishnet, glancing inside to try to see if they knew fish could be broiled or baked, when he saw the balding man take change from the cashier and walk toward the door.

Probably just adding lunch to his errands. But something made Jack watch an extra minute . . .

. . . which was how he happened to see the man take a cellular from his pocket as he left the Fishnet.

Suddenly all Jack's senses jumped into alert.

Shabby and harmless-looking, nothing much to do but mooch around a shopping center — and he carried a cellular phone as state-of-the-art-expensive as Jack's own?

Jack's paradigm flipped, all its elements clanging into their new positions.

Keep your distance. If he's Harry's, he'll know your picture, and a pro could see through your current look.

Act as if you don't care. Don't let him smell your interest.

Jack watched the man's reflection in the restaurant window. The man went to a white Chevy Nova, unlocked it, got in, cracked open the window, and flipped open the phone.

★　★　★

'What's going on?' Harry demanded. 'This was supposed to be over yesterday.'

'We're in Allemar,' Torres said. 'It *would*

have been done by now if you had told us sooner to come here, instead of wasting so much time.'

Harry held his stomach. He hadn't thought Allemar was a possibility, had no clue Sheila still lived there until the call from the librarian. Caron shouldn't even know about her. 'What have you found?'

'Caron's at the house with Sheila now —'

'You're there? You're calling me from there?'

'No. I'm way away, in a parking lot —'

'Is Dodge with her?'

'No.'

'Well, locate him, damn you! If he sees you first —'

'Mr Kravitz, you have to let us handle this. I know Caron is at the house by herself because Ron is in there. He's on the second floor. He can see and hear everything that's going on in or around the house. He has phoned me twice, and I can assure you Dodge is not in sight. I'm heading over there now. Between me and Ron, the women will be taken care of, and Dodge if necessary.'

★ ★ ★

Stinging fluid rose in Jack's throat. At the shock of hearing Harry's name, he had given

441

up the pretense of examining a tire on the far side of the car next to the bald man's. Then his heart had nearly stopped at the next piece of information.

The bald man was backing out of his parking space. Jack's impulse was to jump him, disable the car, shoot out the tires, anything to stop this monstrous steamrolling succession of events.

But he forced himself to duck back down. Impulses were bad.

Think.

All he could think of was Caron in the trap, a killer there, another on the way.

He yanked open his phone, punched Sheila's number.

When the phone rang, Sheila and Caron both looked at it.

Sheila picked it up on the fourth ring. 'Hello?'

Caron watched alarm spring into her eyes. She handed the phone to Caron. 'For you. Why does someone know you're here?'

'Caron,' Jack said. The breathlessness, the panic in the one word, was a body slam, and she fell back against the loveseat as if she had been actually struck. 'Take out your gun. You and Sheila get out of there now and run. Harry's man is inside! He's upstairs, in the house! And there's another guy on his way there, balding, in a white Chevy Nova!'

Her heart banging against her sternum, Caron dropped the phone, tore open her handbag, and took out the gun.

Sheila screamed.

Caron moved to grab her wrist, to get them out without wasting time or energy on words.

Then she saw where Sheila was looking. She froze.

He was in the living-room doorway, the man who had tried to kill her, and the scalpel glinted in his hand.

★ ★ ★

Peter Torres left the Chevy a short way down the lane and walked to the house.

He turned in at the hedge and stopped to listen: nothing. At the front door, all was still quiet except for the low buzz of voices.

But as he edged around to the side to look in at a window, the voices became clearer through a screen, and the one he was now hearing was definitely Brale's.

Shit.

Something was wrong, or Brale would still be a possum upstairs.

Torres moved to the window, positioned himself at the side, and looked in. Brale was standing in the room's only exit, holding the scalpel.

As Torres watched, Caron Alvarez raised her hand, aimed a revolver at Brale's chest, and fired.

'Shit!' Torres yelled, and the word disappeared in the blast. Brale fell, spewing blood, the scalpel clattering across the wood floor.

Torres ran back to the front. The screen door was hooked shut, but he tore it free, just as Caron and Sheila reached it from inside.

His and Brale's orders were to kill Caron with the scalpel, making it appear self-inflicted, and see that Sheila disappeared.

How handy that Caron had the scalpel in her hand now.

Torres wasted no time plugging the other gal, who went right down. Torres was long trained in the utility of the moment of shock following a killing, and he used it now to grab Caron's weapons.

But she recovered fast, though she still looked like she would wet her pants, and arced him a good kick in the crotch.

The pain was inhuman, his breath gone, no yell coming out.

Torres died before he realized he had been shot in the back.

38

The Allemar killings made the news briefly.

Neither of the men carried any papers. The fingerprints of one showed him to be Peter Elkin Torres, a convicted murderer. A Chevrolet parked near the scene was in his name. Investigation of his Bridgeport, Connecticut apartment yielded nothing but the picture of a solitary criminal with no apparent life.

The other man could not be identified.

Both carried cloned cellular phones that had been used primarily to call other cellular phones, making it impossible for any called numbers to be traced.

The woman was a lifelong local resident with no close family.

Because bullets recovered from the three victims did not match, and only the unregistered weapon used to shoot the female was found on the scene, it was clear that there had been others involved. Neighbors had seen and heard bits and pieces that supported this fact.

After a day the news stories piddled down to backpage recaps of the sort that ran when all the players in a particular drama were, or were assumed to be, prostitutes or drug dealers — people it wasn't necessary to care about. Terms such as 'bloodbath' and 'feud' helped that impression.

There was never any suggestion of Harry, Caron, or Jack being involved, because no one knew to make the connection.

★　★　★

Caron yearned to go home.

'Home'. The word was a travesty now. But tentacles pulled her there. If your child falls into an alligator pit, you jump in after him.

But she would be sacrificing herself. Harry couldn't possibly let her live. He wanted her back there so he could obliterate her. Running around loose, she was still a threat. She had to keep using that. She had to hit him again and again.

★　★　★

'Three more bodies, Harry. *Your* victims. You won't be able to explain that away. The blood is on *you*.'

Harry said, 'I don't know what you're referring to, Caron, but it seems to me that if you were present where people died, you are the one who — '

'You don't know? You don't know? You're a psychotic and a liar. I have proof.'

Harry made his tone lie flat. 'That's impossible. There's nothing to prove.'

Caron's hissed words vibrated through the phone. 'Make sure Josh stays well, goddamn you. You won't want to have to explain a dead child in addition to your other sins. *Sheila told me everything before she died. The child rapes, the beatings, all of it. I'll be ready to contact the media very soon. I have the proof.*'

★   ★   ★

'We have nothing,' Jack told Caron exhaustedly as he finished with the cellular. 'Sheila has no history between birth and death. Harry took care of that, or intimidated her into it, or both. The *Galaxy* researchers are magicians, but even magicians can't work with just 'Ron'. Torres is a proven scumbag, but so what?' He sighed. 'They'll keep at it. All we can do is hope they find a connection between Torres and Harry they can use as a starting point, or one between Harry and Sheila.'

They were in the car, parked in the

ever-busy Newark Airport short-term lot. Caron was gritty-eyed from lack of sleep, emotions ribboning through her like poisonous worms. She could not close her eyes without seeing blood and flesh, smelling the sickening reek.

She cried for Sheila, brave Sheila, who would have been a heroine. She saw Sheila behind her eyes as well — Sheila nodding, Sheila weeping . . . Sheila falling, bleeding . . .

Caron blessed the impulse that had prevented her from telling Josh she had found his mother.

Harry's life was a battlefield, littered with dead and injured, and Caron so far was simply upping the numbers.

She couldn't think what she had left to fight with. She had built a good bluff, but she had to back it up fast, or Harry would know she was empty.

20/20 was coming on. Jack had bought a tiny portable TV days before that was barely usable as far from cities as they'd been, but the picture was clear now. A live interview with Harry at home was scheduled.

Maybe she'd be able to see Josh, to appease the frantic ongoing worry that he was already dead. With no contact since that last rushed and frightening conversation, the possibility drilled and tore at her that he was no longer alive.

Suddenly Harry's voice boomed from the television.

'Thank God,' Harry was telling Barbara Walters, 'I've been spared the tragedy in my life that so many people must suffer. But not now. I'm dealing with an awful one now.'

'At least,' Barbara said, 'you must be happy to have your son back.'

The camera pulled away. Caron leaned toward the screen, not breathing.

She collapsed back in relief. There was Josh. He was sitting next to Harry on the sofa in the East End Avenue living room.

He was tight around the mouth and sat defensively, his arms crossed over his chest. The cast was grimy. There was red on his face that the television powder couldn't hide. His eyes were dull and didn't move enough.

Her heart hurt.

Harry was talking again, but the screen showed a longer shot now — long enough so the two other people in the homey grouping could be seen. Harry's assistant Graceann and her daughter shared the loveseat angled by the couch.

Graceann leaned forward as Barbara addressed her.

'You and Lilly are living here temporarily

449

to show your support of Harry, is that the case?' Barbara asked.

Graceann's face in close-up wore an expression of sincere concern. 'Not to show it. To provide it.'

'Then,' Barbara went on, 'you have no concern that you might be in danger? If Dr Alvarez's claims are true — '

'I believe, as the overwhelming majority of people do, that Dr Alvarez is ill and not rational. I have only sympathy for her. But I also sympathize with Harry.'

The close-up dissolved to a two-shot of Graceann and Lilly. Graceann held Lilly's hand.

Then another long shot, and the four of them did look like one big warm family if you didn't know otherwise.

Harry in that apartment with two children . . .

Caron held her stomach.

        ★   ★   ★

The *20/20* taping was the toughest acting job Harry had done. He had carried his role through to the mutually gracious goodbye with Barbara, then the technical breakdown. When the apartment was finally empty but for his 'family' straightening furniture and carrying out garbage, Harry thanked them each with a hug and left to take a walk.

His walks were as necessary as blood now. Only then could he get back in touch with himself.

He had never been this desperate.

He hurried along the park walkway. His hands itched for relief, but he jammed them in his pockets and dug the nails into his palms as hard as he could.

Had it not been for a squib in the *Times*, he would never have known the result of the confrontation at Allemar. As it was, he could only extrapolate from the bits of information given, and the picture emerged of a bullet-ridden cluster-fuck. Sheila was dead, thanks to God, her slate as blank as it was supposed to be — or so Harry had thought. Both Brale and Torres were clearly dead. Neither the excruciating wait following the last call from Torres, nor the tiny article, had yielded any hint as to the condition or whereabouts of Caron and Jack Dodge. Harry had even nursed the hope that they were wounded and dying somewhere.

Until the call from Caron.

What the hell did she have?

With Brale and Torres gone, he himself was back to knowing nothing. He *had* nothing.

Nothing with which to locate and destroy

the barreling torpedo that was Jack and Caron.

Harry was set to go, and all his resources were being wasted on the charade of hiding the wreck he was, the wreck his life and career could become at any moment.

What the goddamn fucking hell was he going to do?

He returned to the apartment just in time to answer a call from Julie Gerstein.

'I saw *20/20*, Harry. You were wonderful. You have a lot of people hosed. But many of us are not. We know you're a vile animal. You will be found out. Why don't you tell the truth now and try to salvage some scrap of human decency?'

She hung up before he could.

He wished he had stayed out in the park.

He was wiping his forehead, staring at the phone, when he caught a glimpse of Lilly skulking past in her bathrobe.

She always rushed now when she had to pass Harry. It was a tacit accusation.

Everygoddamnbody was accusing him.

He leaned way back in his desk chair.

He wanted to pulverize that bag of blood Julie. He wished he could pull her hair out of her scalp in handfuls and stuff it up every opening she had.

He saw Lilly hurry past again, back toward

452

her room, holding a bag of chips. Her hair swished on her shoulders.

The image stayed with him after she was gone, and he saw himself grabbing her hair, tearing, pieces of her scalp coming loose.

In his mind Harry pushed Lilly down on the floor, kneed her fat legs apart, and forced the bloody flesh and hair into her holes.

Loudmouth fucking cow Julie.

He'd put some in her mouth too. Let her taste pieces of herself.

Along with those chips Lilly was always stuffing herself with.

★   ★   ★

Lilly hated how bulky she looked in her terrycloth robe, but it gave her a tiny feeling of being protected.

She saw Harry looking at her as she passed his office, and was glad she was wearing the heavy thing.

She wondered why he was in there so much today. He tended to use his office when he was on the phone, but he hadn't seemed to be talking just now.

As she often did lately, Lilly thought of Harry's agent, that sweet man Mr Wundring. He was always calm and friendly when Lilly happened to answer one of his calls.

453

It was strange that two people as different as Harry and Mr Wundring could be so close.

Lilly had not tried after the first unhappy time to talk to her mother about Harry. But she thought about who else she might confide in who could speak to Harry about stopping touching her, and the person who always came to her mind was Mr Wundring.

She had copied his number from Harry's Rolodex. It was on a Post-it note, stuck to the underside of her dressing table. Once she had started to call, and then she had changed her mind.

But she kept thinking about it.

39

Harry had a lunch date with Paul. They went to Morton's and had steak sandwiches. Harry's appetite was lousy now, but he pretended to relish the meal.

Paul filled his water glass from the carafe on the table and motioned for Harry's. 'You look a little better today. How are you bearing up?'

'Not bad. Thank you for asking.'

'Are you ready to go into production?'

'I've told you. Yes.'

Paul put the jug down and studied him. 'I have to say, Harry, that you still don't have your usual verve. Not that I'd expect it under the circumstances. But you do have to put it out there even though you don't feel it, if you're going to start putting shows in the can.'

'I will, Paul. When I'm on camera, I'm fine. You know that. How soon do you think we'll roll?'

'Soon.'

Harry swallowed. This could all come together, please, God.

The show was going to be magnificent.

People couldn't wait for it to begin. Everywhere Harry went, both industry people and fans were thrilled about it.

Once it was on the air, he'd evolve from a popular personality into a saint.

He'd be his most invincible.

★ ★ ★

Paul had trouble swallowing. The meat and bread stuck in his throat.

Harry wasn't right.

There was something going on, much more than Harry was acknowledging.

Paul wanted to get up, lean across the expensive food, and grab Harry. He wanted to shake some clarity back into his eyes.

He said, 'Is there anything you want to discuss with me, Harry?'

Harry looked at him as if the question was bizarre. 'No.'

★ ★ ★

Caron and Jack slept in the car at Newark Airport.

On Saturday morning, after washing in one of the airport rest rooms, Caron was leaving a terminal building on her way back to the car when a chauffeur-driven Mercedes pulled to the curb and Tomas Valin got out.

His back was to Caron, but she recognized the posture immediately, the arrogant stance, the Mark Cross briefcase.

Her blood seemed to freeze in her body.

For an endless second she was motionless, staring, unable to turn away. Then, just as Tomas straightened, she came to life. She whipped around and hurried off, too shaken to remember not to run.

He must have glimpsed her face before she turned, and recognized her through the disguise, because she heard the slam of a car door — and, a moment later when she risked a glance back, saw the Mercedes following her, Tomas in the front passenger seat.

She darted sideways, across rows of parked cars, where the Mercedes couldn't follow. She ran crouched over, zigzagging, for as long as she could.

Finally, out of breath, she stopped. She stayed hidden between cars. When she finally rose up to sneak a look, the Mercedes wasn't in sight.

Now the reaction set in, the physical shock of running and panting from a base line of stress — no breakfast, no energy, internal resources beyond depletion. Her infection, past being lulled by the juice, needed medication; she was exhausted from fighting it.

Caron sank down on the hot, smelly pavement, hugging her knees, a van tire at her back. The padding in her clothes was wet and uncomfortable. She hung her head, trying to shake off the sick dizziness, the cold-sweat terror.

When she was finally able to stand, she looked around, holding the door handle of the van, trying to get her bearings.

Nothing in the ocean of cars looked familiar. She was in a different lot, one she and Jack hadn't seen before.

Standing on tiptoe, she tried to remember the direction of her run, looking for the way back to the lot where the Century was. But nothing pricked her recollection. She had run and run, but had circled and doubled back so much that she couldn't tell whether she was near the car, or several huge lots away.

She and Jack had to get away from Newark, now that Tomas had seen her. Tomas would have police and airport security people looking for her by now. She had to find the car. It was her only anonymity.

But she had no idea where Jack and the Century were.

★ ★ ★

Waiting for Caron, tapping the steering wheel, Jack mentally replayed the conversation he had just had with Robin.

Finally a piece of news. A tiny opening.

Plus an idea of how they could use it.

He couldn't wait to tell Caron.

What the hell was taking her so long? Had she stopped to have her nails done?

He clicked open his pen and began scribbling doodles in his notebook. The lines were shaky. He was nervous.

No wonder, he mouthed silently, looking up from the page.

Without even turning his head, he could see a police cruiser and two Newark Airport Security vehicles rolling slowly down between the rows of cars.

Looking for someone.

★ ★ ★

'How long ago?' Harry asked urgently.

'Twenty minutes,' Tomas said. 'I asked the airport security to try to find her out there, and they are cooperating, but it took time for them to check me out, so they only just got started. And now I have to make my flight. They'll be in touch with you.'

'Give me the number to call them there.'

'I don't have it.'

'You're certain it was Caron?'

'Yes. She's different from her last likeness. Her hair is red now, and she has glasses and appears heavier. I asked the security people to fax you a copy of her description. But it was Caron. And Harry — she looks quite robust.'

★　★　★

Jack drove slowly up and down the rows, mentally calling to Caron, rechecking the original parking space every few minutes in case she had returned there.

He didn't know for sure that Caron was the reason for the security and police cars. But something tickled about it. Her absence, the slowness of their search, the lack of sirens or derring-do.

Someone must have spotted her.

But why were police looking?

And where the *hell* was she?

He was afraid for her.

And just plain afraid too.

He didn't like her being away from him, not even to go and take a whore's bath in the airport john. And not just because of the threat.

When the hell had that happened? When had this gig become so intensely personal?

At some point his indifference had turned to empathy, and then to devotion. He was shocked to find that Caron was in his fibers waking and sleeping. Not just the story; Caron herself.

He had been flooded with horror in Allemar, knowing she was trapped in the house with Harry's executioner. He lay awake in knots of fright at the idea that she might return to Harry to try to save Josh.

He remembered her in the towel in the motel in Winston-Salem, her glossy shoulders, her bare legs . . .

He entered the next lot, keeping his speed easy, his eyes moving all the time. He tried to slip into her situation, feel what she would do. He used his knowledge of her, of her physical behavior, the way her mind worked, to decide where and how to look for her.

The goddamn security cars were all over the place.

His hands trembled on the wheel.

★ ★ ★

Caron stood in the very narrow space between two parked vans. She could see through the windows of each. With her back and front views, that gave her roughly a four-way line of sight.

Every time she saw a police or security car, she positioned herself as if she was simply locking up.

It wouldn't work for long. Soon she would have to move, or chance being seen twice by the same searcher.

She was pouring sweat in the already humid air. She had to fight to keep from giving in to her panic and just running and running.

She swiveled her head, watching, awaiting a moment when there were no cars and she could move to another spot and keep trying to find her way back to the Century.

It was horribly dangerous to be still at the airport. By now Tomas would have contacted Harry. She didn't dare think about what that would bring.

But Jack and the car were her only way out.

She could only pray the car would still be in the same spot if she got there — that Jack hadn't had to take off.

If he was gone, what would she do? She'd be stranded. How could they find each other again?

Her stomach hurt like hell, curling into itself.

Once again she felt the peaceful prospect of

death as a desirable thing, and bent over with the increased pain the idea brought.

And suddenly, miraculously, there was the Century, there was Jack throwing open the door, and she stumbled toward it, sobbing.

40

Jack grabbed Caron's outstretched hand and pulled her into the front seat. He yanked so hard her shoulder hurt, but she barely noticed.

'Thank God,' Caron gasped. 'I had to run. I — '

'Don't talk for a minute,' Jack said. 'Let me concentrate on getting us out of here before I have to hear there are Sherman tanks chasing us. Those police and security vehicles *are* for us?'

'Yes.'

Driving as fast as he dared, Jack headed for the airport exit. Nearing it, he caught sight from the corner of his eye of a crawling police car. He moved instinctively to insert a disguise element, putting his arm around Caron and pulling her over beside him.

'Don't look right or left,' he told her quietly. 'Just pretend to be my woman. Think it.'

She rested her head on his shoulder.

It felt instantly comfortable, and she realized in that moment that she had known all along that Jack would find her.

She trusted him.

Feeling the point of his shoulder under her ear, she did as he said, thinking her part: she was a wife heading home with her husband from the airport, after a budget vacation.

But he could feel the tremor in her body, and he hugged her closer.

Caron waited for Jack to give up his hold, but he didn't. She turned to look at his face. Then he seemed to realize he still held her, and let go quickly.

'Now tell me,' Jack said. 'What happened?'

'I was leaving the terminal after I washed. Tomas Valin got out of a car right in front of me. I was so shocked I acted like an idiot, first staring at him and then running away . . .'

She was shaking badly, and Jack put his arm around her again. This time she didn't move away.

But moments later she sat up suddenly. 'Why are we going this way? We're almost in New York!'

'Yep. That's where we need to be.'

'But —'

'We were stalling until my office could make headway. Until we had something we could use.'

Caron's head whipped around. 'And? Have we?'

'I hope so.'

* * *

Avoiding the crowded highway rest stop, they went into a Hardee's to use the bathrooms. The men's was occupied, and Jack was still waiting when Caron came out after using the women's.

'Just go in here,' she said, pulling him in.

Then she was astonished to find herself closing and locking the door with both of them inside.

She stood staring at him, watching his eyes watch hers.

Her nostrils and skin and tongue were alive suddenly, her breathing spasmodic. Her body recollected all the sensations she had just experienced in the car. It craved that comfort again.

Her hands were on him, his chest and shoulders, and she moved in, meeting him neck to knees.

* * *

Jack felt the slick tile wall at his shoulder-blades as Caron pressed him back. He froze.

466

Then he gripped her, harder than he meant to.

He was assailed by smells — disinfectant, soap, sewage . . . Caron's hair, her unwashed clothing, his own over-worn shirt. He felt her nails on his skin, under the shirt, and he heard a sound leave his lips just before hers met them.

He had to touch her too. He tugged her top out of her pants. His hands found her buttocks, sticky and sweaty.

After that he didn't, couldn't, think.

★ ★ ★

Jack's fingers were inside her. It hurt and it didn't. She was conscious only of a river of feeling. This part of her body that held the memory of being just a source of pain was now flooded with pleasure.

Her hand found his fly and the rigid erection beneath. She unzipped him and went into his shorts with both hands.

They struggled out of their pants. Caron backed to the wall and reached for Jack as he moved to her.

For an instant Jack's invasive push brought the horror back for Caron. But a moment later he was inside her, thrusting, and her body had not forgotten how to welcome.

467

She moved with him, faster. The rush was so intense she had to push her face into his neck to stifle her cries.

Then the heat and the sweat and their unvoiced emotion peaked with the eruption of their bodies, and they sagged against the wall, holding each other, someone's tears dripping on to the floor.

★ ★ ★

Josh's bedroom TV was on, the Sports Channel. They weren't showing anything he really wanted to watch, but the Sports Channel served the purpose of providing a background of friendly, upbeat voices. He used to love watching the evening news, but that was too upsetting now — even when it wasn't about his own family.

Since he had come home, he needed more and more to create his own background, because the real one was so awful.

His first night home had been nice. They'd sent out for pizza, Dad and Graceann and Lilly and Josh, studying the menu together, choosing and combining. They'd ended up with a ton of crazy toppings, pineapple and bacon and clams.

But in these few short days, his world had spun upside down.

He found himself wondering if he was going to die. All the scary feelings made Josh stay in his room a lot and run the Sports Channel like a calming stream of water.

Today had been especially strange, with Dad grabbing up the phone on the first ring, low-voiced urgent conversations. Enough words floated out for him to know it had to do with Caron, and Josh had to try not to cry, he missed her so. But there was so much about Caron and Dad that he had to push away from his thoughts.

The TV covered the sound of his dad's footsteps in the hallway, and all of a sudden there was Dad standing in the doorway of Josh's room.

Josh jumped, dropping the remote.

His dad had a wrinkled forehead, a worried and angry look, and didn't meet Josh's eyes.

He looked at Harry for another moment, and then got off the bed to find the remote.

It only took him a few seconds, but when he was done, Harry was gone. Josh stepped into the hallway and looked around, but Harry wasn't in sight.

He went back into his room and turned the volume up even higher.

★　★　★

469

It was impossible now for Lilly to imagine how, even a week ago, she had enjoyed sitting and watching Harry on television, had loved it even more when she could be in the studio.

She used to beg for the opportunity.

Now she focused all her effort on being where Harry wasn't, not having to see him or talk to him or watch him on the screen.

She tried to spend her time at friends' apartments, only to be here when her mother or Josh was in.

Lilly prayed every night that soon they could go home to their own apartment, where she could walk around without worrying about being touched or looked at, and where her differences with Graceann were about whether to put butter or sour cream on the potatoes.

Her mother didn't understand. Nobody would. She had given up on her idea of phoning Mr Wundring, had ripped the Post-it to bits and swallowed them. It had been too terrifying to think of Harry finding the number, or Mr Wundring telling on her.

Josh was home tonight, watching a game. Lilly wandered by his room every so often, just to reassure herself he was there. Her ear was perked to hear the door; if Josh left before Graceann came home, Lilly would leave also, even if there turned out to be no one to visit, even if she had to hang around outside one of her friends' buildings.

41

By ten the next morning, Harry was fielding his second phone call about glitches with the new show.

'Our information,' the *Variety* reporter said, 'is that production has been delayed indefinitely with you as host, and that the show will be renamed and David Letterman will replace you.'

'That's hog slop,' Harry said, keeping his tone one of sweet reason. 'This format was conceptualized for me. It is me, and I'm it.'

To the third caller he gave a quotable quote: 'That show without me would be like chocolate chip cookies without the chocolate chips.'

Harry had phoned Paul Wundring after the first inquiry, and Paul had professed to know nothing of Letterman or any problem.

'I told you, Harry, the only question in my mind was your own readiness.'

Harry asked, 'Did you share your question with anyone at the network?'

A pause. 'You mean, did I ask, 'What do you think, is Harry up for the show?' Of course not. I'm your agent. My position is that you're always up for anything.'

Harry phoned Paul again after the chocolate chip call, his hand sliming the phone with sweat. Again Paul downplayed the situation.

* ★ ★

Hanging up on Harry, Paul looked at himself in the hall mirror and saw the weight of his worry in his own eyes.

He didn't like what he was hearing from himself — not the false reassurances to Harry, nor his internal denial monologue.

His alarm was clamoring. He couldn't keep ignoring it.

He had to know.

★ ★ ★

Tomas had been in touch with Harry from Los Angeles the day before as the unsuccessful search for Caron at Newark wound down, but Harry had not heard from him since.

Now, in his Sunday-empty office, staring at the welter of his own idea notes on his usually clean desk, Harry decided he didn't like that silence.

Tomas knew the situation was crucial. He

knew Harry was upset. He should have called.

The thought brought Harry back to one from yesterday: it stuck in his craw that Tomas had phoned to report seeing Caron, then blithely hopped on a plane after merely alerting police and security.

Tomas should have stayed around and seen that through. It was important enough, and his retainer was high enough, even without the long-time personal connection.

Harry was also not thrilled with Paul as the day marched on. Those reports of Letterman replacing Harry had rolled off Paul — as if Paul had more important business than holding Harry's hand.

But Harry wasn't some simp seeking reassurance over nothing. Letterman was no ghost. These were major media reports of no-confidence on the network's part, and Paul should have been more supportive. Should have made press calls, tamped this down.

Why hadn't he heard from Caron again? Was it because her 'proof' didn't really exist? Or because it did, and she was getting set to use it?

He had thought and thought about her last call, and come to the sad conclusion that there was only one way to go. He had to use Josh.

He had to put the boy in bad enough shape to bring Caron running. Then Harry could force her to recant her claims about him.

It wouldn't save her, he couldn't chance that, but it would help his credibility — with the public, and with his associates. With Tomas and Paul wimping around, making cracks about how 'robust' Caron looked, and how much 'verve' Harry lacked, they would snap to when Caron herself admitted, 'Look, I lied, Harry never hurt me.'

Harry pushed back his desk chair and went to the men's room. He used the urinal and washed up. In the mirror above the sink he saw the old white-haired attendant slog in with his mop and evil-smelling bottle of disinfectant.

In a surprising burst, Harry felt the rage that came on him during his walks, when he had to hurt someone.

He stared at himself in the mirror, clenching his teeth, willing the sensation to pass, as the little man inched his mop toward the stalls.

It wouldn't pass. Harry wanted to knock the shabby feet out from under the gnome. Chop at the thin forearms.

He made himself leave the bathroom, and hurried back to his office.

★ ★ ★

By the end of the day, Caron still hadn't called. Harry cursed her in his head during his cab ride to East End Avenue. Caron's statement was exactly what he needed to make Paul and Tomas and the public aware of how he continued to be persecuted.

Once Paul and Tomas understood how she had built this fiction about him, they would bend way over to help him get on with his life and his show. There would be no more lapses. They'd stay on top of every situation.

Josh was in the kitchen when Harry got home, eating an orange. Harry wrinkled his nose at the pervasive smell.

He watched Josh shove a big segment into his mouth.

'Finish chewing before you take another piece,' Harry said.

Josh nodded.

That made Harry angry. He was entitled to a civil answer from his own son.

He looked straight at Josh, and wanted to smash the whole orange down the rude kid's throat.

Just then the kitchen phone rang, and Harry dived for it, but it was the goddamn doorman calling Josh.

Harry gave him the phone. 'Wrap it up fast.

I'm expecting a call.'

Josh finished and hung up. 'I'm going down to put my bike away,' he said.

'Be quick.' Harry watched him leave. As soon as he came back, Harry would have to create the crisis that would motivate Caron to return.

He was looking around the kitchen for inspiration when the phone rang again.

'Harry?'

'Caron!'

'Listen hard, Harry. I'm going to play you a tape. Here it is.'

Harry pressed the receiver to his head until his ear hurt.

'My name is Sheila Dannenbring,' he heard, and he had to drop into a kitchen chair. 'My married name was Kravitz. I am the former wife of Harry Kravitz and the mother of Josh. Contrary to what Harry has said, I am neither psychotic nor a bad parent.

'I gave up my son when he was two years old. I did this after Harry beat me severely and said he would kill me and Josh if I didn't. Harry is a sick and violent man, a batterer and a rapist. I have given Dr Alvarez X-rays of the fractures he caused. I also gave her affidavits from three of his rape victims. Two were eight years old at the time of the rapes, and one was ten. There is a young girl in his household right now whom he has also molested . . . '

★ ★ ★

In her room Lilly heard the front door open and close, and fear tickled up along the back of her neck. That had been Josh going out. Now she and Harry were alone in the apartment.

She hadn't heard Harry's words to Josh, but he had seemed angry. These were the times Lilly had learned to dread most.

Suddenly Harry was at her doorway.

'You're a fucking liar,' Harry said. 'Who the fuck have you been lying to?'

Lilly didn't answer. Harry's rage crawled inside him like snakes.

'*Well?*' he yelled.

Lilly crept backward across the carpet. She was breathing in little bursts. She crossed her arms, then dropped them as she saw Harry look toward her breasts.

'Who the goddamn hell do you think you are, you ungrateful skank? I let you come into my home, and you tell disgusting lies about me!'

Lilly's hands still hung at her sides. The fingers curled and uncurled, her nails poking the palms. The feel of them digging into the tender pads there seemed to be all that was keeping Lilly from passing out cold with the terror.

'*Answer me!*' Harry thundered.

'What?' she whispered. 'What do you want me — '

'Not only are you a liar, you're also a cretin,' Harry said. 'How did your mother manage to get such a dumb kid?'

She started to cry. Harry took a step toward her and she stepped back; then they each stepped again.

Lilly wiped her eyes.

Harry asked, 'Do you know what they used to do with dumb, lying kids in Colonial days? They drowned them.'

Lilly gasped.

'They did,' Harry said. 'They didn't see any point in letting a rotten kid live to become a rotten adult. You're lucky nobody did that to you yet.'

Lilly took a breath and clenched her hands. She said, 'I'm not stupid.'

'Oh, no?' Harry moved closer. Lilly backed up some more. He advanced again, until Lilly was standing with her back to the dressing-table chair — the same chair she had been sitting in when she had tried to tell her mother about Harry touching her.

Harry reached over and pushed his hand between the legs of her sweatpants. He squeezed her groin. 'Anyone with one of these,' he said, 'is not too smart for starters.' His voice shook as his breathing grew harsh. With his other hand he gripped her breast. Then he took hold of her waistband and yanked the pants down.

Lilly squirmed, crying and trying to grab back her pants. He pushed her roughly into the chair and dropped on top of her.

Suddenly there was noise in the hallway, footsteps racing. Big hands, four of them, grabbed Harry and heaved him off Lilly.

*　*　*

Caron gathered the sobbing girl in her arms as Jack Dodge and Ho Plimpton pinned Harry face down on the bed.

'You did brilliantly,' Caron told her, her own tears streaming. 'The camera got it all. You've saved my life.'

Jack scooted around the bed to face Harry, his gun in his hand. 'This is sweet,' Jack said, pointing the gun straight at Harry's nose. 'This is a Kodak moment. Or Ampex, to be more accurate. Say anything you want, Harry, the meaner the better. Say it for your audience.'

480

'You *prick*,' Harry hissed at Jack. 'This is entrapment. You're trying to trap me — '

'Not *trying*. Ho,' Jack said without looking away from Harry, 'I've got this. Tell Schlomo he can make the call.'

'Yup.'

'No,' Harry said, 'wait. Don't call the police.'

'You want to talk to us? Go right ahead. Any details you care to give. How did it feel to murder your own aunt? How many little girls and boys out there have been porked by dirty Harry?'

'You were always self-righteous,' Harry said. 'You know what else you are? Cheap. And underhanded.'

'Very,' Jack said with a hoarse laugh. 'How do you think we got you crazed enough to screw yourself? Who's a better picador than me? I fed out that story of you being replaced by Letterman. Caron wrote the words on the tape she played you, and my assistant voiced it.'

The shock of the betrayal, the slamming lid of the real trap, struck Harry like lightning. He yelled, a high shriek, and tried to lunge out of Ho's grip.

Suddenly Paul Wundring appeared in the doorway.

Harry stared at him.

481

'I had to hear the truth for myself,' Paul said quietly. 'This wasn't the truth I was hoping for.'

'Caron's lying!' Harry shouted. 'She's manipulating you — '

'No,' Paul said. 'I was the one who contacted Caron. I had doubts. I needed to know. I called Jack's office to try to find her, and she called me back. Nobody manipulated me. I was told about the plan for today, and I asked to come along. I saw what you did, Harry. This was no entrapment.'

Caron gave Lilly a last squeeze and moved to face Harry. She made herself look into his eyes. The sensation was sickening and familiar at once. She was jolted back to her first look at Harry, in the emergency room at New York Hospital, the nice dad anguished over his son's fracture. He'd been so attractive, so in charge. So magnetic. The echo of past intimacy jingled faintly still, but recent memory rebutted and rebelled, excavated the fists and the teeth, the blood and semen and the horror, sending waves of nausea through her.

'You steal people's bodies and souls,' she said to him. 'You convince yourself you're somehow noble while you're ruining lives! I *save* lives, but I could happily end yours, Harry!'

482

He made a sound of disgust. 'You set me a trap. You hate me so much you had to destroy me — '

'*You* are the destroyer, Harry! *You* destroyed yourself!'

'*I give pleasure to the world!*' Harry screamed. '*All I wanted was to keep on giving, but I can't! You set it up so I can't!*'

She leaned closer to him, so close that his face became a grotesque caricature, bulging cheeks and eyes, the hair a golden forest. 'You beat your own child! You raped your own wives and nephew and niece!' she yelled, inches from him. 'Can't you hear yourself, you twisted monster? You're justifying inhuman crimes with your blather about television history — '

'*Not history now!*' Harry shrieked. '*It's over! You spoiled it! There's no network show now!*'

'Got your Achilles' heel, I see,' Jack said loudly over Harry's noise. 'Children raped and beaten? No big deal. Network unhappy with Harry? World tragedy. Ho, call the police.'

'No,' Harry yelled. '*Please*,' he said. 'For Josh's sake. Let me go to them. At least have my son know his old man took the high road in the end.'

'You don't know the meaning of the

concept, Harry. You're just playing for time. But there's none left.'

★ ★ ★

It might have been helpful to get out into traffic without the police. Possibly he could have gotten away from Dodge and the black man.

But being escorted out of 114 East End by two uniformed oxen proved to be quite helpful in terms of public relations value. His fans hated to see Harry treated like a criminal. Every day now there were people outside Rikers carrying signs supporting Harry, heralding their love for him. The pictures of the demonstrators ran in all the big newspapers alongside whatever drivel they printed — anything Jack Dodge or Caron felt like fabricating, apparently.

The demonstrators were about all that kept Harry going.

He tried to maintain a brave front. He moved among the prisoners as if he wasn't one. He was charming to the guards. He smiled at the other men's visitors.

But inside he was crumbling away.

Everything he valued had been taken from him.

Letterman had the show. Josh wouldn't

484

visit. Tomas, the scumbag, had run as if Harry was covered in dog shit, pausing only long enough to fling some inbred criminal lawyer in Harry's direction after the arraignment. Paul Wundring had disappeared from his life. Even Graceann, though Harry had been able to make her understand that Lilly had simply been a pawn used to entrap him, had taken a job with Montel Williams.

Harry lay back on the prison bunk, pretending to read a paperback Civil War novel. Prisoners reading were like kids watching TV; their captors regarded them subconsciously as not currently in need of monitoring.

He saw his hands shudder on the book, and knew it wouldn't be long before those hands required use. There was no guarantee Harry would be out on bail at all, let alone soon, since the judge had denied bail at the arraignment. The bail hearing hadn't even been scheduled yet. Harry's frustrations built and built now, with no opportunity for release, and when that happened, there was nowhere to go but the usual.

There would be a way to accomplish that in prison, Harry was sure. Wasn't much you couldn't do in here if you needed to enough.

And there were likely candidates, Harry had seen them — sparse old skeletons who shuffled to and from their cells never looking left or right or up or down ... young brain-dead junkies who wouldn't feel it if their throats were cut.

Harry would just have to find a way to get one of them out of sight for a couple of minutes.

Epilogue

Saturday, October 16, 1993
New York City

Jack jumped over the net.

'That's so cool,' Lilly said.

Jack grinned. He reached out a hand to help her over. 'It's the best part of my game.' He shook hands with Caron and Josh. 'You killed us.'

Caron grinned back. 'Yes, we did.'

'You could at least lower your eyes demurely and murmur sportsmanlike compliments.'

'All right. Your forehand isn't quite as hopeless as it used to be.'

'When are we going to eat?' Josh asked. 'I'm really hungry.'

* * *

They had a Cuban dinner on upper Broadway. Watching Josh chomp down on his fourth spare rib, Caron met Jack's glance and they both smiled. They had been talking about that last night, how Josh's appetite was starting to improve slightly after weeks of weight loss following Harry's death.

'You and I know it was essentially suicide,'

Jack had said to her as they lay listening to music in Caron's new Central Park West apartment. 'You don't live as long and savvy a life as Harry did and be ignorant about prison democracy. Harry must have known goddamn well he'd be taken down for attacking another con. Some day we will have to explain that to Josh.'

Caron had shaken her head against his shoulder. 'Every chunk of his father has been snatched away from him. At least leave him that one tiny illusion. Let him think his father died tragically.'

Jack had shifted her head to his chest, to hold her more comfortably. 'Too bad we can't spread the illusions around. Lilly could use some. She sees life so starkly.'

Caron shrugged. 'It's a stark reality. I probably wouldn't be alive right now if it wasn't for Lilly, but her mother just sees the whole issue as one big betrayal. She thinks Lilly should never have called *Galaxy* to try to reach you. We should never have asked Lilly to let Harry pounce . . . '

'But it was so much more than Lilly,' Jack said. 'How can the woman blame her? Lilly's call was the first break, but if Harry hadn't fallen for Robin's tape, if Schlomo hadn't been willing to smuggle us into that empty apartment and get Josh out of Harry's grasp at the right time, if Ho couldn't be convinced to rig the video . . . hell, if Harry hadn't been an animal to start with . . . Her beloved boss was a murderer and a child rapist and a wife beater, and Graceann is trashing her kid for helping expose him?'

'Lilly is a heroine,' Caron said. 'She was terrified, but she did everything right.'

'We shouldn't let her go back to her mother even if she wants to.'

'She will want to,' Caron said. 'And we will let her. And it might be all right. Graceann has some illusions of her own to get past first.'

Now, in the restaurant, as they passed dishes back and forth with greasy, salty fingers, Jack said, 'How about some illusions for you and me?'

Caron picked up a chicken leg. 'If you mean your tennis game — '

'I mean us. Capital U. I think we should move in together.'

'Uh huh,' Lilly said immediately.

'One vote,' Jack said. 'Josh?'

'Okay.'

Jack took the chicken leg from where it dangled in Caron's fingers. He fixed her eyes with his. He said quietly, 'I promise you will never have to eat another sandwich. I will improve my forehand. I will never, ever hurt you deliberately.' He waited.

Lilly patted her back. 'Say yes.'

Caron said nothing for a long moment. Then, 'I can't yet. I need more time.' She looked at Jack's face, at all there was to see in it. 'Just a little more time.'

Lilly leaned toward her. 'Then you'll say yes?'

'I'm sure I will.'

Jack took her greasy hand and kissed it.

Other titles in the
Ulverscroft Large Print Series:

STRANGER IN THE PLACE

Anne Doughty

Elizabeth Stewart, a Belfast student and only daughter of hardline Protestant parents, sets out on a study visit to the remote west coast of Ireland. Delighted as she is by the beauty of her new surroundings and the small community which welcomes her, she soon discovers she has more to learn than the details of the old country way of life. She comes to reappraise so much that is slighted and dismissed by her family — not least in regard to herself. But it is her relationship with a much older, Catholic man, Patrick Delargy, which compels her to decide what kind of life she really wants.